THE ADVOCATE

RITUAL ABUSE

Dawn Mattox

Morningtide Publishing
PO Box 4262
Yankee Hill CA 95965

MORNINGTIDE PUBLISHING
PO Box 4262
Yankee Hill CA 95965
E-mail: info@theadvocatebooks.com
Website: www.DawnMattox.com

Cover Design: ©Melissa Alvarez
Cover Art: ©Itay Uri
Inside Art: ©Andrey Armyagov

REVIEWS

Dawn Mattox's Advocate Series brings an exciting, honest look at domestic violence and victimization by taking readers on a **nail-biting ride** as Sunny McLane takes on the malicious perpetrators of satanic cults, risking everything and everyone she loves to stop them. **Mattox's characters jump off the page and into your heart** with their tough struggles, self-doubt, and realistic fears as they make life-and-death choices that impact all those around them. ***Ritual Abuse* is one of the few novels this year that I could not put down. I'll be reading every book in this series**.

C. S. Lakin, author of *Innocent Little Crimes*

A Must Read!!! An **emotionally charged** story that grips you from page one with compelling, nail-biting suspense throughout. The story is highlighted with **lush descriptions** of the beautiful and sometimes savage landscape of the high Sierra's, **vivid characters** with whom we can readily empathize, a breathtaking **wild series of plot turns**, and a **blockbuster finale**.

Rabid Reviews

FIVE STARS***** Ever since reading *Ritual Abuse*, **I can't wait to buy the next book** in the series!! I get all excited and then remember – *it hasn't been written yet!!* It's making me crazy.

"Watch out Dawn Mattox! If you don't get that next book written SOON, I will do a *Misery on you!"

Catherine Wolcott; *Heart & Soul Reviews*
{*Stephen King's *Misery*}

DISCLAIMER

This book includes fictionalized accounts of violence against women. They are composed of variations and compilations of the many stories advocates will hear over the course of their careers and is not intended to reflect poorly on any field of advocacy.

Names, characters, places brands, media and incidents either are the product of the author's imagination or used fictitiously. Any resemblance to actual persons, living or dead is entirely coincidental. Any references to events or locals are strictly fictionalized accounts of those events for the purpose of fictionalized entertainment.

The author acknowledges the trademarked status and trademark owners of various products referenced in this work of fiction, which have been used without permission. The publication/use of these trademarks is not authorized, associated with, or sponsored by the trademark owners.

The motorcycle clubs exist, but the characters herein are fictional individuals portrayed as acting outside of their club's purview and are nowise intended to discredit or disrespect the organizations.

All actions taken by law enforcement agencies are fictionalized accounts and are nowise intended to discredit or dishonor the dedicated men and women who work in the field of Criminal Justice.

Only the dynamics of Interpersonal Violence, Human Trafficking, the tireless work of advocacy and law enforcement, the setting in northern California, and identity of the dogs are true.

DEDICATION

This book is dedicated first to Jesus Christ, my forever Advocate, and to those courageous professionals who do not bow to agency pressure, social trends, or influence from the media, but continue to serve the silent population of victims and survivors of ritual abuse with steadfast commitment.

"Do you believe me?"
She asked me from the start.
"Why shouldn't I?"
I answered from my heart.
She's moved far away
from immediate dangers
I sent her away
to live among strangers.
I still hear the terror,
recall her desperate plea
as new faces echo...
"Do you believe me?"

In Memory of Grace

ACKNOWLEDGMENTS

Special thanks and appreciation to:

My husband's inexhaustible patience and support for my work.

My grandson, Chance, who is a budding author.

Kissme, my faithful friend and companion throughout the endless hours of writing and rewriting, and rewriting some more. Laid to rest, October 2015.

Victim

Noun:

1. a person that suffers harm or death from another, an adverse act, or circumstance.

2. a living person or animal sacrificed in a religious rite.

Verb:

to slay as or like a sacrificial victim.

Ritual abuse

Ritual abuse is an extreme, sadistic form of abuse of children and non-consenting adults. It is methodical, systematic sexual, physical, emotional and spiritual abuse, which often includes mind control, torture, and highly illegal and immoral activities such as murder, child pornography, and prostitution.

Also known as RA (Ritual Abuse), SRA (Satanic or Sadistic Ritual Abuse).

PART ONE

Isaiah 21:6
The Lord said unto me;
Go, set a watchman, let him declare what he sees.

CHAPTER 1

਍ ✝ ੴ

There was no nice way to say it—Nina simply scared the crap out of me.

As a crisis worker, I was used to patterns of erratic behavior— from the taut stretch between totally numb to the snapping point of suicide associated with victims of sexual assault, to the cataclysmic turbulence of love and loathing that churned and muddied the emotions of victims of domestic violence.

Then there was Nina. A simple misdemeanor case that left me with a sinking feeling that I was witnessing a scab being peeled back and something putrid was about to be exposed.

"You don't know who you are dealing with! They'll kill me," Nina hissed. She had a look and feel of a feral cat—her gothic styled black hair was spiked, reminding me of raised hackles that perfectly framed her slanting green eyes.

I pulled the county-issue pen from my mouth and leaned forward across the table between us, rolling the pen in my fingers and noting the fresh teeth marks before popping it back between my teeth.

Maybe I've just been missing it, I thought. Me—and a million other advocates.

Delusional? Maybe. But there was something in Nina's razor-sharp words that slashed at my skepticism. Either way, this wasn't a homicide, and I didn't want it turning into one.

I pulled the pen from my mouth again and drummed it against the legal pad. "Who are 'they'? Who is going to kill you? And why?" I asked.

Nina paced the floor of the safe room at the courthouse, her eyes darting about as if looking for an escape route. Then she stopped, grabbed her hair in frustration, and bunched it in her fists, yelling, "They will kill me. And then they will kill you. Don't you get it?"

Nina stared like I was the crazy one. "Look at me! Can't you see my tats?" Then she froze, pinching her brows and shaking her head. "No, of course, you can't. They're white tats. You have to be under a black light to see them." She looked me straight in the eye. "The tat says they own me. It's a pentagram." She pointed to her forehead, then dropped her voice and shoulders in despair. "There's no way out."

I got that. I knew all about tattoos and contracts. They were one and the same. Words or pictures, they're a declaration of ownership that defines the relationship, be it a club, swastika, butterfly, a naked woman, or Jesus. All sealed in ink. Nina had sealed her identity to Satanists.

Nina passed the tipping point and broke into tears, sobbing, seemingly clutched in the grip of a nameless fear. Her thick mascara pooled and dripped, making her look like a mime from hell.

Poor Nina.

I got up and walked around to face her, lifting her chin with my fingers, wiping the smears of mascara from her face and ensuring that she was looking me in the eyes. "I'm not going to lie to you. I really don't understand what you're saying, but if you're willing to trust me, I will help you through this mess. But you have to trust me first. Now . . . are you talking about a gang?"

"Not a gang!" Her black brows tented, and she reached out to me with trembling fingers, touching my shoulder. "You don't know who you're dealing with," she repeated, then lowered her voice to a snakelike hiss. "They sacrifice babies."

My budding headache bloomed. It was almost time for Nina to take the witness stand.

"I have to ask you, Nina. It's a standard question," I hurried to assure her. More like a standard lie. "Have you ever been diagnosed with any mental health issues? Are you under treatment or taking prescriptions?"

Vonda knocked at the door. The court bailiff poked her head inside. "Ready, Sunny," she said. Her gray eyes strayed to Nina, and she frowned. "Everything okay?"

"Please, Vonda, just one second."

"I can give you one minute—but no more." Vonda withdrew, closing the door behind her.

I took Nina by the shoulders. "Listen. Just get on the stand and look at me. I'm your advocate. I'm here for you. I promise that we'll talk after the trial. Trust me," I said as I tried to sweep both hair and mounting anger from her face.

"Bullshit," she said, knocking my arm away. "You think you're so smart." She put her face an inch in front of mine. "If you knew where this road leads, you'd run the other way—screaming."

She pulled back and squared her shoulders, opening the door with the confidence of a death row inmate who had made peace with her fate. Nina strode down the corridor and boldly pushed her way into the courtroom.

The towering door seemed to whisper a warning as it closed with a sigh.

ಬಂ ♀ ಞ

Amanda Cross swept into my office with the look of a two-hundred-and-fifty-pound African American ticked-off tigress that just lost her lunch to a jackal defense attorney. She was wearing her colorful trademark attire—today, a rustic orange-and-brown woven tribal kaftan with a matching turban wrap that layered around her head in folds before tucking into one side. She looked both formidable and magnificent.

"And just what was all that about?" Amanda growled. "You assured me that Nina was ready to go, and now I look like an idiot in front of that weasel, B.S. the Third."

I smiled. Defense attorney B.S. x 3—aka Brecken Stewart III—really was a weasel. He even looked like a weasel with his lanky, too-thin body, ferret nose, and beady brown eyes.

Amanda listened attentively as I related everything that had transpired with Nina. "I know it sounds outrageous, but it wasn't what she said. It was how she said it." I gave a slight shiver as I recalled Nina's words, "They sacrifice babies," and then I shrugged. "She didn't feel delusional."

Amanda arched her brows. "You know what delusional feels like?"

Warmth crept over my face. "No," I admitted, "but I know what honest feels like—and I know how liars feel. She just . . . well, has me wondering."

Amanda's brows knitted together like a pair of thoughtful shuttles weaving a plan on her mental loom.

"Call Danielle Kitch over at Behavioral Health. I'd like you to make time to see her once a week."

"What? You think I'm crazy?"

"Not necessarily," she qualified by flashing a quick smile. "This isn't the first time I've heard stories like Nina's, and probably won't be the last. She may be a survivor of ritual abuse."

"And exactly what is ritual abuse?" I asked.

"For us? When a cult has committed a crime by means of a ritualistic act. Something done repeatedly. They are usually called Satanists, my dear girl."

"Seriously?"

Amanda ignored my question and grew distant, as if she were wrestling with an old memory. "Yes," she concluded, "the more we learn about victim behaviors, the better it will be for all of us. It has to be one of the three C's."

"One of the three C's?"

"She is either clean, crazy, or criminal. Find out which."

Nina wouldn't talk to me after the trial or return my calls. Later, when I heard she was back dealing drugs for her boyfriend, I readily dismissed her dark and disturbing words.

Nonetheless, Nina had been a light—the first light to pierce the dimness of my understanding. The first sharp cutting away of a path that would lead me into a different kind of wilderness—one much different from the high country and the beloved mountains where I lived.

ॐ ♰ ॐ

The annoying sound of tapping pulled me back from sifting through the latest police reports that had been sent up to the district attorney's Special Victims Unit.

"It's me!" Paige sang out all atwitter. My birdbrained intern rapped on my door even as she pushed it open—first peeking, then barging, then waddling over to plop herself on the office sofa.

Oh, joy. If it isn't Pregnant Paige and Wonder Kid.

"Paige," I said, sounding as stern as a judge at sentencing, "I might have been counseling a victim." I pushed back from the desk and swung around to face her.

"But you weren't!" Paige countered in her naturally blond, naturally self-centered manner. "And guess what?" she asked, looking radiant.

It had been ages since Paige resembled anything close to happy, so I relented and swallowed the bait—hook, line, and—

"What's up?"

"He's here!" A glint of mischief sparked behind her clear blue eyes.

"Who's here?"

"The new computer guru. You know—Super-geek? Dweeb? Mega-Nerd?"

I laughed with her, mostly at her childish delight in gossip. Paige frequently acted twenty-three-going-on-thirteen. The Pregnant Paradox was both overly educated and highly immature for her position, but I only had myself to blame for recommending her.

"Let me guess . . ." I played along. Rolling my eyes, I leaned back in my chair and resumed chewing on my pen as I speculated. "Fat? Loser? Pimples? Coke-bottle glasses? Walks like a duck? Dressed in Walmart's finest?"

"Harrumph!" A deep, long throat-clearing "Harrumph" widened Paige's gaze as she stared over my shoulder.

Spinning around in my chair, I rose, startled, to stand face-to-face with six-foot-six, two hundred and fifty pounds of fat-loser-pimples, who wore Coke-bottle glasses and duck-shaped shoes and was probably dressed in Walmart's finest: the new technical supervisor—Super Geek, Dweeb, Mega-Nerd.

Oh, my Lord.

CHAPTER 2

೫ ✟ ೫

"Oh God, I can't believe I just said that," I said, feeling like Wiley Coyote straddling a stick of dynamite.

"Said what?" The stranger's voice suggested innocence that was betrayed by the hardening of his naturally soft features. From behind his Coke-bottle glasses, doe-brown eyes briefly splintered from the painful wound I had just inflicted. His lips—full lips—pinched for a moment above a chin that slightly trembled. He was either hurt or angry.

"Nothing. Nothing at all. Hi, hello, I'm Sunny McLane," I said in a voice even weaker than my handshake. "I am the advocate for the Special Victims Unit, and this is my advocate intern, Paige."

"My name is Duncan. Duncan Harder."

"Pffffft!" Paige spewed between pinched lips, leaning forward, unashamed. "I'm sorry," she sputtered without conviction, swiping the mirth from her eye. "I bet you got beat up in school with a name like that."

"Paige!" I was shocked and embarrassed—Paige's rudeness left me mortified. I would have fired her except that I was the person who got her the job in the first place. That—and the fact she might have been carrying my husband's child. Or my lover's. It was awkward. But she needed the money.

"Oh, come on." Paige shook her head, feigning superiority. "We're all adults here."

"Are we?" I asked, flushing with embarrassment.

Stung, Duncan paused and stared. First at Paige. Then at me. "Chief Technical Administrator for Butte County." He continued his introduction with a solemn air of dignity.

I swallowed hard. When it came to practicing faith, I still felt more like a lost cause than a lost sheep. It was more than not wanting to be a jerk and more than wanting to please my almost-pastor husband. I had been a victim of malicious verbal abuse and knew the pain intimately. I take no pleasure in being unkind to others. But sometimes I'm still a jerk.

"Pleased to meet you," Duncan replied with all the warmth of an auto-responder. His eyes never left me as he continued to stare with an intensity that made me squirm like a worm under his size fourteen shoes. Then he lifted his chin and turned away without so much as a word or a glance at Paige, squaring his broad shoulders and straightening to stand an inch or two taller as he lumbered out the door.

"Oh my God!" said Paige, as Duncan turned the corner—out of sight but not out of hearing. "How did you do that? You described him to a T."

I shook my head in wonder at Paige's stupidity and mine. The only difference between us was that I knew better.

ৎ ♀ ৎ

Waves of sunlight and shadow splashed across the foothills as I drove home from work. Going home was a bit like going to church. Everywhere I looked I was blessed by the beauty of creation, from the cathedral-like spires and domed mountaintops to the face of God dancing in the shimmering waters of the Feather River.

Our home was nestled on a three-thousand-foot-high ridge in the Sierra Nevada mountains with a view across the central valley to the Costal Range mountains. Together, the two mountain chains looked like arms that embraced the northern half of California. Butte County lay in the crook of the eastern arm and geographically included cities and small towns in both the valley and mountains.

"Hello, baby!" I stooped to pick up Kissme, my blond Pomeranian who greeted me with all the passion of a Ukrainian Kazachok dancer as she spun with near hysterical joy. Happiness was a little dog. Little dogs had always been my closest friends. Something, I supposed, about their unabated joy and devotion. "Hello to you too, Miss Mercy," I called affectionately to our German Shepherd, as Mercy came bounding up to me, happy to see anyone after a long day of chasing shadows. I was more Mercy's babysitter than master. Much like me, her heart belonged to my husband, Chance.

Juggling grocery bags, I raced to the kitchen with Kissme on my heels. If I hurried, I would have just enough time to make a pot of chili for the church potluck. I rolled up my sleeves and poured a little wine to soothe my growling stomach. If I didn't bring chili con carne, I would probably be forced to eat Ashley's "tofu con caca." I suppose I could survive being a vegetarian if I was one of those whose diet includes eggs, cheese, milk, fish, and chicken.

The vent over the stove rumbled like an airplane on takeoff, nearly drowning out the phone's ring.

"Oh, Chance—why now?" I complained to Caller ID, eyeing the clock as I stirred garlic and seasoning into the meat.

"Hello? Are you home? Pick up, pick up," the voice called out from the answering machine as I reached for the phone. "Hey babe, I was hoping you were home," said Chance.

"Yep, I'm still here—trying to feed the dogs, put away groceries, and cook chili all at once." Probably best not to mention the wine. That could sound either medicinal or celebratory, and I wasn't feeling either, although work had given me a headache and I was celebrating the end of the workweek.

"How was your day, hon?" Chance's voice was deep, rich, and as warm as a hug.

"Um . . . crazy." That felt accurate. "Hey, Chance, let me call you back tonight, after church? 'K?"

"No problem. Tell Mac and Shane I said hi. I miss—"

The whirr of the can opener sliced through our good-byes as I dumped the contents of the can into the pot and hung up.

"Oh, man—oh my gosh! I can't believe I just did that." The words Julienne Cut Beets jumped out from the empty can where Kidney Beans should have been. Out of time and out of hamburger, I rolled my eyes and poured a little more wine. "What the heck," I said, adding a proper can of beans, a little extra chili powder, and a couple of chopped jalapenos. "It's all good."

There was a new face at church. A very sweet middle-aged face framed with honey-blond curls and wire-rimmed glasses over a pair of blue-gray eyes that had locked onto Mac like a heat sensor on target. Pastor Mac was being his usual self, roving here, there, and everywhere, but the stranger never stopped following his moves.

"Hello, I'm Sunny McLane. I don't think we've met."

The stranger's hand was soft and her voice softer. "My name is Kinsey, but you can call me Oma" she said, never taking her eyes off Mac.

"Alma?"

"O-ma."

O-kay.

Oma must have read my mind as she turned from Mac. "It's a nickname," she said.

Ashley walked up as she finished off another bowl of my chili.

"You're eating meat," I observed.

"Can't help it, Sunny," she said between slurps. "This so good, I can't get enough. You have got to give me your recipe."

"Sure," I said. Positive that I would omit the can of beets.

"This is Kinsey." I *introduced* the stranger to Ashley, skipping the Oma part because I thought it was weird.

"We've met." Ashley greeted her warmly. "Good to see you, Oma." Ashley turned to me. "Oma is a guest of Pastor Mac's," Ashley added, with a tip of her head and a twitch at the corner of her mouth.

So, Ashley already knew about Kinsey aka Oma. I'd been to church almost every Sunday. How could I have missed headline news on the Gossip Gazette? A familiar twinge tightened in my stomach at the thought of being left out of the social loop.

The evening progressed with the majority of the people gathering into the same cliques they gathered into every Sunday morning. The monthly potluck was supposed to be for church folks to comingle with community members, and in the interest of fairness it did happen—starting with the usual icebreakers: "Would you get the door for me?" "Who made this?" "Would the driver of the green truck please move it so people can get out?" And always, "Where's the bathroom?"

I liked the bathroom. It sat apart from the historic little schoolhouse that served as the main building and had a heater hotter than a Pittsburgh furnace. Scurrying inside and out of the cold, I was horrified to find Ashley bent over a toilet heaving her insides out.

"Oh Ash, I am so sorry! It's my fault you're sick," I said, continuing to beg forgiveness as I patted her face with a moist paper towel over the sink. "It was the beets."

Ashley was sweating and trembling, giving me an incredulous look. "Beets?" Her eyebrows peaked in bewilderment.

"Yeah, I'm sorry. I accidentally put beets in the chili."

Ashley digested the information and doubled over again, this time with laughter. She grabbed another paper towel to dry her eyes, saying, "Not beets, silly." She sniffled. "Babies. I am going to have babies!"

"Babies?"

"Twins!

CHAPTER 3

೮♁೪

Tears glistened like so many crystal balls sparkling in the
lamplight foretelling my future. Kissme ignored them, scouring the
back of my hand with her tongue. It was her doggie way of
expressing love. I hoped. Kissme would have made a good mother,
but like me, that wasn't in our future. I'd spayed Kissme because I
loved her, and two pounds was too small to breed. But unlike my
dog, nothing was loving about my inability to bear children.

Life with Logan had gone from bad to worse. It was my
mother's hippy composition and my father's outlaw biker ways—
plus being raised in the woods without electricity—that shaped and
defined my youth. It was all I'd known. It was my life, and it wasn't
all bad. Until I'd gotten pregnant.

Like a pair of pit bulls locked on each other's throats, Logan
and I had gone round and round—he demanding an abortion and I
repeatedly refused. Logan finally won the argument when he
pushed me off the upstairs balcony, crushing our child and any
chance I might have had for another.

Kissme shifted gears from neutral into overdrive as little dogs
are wont to do, exploding into a frenzy of barking at the sound of
knocking. Ashley didn't wait for me to answer the door.

"Sssshh! Kissme—it's okay! Sunny? Sunny?" a soft voice called.
"It's me, Ashley."

No kidding? Only Ashley would be rude enough to walk in
uninvited to my pity party.

"Just a minute." I slipped into the kitchen and quickly washed
the sorrow from my face, like cold leftovers from a dirty plate, and
then shined it with a towel. "S'up?" I asked with a cheerful façade as
I tossed the towel aside.

Ashley never failed to remind me of my mother's peaceful presence in her younger years. Wrapping her arms around me, she said, "Sunny, I know I've hurt you, and I am so sorry."

"Why would you think that? Because I left before dessert? Or because I backed into Ramey's motorcycle in my less-than-graceful getaway?" My stomach churned the mix of resentment and beet chili into a bubbling mess.

Ashley snuggled next to me on the sofa with my traitorous dog jumping onto her lap.

She placed her hand on my shoulder. "Please forgive me. I didn't mean to hurt you. I would never hurt you on purpose. You're my friend, and I love you."

"I'm not hurt," I said, reaching for a tissue. "Why do you keep saying that?"

Ashley paused. "Kissme's head is wet," she observed, petting my tear-soaked dog. We locked eyes and laughed. "Oh, Ash, only you would notice such a thing. Why didn't you tell me you were pregnant?"

Ashley dropped her gaze and puckered her face, looking thoughtful and contrite as she squeezed my hand.

"Because you hate kids. And . . . I didn't want to spoil this time—our time—for Shane and me with negative energy. I've been on a natural high since finding out. It's so awesome! So amazing!" Her voice rose, shining like the sun. "It's like we've been dreaming and planning for this moment all our lives. Shane and I are thrilled beyond words."

Shane? Her husband was one of Chance's closest friends. The ugly thought slithered in. "Has Shane told Chance?"

"Yes. Of course."

Of course? "So . . . everyone knew but me—your closest friend?"

"It's because I'm your closest friend that I didn't want to tell you! I know you lost a baby once, and that must have been horribly painful for you . . . to leave you so bitter toward children."

Painful? She had no idea of the horror, the agony, the utter hopelessness in the months following the miscarriage. What it was like to be sucked through a wormhole into the dark place. I had prayed for death.

"I don't hate kids. I just don't need them." I pressed my lips into a tight line and blinked. "So, when are you due?"

"Four months." Ashley's face grew luminous as if a dimmer switch had been turned from soft to radiant. "Twins!" she exclaimed in a burst of joy. "I am going to have twins!" And she hugged me as if I cared. As if I could catch pregnancy like the flu.

I opened my mouth, but no words came out. They sank, feeding the toxic brew that still churned in my stomach. I tried again without success. This time the words were trapped behind a huge lump in my throat. All I could manage was a meaningless utterance—"Ungh"—and a nod to fill in the gaps.

"Isn't it fantastic?" Ashley rose to hug me, chatting for three all the way to the door. Nausea threatened. We hugged again and this time, "I'm happy for the both of you" slipped out of my mouth like a shadowy wisp. Then I closed the door and retreated to my familiar world of disassociation.

How can I help others when I can't help myself? I warred myself as I turned to walk down the hall.

Healing is a process, not an event, I reminded myself. Physical wounds heal, but emotional scars last a lifetime. Every time I thought I'd recovered, a new test would come. A new kind of punch—from someone I loved, leaving a different kind of bruise, a different kind of scar.

Disassociation is a survival mechanism for victims of prolonged abuse. The mind packs its bags and checks into a different reality and in extreme cases, a different personality. When my father would beat my mother or Logan would hit me or pull my hair. When hurtful words crushed my self-worth, or I was overwhelmed with sadness, I would withdraw. Sometimes into books and daydreams, and sometimes curled into a fetal position, hugging my knees to my chest and embracing the darkness that wrapped around me like a celestial womb.

℘ ♀ ℭ

Gayle called from reception. "Sunny, Amanda is waiting in the conference room. The first applicant has arrived."

I hurried to the conference room filled with mixed emotions. It was a bad time to remember that I had forgotten to call Chance back last night.

The meeting in the conference room would begin the first round of interviews for the Investigative portion of our vertical prosecution team. The team called for one prosecutor, one advocate, and one investigator. Vertical prosecution is a system that prevents cases from being handed off to multiple attorneys and increases conviction rates as victims are supported and stabilized They become part of the process instead of impartial witnesses. The former investigator for our unit, Travis Winslow, had returned to his position as a field operative at the Alcohol, Tobacco, and Firearms office in Oakland after finishing his work here. Now Travis was back working with his former father-in-law—Paige's dad.

Amanda, a deputy sheriff named Jax, and I seated ourselves behind a long table looking official and formidable as the first applicant shambled in.

Fred Edwards had worked for the Glenn County's Sheriff's Office since the beginning of time. Watery eyes peered out from bushy brows that reminded me that my lawn needed mowing. He probably had a barrel chest once, but now looked as if it had slipped beneath his belly button. Fred kept running his fingers through nonexistent hair, swiping at his head, which reminded me of the soft-boiled egg I'd had for breakfast.

Amanda ran through her list of questions and answers, then straightened the papers before her, to indicate that the interview was finished. She concluded with the traditional "Do you have any questions for us?"

"Where's the restroom?" Fred asked as he hitched up his pants.

The next person was a recent graduate from the law enforcement academy at the local community college. Duane Pickett wore multiple earrings and sported colorful tattoos that peeked from beneath his cuffed shirt. Too perky. Too trendy. Too green.

"Do you have any questions for us?" Amanda wrapped it up with the standard question.

"Do I get a car and a gun?"

Next.

A stunning black woman with the elegant name of Jewell Johnston entered the room. Tall and graceful, she exhibited a professional demeanor that belied the lack of experience on her résumé. She carried a black leather portfolio and handed out copies of her college transcripts and letters of recommendation. Her answers were accurate and concise. Her references were as impeccable as her attire.

"Do you have any questions for us?"

"When can I start?"

Amanda headed for lunch with a happy glow. I skipped lunch with a pounding headache.

ဢ ♀ ᘓ

"Excuse me, Mrs. McLane."

"Duncan." I bolted upright at my desk with a warm smile for the master computer tech. "You can call me Sunny. 'Missus' feels funny. Anyhow, my husband and I are sort of separated."

"Oh. I'm sorry." Duncan looked flustered, and I hurried to make him comfortable.

"Please sit down," I said, pulling out a chair.

"I'm here with your new laptop. I'll connect you back up to the county intranet, and of course, you'll be able to get online as well. Oh, and I'll show you how to download drivers for the office printer. It's easy."

"Won't you stay? I'm bound to mess up." I threw him a warm, adorable puppy-dog look. I was determined to give Duncan back the self-esteem I had so blithely stripped away before our first hello.

Duncan proceeded to walk me through the process of setting up the new laptop in place of my old dinosaur desktop computer. My workshops and outreach were going to be a lot simpler to prepare and present with just one computer.

"Oh, by the way, the projector should be here any day," said Duncan. He brushed by me on his way out the door.

"Duncan. Is that. . . Eternity I smell?" I recognized the crisp scent of jasmine, sweet basil, and sage that I had given to Chance as parting joke-gift when he left for seminary school.

A blush crept up from under the head tech's starched white shirt, and laugh lines deepened at the corners of his mouth. "Yes. It is. Thank you. . . um, I'll show you how it's done. Uh, the uh, run the projector that is."

"Thank you, Duncan." I kept him there for a few more minutes making small talk: asking how he liked his job, where he used to work, etc. etc., then sucked down half a dozen M&Ms and a

Tylenol, thinking all the while that a half-dozen Tylenol and one M&M might have been the better choice.

Halfway back to the conference room I pulled up short and slapped my forehead. Oh man, I still haven't called Chance.

How had my husband slipped to the last place on my list of to-dos? While I was still working on the process of complete forgiveness, Chance's decision to move to San Diego and attend seminary school last September had come with a washtub of mixed emotions that I was still sorting out. I was proud that he felt called to be a pastor but sad that he might give up his profession with law enforcement and search and rescue. I was glad to have my independence but sad that Chance had moved away.

Pulling my pen from my desk, I hastily jotted *Call Chance* into my appointment book and let my fingers linger over his name, then hurried back to the interviews with a lighter step.

Two more applicants to go. One as soft as pudding. The other as hard as nails.

Bonita Esquivel was not as large or grand as Amanda, but she would make a formidable contender if they were mud-wrestling. Amanda seemed regal compared to Bonita's roughness. My father would have said Bonita was built like a "brick shithouse." I tried not to talk like that, but the image came to mind nonetheless. She wore her chestnut-brown hair buzzed short, and there was a mustache on her lip as sure as there was a gun on her hip. Bonita's background was in corrections, and throughout the interview, I kept wishing she were assigned to guard Logan. If Logan messed with her, she would probably beat him to death with her baton. I liked Bonita. A lot.

As always, Amanda asked her if she had questions for us, to which Bonita replied, "Can I ride my motorcycle to work?"

The last person for the day was Jas Wheeler—wearing pants that were tighter than Paige's pre-pregnant spandex outfits, loafers, a hot-pink shirt, and smelling like a bowl of French vanilla pudding. He did not have a gun or a portfolio, but he did have a pack. Not a military commando-style pack or a messenger bag, but a man purse. Okay. Not a problem. If he could have talked without a lisp and effeminate hand gestures, he might have been a consideration. But the job of Investigator for the Special Victims Unit sometimes included interviewing brutal wife beaters, and frankly, I didn't want Jas to become the next victim.

Amanda asked Jas the final question of the day, "Do you have any questions for us?"

"What is the dress code for transgender employees?"

ରୀ ⚇ ଔ

I needed an appointment with mental health. Not as a client—yet—but regarding Nina's case.

"Dano speaking."

"Danielle Kitch?" I asked.

"Yes, this is Dano. How can I help you?"

Dano? Drano? I rubbed my tired head as I briefed her on my encounter with Nina and requested a consultation. My request was followed by a weighty pause on the other end of the line.

"How fast can you get over here?"

I had a few more hours until "quittin' time," so I agreed to hurry over.

Dano and I swapped credentials as a formality. She was pleasant and easy to talk to. No rooster-strutting or hen-pecking ego trips arose. Her eyes sparked with anticipation.

"Impeccable timing," she said from behind her desk. "I have a client scheduled in about . . ."—she glanced at her watch—"fifteen minutes that I think you will find interesting, to say the least. I've been seeing this particular client for about three months now. Her name . . . well, one of her names is Taylor."

One of her names?

"Taylor is the only case of multiple personality disorder—also called DID for dissociative identity disorder—that I've ever treated. I think you will find her . . . interesting. Taylor has made some extraordinary legal claims, and frankly," Dano said as she tapped her pencil on the desk, "I don't have a clue how to proceed with the legalities. But we can talk about that after her session." Then Dano asked me the magic question that would forever bond us as friends: "Latte?"

Dano definitely had my interest. "So what does a case of dissociative identity disorder look like?" I asked as she mixed some instant mocha lattes for us. We settled back in our chairs as she briefed me on her client's background. "DID is a severe form of dissociation that produces a lack of connection in a person's thoughts, memories, feelings, actions... even their sense of identity.

Think of two or more complete, distinctive individuals sharing the same body. They may not be the same age or even the same sex, and only one personality can emerge at a time. The presenting personality controls the person's behavior. The *different people*," Dano made quotation marks in the air with her fingers, "have varying degrees of knowing about the other one's existence."

"It sounds like science fiction or something out of a bad movie, like Invasion of the Body Snatchers," I said, taking a weak stab at humor.

"Yes, it does, doesn't it? But of this, I am certain," said Dano, as she thoughtfully licked the last traces of the sweet beverage from her lips, "after three months of clinical observation and evaluation, I can say that my client has no chemical dependencies, and I have ruled out delusions, psychosis, and paranoid schizophrenia."

"Just how many personalities does she have?"

"Watch and see."

Taylor Jarreau was a large woman, but her slumped shoulders, downcast eyes, and the stealthy way she slipped into the room would make her presence diminutive in any social setting. Her caramel-colored skin and honey-colored hair only added to her mystique.

"Hello, Taylor. Nice to see you again," said Dano, to which Taylor nodded an acknowledgment but did not raise her head. "Taylor, my friend Sunny is with us today from the district attorney's office. Can you say hello to Sunny?"

Taylor had hunkered down into a hardback chair, her upper body slowly curling into her lower half as she rolled forward, her brown eyes darting about like startled quail from beneath her long thick lashes. "Hello" she mumbled in a soft, childlike voice and a tentative wave of her fingertips.

"Is it okay with you if Sunny stays with us through our session?"

"I like your name. It's pretty," said Taylor.

"I like your name too, and your hair. It's beautiful," I replied with a smile.

Taylor's chin tucked into her chest. "You can stay," she said as she crossed her arms to hug herself.

"Taylor, I would like your permission to speak with Pat today. Would that be okay with you? Sunny would very much like to meet

Pat." Dano raised a watch this eyebrow in my direction as Taylor appraised me with caution.

I gave Taylor an encouraging smile and nod as she continued to rock herself, back and forth. Taylor paused and cocked her head as if listening to a voice that only she could hear. "Uh-huh," she acquiesced.

Taylor unfolded like a time-lapse camera that had captured the unfurling of a blossoming bud. Or perhaps more accurately, like a frame-by-frame slow-mo of the scene in the classic horror movie The Exorcist, when twelve-year-old Regan's head spun around backward. Slowly, with feet reaching for the floor and arms unwrapping from her torso, Taylor grasped the arms of the chair and pulled herself upright. Her chin came up, and her eyes popped wide open with a look as sharp as an axe. The transfiguration was mesmerizing, paralyzing. But what rocked me was the deep, throaty, authoritative voice that boomed forth with startling clarity.

CHAPTER 4

᪻ ☦ ᪺

Where is a camera when I need one?

Smiling with an air of confidence, Taylor leaned toward me and extended her hand in friendly greeting. "Hello," she said. "I'm Pat. Pleased to meet you." The scene was mind-numbing, and I reacted by shaking her hand on autopilot. Her grip was firm, her handshake solid. It was hard to conceive—yet impossible to deny—that a different person now inhabited Taylor's body.

Dano began the session, and soon Pat was zigzagging through her life like a bloodhound tracking her most powerful memories, starting at around age five and spanning over thirty years.

"My mother, Deirdre, is a high priestess," said Pat with her chin up and chest out. "She is very powerful and influential." Pat stared at me as though gauging my reaction. "She was a judge in Southern California."

She got no reaction from me. Maintaining a poker face was part of my job description.

Dano carefully guided and questioned Pat. "Where was your mother a judge in Southern California?"

"San Bernardino. But she has disciples everywhere."

"And the priest? What can you tell me about the priest?" Dano asked.

"My father? He's the most important person." Taylor Jarreau drew herself up, sitting tall. "He lives with my mother. They moved to Jenner after the big scare in Butte County. I grew up in Berry Creek. Now they live on the Russian River, in Jenner—where the river meets the ocean."

I knew her parents had to be rich to live in a town where home prices started in the million-dollar range.

"Tell us more about Berry Creek, Pat. What happened there?"

Pat gave a coy smirk. "I was their prize. They dressed me in white, and only the most honored and powerful people, could have me."

"How did they have you?"

She looked up suggestively through half-closed lids. "High Mass," she said. "They would blindfold me and usually drive to town, but sometimes out in the woods. Sometimes I'd go down a ladder. Sometimes steps. But usually deep underground, into the tunnels, beneath Oroville. There were people. Lots of people. Wearing black robes and chanting in some weird language. Then they would lay me on an altar and remove the blindfold . . . and other things," she added, suggestively tracing her finger along her breastbone, coming to rest halfway to her navel.

Dano leaned forward over her desk and asked Pat, "Where was Taylor while this was happening?"

Pat flinched and gave a dismissive shrug. "Taylor's weak and stupid. She would never survive down there. She's not like me," she said with a curl at one corner of her mouth. "It's just a game."

Pat went on to talk about the sexual depravity the honored guests would engage in and of sexual perversions between cult members. She seemed to enjoy giving explicit details of her parents as they performed ritual animal sacrifices.

The pictures Pat painted sent chills racing up my spine and left me wavering between shivers and nausea. To hell with survivors, I thought, positive that I wanted nothing more to do with the occult or its victims.

An hour later Dano said farewell to Pat, and with the delicate precision of a surgeon's knife she invited Taylor's persona to return. Dano concluded the session by setting a new appointment with the now present, introverted, and insecure Taylor, and then bid her good-bye. Taylor rose to her feet and took the appointment card, hugging it to her breast as she padded silently to the door.

Aghast, I turned to Dano. "You've seen this before?"

"Not like this. Not where the abuse was so extreme and prolonged the other personalities splintered into new identities."

"Are these different personalities aware of one another?" I asked.

"Yes and no," said Dano, slouching in her chair.

That made me smile. "You'd make an excellent defense attorney."

"No thank you," Dano wrinkled her nose. "Sometimes the personalities have no knowledge of another one's existence, and sometimes it's limited. For example, it was safe to say that Taylor has never been to a gathering. Pat is a stronger personality, and so she goes in Taylor's place. Taylor knows about Pat, but has no knowledge of Pat's experiences in the tunnels or woods."

The office was warm, and yet I continued to shiver in spite of the thick cable sweater I wore over my blouse. I pulled my neck scarf higher and flicked one end over my shoulder to trap the warmth.

Dano gave a deep sigh and looked at me thoughtfully. "Any thoughts on how to proceed legally?"

"I'm sure it's loaded with legal implications. There's always a myriad of problems associated with delayed reporting of any kind. You're not going to want to hear this"—I winced—"but my partner, Travis, and I once had to tell a woman who had been chained, naked, to a tree for an entire summer that the evidence she gave was too old and the witnesses too cold to substantiate the facts. There was not enough evidence for prosecution.

"You see, it isn't whether a case happened in fact but whether the facts can be proven. The burden of proof for the prosecution was beyond a reasonable doubt. For the jury, delay and doubt are usually proportionate and . . . um . . . there's the matter of Taylor's mental health history. That would likely increase uncertainty and decrease credibility."

Dano mulled it over. "It occurs to me that Mental Health could use some training from your department on the topic of ritual abuse. It's long overdue. You'd be surprised at how many clients we get claiming to be cult victims. It's been a taboo topic since the witch hunts of 1970's infamous 'Satanic Panic.' We don't talk about it much here at work, but the problem hasn't gone away. We still have client-victims."

I wasn't sure what she meant by "Satanic Panic," except that the very term made me feel panicky. However, I was curious enough to overcome my revulsion and cautiously ask, "By the way, about how many allegations of ritual abuse do you get in a year?"

Dano tipped her chair back and looked up, calculating. "Twelve . . . maybe fifteen."

I stared, eyes wide, mouth open. "Per counselor?"

"No." She nodded. "Between the six of us."

Still, I wanted to run. Thanks, but no thanks. Rising, I thanked Dano and gave her my card. I looked forward to seeing her again but determined that I would limit future visits to general education, like Mental Health Diagnostics 101. I wanted nothing more to do with multiple personalities or bizarre cults.

My life was crazy enough.

I had a psychopathic ex serving time in prison, a repentant husband serving time in seminary, and an intern I resented about to give birth to a baby that I hated, fathered by someone I loved.

Sigh . . .

ഇ ⚕ ന

I sent Chance a text message from my office, apologizing and promising to call him when I got home and signed it with Xs and Os. Then my mind turned to M&Ms. My stomach rumbled like the sound of food dropping inside of a vending machine. Somewhat embarrassed at the thought of being seen porking out on junk food for the second time in one day, I headed for the relative seclusion of the downstairs break room contemplating the question of the age: Do calories count if no one sees you eat them?

My fingertips had just wrapped around the doorknob to the break room when I froze at the sound of a heated argument. Familiar voices triggered a buffet of emotions that swept away all thoughts of anything sweet.

"I won't. I won't! And you can't make me!"

Paige, for sure.

"It's my right!"

Travis. Oh, my.

"Screw your paternity test! This is my baby! I know the law, and you can't make me do anything I don't want to do." Paige's voice had the ear-splitting quality of feedback screeching through a microphone.

"You are one heartless bitch. You take the word selfish to whole new level. Everyone wants to know. Your parents want to know. Chance and I need to know. Probably even your old boyfriend Mark would like to know." Travis sounded like a revved-up engine. Then he popped the clutch. "Is that why you won't take a paternity test? Still playing head games, or is this just another power trip?"

"Mark could care less. Besides, he's . . . fixed."

"Fixed? Good God, Paige—you think men are dogs?"

"Vasectomy," Paige corrected herself. "And don't think my parents—with all their money—can force me to take the test either. You don't need to drag them into our problems."

My heart was thudding in my chest and roaring in my ears. They were bound to hear it, unless I passed out and fell through the door first.

Travis lowered his voice. "I need to move on. If it's my child, I want to honor it. If not, I need to know. I'll get lawyers and a court order if necessary."

"You just try it, Travis," Paige snarled, "and I'll—"

"You'll what?" Travis's words were sharp and clipped. Furious.

Travis was not a man to lose his temper. Letting go of the doorknob, I drew breath.

"I'll get an abortion!" Paige hissed.

Easing away from the door, I fled to the safety of my office.

ℬ ♀ ℭ

I reached up to touch the smooth particleboard cross lying warm against my neck. Particleboard is a manufactured wood product composed of shattered fragments that had been reformed into a product many times stronger than the original slab. Chance had made it for me to symbolize that our broken marriage could not only be repaired but made stronger. I wanted that to be true. I did. With all my heart.

"Everything okay?" Chance asked. Dinner was in the oven, and it was time for our daily phone hug. "I know you can take care of yourself, but I still worry about you."

I have had to eat those words—I can take care of myself—every day for the past three and a half months. I really could take care of myself. Mostly. But I still regretted throwing the fact in my husband's face. When Chance was here, I didn't want his protection. Now that he was gone, I felt exceedingly vulnerable.

The quiet magnified as I wandered through the empty living room while talking with my beloved husband. Maybe it is me that feels empty, and not the room. I hugged the phone to my ear and let my fingers affectionately trace Chance and Mercy's display case, filled with medals and citations for valor in their work in search and rescue and the Army Special Ops. *This box is like the man;* the thought made me smile. It was hard on the outside, lined with soft satin padding, and filled with a lifetime of commemorative acts of service and self-sacrifice.

"Yeah. It's all good," I continued. "I've just been distracted with all the interviewing going on at work." I laughed and joked as I told him about the various applicants.

"Travis is going to be hard to replace." Chance's remark caught me off guard. Just hours ago I had dismissed the idea of telling him about the argument I had overheard between Travis and Paige. I hadn't seen Travis since September at Logan's sentencing—which started me thinking about Logan.

It felt wrong that Logan was only two hours northeast of my home, housed at High Desert State Prison. He was too close—even if he was behind bars and rolls of barbed wire for the next thirty years. He should be in Cambodia, or maybe Siberia.

I didn't want to talk about Travis, and I sure didn't want to dwell on Logan. Taking a deep breath, I chose my battle.

"I saw Ashley last night. She came over after church."

"How are they doing?"

"They? You mean—the four of them?"

There was a long pause, and I could hear Chance release an even longer sigh.

"I guess she told you, huh? About the babies."

Chance waited for a response that I wouldn't give. I was glad he couldn't see the hurt that I felt etched on my face: lips superglued together, twin furrows that plowed between my brows, and the sharp sting of mascara in the corners of my eyes.

"Shane told me," said Chance, sounding like a confession.

"And I suppose he asked you not to tell me?" More hurt.

"Not exactly. Shane asked me to let Ashley tell you when she was ready."

"And when was that supposed to happen? At the twins' first birthday party—when I ask them, 'Whose kids are those?'"

Another sigh stretched across the miles and lingered.

"If you give Ashley a chance, you'll find out how much she loves you. Right or wrong, it's her way of trying to spare you."

"Oh please, Chance! I'm sick of you and everyone else *sparing me* with lies."

A chill crept through the phone as I stood at a familiar crossroad. This conversation would either move us backward or forward, and back would take us nowhere.

"I went to Mental Health today."

Silence. "I'm sorry. Did it help?"

This was why I was reluctant to call. I was tired of walking a tightrope between the past and the present.

"Not for me. It was work related." And I proceeded to tell Chance about Nina and Taylor and the unnerving manifestation of multiple personalities I had witnessed at Mental Health.

"I know this won't sound professional or politically correct, but Taylor totally creeped me out. It was like a real-life horror show. I've never seen anything like it . . . and I don't ever want to again."

"Maybe God is bringing you a special assignment: people that no one else will help."

"What if I don't want God's special assignment? Don't I ever get a say in my own life?" I gripped the phone, pinching my words.

"Then . . . He will find someone else who is willing."

And I get damned? I fumed. Jeeze-iz! "Why do you have to spiritualize everything? Can't I just be creeped out?"

Sometimes I wished my husband loved me half as much as he loved the Lord. I hung up the phone more frustrated and confused than when I'd started.

Before I went to bed that night, I sent Chance another text message. "I'm sorry I hung up on you. I love you, Chance."

He didn't reply, and I didn't blame him.

ഇ ☥ ര

Three days of work interviews passed in pretty much the same fashion, with applicants falling into one of three categories: Interesting, Maybe, and No Way in Hell.

"Bonita. She's the one," I said with great conviction.

Amanda's shrewd eyes narrowed, pinning me like a butterfly to a mat. "Why her?" she asked, her voice tight and somewhat accusing. "I happen to favor Miss Jewell myself." Amanda hurried on, flipping through Miss Jewell's letters of recommendation. "She was an investigative intern with the Department of Justice."

"Bonita was a CO and investigator with the Department of Corrections," I countered.

Amanda huffed. "It's because she's black, isn't it? Go ahead. Admit it."

No, it's because she's young and beautiful, and I don't need my husband whoring after another coworker.

"You got me, Amanda. You're right. I don't want Jewell because she is black." I called Amanda's bluff and laughed to myself as she bolted upright, her eyebrows knocking holes in the ceiling.

"What did you say?"

"I said, 'I don't want Miss Jewell because she is black.' What this unit needs is an experienced bilingual Hispanic." Not to mention possibly bisexual. Bonita didn't feel like a threat to my marriage.

Amanda acquiesced by lowering one brow, followed by a "Humph."

I blinked innocently and stroked her ego. "I hear they're interviewing for a new 'gator over in the Bad Check unit. I bet Jewell could get that position if you use your persuasive skills."

This is why I get paid the big bucks.

Amanda "Humphed" again, and Bonita got the job.

CHAPTER 5

ॐ ☥ ॐ

Paige dabbed at the tears that trickled along her soft round cheeks. Today she had that mystical glow that sometimes highlights pregnancy, although lately her light was periodically overshadowed by dark smudges under bewildered and sometimes vacant eyes.

I wondered for the millionth time how this could possibly be the same woman who, in her pre-pregnant state, dressed like a hooker, walked like an exotic dancer, and dripped oil and vinegar from her tongue.

"Oh, Sunny," Paige sniffled, "how can you be so nice to me?"

Good question. I had transitioned over the past two years from genuinely admiring Paige and wishing we were girlfriend close to loathing her, to indulging in occasional fantasies of strangulation, to finally—with God's grace—working on forgiveness and even engaging in occasional random acts of kindness. Our relational journey had been forged through trials of fire and ice. The road Paige and I traveled was a rough road; full of twists and turns, potholes, washouts, and fallen rocks. But I tried—on occasion.

"Oooh, Pandora charms! My favorite! They are totally adorable," Paige cooed, clasping the box to her chest as she threw me a radiant look of appreciation. "You are spoiling me."

I winced. Pandora had been fresh out of morning-after pill charms and Planned Parenthood logo charms, so I had gone with cutesy baby charms.

"Let me help you," I said, popping off her Pandora bracelet to add a silver pacifier and a tiny heart etched with baby footprints.

"Do you know if it's boy or a girl yet?"

"No." She sniffed. "I don't want to know."

A new thought occurred. "Paige? Have you even been to a doctor?"

"Nice to see you two hard at work."

I dropped the bracelet, sending charms bouncing across the room at the sound of Jack Savage's deep voice. My panic got a laugh out of him.

"Nice to know I'm a cheap source of entertainment," I said, throwing a mock scowl at my boss. "You startled me."

Jack rolled his eyes. "I wouldn't say, cheap." He looked distinguished for a man in his fifties. Today he wore a white shirt and tailored black suit that accentuated his salt-and-pepper hair. Jack looked more like a Supreme Court judge than Butte County's District Attorney.

"Sunny, I got a call from the director of Behavioral Health this morning. They're requesting that you put together training on working with crime victims who have mental health issues." He paused, his brow forming a question mark. "Something about cults. Anything I should know about?"

"I had a victim who made some bizarre claims. Amanda suggested that I consult with Mental Health."

Jack nodded. "Good idea. I like it. Put together some outreach for the various social services."

"I'm not qualified." That, and I would be the laughingstock of my coworkers. A certified nut.

"Maybe not, but you'll get there. Keep consulting with mental health." A jittery attorney danced behind Jack, looking as if he was about to hang himself by his necktie, so Jack moved on.

"What was that all about?" Paige asked as she picked up the last of the charms and put them back on her bracelet.

"I worked with a victim last week who claimed to be part of a cult, or drug dealers, or something."

"You always get the cool cases. Let me help. Please?" Paige looked . . . charming.

I hesitated and then agreed. I wanted her on my good side before moving on to the next topic.

"I thought I saw Travis on my way out last night. Was he here?"

Paige froze, fumbled, and almost sent the charms rolling again. "Travis? Uh-huh. He was here."

"How is he?" I enlarged my eyes, feigning innocence, even as Paige narrowed hers. As her divorce from Travis was drawing to a conclusion even as the matter of paternity escalated.

If I had a piece of chocolate for every hour I'd spent lying awake at night, puzzling over Paige's obsessive refusal to disclose the sperm donor, I'd be a walking pimple. Maybe Paige really was on a power trip like Travis said, but sometimes I thought not.

"Travis is okay, I guess. It's just a guilt trip he's on, wondering if it's his kid."

"Is it?" I tried to maintain an aura of innocence as Paige rolled her eyes in exasperation. We had never talked about my feelings for Travis. Perhaps she felt she had no right to ask me after having an affair with my husband. If that was so, then Paige and I finally agreed on something.

"Give me your cult cases. I love that stuff," Paige said as she rose to leave. "That would be so sick"—which I took to mean "cool."

It was totally uncool; sick-sick, and I hated all that "stuff."

I wanted no part of it but grudgingly set about trying to figure out some kind of training module for social services.

℟ ⚜ ℜ

Bonita barged in as Google brought up 286,000 results to the question "What is Satanic Panic?"

"Got a victim?" she queried as she repositioned herself to see my screen. I noticed Bonita was nicely dressed in a dark pantsuit and white collared shirt. I wondered if she had tats on her biceps like Logan's entwined snakes, imagining her with death heads and a Mexican flag under that unassuming polyester outfit.

"Maybe." I shook my head, sweeping away thoughts of tattoos. "What do you know about satanic cults?"

"More than I'd like to. You see a lot of that stuff in prison. The problem is that no one believes anything an inmate says."

Bingo. "Really?" I tried my no-fail eye-batting technique. "Maybe you can do this training for me."

"No gracias!"

So much for no-fail.

Bonita slapped me down momentarily with a definitive slant to her right brow that acted as a counterweight to the left side of her mouth.

"But I have a friend who might be able to help you. Old 'Witch-Hunting Wally' and I worked together at the Leo Chesney facility in Live Oak." Bonita wrote a phone number on my Post-it pad. "He works in Glenn County now," she said, "but he investigated a lot of that stuff back in the day."

I called Old Witch-Hunting Wally to talk about "that stuff," and he graciously set an appointment for Thursday.

I spent the next few days bouncing between court and research for my PowerPoints. Thursday came quickly.

The stack of boxes on the dolly was almost taller than the person wheeling them into the office. A happy-looking man popped out from behind the stack wearing a cheery smile and a pair of wire-rim glasses that rested on his fleshy red nose. He extended his hand.

I'm not sure what I was expecting, but Wally wasn't wearing a cross or a string of garlic around his neck, and he wasn't as large or old as I imagined either. However, he was packing heat, and I briefly considered the possibility of a silver bullet.

"Hi, there! I'm Wallace . . . Wally. I brought you a little something," he said with a smile that stretched from ear to ear. "No need to return them," he asserted. "They are all yours," he said, patting the stack farewell.

My eyes rounded like a pair of full moons on an alien planet. The boxes contained the remnants of past criminal cases: reports, recorded interviews, and crime scene and evidentiary photos that spanned over twenty-five years of investigations. What I found most disturbing was Wally's exuberance in unloading them.

"Tell me, Wally—how did you ever get into handling ritual abuse cases? And so many?"

"See this?" he said, lowering his laughing eyes and pointing to his head. "I had hair before I took on these cases. Back when I was an investigator in the sheriff's office."

Wally glanced at his watch. "Got time for lunch?" he asked, all shiny-faced and expectant.

Within minutes we were headed for a local café. Wally ordered enough food for himself and his clone—and his clone's clone—while I picked away at a dismal-looking salad.

"The years went by seeing the craziest things," said Wally, as he thoughtfully chewed on a side of beef. "Pentagrams on barn floors, dead animals that had been surgically dismembered, altars built from piles of stones out in the woods . . . with black candles on top." He swallowed and continued. "All covered with animal blood. And then the local cemetery—God, the cemetery was a total nightmare. Bodies dug up, fresh graves dug with grave liners placed inside."

"What's a grave liner?" I asked, thinking that Wally would've made a fine forensic pathologist, doing autopsies over lunch.

"It a liner that looks like a coffin. The coffin actually sits inside of it. But local Satanists used them to bury people alive and then dig them back up again as part of their rituals."

I swallowed hard, feeling as if a cherry tomato was stuck in my throat.

"That kind of stuff never made the papers," said Wally, jabbing his fork in the air emphatically, and then he calmed down to muse, "That—and even worse. Like the refrigerator we found with jars of body parts—disgusting." He shook his head and took another bite. "That never made the papers either. It was like nobody wanted to talk about it because it was so damned uncomfortable. So . . . unconscionable."

Wally seemed to snap out of his muse. "Sorry," he said. "I guess you're new to this, huh?" And then he gave a little shrug and smiled a mischievous little smile, adding, "I feel sorry for you. It's a dirty job, but—"

"No witnesses? No prosecution?" I asked.

Wally tipped his head dismissively. "Yeah. Sort of. It's just that things changed as years went by. Nobody talks about it anymore. The crimes didn't change—don't change—just the way we respond to them . . . or don't respond to them, I should say. The era of Satanic Panic was the best thing that ever happened to a Satanist."

Later that day, I drove back to the office with a trunk full of information—but zero understanding of that remark.

ॐ ♀ ℞

Grace took a seat on the office sofa, shaking her head as she declined my offer of something to drink. Staring quietly as I read the police report, she played with the zipper on her hoodie, tugging it up and down, up and down.

"Do you believe me?" she pleaded in a hoarse whisper.

I held up a single finger to indicate that I needed another moment to finish reviewing the police report.

Another domestic violence case. Or so I thought.

I didn't meet with perpetrators, but, then, Grace wasn't at my office with the usual request to drop charges. All she wanted was for someone to believe her.

Not me. I was hoping she was no more than a byproduct of being immersed in Wally's files.

Grace's story did not have me by the heart at first, but she did have me by the gut. My intuition and indigestion told me that she was telling the truth—a very uncomfortable truth.

The police report stated that Grace's boyfriend, Nate, had called 911 to say that Grace was tearing up his home and he needed police assistance. Nate had met the responding officer out on the lawn with a good buddy attitude, gesturing over his shoulder toward the house and the sound of screaming and breaking glass, saying, "Check this bitch. This is what I have to put up with."

Nate went on to show the sympathetic officer scratch marks on his cheek, whereupon Grace was promptly arrested for misdemeanor domestic violence.

"The report says you smashed out the windows in Nate's home."

"I did," said Grace. "I was trying to escape, but the officer didn't believe me."

"False imprisonment is a serious crime. Tell me more. How did you meet Nate?"

"I was on a softball team with Feather River Parks and Rec, and he slid into me on third base. The next day he showed up at the pizza parlor during my nephew's birthday party. My nephew, Runny, was turning seven."

"Runny?"

"It's Ronnie's nickname. Anyhow, Nate talked to me for a while and then offered to buy us a pitcher of beer. I said, 'No thanks,' but then he got really freaky. He started telling me all kinds of details about Runny—like, where he lives and who his friends are, where he goes to school and stuff like that. Then Nate said that if I ever want to see my nephew alive again, I'd better go with him to his car. So I did."

"Where did he take you?"

"He took me to a motel." Her blue eyes clouded over and threatened rain.

"And then?"

"I was there for a really long time. Nate kept me tied me to a bed, and they would come in and take turns whenever they wanted."

"Who took turns, doing what?"

"His stupid little Devil friends wearing rubber Halloween masks. They fucked me for three days and nights and said I belonged to them. They told me no one would believe me"—Grace hung her head in despair—"and they were right about that."

"Did you go to the hospital?"

Grace gave me an incredulous look. "No way. If they would kidnap and rape me, what do you think they would do to Runny?"

The tears fell, and Grace panicked when I suggested we get our investigator involved.

"No cops. They'll kill me!" Her voice ratcheted with tension. "I just needed someone to believe me." She cast about the room as though Satanists would come out of the woodwork. Again she whispered, "Do you believe me?"

God help me. I did. And in doing so, I stirred a pot of memories best left behind.

೫✝౩

"Mom? You got a few minutes?"

"Sure, baby. What's up? "Starla took a long pull off a joint and offered it to me.

"No thanks. Um, can we take a walk?"

"Yeah. Sure you don't want a hit?"

"No, Mom. I don't smoke."

Starla sniffed a rebuke and then went inside, interrupting her latest boyfriend and Logan in the middle of a business transaction to say that we were taking a walk. We strolled through the orchard, down to the Maidu grinding stones.

Starla didn't look overjoyed at our mother-daughter reunion. Her infrequent visits had grown scarce. I hadn't seen her in months, and here she was with someone new. Always someone new. They were looking to score drugs from Logan.

We climbed up to sit together on the moss-covered boulders in the cool forest shade.

"He knocked you up. Am I right?" Tact was never my mother's strong suit.

"No, Mom—he knocked me out. He used to just push me around. Last month, he punched me in the head and knocked me out. Unconscious."

Starla stared for a moment, then flitted her hands in the air as if to brush away an annoying insect. "Oh, Sunny. You are so melodramatic. You always have been. That's your problem. You're just saying that because your dad used to beat me."

Starla relit her joint and took another hit. "You just want me to feel sorry for you. Logan's not so bad. If you weren't so damned prissy, you wouldn't be having these problems. You need to lighten up and stop pissing him off. Logan's wild—but he wouldn't hurt you."

Mom was partly right—I was looking for sympathy. I was also looking for compassion. Hell, I was looking for a ticket out. My mother offered none of these. In the end, Starla drove away leaving me feeling even more helpless and hopeless than when she had arrived.

I sighed, recollecting and resurrecting old wounds. The anguish and disregard felt as fresh and raw as a newly picked scab.

I concluded that there was no greater loneliness than having your biggest fear dismissed. There was no deeper feeling of hopelessness than abandonment. There was no more lasting sense of rejection than being called a liar in the face of your truth.

CHAPTER 6

ഇ ✢ ೧

If I hurry, I'll have just enough time. I pulled into Babies "R" Us and glanced at the time. Ashley's baby shower started at noon. I tried to beat down feelings of resentment as I gathered my purse.

Not much different than having your best friend win the lottery—you want to be happy for her. But what if she won the lottery the day after my home was foreclosed? Or was getting married as I was filing for divorce? Or landed her dream job the very day I got fired? I may have been Christian, but I was only human.

Watching other people's dreams come true felt like another test. The old theme of God loves Ashley more than He loves me seemed to grow along with my best friend's waistline. She would get two kids—I would get none. I shut the car door with a sigh. Sometimes it was hard to know the difference between an act of God and Lady Luck, but then, I guess I was still young in the faith. Or perhaps, growing in faith took a lifetime.

That said, throwing Ashley a baby shower turned out to be easier than I'd ever imagined. That was the nice thing about being part of a church and having Christian friends. Logan once said that getting Christians to do good deeds was as simple as baiting a hook, that you "only need to dangle the promise of a good deed and they will snap it up." But that was Logan, not me.

Once I put the word out, the generous souls of the church were more than eager to help spread the joy and love of welcoming a new child into the world, and soon I had promises for more than enough food, half a dozen offers to bake cakes, and her newest best friends offering to come up with some fun games to play at the party. All that was really left for me to do was buy some decorations and a gift, and get the guest of honor there.

Still, I wasn't looking forward to the event. I resented the obligation to celebrate her deceit. I was certainly not jaded. A little negative, I supposed, but Ashley hadn't been a very good "best friend" lately.

It's like finding out on Facebook that your sister is pregnant.

Holding up little matching pairs of baby overalls, one forest green, and one autumn brown, I once again felt those unwanted emotions swelling in my throat. I fought them back by boldly speaking my mantra out loud: "Kids suck."

Shoppers froze or hurried down other aisles. A woman with a toddler happily chewing her purse strap in the seat of her cart did a U-turn in the aisle. Fortunately, I wasn't arrested by the baby police or escorted from the store, but if looks could kill . . . well, I knew why women made formidable soldiers.

I stuffed the overalls into an oversized gift bag and topped it with a pair of teddy bears wearing doo-rags and dressed in Harley biker leathers. At least the bears brought back happy memories. Driving back up the hill, I recalled the day my father had given me a bear. A bear just like the ones I'd placed in the bag.

𝕊❦ℂ

Lefty plunged his Buck knife into the back of my teddy bear as I watched in amazement. "We'll hide it in here," he assured me, "where no one will ever find it." He pulled out some bear stuffing and slipped in the .22 pistol he had just given me for my tenth birthday. I watched in awe as Lefty worked, his right hand in coordination with his left hook, finally using Velcro and Super Glue to seal the gash in the bear shut and replace its little leather coat.

"I can't always be here to protect you, but Harley Bear will." Lefty kissed me and gave me a warm hug. Then, gripping my shoulders, he kneeled down so we were eye to eye, his gaze burning with a fierce love as he told me, "There are evil people in this world, baby girl, and they aren't always who you think they are . . . or who society says they are."

"How do I tell good people from bad, Daddy?"

"You'll know evil when you see it. You won't need your eyes." He pursed his lips and winced. "You can feel it."

I thought my dad was talking about his years as a POW in the Hanoi Hilton. And maybe he was. It was evil that had cost him his hand. But I never knew for sure which uniform it had been wearing.

80 ⚓ ⍵

Three cars were already parked outside of our picture-perfect church—a historic little one-room schoolhouse with a tall steeple, nestled among sighing pines, painted white with green trim, showcasing a black cast-iron bell in front. Today, the building was skirted with antique gold, faded lavender, rust, and pumpkin colored mums.

Entering by the back door, I put the plate of cookies in the kitchen and peered through the little window into the sanctuary. There was Ashley, looking like a butternut squash under her tan suede skirt and matching boots, chatting away with two other pregnant women.

Jealousy cut like a two-edged sword. My best friend had moved on, headed for the promised land of motherhood with new friends, and I had been left behind.

Everybody was pregnant except for me. "It's not fair," I whispered to God, but doubted that God was listening. I shrugged and opened the door to hear Ashley and her friends talking about Pastor Mac's new girlfriend.

"I hear she has a son in prison."

"Oh my God. What for?"

"I heard it was murder."

"No way. Who did he kill?"

"An entire family."

"What?!"

The gossip came to a screeching halt as I entered the room. Guilty looks were briefly exchanged, and for a moment, I was the outsider again—the weird kid from the mountains that grew up without electricity, the one who rode to Sturgis with Hell's Angels while my classmates shopped for prom dresses.

"I heard . . . she's an ex-prostitute," I said, laughing aloud as I tossed them a bone.

The women embraced me in a heartbeat, and I added details as sweet as the frosting on the party cake.

"You know, O-M-A stands for Only Marries Alcoholics."
Everyone got a laugh out of that since Mac was a recovered
alcoholic. I felt accepted for a moment, and then we quickly
changed topics as more people arrived with shouts of
"Congratulations!"

The party was a great success. Ashley got what she wanted—
and so did I. Friends.

ॐ ✙ ☙

"Tell me you are coming home for Christmas."

I heard that familiar pause at the other end of the line that gave
me the answer before Chance could voice it.

"I know I've disappointed you again," said Chance, and for a
moment he sounded contrite. Then excitement crept into his voice.
"I'm going on a mission trip to Mexico . . ." and he rambled on
about the poor and needy people living in squalor in the city of
Colonia Morelos, just south of Mexico City. "We're going to add a
wing to the medical facility—just a shack really . . . feed families . . .
provide needed—"

"What about me?" I cut in. "That's not fair. Isn't it enough that
you worked the soup kitchens over Thanksgiving? Let someone
else go. I don't want to spend Christmas alone. I miss you, Chance.
Mercy misses you. Kissme misses you."

"And I miss all of you." Chance hastened to reassure me.
"Listen, I have an idea. School doesn't start again until mid-January.
Why don't you put in for vacation time, and we'll do something
together. Take a trip over to the coast or go up to Lake Tahoe. Or
. . . or maybe just stay at the house, naked, in front of a fire, on top
of some sleeping bags."

Heat shot through me in places that had been cold for a very
long time.

Chance lowered his voice. "Bottle of wine, a bottle of baby oil
. . . anything could happen . . ." And it almost did, right there. I let
out a little gasp and heard his warm chuckle. "God, I miss you,
Sunny." His voice was deep and a little rough, like our lovemaking
when we'd been apart for a long time.

My body stirred, alive with the memory of his strong arms and
kisses that literally sucked the breath right out of me. And our
passionate lovemaking—oh—the lovemaking that began at sunrise

and was repeated with the rising moon. On the bed, in front of the fire, on the deck. On beaches, mountaintops, and meadows. I missed my husband with an overwhelming ache and a pang.

"Then why don't you come home? I haven't seen you since September. You promised me that you'd be back."

"And I will. And I promise I'll make up for every minute we've been apart."

ഇ ♀ ൸

I intercepted Duncan on his way to lunch and asked him to check on my laptop. An image on the screen had frozen, eerily suspended in time and space. My training module was turning into the project from hell, and Duncan didn't look too happy at the prospect of spending another hour working on my computer. As lead technician, working on my laptop wasn't his job, but the rest of the geek squad kept making excuses. One would have thought my computer was infected with Ebola. Not that they feared a lethal virus, but maybe they were avoiding sickness of another sort, something much more invasive than pervasive. Something darker.

And it was hard to imagine a darker world than that of Criminal Division where the daily grind can include glossies of grisly human remains, or pictures of women who have been beaten, broken, or set on fire. Pictures of hollow-eyed children who saw Daddy kill Mommy, or the vacant stare of a victim who has been raped and sodomized, shutting down their minds to reality and sending them somewhere else, somewhere safe. But even those images seemed tame when set against the bizarre, otherworldly pictures and facts that had found their home on my machine.

This was our world, but the last image Duncan wanted to see was now staring at him from my computer—an arresting face whose dark expression was both mesmerizing and foreboding.

"That's it!" Duncan fumed as he grabbed the cord and jerked the plug viciously from the wall. "Enough already!"

To our great dismay, the image remained on the laptop. With the stealth of a stalker moving in for the kill, Duncan flipped the laptop over with a vengeance and ripped the battery pack from the heart of the machine. "Now I've got you. Yeah! Take that!" he declared, triumphant. I fully expected blood to flow from the computer when Duncan's flush of victory paled to incredulous and then melted into horror.

"That's not possible. There's no power source left." Duncan turned an accusing glare on me that felt like a finger as he jabbed, "It's that stuff you have on it. Who is that guy?"

"Anton LeVey—father of modern-day Satanism."

Duncan blinked, looking like a plastic doll whose eyelids blinked when you turned them sideways. "He started the church of Satan in San Francisco and declared 1966 as 'year one' of the age of Satanism."

The picture continued to hold us, entranced.

"Duncan, look!" I said, placing a hand on his shoulder. "Look, it's fading."

I felt the big guy give an involuntary shiver.

We stared at each other in stunned silence for a minute. Duncan's pale face whitened another shade. I was just as rattled, but years of hiding my feelings from victims and perpetrators had made me a master at hiding my true feelings.

"Hey, what do you say I spring for lunch? Come on, Duncan. I owe you. Let's go."

Duncan swallowed. "Chow Mein Charlie's?" he asked.

I hesitated. The restaurant brought back memories of Travis. "Sure. Okay."

Duncan proved excellent company. He had a delightful sense of humor, and in no time we were laughing and joking about the awful topic of my upcoming training. Then he told me about a drunken frat party that almost landed him in jail, and I told him that both my dad and my ex had been members of Hell's Angels. Duncan said he wanted a Dodge Viper and I said I rode a Harley Fat Boy. By the end of lunch, we had the beginnings of a great friendship. That was good. I could use a friend.

Later that night I sat on my couch hugging my dog, both of us jumping at every small sound the house made. This is ridiculous. The surreal experience with my laptop, coupled with spending the past weeks buried in images and stories of such evil, was starting to affect me. "I'm a Christian, for God's sake!" I told Kissme. "Isn't dabbling in this occult stuff against my religion?" Her ears perked up, but no answers came. Perhaps I needed to ask the right person.

ॐ ☥ ॐ

I listened for the sound of Mac's Harley as I paced the deck that wrapped around the church. Mac was still a biker, only now he lived and rode for the Lord.

Mac was more than my pastor. He had been a counselor and friend to both Chance and me during our separation. Chance and I weren't exactly separated, but then we weren't exactly together either. It was good to know that I could always go to Mac for a second opinion.

"Mac. I have a problem." I hit him up even as he shed his leather coat.

"Hello to you too, Sunny." His laughter rose up and sparkled from his clear blue eyes.

A second biker pulled in riding a white Victory, catching me off guard and drowning out the sound of our voices. The engine shut down, the helmet came off, and honey-blond curls spilled out. It was Oma, the "ex-prostitute."

Face scorching, I cleared my throat and hurried to say, "I'm sorry, Mac. I should have made an appointment. I'll come another time."

"Freeze! You're not getting off that easy, Sunny McLane. I'd like you to meet my friend, Kinsey. Her friends call her Oma."

"Oma." I swallowed hard. "We've met. Hello."

Good-bye would be better.

I danced around Kinsey-Oma, helping with the chairs until she gracefully retreated into the kitchen so Mac and I could talk.

"Mac, can't I tell my boss that dabbling in satanic stuff is against my religion?" Mac listened patiently, as always. "Chance says if I don't accept these cases, God will find someone else. And honestly, anyone else doing these cases works for me. I can't do it. I'm not qualified."

My excuses hadn't worked with Jack Savage, and they didn't work on Mac either. Mac shook his head, but his eyes filled with sympathy. "You know, Sunny, God doesn't call the qualified. He qualifies the people he calls. You may not have asked for these cases, and it's obvious don't want them, but I have no doubt that God has chosen you. And yeah"—he shrugged with a sigh— "Chance is correct. If you refuse, God will find someone else."

I breathed a sigh of relief. "So . . . I can tell Jack that this training is against my religion?"

Mac placed a comforting hand on my shoulder that was anything but comforting. I sensed that it was more like the calm before the storm.

"Sit down, Sunny." We scooted the metal chairs that made a hollow echo in the empty room, then sat across from each other. "That, my dear, would be a lie—because, in fact, that is exactly what we, as followers of Christ, are called to do. We are not called to follow but to lead. We don't just sit under the blessing tree and wait for the fruit to fall; we dig the ground and plant the seed, then tend it with sacrifice and hard work. Never confuse 'meek' with 'weak.' There's a lot of sweat and dirt involved in our work. The Bible tells us that we not only battle flesh and blood but also powers and the rulers of the darkness of this world. And that, my girl, calls for courage and strength."

Courage and strength. "Where do I find those?"

"And I quote," said Mac, "'I can do all things through Christ who strengthens me,' and hundreds of others Scriptures about strength and our God who fights battles for us and through us. No one ever said that being a Christian was easy. Jesus himself and eleven of his best friends were tortured in life, and all but John died agonizing deaths."

"Eleven friends?"

Mac's mouth turned up at the corner. "Judas wasn't exactly a friend at the end."

I winced, feeling like a Judas. As if I had just received a terminal prognosis from my doctor. "Good thing no one told me about the horrible death part when I converted."

And my joyous Mac was back with his reassuring smile and sunlight in those dazzling clear blue eyes. "If they had told you, would you have chosen differently?"

I didn't jump on the correct answer. I never do. The question was too deep to lightly dismiss, although it did raise a lump in my throat. "No." My answer elbowed the lump aside. "I guess I would still be a Christian. I would rather live and die for something I believe in than live and die for nothing."

Mac glowed like a votive candle. "God loves you, Sunny. If He wasn't using you and you weren't resisting, I would wonder about your relationship with Him. But know this, my sister. God isn't just dumping his work on you and leaving you to shoulder it alone."

"It feels like it."

"Yes, sometimes we do feel abandoned by God. We might be praying and weeping and begging to hear from God when what we really need to do is shut up and listen. Remember the Scripture that tells how God was not in the thunder or the fire, but in 'a still small voice.'" Mac gave a little laugh. "Sometimes God answers me through something as ridiculous as an infomercial, or a weed I'm pulling out of my lawn. It's pretty fun once you get the hang of it— learning to listen for God's voice. He left each of us two promises: that he will never give us more than we can handle and he is always with us. God will go on loving you, no matter what you decide."

Mac prayed a prayer of protection for me, and while I immensely welcomed his prayers, I asked him not to post it via e-mail to the church prayer chain. Right or wrong, I found it embarrassing to be immersed in a type of work that felt like a cheap Hollywood movie, and I didn't want people laughing at me.

Later that night, Kissme and I sat watching the evening news with our good friends, Ben & Jerry. Tonight featured Coffee Toffee ice cream. Caffeine didn't seem like a big concern since sleep felt elusive anyhow. And it probably didn't help that Fox News did a segment on an exceedingly rare upcoming series of lunar eclipses known as "blood moons."

CHAPTER 7

ॐ ☧ ∞

There was a high probability I was conceived on the back of a Harley. If you think that's not possible, then you don't know bikers. I believed it was true because of the way my blood heated up at the sound of motorcycles revving their engines, my pulse shifted internal gears, and something not-so-Christian deep inside me yearned to howl like a wolf calling its pack. I couldn't explain it, but I'd have bet Pastor Mac and a quarter of our church flock could have related. All that Christian bikers could say about that primal urge was, "Pray for us." My father understood the pack. Before he went to Vietnam, he was all about the team when he quarterbacked varsity high school football. In the Army, he was part of a band of brothers. After the war, after his internment as a POW, his pack, his family, his new brothers were Hell's Angels. I guess I was Daddy's little angel.

Perhaps it was a longing for the pack that led me to join a Christian motorcycle ministry called Heaven's Horsemen. Or else I was trying to engage in a ministry and relate to my husband.

I backed my Fat Boy in alongside the other bikes that sat like a row of polished dominoes lining the street in front of the Gold Pan Diner. My stomach rumbled like my Harley at the intoxicating smell of motorcycles, leather, coffee, and bacon as I went inside.

"Good morning everyone. Let's bring this meeting to order." Mel rapped the gavel on the sounding block. "Breakfast is getting cold, and we have a lot of ground to cover, so let's bless the food, the bikes, and one another."

Everyone certainly loved Mel, the chapter president—all two hundred and fifty pounds of him. Possibly three hundred pounds if you counted the pins and medals turning his vest into an armored car. Mel was bulletproof. Like my dad, after the war, Mel became another Vietnam veteran-turned-outlaw-biker. Unlike my father,

Mel had been set free from his anger and bitterness by the grace of God. The medals on his vest were evidence that he had been riding for many years. Bikers got pins, badges, and patches by attending various runs and events. Simply put, a five-star general couldn't boast more metal than Mel.

Breakfast was as basic, warm, and satisfying as the natural friendliness of the club members. I was pleased to be invited to join them on their traditional after-meeting run. It was a typical Northern California winter day, cold and dry, but as Shane had often said, "That is why the good Lord invented leather." A little cold never stopped hard-core bikers. So I hit the restroom and headed for the door.

"Oh my gosh. Duncan. What a surprise."

Duncan's butt was parked in a booth near the door, a napkin tucked under his chin, wearing a baggy, grease-stained sweat suit, eating a breakfast fit for a king. And a queen. And a couple of growing princelings.

"Sunny!" Duncan choked my name into his napkin. "I thought that looked like you—getting off the Fat Boy, right? Wow—that is so neat. I always wanted to ride a motorcycle." His round eyes enlarged with admiration from behind his thick lenses, making him look like one of Margaret Keane's big-eyed pop art puppies so popular back in the 60s.

"So why don't you get one? You'd look pretty tough on a Harley," I said with an encouraging wink. *Or not!* Second thoughts ran roughshod as I imagined Duncan as a counterpart for Dudley in Wild Hogs more than Jax in Sons of Anarchy.

I felt sorry for Duncan. Especially after hearing the secretarial shark pool snickering over Paige calling him Duncan Dumbnuts behind his back. At least I hope it was behind his back.

Poor Duncan. He fell straight into my need to rescue the hurting people of this world—one person at a time.

Bikers walked past us, heading out for the group ride up the canyon. I needed to get going, so I parted with a friendly pat on Duncan's arm and quick words of encouragement. "Got to live the dream. Catch you later, big guy."

I saddled up and throttled up, stirred as always by growling engines as they caught and the roar of metal beasts as they sprang to life. Duncan gave me a thumbs-up through the café window.

Nine bikes is a good-sized pack, and the rumble of the bikes echoed off the walls of the winding Feather River Canyon. For seventy miles we rode; climbing over four thousand feet in elevation, sometimes running level with the mighty Feather River and sometimes looking down as it faded into a distant silver ribbon that shimmered along the bottom of the steep-walled canyon. A long train pulling black-and-gold rail cars along the tracks snaked its way around twists and turns as it slithered through tunnels, giving us a mournful cry of greeting as we passed.

My body clenched when we passed the site of my motorcycle accident, four—almost five—years ago. Broken and half drowned in the swollen river, I had looked up into the eyes of my future husband, a search-and-rescue worker with the sheriff's office. At the time I'd thought of Chance as my guardian angel. I smiled a sad smile as I flew past because now I thought of him as my fallen angel. I missed Chance and wished he were riding next to me on his VTX. I missed "us."

There are few things slower than a line of women wearing thermals under heavy leather chaps waiting to use a single stall toilet at a gas station. But having emptied bladders and filled tanks, the group finally turned to the high country and the clean, crisp pine scent that permeated the thin air. Climbing another two thousand feet, we crossed the mountains and descended on the little historical gold-mining town of La Porte, then line-danced our way through the backwoods before descending into Feather Falls, about twenty-five miles above Oroville.

I waved good-bye to the group and powered away, turning onto the paved road that headed toward the scenic six-hundred-and-forty-foot waterfall that the community is named for, and then turned onto the narrow dirt road that led to the cabin where I was born.

To my knowledge, no one had been to the cabin since Logan went to prison. I didn't worry much about it since Joyce and Kenny, who were both neighbors and my "surrogate parents," lived past the cabin and were happy to keep an eye on it.

It was the law of nature: things don't go to waste in the wild. An empty cabin was an open invitation for meth labs, vagrants, and looters that might move in, or just as bad—neighbors who could dismantle a building faster than the Army Corps of Engineers and haul it away just as quickly to use on their next remodel.

"Jesus, don't let it be Mexicans or meth heads," I prayed as I followed the single motorcycle track that cut down the driveway.

I did not fear the Hell's Angels. They were my family, no matter that my father was dead. But Logan had been an outlaw among outlaws. He had gone rogue when my dad convinced the club not to back Logan's plan for a major gun heist. Logan had rebelled, teamed up with rogue members of rival gangs, and gone on to rob the Silver State Armory.

Not only had Logan gone against the club, he later instigated a shoot-out between the Hell's Angels and the Mongols down in Laughlin, Nevada, to cover the hit he had taken out on Lefty. Logan had hired a renegade Mongol—as dirty as himself—to waylay my dad out in the desert. Lefty's murder had been a double betrayal to the club because part of Logan's duties as sergeant at arms for the Oakland chapter required that he protect Lefty.

Ever treacherous, Logan went on to cut another deal by paying a Bandido gang member in stolen guns to blow up the Mongol clubhouse—thus taking out the only link between himself and my father's murder—misreported later in the paper as a biker gang war between Mongols and Banditos. Logan came out of the filth as bright and shiny as polished chrome.

Probably good news for Logan was that ATF had busted him before he could pay his debt, handing off the guns to the Bandidos. Now there were wealthy, powerful drug lords in Mexico who had an interest in getting Logan out of prison. They wanted their weapons and money.

A cold sweat dampened my doo-rag as I eased up to the cabin. Anyone could have been waiting. Logan had sworn to kill me, and he could easily have taken out a hit while behind bars. Or it could have been the Mexican cartel that persisted in thinking that I still had a relationship with Logan. They thought I knew where the guns and money were hidden. Then again, it could have been a druggie or squatter who owned a bike.

Not knowing who might have been waiting inside the cabin sent chills up my spine.

"Ready or not—here I come," I whispered to myself as I turned off the engine.

The possibilities were terrifying—but not nearly as frightening as the bloody knife someone had stabbed into the heart of the front door or the blackened pool of blood that puddled beneath it.

CHAPTER 8

֍ ♰ ֎

Bonita strolled in, this time dressed in a pantsuit, neck tie, and matching loafers. I wasn't sure if she was making a fashion statement or a gender statement and I didn't really care as long as she wasn't making a slut statement.

"Pollo." She answered my unspoken question.

It took a minute to register. "Chicken?"

"Sí," she joked. "Chicken blood. No prints on the knife. No fork. No salsa." Her smile faded, and brown eyes darkened. "Hey, you okay, chica? Rumor has it you have a long history with outlaw biker gangs. Wanna talk?"

No. "Yes. I would like to know who you've been talking to about my personal life." Bitterness stirred, tasting like a late-afternoon cup of gas station coffee.

"Bonita gave a dismissive shrug. "Paige told me that both of you have been married to outlaw bikers."

I chewed my upper lip and glanced toward heaven. God, give me strength. And he did. It was obvious that Bonita meant well.

"Paige's ex-husband is Travis," I explained. "The guy whose job you now hold. He was working undercover inside a motorcycle gang for ATF when they met."

Bonita slowly nodded her head and parked herself on the corner of my desk.

"To be honest, I looked into the people I'd be working with before I took this job. What Paige told me wasn't all news," she said with an eye roll, "except for the fact that she'd been married to a biker. I already knew quite a bit about you without help from Paige. Sorry about the prying, but I wanted to know what I was getting into."

She leaned into me and said, "Seems to me that ATF should be notified. The knife is a serious threat."

I eyed her warily. "Bonita, I'm sure it's nothing. Just some bored mountain kids acting stupid."

"Yeah . . . that, or Davey Crockett out hunting chickens in the woods." Bonita wasn't that easily put off. She had a bulldog streak in her that led all the way back to her roots in East LA.

"Please, Bonita. I'm asking you as a favor. Don't call them. Don't bring ATF back into my life."

"Chica, you gotta know your limits."

Bonita left, and I went hunting for Paige.

"Seriously?!" I upbraided Paige, my nose just inches from hers, thinking, I hate you. I hate you. I hate you.

"Don't have a stroke," said Paige. "It's not like Bonita wasn't going to hear about it anyhow."

"My life is no one else's business. Stay out of it."

"Oh really?" Paige's brows arched, ready for a cat spat. "Is that what you really want?" Her words trailed like a cat snapping its tail.

I hated her more. Paige staying out of my life was not really an option, and she knew it. I took her meaning and bit my tongue. She knew I could walk away from her but not the blasted question of paternity.

"Don't talk about my private life with other people again," I warned.

"Too late," said Paige with big-eyed innocence. "I called ATF this morning. I thought they should know about the dead chicken— and the knife, for God's sake. It's an ongoing investigation."

"How do you know about the chicken?"

"Everybody knows."

I squeezed my eyes shut and then opened them. "Did you tell Travis?" The words crept out from between clenched teeth.

Paige cocked her threaded brows above her pouty expression. "Travis and I aren't speaking. I told my dad. And before you have a seizure, Bonita agrees with me."

ഔ ♀ beta

Gina from Child Protective Services and I sometimes shared cases involving child victims from homes where there was domestic violence. This case was different. No parents. No home. Just two babysitters arrested at the Thunderbird Motel and a two-year-old boy abused by the sitters and dumped out the motel window.

"Two girl perps," said Gina. "A fourteen and a sixteen-year-old. They were, and I quote, 'practicing Satanism.' I thought you'd want to know since you're the resident cult expert."

"I'm no expert. Jack's making me do this. I hate it." The antiseptic tang of the hospital could not cleanse the stench that lingered in my nostrils. I could still smell the feces that had oozed from the refrigerator at the scene where the sitters had kept the boy locked up for part of the day.

"Will the little guy be okay?" I asked.

"Are you sure you want to know?" Gina was serious.

No. "Tell me."

"Looks like they tied him up and gagged him, then heated a nail over the stove in the kitchenette and tattooed a pentagram on his butt. He must have been screaming, so they let him chill in the refrigerator for a couple of hours before tossing him out the window."

Minutes had passed before I regained the power of speech. "How many cult cases do Child Services get a year?"

"I can only speak for myself," said Gina, "but I guess I've seen . . . maybe two or three a year. The abuse isn't always a direct result of some kind of ritual, but it's safe to say the parents are either Satanist or wannabes.

"And, by the way," she continued, "a reporter told me The Church of Satan in San Francisco has already denied any involvement."

My lips curled into a snarl. "They sanction this crap by their very existence."

"What do you mean?"

"I mean, people like these girls do God-awful acts in the name of Satanism whether they belong to that white-washed church of Satan or not. I've read the cases, Gina. I've seen pictures taken at crime scenes." I shuddered. "Whether you believe in white magic or black, a real Devil or not, Satan represents the epitome of evil. How can anyone say, 'We only follow and support good evil'? It's just a smoke screen to blind the public to what's real."

Gina blinked. "Good luck at the seminar. You're going to need it."

ॐ ☥ ೞ

Another drive home. Another soulful meditation. The whole crossover between cult and occult had me thinking. "Cult" referred to a group that worshiped something religiously outside of social norms. The word could also reference the members as a whole that belonged to the cult.

My thoughts rambled.

Biker gangs were cults. As a Hells Angel, my dad had practically worshiped bikes and all that the outlaw biker lifestyle entailed. But for all that Lefty had taken great pride in living outside of the law, he had freely submitted to the rules and authority figures that guided the club. Go figure.

My mother had been part of the hippie cult. A spiritual woman open to every kind of spiritualism and mysticism from consumption of datura—called "moonflower"—to munching baggies of peyote, to an in-depth study of astrology. She often justified her behavior saying that she was "born under the sign of Aries," whose ruling planet is fiery red Mars that represents anger, energy, and sex. That would be Mom. I nodded to myself. Aries also represented the first sign of spring, which was supposed to explain her "me first" attitude.

Maybe there is something to astrology after all.

I sighed for the millionth time regarding the mystery that was my mother. While Starla's brain had zoomed through the cosmos seeking God, she remained adamant in rejecting Christ. I thought that was sad because they could have been close friends—my mother and God—but no, she had lain, dying in her hospital bed, brushing me off with a wave of her hand when I had tried to tell her about Christ. She crossed her arms with a dismissive snort and then sneered. "What do you have that I don't have?"

My heart had swelled with pity and compassion as I took her hand and offered a weak smile. "That's an easy one." The answer came softly. "Hope. I have hope—and you have none."

ॐ ☥ ೞ

"Don't get sticky stuff on the sofa," I cautioned Paige as she munched a jelly donut, powdered sugar falling like flakes of dandruff on my dark sofa as we talked between bites.

"I played with Ouija boards and read tarot cards and all that stuff when I was a kid. In fact, I did that and a whole lot more. I was really into Halloween costumes and everything," said Paige.

I didn't have any problem imagining Paige as a witch.

"It was fun. My friends were all into it," she said.

I gave Paige a careful look.

"It's not like I sacrificed animals or anything," she added.

"That's what they all say," I mused. "Do you have a head count for today?"

"Yeah. Crazy. We have the usual social services and nonprofits. Even two police departments, probation, and Mark from the sheriff's office." Paige paused at Mark's name as if trying to shake, or possibly embrace, the memory of her former lover. "But what's crazy is I only sent one invitation to the county's Office of Education, and we have six school counselors attending." Paige squirmed, looking uncomfortable.

"I'll be right back," she said. "I have to go to the bathroom." And she scurried down the hall.

"Ready ladies?" Duncan barged in, his face flushed. It had to be caused by more than the weight of the new projector he had acquired for my presentation.

"Almost. As soon as Paige and Wonder Kid get back from the bathroom," I said.

Duncan gave me a puzzled look. "Why do you always refer to the baby as Wonder Kid?"

I threw him an eyebrow shrug. "Because she keeps everyone wondering whose kid it is."

The big guy gave a huge scowl. "That's not very nice."

If only you knew. "No, it isn't."

Paige came back ready to roll.

I grabbed my bag and did a double-take. It took a minute. "Duncan. You look . . . different. Is that a T-shirt under your coat? And . . . Oh, Lord . . . a gauge in your ear?" His sense of adventure seemed to have stretched along with the enlarged piercing in his ear.

The pink on his face deepened to red. "You think it's okay? It's a fake one. Not like I'm going to court or anything. I'm just running the projector."

"Dumbkin, come here, let me have a peek," said Paige. I gasped at Paige, but Duncan just blushed harder as she lifted the corner of his sport coat. "Ohmygod, it's a Harley shirt." She squinted. "With skulls and flames. Well, you're certainly dressed right for the occasion."

"You're wearing a Harley shirt to work?" I laughed in disbelief and merriment. "You're a new man."

"Yeah," he said. "I'm living the dream!"

I jumped in before Paige could turn his dream into a nightmare. "Awesome. I love it. Better keep it under wraps!" I added with a warm pat on top of his new coat.

Bonita strode in jangling car keys like Paul Revere sounding the village alarm. "Saddle up. Let's ride." We gathered our equipment and headed for the conference, stuffing ourselves in the county's new hybrid chuck wagon with Bonita at the reins. Duncan and Bonita were crammed shoulder to shoulder in the front seat, and I was wedged next to Paige-and-a-half in the backseat. Our county spared no expense to save a dollar.

I was nervous. Afraid, actually. Not like fearing for my life when I was with Logan, but terribly afraid of being ridiculed by my colleagues. Paige passed out the informational folders she had prepared: Cult Symbols and Holidays, Survivor Symptoms that Characterize and Contrast Satanic Ritual and Sexual Abuse, Psychological Indicators for Children and Adults. And for law enforcement: Evaluating Evidence for Ritual-Based Criminal Activity.

I prayed for the first time in days and was grateful to remember that God didn't keep score. I was comforted in knowing that the God I worshiped was more faithful to me than I was to him.

"I don't want to do this, Lord, but here I am. Can you help me out?" For the faithful, God says not to panic. When the time comes, he will have your back. I had not prepared for what came out of my mouth next, but I am pretty sure it was answered prayer.

⋙ ☤ ⋘

"This presentation is not about you. It is not about whether you believe in black magick or if the Devil is real but whether you believe that there are others who sometimes act out such beliefs through criminal activities.

"This is not about whether you are a Christian and believe in heaven or hell but whether you understand that cults exist and they espouse opposite values of Judeo-Christian beliefs, particularly the ceremonies that are sacred to the Catholic Church.

"This is not about witches, Wiccans, neo-pagans, agnostics, or atheists. Neither is it about freedom of speech or freedom of religion. It's not about heavy metal music or current trends that lead to destructive behaviors.

"We are here for the victims of ritual abuse and the roles we play—either in their rescue or their continued victimization.

"We cannot address a problem until we admit that a problem exists."

The room was silent. Somewhere along the opening lines, my palms had dried, my knees stopped shaking, and my voice returned to normal, acquiring a tone of authority that I did not feel.

"The purpose of today's training for law enforcement is to affirm the existence of ritual abuse as it relates to unlawful activities. For mental health providers, to consider Dissociative Identity Disorder, commonly known as multiple personalities, and code §5150; the Welfare and Institutions Code that allows law enforcement to place a person suspected of being suicidal, homicidal, or gravely disabled, into the restrained custody of a mental health facility for up to seventy-two hours of observation. For prosecutors, we will talk about evidence and legal response.

"And, last but not least, for advocates—how to identify the presence of ritual abuse activity, validate the victim's story, and provide appropriate referrals."

Welcome to the ritual-crime buffet, serving a little something for everyone.

Power Points fulfilled the promise. The presentation was enriched with pictures and case studies, thanks to Old Wally the Witch Hunter.

Gaining confidence and finding my stride, I emphasized, "The greatest obstacle to helping victims will always be agency disbelief. Without the support of your office, it is hard, if not impossible, to provide help."

A metal chair scraped as it scooted backward over the hardwood floor, clanging and echoing as it banged into another chair. Chief Probation Officer, Marianne Marshall, stood, an imposing nearly six-foot-tall figure. Curious eyes turned to track her departure, her heels tapping a sharp cadence as she retreated from the conference room, followed by a slight jolt when she slammed the door.

Stunned silence reigned as all eyes shifted back to me. It was a defining moment as I fought a rising tide of panic. I didn't know what to say. And then . . . God bailed me out for a second time.

"Thank you! Thank you, Ms. Marshall. I intend to send Ms. Marshall a formal thank-you card for her outstanding demonstration. She proves my point more than words ever could. Let me repeat; "Without the support of your agency, it is difficult, if not impossible, to provide help for victims of ritual abuse."

Then I went on to fulfill my training objectives.

∞ ♀ ∞

"Way to go. Damn fine job," Duncan said as he took down the set. "I don't know how you do it, Sunny. That stuff is downright disturbing. I prefer fantasy entertainment—you know, with wizards and zombies." He packed the coils of cords into a crate. "The real stuff sure takes the fun out of it."

Out of the mouths of babes.

"Maybe you're onto something there, Duncan. If people understood the real horrors of ritual abuse, they would probably have to change their concept of entertainment."

"Then again," Bonita joined in as she opened the trunk to the car, "people award murder and mayhem at the Oscars every year. Where would Hollywood be without violence?"

"I got into the occult," Paige said defensively, "when I was a kid," she hastened to clarify.

We all turned to stare at her since she still looked like a teenager.

"I didn't kill anyone."

Her words were like an appetizer, and we all waited expectantly for more. It didn't happen.

CHAPTER 9

❧ ✠ ☙

It was hard looking my boss in the eye as my gaze kept straying to the veins that beat like war drums at his temples. Chief Probation Officer Marianne Mitchell stood behind him.

"Sunny—a word please." Jack stood tall while I cringed behind my desk. Paige bailed from my office like the rat she was, and Duncan shrank his massive body to invisible as he narrowed his focus on repacking the box of cables we had brought back from the presentation. Only Bonita leaned forward with interest.

"Ms. Mitchell says your presentation on ritual abuse was an embarrassment to this office." Jack frowned, looking like a judge handing down a sentence for mass murder. "She says it was highly inappropriate and unprofessional. I'd like to hear what you have to say."

My heart stopped, and my tongue cleaved to the roof of my mouth. The corners of Marianne's mouth inched up her eyes and flashed like sunlight on shards of glass. Much to her disdain and satisfaction, she seemed to enjoy watching me swallow the lump of fear in my throat and my need to wet my lips.

Don't be a wimp—think fast. Better to go down in flames.

Pulling myself upright to sit tall, I clasped my hands on the desk in front of me and looked Jack in the eye and countered, "I would say, sir, that, in my opinion, Chief Probation Officer Marianne Mitchell is the one who behaved unprofessionally. She created a scene when she walked out." I pointed to Exhibit A and tapped my pen on the stack of papers sitting on my desk. "I have about forty reviews right here. I'd say about two-thirds are positive and the other third neutral. No one else walked out. I believe that Ms. Mitchell was the embarrassment—to both our offices."

A smile played on Jack's face, and I was rewarded with a look of respect. Ever the politician, Jack turned to the Chief Mitchell and said, "Thanks for stopping by, Marianne. I'll take your concerns under advisement."

Within days I received notice that I would be attending the National Victim Assistance Academy in Fresno the following week—with Paige.

℮✝ℬ

Shane waved as he cruised past on his motorcycle. Ashley was expanding the women's Bible study group to include the first Saturday morning of each month, and I imagined that Shane would rather be at his Harley shop surrounded by burly bikers than trapped in a house full of chatty women.

Since Ashley and I seem to be on a no-need-to-knock basis, I opened the door and slipped inside to the sound of laughing women and boisterous children.

"I wonder what it's like being married to a pastor," a musical voice sang out from the den.

"Always doing it in the missionary position?" came a giggling reply.

"Thank God he's in the mood!" quipped another.

"Praying for the big one?" added Ashley.

"Screaming Oma God—Oma God," I chimed in, not considering for a heartbeat that one day I would be a pastor's wife and the butt of hurtful, blasphemous remarks.

Everyone froze, and then rose laughing and joking as they greeted me, embracing me and making me feel like I was one of them. Which I wasn't. And never would be. But the feeling of acceptance was intoxicating.

The woman with the musical voice had been bottle-feeding a baby. The second woman had a toddler clinging to her skirt and claimed another one that was bouncing on the sofa. Then there was Ashley, looking like she had swallowed a big blue exercise ball.

"I'm so glad you could make it," followed by chants of "Sit down, sit down."

"Oh, I can't. Thanks anyhow. I have to go. I'm just dropping off some scones. This is such a terrific idea that I wanted to support all of you." The lie slid as easily as oil on a baby's bottom. The heartache didn't come until I cradled Kissme back in the safety of my home. I had never felt more alone.

When the tears had dried, there was nothing left to do but wash my face, wash my car, and wash my clothes for the trip to Fresno. The best cure for internal pain was external action. It was never what I want to do. I would much rather have eaten a bag of potato chips and crawled under the covers into the safety of the void. The problem was when I'd finally crawl out, I would still be here, and nothing would have changed. At least this way my car would get cleaned.

It was times like these that I could still hear my dad's instructions: "You got to toughen up, baby girl."

ഈ ♀ ൫

Rule #1: Never go into the eighth-grade bathroom until you are in eighth grade.

It didn't matter that the other bathroom was down by the little kids' rooms or that your knees hit your chin whenever you sat on their tiny toilets. There were some tough girls at our school, and they ruled the eighth-grade bathroom with the same fervor that Crips and Bloods ruled LA. As long as you followed the rules, nobody got hurt.

I broke Rule #1 when I dashed to the nearest toilet. When you got to go, you got to go. Three big girls were waiting when I left the stall.

When I say "big", I don't mean older, even though they were. The two Maidu girls were built like skid loaders, and the freckle-faced white girl was third generation logger stock. The girls left the bathroom with me curled up on the floor holding my ribs when the bell rang. When I got up, I didn't run to the principal's office. I limped home.

Lefty bristled like a wolverine when he saw the tears flowing from my swollen eyes. He held me close until the tears stopped, then washed my face and led me out to our little lawn. I didn't want to learn hand-to-hand combat. I wanted to be rocked until I fell asleep.

"You got to toughen up, baby girl," he said.

"Daddy, I don't want to—"

"I know, I know. Those are the times when you have to make yourself. Always remember, Sunny: offense is the best defense."

I was never sure if he learned that line playing football or as a POW, but that afternoon Lefty taught me how to gouge out someone's eyes with my thumbs, "doorknob" them in the boobs (or scrotum), jump on their feet and shove them, rip off an ear, throw dirt in their eyes, and, finally, how to kill someone by ramming their nose through their brain with the heel of my hand. But he made me promise never to kill anyone at school.

The following day I ambushed the largest girl as she walked home. After strategically placing a crumpled dollar bill on the dirt road near her house, I waited for her to bend down and pick it up before springing out from behind some shrubs and charging her from behind. She launched like a bird in flight, straight into an ancient thicket of blackberry brambles—where gnarly old vines clamped around her limbs and tore her skin like steel teeth on a bear trap. The harder she struggled, the deeper she sank.

My dad had been right. No one messed with me at school after that. Still . . . there were times when I wondered if the decision I made that day marked a turning point that would set me on an irrevocable course with destiny. Had I crossed the line and become an outlaw like my father?

In the end, I could have taken her place in the badass hierarchy and become the newest school bully. But I didn't. I still preferred the company of the little kids.

ॐ ♀ ॐ

Getting "tough" was sometimes easier said than done.

Casey had been born blind, but she wasn't disabled. Casey lived in her own apartment and attended school at Chico State with the very noble goal of becoming a counselor for the blind. But for all her intelligence, all her courage, and all her skill at living independently, she had been a repeated victim of rape by different men.

Casey learned that when she didn't fight and didn't struggle, she didn't get hurt. By contrast, I had frequently fought Logan, often struggled, and was repeatedly punched or sexually assaulted. Maybe Casey wasn't completely wrong. Different people employ different mechanisms for coping and surviving.

There was that time with Logan.

It seemed like fun. Daring. Erotic beyond belief—when Logan had taken me behind the high school. He had picked me up on the motorcycle and cruised around to the far end of the baseball field, where he dismounted and told me to remove my gym shorts.

Hormones exploded like the grand finale on the Fourth of July as I looked around, fearful and searching. I was eager, embarrassed, terrified—of being caught by the school and also of not obeying Logan's directive.

He took me there, behind the dugout, where I writhed and moaned in ecstasy until the sound of voices pierced the haze of passion as efficiently as a bucket of wet sand dumped on a bonfire.

"Stop! Stop. Logan, stop. Please. People," I panted as I struggled in the dirt to escape from beneath him.

Logan looked up. What he saw only fueled him to greater heights. Logan went crazy—and I went limp. When he was done, he stood up and laughed, wagging his man part at the girl and boy who had frozen, gaping in horror. They turned and ran hand in hand as hard as they could.

For Logan, it was all about his lust for power and control. But like Casey, I felt responsible for agreeing—up to a point.

Shamefaced, I became the overnight subject of gossip; ridicule and sneers from bitchy girls, lusty leers and obscene notes from the boys.

It was a relief when I was finally questioned and suspended from school. I didn't try to deny that I had engaged in sex on campus, but I would not disclose who my partner had been.

I was tough, but I didn't have a death wish.

ഓ ☥ ൈ

Driving to Fresno was about as exciting as sitting on a boat in the middle of the ocean—except you were looking at rolling waves of golden hills instead of water, the scenery occasionally broken by schools of big rigs and island farms. Behind us, a motorcycle traveled close enough for me to hear his tailpipes, breaking the hum of the monotonous flow of trucks and cars.

Paige idly pressed buttons on the radio, the channels jumping from droning Christian sermons to energetic conservative talk shows, to mysterious ethnic stations of unknown composition. Then, for whatever reason, she hit the CD button, and I freaked, overcorrecting and narrowly missing the truck and trailer to my right.

"One way or another, I'm gonna find ya . . ." The car filled with the squealing of tires and acrid smoke of burning rubber. *"I'm gonna getcha, getcha, getcha, getcha . . ."* Bump, bump, bump as we spun across the median strip. *"I'm gonna meetcha, meetcha, meetcha, meetcha . . ."* The piercing sounds of Paige screaming mingled with the throbbing beat. *"One day, maybe next week . . ."* I screamed in rage. *"I'm gonna meetcha . . ."* And then:

> *I will drive past your house*
> *And if the lights are all down*
> *I'll see who's around . . .*

"Turn it off! Turn it off!"
Hysteria made me lose it. Rage helped me refocus.

> *One day, maybe next week . . .*
> *I'm gonna give you the slip!*

Cursing, I slammed the Eject button, and the disc slithered like a cold-blooded wraith under a door into my hand. I didn't wait to open the window but jerked the car door open, jumped out, and threw the vile thing into oncoming traffic, panting and watching as a line of untroubled cars demolished it.

My head was still spinning even as the dust settled.

Logan is in prison. Behind bars.

I leveled a vicious glare at Paige and demanded an answer. "Did you do this? You! Is this your sick idea of a joke?"

Paige sat there wild-eyed, petrified. "You're crazy! You know that? You should be locked up with your psycho ex! You almost got me killed!"

Back in the car, I clenched one hand on the steering wheel and one on the back of the car seat to keep myself from tearing out her throat. "Did you put that f-ing disc in the car or not?"

Paige struggled to compose herself. "A freak. That's what you are. A psycho freak. If I put a disc in this car, it sure as hell wouldn't be Blondie. I'm not that old."

I exhaled, shaking my head, stupefied. Only Paige could come up with an answer like that. I didn't know what to think. It was a message from Logan, but I had no idea how it got there.

In the end, there was nothing to do except get back on the freeway and rejoin the endless stream funneling south. Hours and miles slipped away in stony silence.

I-5 was a long north-south freeway alongside which gas stations, coffee shops, and bars were scarce. Bikers usually preferred Highway 99 that ran parallel to I-5 and hit every town down the central valley.

Bathrooms were also scarce on I-5, but Paige needed to stop at every one, adding two hours to our four-hour trip and landing us in rush hour traffic. Okay, I admit, central California wasn't New York or Chicago or LA bumper-to-bumper traffic, where cars moved slower than a fat person in a power chair, but the cars did bunch up, shoulder to shoulder and nose to tail as you neared Fresno.

"Can't you hold it?" Stress had taken its toll. I was tired and anxious and somewhat disassociated. Like a turtle, I had pulled my mind into the dark shelter of my shell, telling myself that I would think later about the CD and Logan how the disc got in the car. We were still ninety minutes from Fresno State with the check-in time in sixty.

"I can't help it. I'm pregnant. Look, there's a Pilot truck stop up ahead."

It couldn't have been worse. Pilots were like the Disneyland of gas stops—sort of a gas station-Walmart-fast food-Good Sam campground for big rigs all rolled into one. Paige would probably take a shower and shop for baby clothes on her way back to the car.

I took a deep breath, relaxed, and used the time to call Chance.

"How's my sexy Sunny?" Chance's voice was Sam Elliot deep and as suggestive a slow dance on a hot summer night. Soft. Soothing. Healing. My breath caught, and needful feelings stirred.

"Don't start anything you can't finish, Romeo. I'm sitting here at a gas station in the middle of nowhere, not our bedroom."

Chance didn't laugh. He groaned, low and slow. "I woke up dreaming about you this morning . . ." He let it hang between us with a pregnant pause. "And I came up with a brilliant idea."

"Umm . . ." Two can play this game. I sugarcoated, "Do tell."

"I was thinking—since you are going to be halfway to LA, how about I skip a couple of days of school and take the VTX for a ride?

Then take my wife for a ride? Get a room for two. A shower for two. Maybe a bottle of champagne and two glasses?"

It was a hallelujah moment. God, I loved that man! Then, like a cresting wave, hope broke with the reality check. There was no way this could possibly work.

I already had a room reserved for two and a half, and there was a fifty percent probability that Chance was the father of the "half" growing inside Paige. There was no way I was going to share a room with my husband and his pregnant ex-whatever.

Where there is a will, I will make a way. Little things—like being stalked, almost being killed on the freeway, and having Paige with me—were going to have to wait. I'll tell Chance all that later—after I have my way with him. So I made some sexy, suggestive noises in reply.

The joy in Chance's voice was unmistakable. "I can be there by Thursday. I'll leave early, between two and three."

"I am already 'ready.' I'll be waiting." I felt as giddy as a schoolgirl, which seemed appropriate since we'd been assigned dorm rooms on the Fresno State campus.

Paige finally made it back to the car, carrying a large Pepsi, a large bag of Doritos, Fig Newtons, and probably a dill pickle.

"Thank you, Lord!" I prayed with exaggeration as if I had been impatiently waiting on her. I hoped God would forgive me, but sometimes I liked to pray out loud just to annoy her. "Please part the waters and get us there before registration closes." I was rewarded with a scrunch on Paige's face.

God answered prayer. Cars parted before us, paving the way like the Red Sea had parted for Moses. I cut off the I-5 freeway, heading back toward Highway 99 and Fresno, and was surprised to see the mysterious motorcycle tailing us once more. I studied him in the rearview mirror, noting that the rider was dressed in traditional black leather, and his facial features were hidden under a full helmet with a tinted visor.

Just another biker, I hoped, but prickled with suspicion. I quickly maneuvered the car between a pair of big rigs, forcing the biker to pass me and enabling a closer inspection. Nothing to see. No patch, no logos on the bike. He was not only blacked out, he was murdered out—the biker term for all black with no identifiers.

No looks, no nods, but the rider mirrored my move and pulled in front of the lead truck and waited for me to pass him before taking up his position behind me once more. It was disturbing to think that the biker had seen us spin onto the median and hadn't stopped to see if we were okay. But, then—I gave a mental shrug—neither had anyone else. I wasn't sure exactly at what point he had rejoined us, but I knew it was sometime after the last gas station.

We exited into Fresno, and I found myself smiling with satisfaction as I blew through a series of stop signs and green lights, noting that our tail was slowly fading into the distance. A couple of deliberate detours later and we finally slid into the university parking lot with minutes to spare.

"Hey!" a voice called out. Apparently, we weren't the only late arrivals. "Your lights are on!"

I looked back at the county car and was startled at the sight of the woo-woo lights blinking with more strobe than a disco dance floor.

"Wow. No wonder we made such good time," said Paige as we walked back to the car. "Maybe there is something to that prayer stuff after all."

I rolled my eyes but didn't forget to thank God while they were still in the up position. I figured later that my knee must have bumped the toggle switch located under the dashboard while I was at the gas station, but it still felt like a miracle.

Classes started right after a cafeteria-style breakfast and warm reception from the keynote speaker. I probably could have taught most of the classes scheduled for day one as the workshops all related to the criminal justice system. I cut an afternoon class to keep an appointment I had set with the National Victim Assistance Academy program director.

NVAA was a national training, and I was excited at the prospect of meeting advocates from across the country. Now that I was out of the closet with my newest training module, I intended to take advantage of the time and place to tap into my colleagues' experience of working with victims of ritual abuse.

Taking a deep breath, I stood tall in an attempt to shoulder some courage. Once again, I was risking the sting of professional contempt. I needed permission to distribute a short questionnaire that related to social services for victims of ritual abuse to about one hundred attendees.

"Hmm. Interesting," Sondra Klein mused, looking as rigid as any attorney as she scrutinized my questionnaire. She looked up and leaned back in her luxurious leather chair. "I don't have a problem with this," she said. "Just make sure you send me a detailed summary of the results. And, Ms. McLane . . ." She relaxed, smiling. "You might want to meet Dr. Shelton, the chief medical officer from Utah's Department of Corrections. He's our Friday morning speaker before we break into workshops. Would you care to join us for breakfast?"

"Thank you. I'd love to," I said with a mental grimace, thinking I'd much rather dine on my husband Friday morning.

The second and third day continued with workshops put on by the various agencies that respond to crises: victim witness, rape crisis, domestic violence, LGBT, tribal health and other minority populations, each with a unique set of issues when providing appropriate support services to victims.

I stretched and yawned, looking at the clock, happy that this morning's erotic dream would soon be replaced with the real thing. My body fairly throbbed with the love-lust of a young woman who had been separated from the man she loved. Only a few more hours. I kicked back the covers with a reluctant sigh. I had to distribute the survey and explain my objectives to an early-morning leadership workshop.

"Good morning, Lord Thank you for this day!"

Mission accomplished. As soon as the group had given me the green light, I sped to the closest copy place and got one hundred copies from Staples and a bottle of champagne from Crazy Jimmy's Liquor Barn. I figured Chance and I would make do with the plastic cups in the dorm bathroom.

My phone buzzed as I pulled into a parking spot. Chance? Really? Chance hadn't used text messaging since the day I found the messages he'd exchanged with Paige during their affair. But there it was: Get ready—Get ready—Get ready; ice for the champagne and a fire extinguisher for the bed. I replied with my room number.

Paige had befriended an advocate on day one—a pregnant young woman from Southern California—and they were taking the same workshops and enjoying their spare time together. I knew I wouldn't be seeing her again until just before dinner, around five p.m. Chance and I would have plenty of private time together. Floating on air, I dropped off the stack of questionnaires with attendees at the upper management classes. First I slipped back to my room, then slipped out of my clothes, and then into and out of the shower. Warm. Wet. Ready.

Anticipation reached its climax at two thirty with a hard knock at the door. Like a star in an Oscar-winning performance, I sprinted naked across the room as the door swung open and leaped into Chance's strong, eager arms as he kicked the door shut behind. Wrapping bare legs around his waist and my arms around his neck, our lips molded and melted together.

I came up for air just long enough to gasp out a warning, "Oh, baby, I have to tell you . . . Paige might . . ." but the words went up in flames as Chance reclaimed my mouth, literally sweeping me off my feet as he quickly carried me across the room to my bed. I was home. I was the leading lady and Chance my leading man.

Our appetites were voracious as we feasted on each other in ways that only married people can fully understand—a mating of body and soul with a certainty that we were experiencing a glimpse of heaven.

Some "Oh-God, Oh-God, Oh-Gods" and few "Yes-yes-Oh-Jesus, Jesus" and "Baby-babys" commenced, hot breath mingling, ebbing and flowing between entwined arms and legs as we cried out impassioned names to the one who had made us "both male and female."

Looking back, it doesn't seem at all blasphemous. He didn't need to make us so soft or so desirable or our passion so exquisite. I thank God he did!

"I love you, Sunny," Chance panted.

"Me too," I gasped.

And we started round two.

CHAPTER 10

৪৩ ✦ ৎ৩

Slower this time.

I lay in the arms of my gorgeous husband with my fingers combing through his thick blond hair, then trailing along the rough stubble of his jaw, down his neck, and along the hard muscles of his biceps.

Oh, what I am going to do with those biceps!

Chance responded with feather light kisses that followed a path across my eyes to my ears, where he nipped and tugged on the edges of my ears. "Oh, baby," Chance breathed into my ear, reigniting my already heated blood.

Chance's chest was smooth and hard, and my fingers wandered happily to the smattering of hair at midpoint and then turned to follow the velvety trail south. My husband's kisses also moved south, along the side of my neck, to my throat, still heading south—his lips both demanding and infuriatingly slow at the same time.

Heavenly. Divine. God, don't stop.

My body thrummed in anticipation as I reached around to skim the muscles of his back and caress his bottom, so heart-stoppingly smooth.

Chance rubbed my back in languid, possessive circles while his eager mouth continued its exploration.

"Oh, Chance. I've missed you . . . missed you . . . need you . . . Ohh . . . There."

His scent was intoxicating, robust and masculine, uniquely Chance, and it set my head spinning. Our desires quickened in time as we moved to the beat of drumming hearts.

Oh . . . Chance was positively decadent. He was more delectable, more satisfying, and more addicting than a truck and trailer of Ben & Jerry's. I was in heaven as he gathered me in his arms, and I melted under the sweet fullness of his embrace.

"Rock me . . . rock me, baby," I pled, and Chance responded.

The world faded away—always narrowing. The room grew dim, the bed melted, and the insatiable mysterious flame burned bright and hot, reducing the two of us into one. One heartbeat, one gasp, one passionate agonizing cry—one flesh.

Umm . . . My mind wandered in the afterglow as Chance and I lay tangled, entwined in each other's arms and legs. I didn't know what sex was like before Eve was taken out of Adam, back when Adam was still both male and female, but I was thinking that Adam must've been one happy guy.

The cork popped as my Brad Pit husband came sauntering back from the bathroom with plastic cups and the bottle of champagne that had been chilling in the bathroom sink.

"You cut your hair," I said, my eyes aglow with appreciation. "It looks—"

The door flew open, and Paige burst in. Yet another episode in the series called Life's Most Awkward Moments.

Paige froze, her eyes popping as they took in my naked husband. Not for the first time.

"Paige? Jesus . . . oh . . ." Chance dropped the cups and snatched a pillow to cover his man parts. "What the hell are you doing here?"

We waited expectantly as Paige stared, open-mouthed.

"Number two," she said as she scurried into the bathroom, slamming the door behind her.

ॐ ☥ ☪

The flu took out kids like a modern-day medieval plague. I was in fourth grade, and the day had started out okay, but by the time we had pledged the flag, my stomach was doing flip-flops. One glance from the teacher at the red flush under beads of sweat bought me a fast ticket home. The school nurse had driven me to the cabin and left me at the gate with a sympathetic "Hope you feel better soon."

Crosby Stills and Nash blasted from the upstairs window: "If you can't be with the one you love, come on and love the one you're with . . ." I recognized Dirty Dan's bike in the driveway. I liked Dan. He was nice, and so was his old lady.

I gave Frito a tired hug before trudging inside. Starla had thrown Frito outdoors again. She didn't like him or me indoors much. Mom was upstairs. As it turned out, so was Dan. And so was

Dan's old lady. Mom got out of bed, saying, "God, Sunny, grow up! It's not like you've never seen me naked before."

That was true. I had seen my mother do yoga in the sunrise naked and swim naked in lakes and rivers, and once I even watched in awe from the upstairs window as she danced naked in the moonlight out in the orchard. Starla had been hypnotic as she swayed in time to a remembered song, or perhaps she danced to the rhythm of the wind that sighed through the trees as the earth spun on its axis to a tune that only she could hear.

Seeing my mother, Dan, and his girlfriend... all in bed together had triggered the first of many times that I would vomit from stress. While I sometimes still got that familiar wave of nausea, I discovered additional methods for purging pain. Ben & Jerry's was one. A glass of wine was another. Seeing that the bottle of champagne was so close at hand . . .

I took a hit of champagne straight from the bottle. Followed by another. And another.

Chance jumped into his pants and shirt. I slipped into my pants and was buttoning my blouse when the toilet flushed, and the pregnant princess made her entry.

"Should I leave?" I asked.

"No." Chance and Paige replied in unison.

I looked at Chance first. "The county sent both of us here for training. I was going to tell you."

"When?"

The clothes on Chance's body were dark, but not nearly as dark as the expression he wore on his face.

"Umm . . ." I tipped my head and arched a sassy brow, replying with a playful smirk, "About the same time you were going to tell me about the twins."

"I'm not having twins," said Paige.

"We know," Chance and I responded.

"Listen. Enough." Chance ran his fingers through his hair and took charge.

"You." Chance pointed to Paige. "Shut up and sit down."

Paige sat.

"Are you carrying our baby or not?"

Would that be yours and hers—or yours and mine? I wondered.

I settled back in bed and took another hit of champagne and watched them do a remake of the Travis-Paige whose-baby-is-it melodrama that I had overheard at the county break room.

My eyes shifted first to Chance with a drawn-out mental sigh. You just had to knock her up. Then to Paige: I hate you . . . and I especially hate that baby. After all, the affair had ended nine months ago, but the consequences of the pregnancy would last a lifetime.

True to form, their argument devolved from bad to worse. I stayed out of it, happily nipping at the bubbly and somewhat entertained as I tried to convince myself that it wasn't my problem.

The room was starting to spin about the time I heard Paige snarl at Chance, "You got what you wanted! And I got what I what I wanted!"

Her expression didn't reflect the touted joys of motherhood. She had me wondering what the heck it was she really wanted.

Paige threw her package of Fig Newtons at Chance, Chance threw his hands in the air, and I threw up on the rug.

ℰℐℰ ♀ ℰℐℰ

It was a good thing Chance had slammed the door last night instead of this morning. Even the sound of my toothbrush reverberated like a jackhammer in my head. I looked at the stranger in the mirror and groaned. An hour in the shower had failed to rinse the grit from my eyes or the stink from my skin. Pride had washed down the drain a long time ago, so there no was use looking for that.

I rubbed my head in regret, trying to massage away the pain. I hadn't drunk like that since the day I learned about Chance's affair, and neither drinking binge had changed a thing. The only thing I gained was a head filled with more throb than a Southside boom box, and a churning stomach that kept time with the beat.

I wanted to go home, but there was the matter of a breakfast meeting with Dr. Shelton and Sondra Klein. Then I had to pick up the results of the survey from the Ethics in Leadership workshop and find Paige. Paige had left the room shortly after Chance, and by the looks of her bed, slipped back in sometime during the night, and left again before I woke. I figured I would probably find her somewhere between the cafeteria and the women's bathroom.

Dr. Shelton was an impressive man—not only because he held a master's degree in forensic psychology but because he was a strikingly handsome man with silver hair and a goatee, austere features, and laughing gray eyes. But it was hard to appreciate his noble Grecian features when mesmerized by the pale, rubbery eggs that quivered under blood-colored ketchup on his fork.

My stomach did a slow churn, and I tried to hold my breath and talk at the same time. It wasn't working very well. But I made it through introductions and learned that he not only currently worked within the prison system but had authored several books on the topic of serial killers.

He popped a corpse-gray sausage into his mouth, and I had to fight to hold down the champagne residue that still bubbled in my stomach.

"I would estimate"—the good Dr. Shelton ran his tongue across to his teeth—"that as many as forty thousand to sixty thousand people are ritually murdered each year."

Sondra must have recognized the impending crisis as Dr. Shelton talked, and she moved to avert it. Excusing herself, she left for a few moments and returned with a hot cup of coffee loaded with cream and sugar and a piece of toast that she wordlessly slid in front of me.

I threw her a look of appreciation and nursed the coffee throughout the interview.

"And that doesn't take into account the increase of murders along our border towns that directly tie back to La Santa Muerte—the Holy Death cults. Those people have taken over Mexico and infiltrated the United States with the flood of illegals.

"Santeria is the other large religious cult. Drug dealers believe that blood sacrifices, including those of humans, gives them power over their competitors."

I will never, ever, ever get drunk again.

"And, of course, Santeria's ritual animal sacrifice has been ruled legal in the state of Florida."

That got my attention. "Animal sacrifice? In America?" Home of Bambi and Thumper? I was skeptical. America had had animal shelters long before it had shelters for battered women. Where is PETA when you need them? "I find that hard to believe."

"It's true. The Supreme Court ruled that it fell under religious freedom. The river's cleanup boat picks up about a hundred animal carcasses a week down in Miami."

"So, Dr. Shelton, would you go so far as to say that ritual abuse is prevalent in today's society?"

Dr. Shelton finished chewing his food and swallowed. "Absolutely."

"And that abuse is an integral part of certain religious cults?"

"That would be correct," said Dr. Shelton, nodding in agreement.

"And those cults are not limited to our traditional concept of Satanic worship?"

"Correct in fact, although theologically speaking, they may be considered one and the same."

I thanked Dr. Shelton and Sondra and tried not to lose my dignity, by walking instead of crawling back to my room, when I was accosted by two advocates I had met in a workshop.

"Sunny! Hi. Join us for breakfast?"

Just shoot me. "No thanks. Nice of you to offer, but I just ate."

Charles and Terri were victim witness advocates from West Virginia. Charles motioned for me to join them. "You can sit with us while we eat."

Ughh . . .

Charles and Terri returned with full platters loaded down with a pair of women's breasts for him and scrambled brains topped with bloody salsa for her, and dead pig parts for both.

God is punishing me. Okay, maybe not.

"Yes?" My little way of telling them to hurry up.

"Well . . ." Charles stopped to take a bite from the poached eggs that wouldn't stop looking like a pair of boobs. Thoughtfully chewing, words and food mingled, spilling from his mouth. "Oops. Excuse me." He swallowed. "Terri and I have been talking about your survey questions and, well . . ."

"We haven't had any ritual abuse cases in our county," Terri cut in, dabbing at the blood-colored salsa at the corner of her mouth. "But what we have had is—"

"Quite a few cases that involve dead animals." Charles finished.

"Dismembered," said Terri, ripping a piece of fat from a bacon strip with her teeth. "They were noted by the brand inspector."

And they think they don't have ritual abuse in their county. They had missed all the signs of ritual sacrifice just as I once had, and no doubt, countless other advocates across America and around the world.

ℳ ♀ ℭ

Paige was busy packing her suitcase, folding each item with meticulous care as I crammed all my stuff into my bag in a matter of minutes. Home was calling.

"Here. You look like you could use a couple of Tylenol," she said, handing me a bottle.

That was Paige's apology, and I graciously accepted it. "Thanks," I said, bridging the gap as I shook three into my hand.

"I picked up the survey results for you." Paige continued as if nothing had changed. And sad to say, nothing had.

It is what it is. The two of us had become pretty good dance partners over the past year, skirting and stepping around each other, avoiding the obvious and being careful not to step on each other's toes.

"Want a look?" she offered.

Yes and no. I felt stupid that I had completely forgotten all about the survey—what with the vicious hangover—but I was burning with curiosity and a little foreboding. "Yeah, sure."

So we sat on the edge of the bed and sifted through the stack of papers, then Paige compiled the results while I wrestled with luggage.

Paige was good at math. Better than I could ever hope to be. "What's the verdict?" I asked as I wheeled our luggage to the door and piled our coats on top.

"Okay," she said. "Here goes: for the advocates, about fifteen percent have seen police reports that included ritualistic activity in the form of animal sacrifices, gatherings, altars, or graffiti."

I stroked my chin and nodded thoughtfully. "That makes sense. Advocates working at shelters typically don't have access to police reports."

"That's true," said Paige, "but get this: about twenty-five percent of the advocates at this conference have either worked directly with clients who claimed to be victims of ritual abuse or had coworkers that worked with RA survivors."

"That's more like it. That's what I would've guessed," I said, returning to sit next to Paige.

Paige glanced at her notes. "Georgia had the most annual cases. The cop from Atlanta has responded to ten cases in his career. Hmmm . . . wish I knew how long that was. The two reps from Macon Victim Witness averaged ten reports a year—five sent directly to them by law enforcement plus an additional five claims from victims outside the criminal justice system."

The sun set early in December, and it was almost dark by the time we returned to I-5 North. Paige cautiously checked the CD player and then opted for some soft music on the radio before drifting off to sleep.

As we passed the general area of the spinout, I realized that the promise I had made to "think about it later" had arrived, and I began to speculate on the various ways Logan might have arranged for stalking music to be planted in the car.

So many things to consider. My mind wrestled with possibilities. Logan was in prison and had no way of knowing that I was going to San Jose, but then, his friends had learned to break into cars while still in high school. Paige could have slipped the disk in when I wasn't looking. But why would she do that? And who was the mysterious biker that had tailed me down to the conference? Was it Travis?

Traffic thinned. More people traveled south on Friday nights than north. Somewhere near Stockton, I became aware of a light bar in my rearview mirror—the kind of lights that mount on the forks of motorcycles. I rolled down the window and listened with fear to the distinctive growl of a heavy cruiser.

CHAPTER 11
༄ ✚ ༅

The engine idled, lights off and heater on high to keep We were hiding behind a Taco Bell in Chico that caters to midnight munchies. Paige tapped her fingers on the car panel time to the beat... *"I need two supreme tacos and hold the sour cream—it makes me vomit, and it's an ugly scene..."*

I cut her off. "What is that you're singing?"

Paige threw me a dirty look. "YouTube: Taco Bell rap about food, since you won't let me get out and get some. I'm starving!"

"You don't look like you're starving."

Paige threw me a dirty look.

I was tired and frustrated. "It's for your safety as well as mine." I glanced again down Main Street. I had doubled around the block and cut through an alley in hopes of losing the motorcycle that had tailed us for the past three hours. "I won't risk anyone seeing you."

"I have to go to the bathroom."

"Five more minutes, and I'll take you home. It's not that far. You can wait." And she did.

I was still congratulating myself as I approached the observation point just below my home when a rack of headlights popped on and eased out onto the road behind me. It was three a.m., and I had less than five minutes to make up my mind about what to do next.

It's Logan! I feel it. I know it. He's escaped. Or worse—he's been released. It was only a matter of time.

I was tired of running—sick of feeling afraid. Victims live in a constant state of fear. I have worked with victims that still tremble in fearful anticipation of encountering a long-deceased abuser. Tonight, I opted for anger. Advocates weren't supposed to get angry, but personally, anger was a fuel that had saved my butt more than once. Sometimes anger could be a good friend.

Done running. I gripped the steering wheel. I sped the last half mile driving like a crazy woman to my corner, one hand on the wheel and the other rummaging through my purse—frantically searching for my house key that I wished was a gun. I fishtailed onto my dirt road and skidded to a stop in front of the house, burying my pursuer in a California version of a Middle Eastern haboob.

"Mercy!" I called. Racing to the dog pen, I released our dog of war with a single move and sprang toward the house with the great dog at my heels. From within the wall of dust, the motorcycle's engine cut.

Not missing a step, I unlocked the door and raced through the house to retrieve my Glock—always loaded, always chambered with a bullet that carried Logan's name. It felt good— cold and powerful as I gripped it, crouched low, and took aim—almost shooting the man who was coughing as he wrestled with an enthralled Mercy.

"What the . . . ?" followed by a slight, tight cough. "Are you trying to kill me . . . ?" I heard him clear his throat. "Again?"

I collapsed on the sofa, overwhelmed with the staggering realization that I had almost shot my husband. He's right. It wasn't the first time.

Getting to my feet, I stood over Chance and Mercy, shrieking, "Goddamn it! Are you out of your fucking mind?"

Chance reached out and caught my hand en route to his face.

I kept shrieking. "You're crazy! You know that? God . . . I nearly . . . I nearly . . .." Screaming. Shaking. Sobbing. Exhausted.

I could have killed him. But I clung to him instead.

ဆၜၐ

It wasn't the first time I had nearly mistaken Chance for Logan. Between the roar of the motorcycle, the black leathers, and the powder coat of dust. All I had seen was tall and scary.

"It was you—following me home? Oh, Chance." My voice caught. "I thought you were Logan."

Still rubbing dirt from his eyes, Chance was in no mood for excuses. "You're the one who's crazy. Logan's in prison," he sputtered, spitting a piece of dirt from his mouth. "Why in hell would you think I was Logan?"

The gun slid from my hand onto the sofa, and the other covered my mouth as I cried, "I'm sorry, I'm sorry, I'm so sorry." Still holding my arm, Chance drew me close to envelop me in a tight, protective embrace. His rough cheek pressed into mine as he nuzzled my hair.

I heard him take a deep breath and sniff back some emotion.

"After I left you, I got a room in town and . . . and I missed you, babe. I felt so sorry about everything. I never meant for Paige to come between us again. I just wanted to be with you. Then, I saw you drive by. I was at a parts store . . . having a little trouble with the bike . . . and there you were, driving past. I decided to come home. I need you, babe. Sweet God, I need you. I love you—I love you."

His words melted into kisses as they trailed down my neck. No sense wasting all this adrenaline. Talking could wait. My husband was home and back in our bed, at least for tonight.

Sunshine painted bars across our bed—bars that kept us prisoners of winter, until almost noon, when the light finally crept across our swollen eyes. Snuggling deep into each other's warmth, I started my day with thanks: Thankful for my home, thankful for my life, and thankful for my husband's sexual prowess. The night was now a lingering dream, shattered all too soon by life.

I bolted upright in bed. "Uh, Chance. I have a question." I pulled the quilt around my shoulders. I felt the elevens between my eyebrows deepen as I twisted around to face him. "You said that you followed me home from Fresno." The question was unavoidable. "Uh, did you happen to tail me on the trip down there also?"

Chance sat up, frowning as he rubbed the sleep from his eyes. "What are you talking about? Are you saying someone followed you to Fresno?" His handsome, rugged face tightened, causing a shadow to fall across my heart. "Why didn't you tell me?"

"I just did."

"Nothing ever changes with you." Chance's voice tightened. "This is the problem with our marriage. You don't trust me. Never have, never will. You should have told me everything when I saw you in Fresno."

I didn't mean to raise my voice, it just happened. "You mean, like, instead of having sex?"—I jabbed a finger at him—"Or was I supposed to tell you in the middle of your fight with your mistress about your baby?"

Chance rubbed his head. "God, I don't want to fight. You know I'm done with Paige." Chance swung his legs off the bed and into his pants. "I know Fresno was another mistake, but I'm here now, trying to make it right. You're beating a dead horse," he growled. He shrugged into his T-shirt, yanking it down over his head.

Chance leveled an icy stare and pointed his finger back at me. "I will always regret my affair, but hear me now," he said, raising his voice. "I am done apologizing. Got that?"

I warmed to the occasion. "Oh . . . excuse me if your whore is in my face every day." The next words oozed like festering shrapnel long after the battle. "Now you have your damned baby."

Chance turned away with a huff and stalked into the bathroom. We didn't talk again until we sat down together over a hot meal at a cold table.

"I called the prison just to be on the safe side. Thought you'd want to know that Logan's still in custody."

"Thanks." I meant it—even if it didn't sound like it.

Chance picked up a piece of toast and then set it down again, peering at me through tousled hair and two days of stubble sprouting on his face. "Anything else you want to tell me?"

It sounded like an accusation.

No.

I stabbed my fork in the egg yolk pretending it was his eye and smiled when it exploded. The weekend was devolving into a familiar duel of hurtful remarks.

I took up the sword. "Not a thing," I said, my voice razor sharp.

Chance's eyes kindled as he pushed the plate away. "Really?"

"Really." My brows peaked, feigning innocence.

I noticed the muscles that tightened along the curve of his jaw were quivering and straining with restraint. I thought his jaw might crack.

"This is bullshit." Chance pushed back from the table and rose. I froze, fork in midair. "Someone nails a bloody chicken to your front door, and you call it nothing?" He gripped the back of the chair, white-knuckled. "That's why you thought Logan was tailing you. Am I right? Am I?"

I heard my fork hit the plate. "Who told you about the chicken?"

"What difference does it make? I'm sick of this." He pushed the chair against the table with finality.

"Who told you?" I shouted, hitting the table with my fist and making it tremble.

Chance spit the word, like a bad taste, out of his mouth: "Travis."

℘ ♀ ℃

"You're leaving? What happened to spending the weekend together?"

"I can't take it anymore." Chance had spent the afternoon splitting firewood, and now he was busy packing clean clothes into a suitcase.

"Can't take what? What are you saying?"

He dropped his shoulders. "I'm saying I'm sorry and I have to go."

Desperation bloomed in my throat. I was driving him away again. "I'm sorry too." I choked out the words. Words that seeded panic across a field of emotion as my eyes prepared to water them with regret. I didn't want Chance to go. Not now. Not ever.

Chance reached out and drew me close.

"Please don't go," I whispered.

He let me go and stepped back. "I need to get going. It's a ten-hour drive. I'm leaving the bike and taking the Dodge. It's freezing out there."

"I know." It was cold inside too. "It's almost Christmas. I want you here, with me. Please—please change your mind. Come home for Christmas."

"I already told you. I'll be in Mexico—but we still have a date for January, right?" Chance added with a weak smile of encouragement. "You put in for a vacation like we talked about?"

"Sure." Monday. I refused to cry in front of him. Tears would come as soon as he was out of sight.

"Okay then."

And then he was gone, and I was alone—again.

℘ ♀ ℃

"Mommy? Momeee!" I heard the distant words while still trapped in the nightmare, although in my dream age I was too old to call Starla "Mommy." In a blink, I was hugged and comforted by Joyce's strong brown arms and soft words. My friend and neighbor, Joyce, was more of a mother to me than Starla ever was.

Joyce and her husband, Kenny, lived about a half mile down the dirt road past our cabin. That was the end of the road before dropping into the Feather River Canyon. It was Joyce who took care of me during the school week after Starla left, while my dad was in Oakland. The arrangement worked for Lefty, knowing I was safe—either with Joyce and Kenny, in school, or at home with Frito. Lefty gave Joyce and Kenny money for their trouble, but I know they would have taken me in regardless.

I spent almost every Sunday through Thursday between fifth and eighth grade with Joyce and Kenny. But when I reached high school, I felt grown-up enough to stay at the cabin by myself, knowing that they lived just down the road with an open door, a hot dinner, and a warm bed. Joyce and Kenny were my friends. It's just that I needed to be home— in case my parents returned.

৪ী ⚥ ৫৫

There were people at the DA's office who thought that living apart from one's spouse would be an ideal living arrangement. On the bright side—and it wasn't all that bright—having Chance gone meant half the usual laundry. I slept on one side of the bed and then switched to the other instead of changing the sheets. A little blessing I would surrender in a heartbeat, I thought, as I dragged my pillow, blanket, and dog out to the sofa. Sometimes, no matter what I did, the bed still felt dirty.

I tried to sleep, but sleep didn't come. I wanted to cry, but my tear tank was past empty. Soft purple shades of evening spilled through the sliding glass door and found me still on the sofa, staring at the phone.

I have options.

Temptation wrapped its arms around me and whispered in my ear, as satisfying as chicken and dumplings to a fat man. As needy as a drink at an AA meeting. And as alluring as a shiny apple dangling in front of Eve.

Travis would always be my temptation, and now, after months of not speaking with him, I actually had a justifiable reason to call. He had been my friend, my adversary, my coworker, and my lover—at least for one exquisite night of unforgettable passion.

Talking couldn't hurt. Reaching out with trembling fingers, I pushed the buttons and held my breath, each ring lasting an eternity.

"Hello?" A soft, lilting voice answered. Female.

I hung up, disconnecting from my heart, feeling stupid, embarrassed, and an irrational stab of jealousy.

Within minutes the phone rang, rang again, and again before I picked up.

"Sunny, it's me." I thought I might pass out for a second. "Babe." Travis's rich voice was filled with concern. "Talk to me."

And I did. Discarding all pleasantries, along with curiosity and resentment that surged from the pit—of my stomach, of hell—maybe both—I determined to turn defeat into victory. I demanded answers. I wanted to know the names of people feeding him information about me, and why the hell he was talking to Chance.

One hundred channels to choose from and all I could play was reruns. Even I was tired of hearing myself.

Travis took my questions in his usual restrained, self-disciplined, self-controlled manner. There wasn't much that ruffled Travis, including me. His words were careful, draped in a tone as smooth and tailored as a set of karate silks.

"You don't think an animal sacrifice on your doorstep is serious?" he asked.

"Why do you care?" That one made him pause.

"I care," he said. "Besides, the investigation isn't closed. The cartel will be after you as long as they think you can lead them to the guns Logan owes them."

"Why did you have to tell Chance about a stupid chicken?"

"You're right. You're the one who should have told him." Travis let that hang for a minute. "He's looking out for you. He loves you."

"Right." I laughed—a short, derisive laugh. "You know nothing. If Chance really cared about me, he would be home instead of running off on some missionary trip. I don't need him. I can take care of myself."

"I know. I know." We both knew. It was a lie.

"And now you're being followed?"

Chance had already called him.

"Just forget it," I said.

"No problem. If you want to kill yourself—go ahead and do it. Grab that Glock of yours, stick it in your mouth, and pull the trigger! Just stop forcing the people who love you to watch you choke to death on your pride and pain!"

I was still staring at the phone in my hand when the dial tone reminded me to hang up.

Travis was right. Chance was right. Sitting on the edge of the sofa, I cradled my head in my hands and massaged my forehead. Life was so damned confusing.

I had always taken care of myself. Shit, I probably had changed my own diapers. The day I failed to take care of myself would have been the day my parents got rid of me forever. So I worked hard, taking care of the house and nursing my mother. I showed my father that I could feed myself, make a fire, and not be afraid of anything. And he had loved me for it.

I'd had to take care of myself or die. My mother had repeatedly left me. And even Logan had spent most of his time in Oakland and San Bernardino. Independence was synonymous with love. Weakness could only result in permanent abandonment.

The days were cold and the nights colder still. I got up and added a log to the soapstone heater, then returned to the sofa. Tucked under a fleece throw, cuddling with Kissme, I watched the flames entwine behind the glass, dancing like an orgy of drunken spirits.

$$\wp\,\maltese\,\wr$$

Taylor hunched over, balled up like a pill bug, her hands over her face, her long hair threaded through her fingers. As fast as she coiled, she rebounded. With startling swiftness Taylor grabbed her hair in her fists and jackknifed up, her nose touching mine—except it wasn't Taylor's face, it was Logan's—dark and sinister, painted like Batman's adversary, the Joker. Menacing words slithered through his lascivious grin. "Hello, Sunshine."

If Logan died tonight, he would still haunt me all the days of my life. It's not that he's immortal, but the evil that inhabits him has been around forever. Always was, always will be, until the Lord comes again. Daylight memories and nightmare fantasies. I wonder if I will ever find freedom this side of heaven.

CHAPTER 12

ఴ ♁ ಏ

A slice of moon hung in the sky, peeking through the corner of the sliding glass door. Shadowy shapes of furniture looked threatening in the dim light. Kissme whined, and I held her tight to soothe the thumping in my chest and calm my ragged breath. The dog kissed me, and I kissed her back as her love chased the nightmare that was Logan away. Swallowing hard, I breathed a one-word prayer: "God."

There was comfort in God, the dog, and the moon. Somewhere in the jumble of my tangled thoughts, I found myself wondering about Nina and Taylor. What evil invaded their dreams? Where did they turn for comfort in the night? To whom did they pray? As haunted as I was, I gazed at the moon and prayed for them.

ఴ ♁ ಏ

Paige had left a stack of summaries on my desk. I flipped through the stack with interest. Numbers didn't lie. No surprises on the NVAA stats, but I did a double-take on the results from the one-question survey I had sent around to some local agencies. The inquiry was comprised of a single question: How many claims Satanic or ritual abuse does your office receive annually? The results were unnerving.

The sheriff's office reported six to ten, Rape Crisis kicked back six, the local domestic violence program noted three to five, Victim Witness, one to two, and Dano responded with the ominous number thirteen from Mental Health. There was no denying that a problem existed. Shrouded in dark thoughts and growing paranoia, I headed for the intake office and reached up into my box.

"Ahhhhhh!!" I screamed like a girl. No big surprise there—I sounded like someone had just stuffed a snowball down my shirt.

Heads jerked up like a dog pack catching the scenting of blood, followed by an explosion of hilarity—as a coal-black red-eyed white-fanged king-sized OMG hideous rat tumbled from the in-box and landed on my face, pulling a stack of police reports with it that spun and flitted to the floor like so much confetti at a Macy's parade.

It took a couple of seconds and a few hundred heartbeats to realize that the rat was a fake. Nevertheless, I bent down and cautiously picked it up by the tip of the tail.

Breathing fire, I flipped my hair out of my face and scanned the room. My gaze alone should have torched the place. One hand on my hip, with the other dangling the rat by the tail, I demanded, "Alright, who's the clown?"

The secretaries met my glare with wide-eyed innocence, dismissive shrugs, chuckles, and smirks.

"Funny. Real funny!"

My coworkers had clearly thought so.

Duncan walked in and glanced at the rat, scrunched his face, and bent to gather the scattered papers. "What's that?" he asked, nodding toward the rat.

"Office humor, Duncan. This place is a joke." My eyes narrowed with suspicion. "Did you do this?"

His baby face looked startled. Hurt. "Me? Heck, no. I wouldn't do that."

Stalking back to my office, I passed Bonita. "Was this your idea?" I demanded, thrusting the rat in her face.

Bonita inspected the rubber rodent.

"Made in China."

"No shit, Sherlock."

"Ouch—someone have a bad night?" Bonita looked pained.

As a matter of fact, I had. "Did you put the rat in my in-box?"

Bonita seemed to chew the question like a chunk of tripe in a bowl of Menudo. "Yo no. But—"

"But what?"

"You know, Sunny, you're going to get some heat for doing these ritual abuse cases. Right?" Bonita's words were a lot like the Kevlar on her bulletproof vest—tough and yet protective. "Laughter is how some people deal with fear. You should know that, Chica."

I did know it. I had just forgotten. Maybe that's why I was so darn angry. Pain and laughter were neither opposites nor twins. They were often just ugly stepsisters. When it hurt too much to cry, you laugh. The degree of horror inflicted on victims of ritual abuse is typically so bizarre, so egregious, so outside the norm of social boundaries that pain and laughter become both crime and shield.

Between TV and responding to crime scenes, there isn't much left to frighten anyone working criminal division. Perhaps investigators need to believe that no atrocities exist outside of their control, so they joke about witchy-poos, goblins, and things that go bump in the night.

Bonita tipped her head thoughtfully. "Maybe the rat connected to the . . . joke . . . in Feather Falls. Have you thought of that? Chickens nailed to your door. Rats in your in-box."

Yeah, and hemorrhoids might be related to too many donuts, but I'd rather not think about it.

Paige rolled past clutching her belly as if it were a lifesaver hanging on the side of a cruise ship. I thrust the rat in her face, and the resulting screams got her off the hook. Paige only associated with two-legged rats.

Bonita laughed and moved on.

There was only one outreach program planned for this week—an odd one, with a foster-child agency. Ducking into my office, I grabbed the laptop with the implications of Bonita's words still firing through my brain with the force of my 9mm. If the rat wasn't the insufferable prank of a coworker, then who . . . ?

No time for meditation or contemplation. I was late.

Briefcase in one hand, laptop in the other, I hurried downstairs and was startled to see Bonita in the parking lot hugging a rough-looking woman who was straddling a really sweet motorcycle.

Each to their own. I shrugged, congratulating myself for hiring a woman who would never pose a threat to my love life—if I had a love life.

The people at the foster-care agency were kind and forgiving. They graciously took a break without any remarks or raised eyebrows when the overhead lights were dimmed and the screen remained blank. The computer ran, but the projector wouldn't project. Lights back on, I spent fifteen minutes rechecking everything—cords, connections, links, everything—twice, before panicking.

Duncan dropped everything and rushed across town to rescue me. Jittery, suspicious, and completely clueless, I apologized again to the attendees, who smiled politely and went back to talking with their friends.

Duncan found the problem in less than a minute. "The lens cap is still on the projector."

Duh!

"You'd be surprised at how often that happens." Duncan kept his voice down and gave me a reassuring pat on the back, then stuck around to give me moral support.

"Technical problem solved," Duncan announced as the people filed back in to take their seats. The lights went down, and the show began.

"Come on, good buddy. I'm treating you to lunch," I said to Duncan, with a warm rush of gratitude. Duncan was easy company, and I considered him a friend.

"You've had a rough day," Duncan sympathized as we worked our way through a pair of hamburgers at Jake's Burger's that came with enough fries to end world hunger. "Sunny," he said with a hard swallow while staring at his double-decker Jake-burger and dabbing at his mouth with the checkered napkin, "I was thinking, um . . ." he cleared his throat again and chased it with some soda before continuing. "About . . . what would you think . . . ?"

"Go ahead, Duncan. Spit it out." I munched another fry. "Anything for my favorite guy." He was teddy-bear cute.

"Would you go out with me?"

"Out?" I didn't understand. "Out where?"

Big eyes flashed with hope from behind a new pair of designer glasses. "Dinner? Dancing? Movie?"

The fry stuck in my throat—and the fry, my throat, or both swelled. Unable to breathe, I gasped, sucking the fry deeper into my lungs. My eyes popped as I gagged, my hands flailing at my throat as if I could somehow shake it loose.

The chair bounced off the floor as Duncan rushed behind me, half lifting me out of my seat. His tree-trunk arms wrapped around me, and he locked his hands high under my breasts—too high—repeatedly thrusting against me until the fry dislodged and flew across the table, landing squarely in his lunch basket.

Awkward. I didn't want to live. I prayed for death—or at least an asteroid to hit me.

Duncan looked ecstatic, rhapsodic, like he had hit all six numbers on a Mega Millions lottery ticket, or we had just finished having gorilla sex. I could see his dreams unfolding in his expression: our wedding, Duncan Jr. and his five baby sisters, Sunday picnic baskets full of KFC.

Oh. My. Lord.

"To tell you the truth, Duncan," I said weakly, "you're a sweetheart, but I don't feel so good. Can we talk about this later?"

Duncan offered to drive me back to the office, and when I declined, he shepherded me to my car, where I thanked him again for saving my life and patted him on the cheek, and he left me with a fond farewell.

೫✝ಜ

The Chinese celebrate the year of the horse, the year of the dog, the year of the dragon, and so forth. If I could name the year ahead, it would probably be the year of the baby. It was worse than the Asian flu that everyone pretended was not from Asia in order to avoid offending Asians. Why couldn't everyone pretend they weren't pregnant and not offend me?

I sighed, realizing that Ashley had tried to do just that. She had tried to spare my feelings, but I ended up hurt anyhow. Some people see flying monkeys, I was seeing flying babies.

"District Attorney's Office, this is the advocate speaking."

"Hello, my name is Vicki—Victory West." That was her name, not her street.

"Vicki, how are you?"

I recalled that Vicki had been a victim of domestic violence during her pregnancy, and her husband had been sentenced to three years in prison. It was an unusual case that included some hazy allegations that her husband, out on bail, had tried to sell their baby on the day it was born. He had walked out of the hospital with the baby after placing a phone call that Vicki overheard. Paradise Police located her husband in the hospital parking lot holding the newborn child. No one else was in sight. While his bail was revoked, no additional charges were filed regarding the baby.

"I need to see you," said Vicki. She sounded rational. No panic or fear in her voice.

"Would you like to come into the office or . . . ?"

"Can you come to my home? Please. Like you did last time? There's something you need to see."

I slid out early and headed for Paradise on my way home.

Vicki lived in a nice trailer park in an area called "The Pines." Her modest home was neat and clean, completely incongruous with a mysterious stink that permeated the air.

"Please. Sit down." Vicki was a thirty-something redhead, neat and trim, wearing designer jeans and a Redheads Not Warheads sweatshirt. She left the door open in spite of the chill wind that slipped in behind me.

Vicki took up her story after I declined her offer to get me something to drink. She politely briefed me on her son, Kyle— "three years old now"—and her career—"one more year of college"—then she got to the point. "I got rid of the old couch—the one Jack carved all the pentagrams on."

Pentagrams? I had forgotten about the pentagrams. What I remembered was Jackson West had poured charcoal lighter fluid in Vicki's hair and then repeatedly flicked a barbecue lighter over her head as she cringed in the corner of their yard. Another time, he had held his electric shaver as she sat in the bathtub, threatening to drop it in and light her up. I had almost forgotten the allegations regarding their baby.

Anxiety flashed through Vicki's determined features, a chink in her tired armor. "Jackson is out of prison." Vicki's hands shook as she lit a cigarette. "I took Kyle to my mom's house this morning. I'm scared to death that Jackson will sneak in and grab him when I'm not looking—like when I'm on the toilet, sleeping, cooking, anything. Christ only knows what Jackson will do."

Her freckles looked as if they'd been applied with a Sharpie against her pale skin. Her lips quivered. "I did some housework after I got home this morning and then lay down for a nap. I haven't been able to sleep since Jack got out. I woke up coughing; the house was full of smoke. I thought it was on fire." Vicki stood up and gestured. "I want you to check this out."

She led me outdoors, around the mobile home, past a plastic Big Wheel parked on the sidewalk. I paused to stare in wonder as we passed a play area. It held a treasure trove of timeless action figures with their trusty land, animal, and space vehicles, along with a pile of assorted armament, a plastic dump truck, a shovel, and a soccer ball.

It was the toys that had changed my reluctance to handle ritual abuse. Toys. The wondrous magic of a child's world that made my heart melt and throat swell. Toys. Lying there, as silent as a graveyard without children to give them life and purpose. I swallowed, and for a brief moment I was Vicki, and Kyle was my little boy at risk of being kidnapped and sold. I felt for her—her anguish, terror, and guilt over picking a bad dad for Kyle. I blinked. Vicki was every mother, and Kyle every child.

Vicki didn't seem to notice my distraction. She was intent on the sodden black mound that she had hosed down to squelch the threat of fire. "I found this pile of feathers and leaves"—Vicki kicked at the pile—"and probably dog crap stuffed under the corner of my house. That's my bedroom, right there. It was still smoking when I found it." Her voice caught, and then she continued. "I—we—might have burned to death."

I shook my head at my own stupidity. How was it that I could see the risks and have so much concern for a stranger, and yet have so much hostility toward Chance and Travis, and even Bonita—all of whom took the threat up at the cabin more seriously than I? The incident with the chicken and the knife had been staged to send a loud, clear message. The problem had been that the message was delivered in a language I didn't want to hear.

Wetting my lips, I turned to Vicki. "We need to call the police. This is arson. If you report Jackson to the police, his parole might be revoked and he'll be sent back to prison."

"Please don't do that. That's why I called you. I don't want the police." She shook her head, sending her copper curls bouncing. "I don't want to get into it again with him. I want to be free of him, not in court with him. Jackson's terms of parole say that he isn't supposed to come within five hundred yards of me. But somehow he managed to get released to Magalia. There's only one road out of the mountains, and it goes right past my house. He drives by my house every day—to shop, to see his parole officer, to spy on me. It's not right."

Vicki waved her hands in frustration. "How can they do that? How can they parole him right back to the cult? Those are the same people he tried selling our son to pay off his drug debts. The very same people!"

Tears broke through her defenses, and she swiped them away in anger. "I need your help, not the police. I need you to call the parole board. Get him moved to Chico. Or San Ysidro. Or the moon. I don't care."

I smiled. San Ysidro was the southernmost city in the state before crossing into Mexico, but personally, I thought that paroling Jackson to the moon was a better idea. Vicki confirmed my belief that releasing people back to the county of origin was the worst possible policy. Good intentions did not negate reality. The intent might be to parole inmates back to the support of family and friends, but the reality was that the person was also back in the land of familiar—old habits, old haunts, old addictions, and old patterns. Sending parolees to a different state could at least offer hope for a new beginning.

I spent hours on the phone the next day calling everyone short of the president of the United States, who was probably busy golfing anyhow. I labored up the food chain through agents, chiefs, deputies, and directors until I finally reached a person in the Department of Corrections who did not ask for confirmation of my position and details of my duties—or dismiss me for wasting his precious time—time better spent addressing real concerns. True to his word, the administrator that finally listened called Jackson's PO, who in turn called me. I provided him with additional background on Jackson's involvement with a satanic cult and the geographical dynamics that necessitated him breaking the restraining order on a daily basis.

I guessed it really was the season for miracles. The officer modified terms of Jackson's parole to read "Chico," located in the valley, and detailed further provisions to protect Vicki and Kyle. The presence of Satanists did not surprise Jackson's parole officer in the least. He concluded by saying that he was acutely aware of pervasive cult activity in our county.

Sometimes I felt like I was just another citizen who didn't want to admit that ritual abuse existed in my backyard. According to my statistics, law enforcement and social service professionals all had direct knowledge of cults and cult survivors. They all handled silent caseloads of perpetrators and victims, and yet, with the exception of Jack Savage, who thrived on conflict, it remained a taboo topic. It was as though the national response to Satanic Panic was Satanic Repudiation.

CHAPTER 13

⚜ ✝ ⚜

One more baby shower and I will hang myself.

It was Sunday afternoon, and I drove up the hill to Ashley's house. It was the last thing—even if it was the right thing—that I wanted to do. More than being motivated by my Christian duty, if I dug deep enough beneath the festering mounds of garbage in my soul, I knew I was arranging this baby shower for the secret sire, be it Chance or Travis, rather than the miserable mom.

I wasn't sure where I would fit into the picture should Chance turn out to be the father. Our conversations never seemed to get that far. Now the question dangled between us, unspoken and perhaps unnecessary, waiting on Her Highness to bestow the truth on her servants-in-waiting.

Maybe I should have given Paige two baby T-shirts, I mused with a grin—one with a little search-and-rescue emblem and the other with an ATF logo—and watched to see which one she hugged and which one she threw in the trash.

"Out! Stay! Good boys!"

"What did they do?" I asked, petting Ashley's dogs before entering her home.

The usually trim Ashley had continued to expand—from looking like an exercise ball to resembling my Volkswagen.

"The dogs stay outside now. I'll have enough to deal with later."

Her answer surprised me since I'd rather have had dogs in the house than kids any day. "Why? Are you afraid they'll go rogue? Eat the babies?"

Her gray-green eyes were not laughing. "Germs. Germs and pet hair," she said, closing the ornate door on her two sad-looking dogs.

"What's a little hair between friends? I sleep with Kissme."

"Yeah, but you're not . . . you don't . . ."

Shane came to the rescue. "Good mornin', Sunshine! About time you came over." He swept me into a bear hug, intentionally tickling my neck with his shaggy brown beard until I laughed and playfully shoved him away. Shane's beard, a few tattoos, and owning the Harley shop in Chico still evidenced his biker roots. Shane reminded me of my dad's friends that would ride up on weekends. Rough and tender, formidable and fun—crazy contradictions, but they were family.

Ashley brought out the blender to make us nutritional smoothies for breakfast, which included fresh fruit, yogurt, and more supplements than a Chinese apothecary. There was a time, not long ago, when it would have been lattes for two, but now she had sworn off caffeine. I watched Shane as he headed outdoors and wondered dryly if she had sworn him off too. Germs and hair.

Ashley lectured me about nutrition and thanked me again for her baby shower.

No problem. And it hadn't been a problem. The ladies at church had done it all. I flooded with guilt even as I basked in Ashley's appreciation.

"Follow me," said Ashley, leaving her half-finished drink on the breakfast bar. "I can't wait to show you the nursery and all the gifts." Ashley was as wound up as a mobile dangling over a crib.

"So, Ash," I said, trailing her down her hall, "since you're on top of this baby thing, you think you can help me throw Paige a baby shower?" I knew she had to say yes since I had thrown her one.

Ashley froze, turning in the hall. She stared in surprise, and then wrapped her arms around me. "Oh, Sunny, you are unbelievable. How . . . forgiving . . . how thoughtful of you to throw Paige a party." She held me at arm's length. "You are one strong woman. That must have been a tough decision."

"Complicated," I corrected her.

Are those tears in her eyes?

"No wonder Chance loves you so much. I really admire you."

I winced through a smile of appreciation. "Thanks, Ash. You're a good friend."

If I'd been a Catholic, I'd be burning rubber headed for confession. I didn't know why I continued to go to church. Maybe I was hoping that the spirit of Christianity, now exemplified by

Ashley's genuine compassion, would eventually rub off on me. I seemed to be driven more by guilt than goodness. I knew I didn't deserve her praises, much less her friendship.

"What will you do if the baby is Chance's?" she asked me in a voice as soft as the shadows in the hallway.

"Chance will do the right thing," I said. "He'll make a great father."

Ashley reached out and caressed my arm. "I asked, 'what will *you* do?'"

Silence.

"I don't know what my options are yet. Whatever I do will depend on what Chance does. And ultimately, what Paige decides."

More silence.

"It must be awkward, going back to Step One. But I guess life is a series of Step Ones, huh?"

"Step One?"

"Codependency. Remember? Giving Chance power over your happiness."

Ouch. Ashley was good at sticking her fingers in sore spots. I think that was part of her attraction. The best healers seemed to have a natural instinct for targeting pain.

"Thanks. I'll try to remember that."

Church isn't always where you think it is. Sometimes it comes to you, I thought. Indeed, the narrow hall did feel like a confessional, a safe place to release my deepest fear.

"I want to be with my husband," I whispered. "I've always wanted to be with Chance. I just don't know for sure that he wants to be with me. If Paige is carrying his child, maybe he'll want to be with her."

Ashley took some time to absorb that.

"I love you Sunny," she said, "and I don't have any answers. But I'm sure of some things. I'm certain that Chance loves you, and I know that God has a plan for something good to come out of all the chaos. I will pray for you, every day." She hugged me again, and I thought she might cry. Instead, she drew back and gently tugged at my sleeve. "Come on—wait till you see what I've done with the nursery."

The nursery looked like Sunday school with pictures of lambs, doves, and Jesus surrounded by children. Crayon-colored furniture and blocks with bright ABCs bordered the ceiling. Soft toys were scattered about the room as if she expected the twins to pop out of her ready for recess.

"What's that?" I pointed to a walkie-talkie cradled on top of the colorful dresser.

"It's an audio baby monitor. It lets a parent listen to the kids from another room. Ashley lowered her voice. "It was a thoughtful gift, but already a bit outdated. Shane is buying a Wi-Fi system so we can keep an eye on the babies through a streaming live app on our phones."

I studied the gifts still piled in the cribs. Safety equipment seemed to be running second place to stacks of diapers, followed by matching twin outfits. I fingered cushiony bumper guards of every type; a fireplace screen; locks for the TV and PC, stove, refrigerator, dishwasher; cabinet locks; colorful switch plate covers, and a set of Mommy's Helper Soft Corner Guards to pad the sharp edges on everything from furniture to corners on walls.

My nose wrinkled in resentment and disdain. There had been nothing to protect me from the sharp corners and hurts of my childhood.

ঙ ✚ ଓ

A bouquet of wildflowers—long spears of wine-colored lupine, lemon-yellow clusters of Spanish broom, and a small branch of delicate sweet birch that looked like billowing cumulus clouds—the type that precedes thunderstorms—were clutched in my grubby little fist as I climbed the stairs to my mother's bedroom.

Sometimes nightmares were real. Just last night I had hidden under my parents' bed as my cherished father had beaten my cold-hearted mother. Then the living nightmare receded as her screams began, and I retreated to my safe, dissociative place.

My inner child took flight as I mounted a wild stallion that "no man could tame."

"I am not a man," I declared, clutching his thick black mane and leaping onto his muscled back. The stallion and I had raced as one into a far land where the mountains met the ocean, and the soft sound of waves had eventually rocked me to sleep.

Starla's eyes were as purple as the lupine, her skin whiter than the sweet birch. She had set the flowers to one side, telling me to hurry or I would be late for school. I knew that the flowers, so vibrant with life, would wilt on her pillow by the time I got home. I understood the cycle of violence long before I knew it had a name. At least, it was my childlike understanding of the cycle of violence: my mother would disappear, and I would be alone until she accepted blame for her part in the fight with my dad. Then she would return, and we would be a happy family again. Until the next time.

Ashley's kids don't stand a chance, I thought bitterly. They will grow up soft and pampered. She will raise them to become the next generation of victims. At least I had grown up learning how to take care of myself. Maybe that was what my mother had intended all along.

₭ ⚇ ℞

I told Chance about Paige's baby shower during our evening phone call, and I guess it was no stretch to say that there was a pregnant pause between us.

"Sunny, I love you. I don't know what to say except that I'm sorry about this morning, hon. You are . . . the most incredible, the most amazing woman in the world."

He would have been amazed alright, if he really knew. My deceit felt like a form of adultery, taking praise that was not really mine. I took it, but I didn't deserve it. His approval was intended for the woman that he thought I was… the woman I wished I was.

Pressing the phone next to my ear, I snuggled under flannel sheets and the thick quilt that covered me with appliquéd bears, deer, and evergreens. Kissme burrowed next to me, and I stroked her head absentmindedly, enjoying the sound of Chance's deep voice. It was the closest thing to pillow talk that we had shared in some time.

Monday morning arrived. Nothing dead or alive leaped from my in-box, and for that I was grateful. Bonita had been on hand to check it for me. More likely, she was preventing me from disturbing a potential crime scene. She gave me the "all clear," and when I returned to my office, a mysterious venti-sized latte from Starbuck's was sitting next to the blinking light on my message machine.

"Playback all messages," the automated voice intoned. No message. But a song called "Poison" played.

That girl is poison, poison
If I were you I'd take precaution
Before I start to leave
Fly, girl . . .

Oh God—not again.

She'll drive you right out of your mind
Steal your heart when you're blind
Beware she's schemin', she'll make you think you're dreamin'
You'll fall in love and you'll be screamin' demon ooooooooh . . .

CHAPTER 14

☙ ✦ ❧

I tried to stifle a scream, but the sound rammed through my fingers like a muffled death cry.

It has to be that dirty piece of—

Duncan hurried in, his smile twisting into fear, than rage. He threw a huge protective arm around me. "Sunny. Dearest. What?!" sounding like Shrek, preparing to do battle for the love of his life.

"Bonita! Bonita. Get in here!" Duncan bellowed as she breezed past my door—and there came Fiona to the rescue.

My office became a beehive of activity, all for nothing. In the end, the coffee had contained nothing except caffeine and that deadly combination of cream and sugar that Shrek, aka Duncan, had put on my desk, and a phone message that couldn't be traced. When the excitement slowed, my office felt like a football locker room at halftime.

Homing in on the action, Paige drifted in and listened to the recording that Bonita was playing for the twentieth time. We made eye contact, and she gasped, the blood draining from her face. "Ohmygod—it's like what happened in the car," was all she said before turning heel.

"Don't"—I tried to shout over the hubbub—"call Travis!" But she was already through the door, leaving me with that familiar feeling of anger, frustration, and hopelessness, knowing that Bonita would probably rat me out, even if Paige didn't.

I haven't actually seen Travis in months, I thought. The horrible phone call and his fight with Paige don't count. The months felt like years. Travis was more like a memory. Like an old love letter hidden in the recesses of . . . not quite a trunk in a dusty attic, but more like the Rubbermaid tub where I keep clothes that didn't quite fit anymore. I wondered how Travis would look and feel if I dug him out and tried him on again.

There had been plenty of recycled relationships in my youth.

ဗ‍ဉ ⚲ ဗ‍ဉ

I wasn't excited to see her. My heart no longer beat a welcome home song. I did not run to my mother and throw my arms around her this time, burying my face in her long paisley skirts that always smelled of patchouli oil.

How long has it been this time?

I had brought her wildflowers on the day she left, and last Sunday Lefty promised to bring home the "biggest goddamned turkey on the planet" for Thanksgiving.

"Don't just stand there looking stupid," said Starla, who had picked me up from school. "Get your butt in the house. What's wrong with you, Sunny?"

I followed her inside the cabin, closing the door behind me. Angry and sullen, I shut the door and stood, staring, trying to understand.

"So... you're back for a visit? Run out of drugs? "

"Well, aren't you the little smart mouth these days?" Starla sat in Lefty's chair, tapping the ash from a joint into his ashtray with one hand and waving smoke from her face with the other. "I've been in the redwoods. If you really want to know, I've been living up in a redwood tree, one of the largest and oldest trees on this planet, and I"—Starla put great emphasis on 'I'—"have been keeping it safe from loggers for months."

Is she talking to herself or to me?

"My family brought me food and blankets and books . . . and pot." My mother was smiling as she chatted on, fairly glowing with self-illumination. "I learned to play the recorder, and . . . are you ready for this?"

No.

"They even wrote about me in Mother Earth News."

My mother was clearly expecting me to bask in her glory.

"Your family?"

"My commune family. The beautiful people. I don't expect you to understand."

"You got that right!" School books hit the floor, and my mother hit me.

"You think you're so smart. You think you know everything," she hissed and drew back her lips into a sneer. "Well, you don't! You have no right to judge me."

I cried, and Starla stayed until spring.

℘♀℃

It was about time I got my phone back.

"Thanks, but no thanks," I told Bonita. "I do not want my phone tapped or client conversations recorded." I quoted HIPPA laws regarding confidentiality. Being classified as a Mental Health counselor had its advantages.

The day was young, and there was still another surprise phone call. This one from Enloe Hospital in Chico.

"Ms. McLane? This is Dr. Jones."

I smiled for a nanosecond, wondering if the call was a prank and "Jones" was an alias, and then frowned because the man was clearly upset.

"This is Sunny McLane, advocate for the district attorney's office. How can I help you?"

"I need to begin by saying that I am making this call on behalf of a patient of mine, who is also a client of yours. She has been admitted anonymously under the name of Jane Doe for safety reasons. If you come to the hospital, be sure to let the desk know that you are from the district attorney's office. She said to tell you that her name was Grace.

I gasped and gripped the phone. "Not Grace." The haunting question she had posed, *Do you believe me?* could be the tagline for every ritual abuse survivor. On top of it all—adding insult to injury—Grace had been labeled the perpetrator.

"What else can you tell me?" I asked Dr. Jones.

"First, I need to ask you a question." The doctor's voice sounded accusing, taut, as if the phone were about to snap.

"What is it?"

"What the goddamned hell happened to this woman?"

The doctor's voice came like a slap. "I don't understand. What are you saying?"

"I am saying that her injuries indicate that she has been subject to torture. In addition to over a dozen scars, including some large puncture wounds, it appears that at some point she'd had a basement cesarean. A botched job, to say the least."

"I'm sorry, Doctor. I am not able to elaborate on that. Domestic violence charges against her were recently dropped."

"Charges against her?" His voice raised and thundered in my ear.

"I am trying to protect her, sir. Please tell me why she has been admitted to the hospital."

"I had to medically clear her of any physical issues before she could be transferred to Mental Health. Her physical condition is appalling. She is in bed, wearing a hospital gown and a pair of tennis shoes—her running shoes. And I assure you, Ms. McLane, she is not a jogger."

"I'm on my way." I hung up the phone with my right hand, grabbed my things with the left, and hurried down the hall of the atrium toward the stairs, passing Duncan as I went.

"Sunny, wait," he called out. "How about lunch when you get back? Our restaurant. My treat!"

"Sure. Fine," I said, distracted. "Later." And I blew past, skipping down the stairs to the parking lot until my mental Duncan-warning blinker flashed, bringing me to a halt even as Bonita intercepted me on her way back from the courthouse.

"You okay after this morning?" Bonita was being considerate, and I responded with my usual.

"Sure. Fine. I'm okay." The lie rolled off my tongue with the practiced ease of an acrobat. "I'm in a hurry to meet with a client." I threw her what passed for a look of gratitude, and popped the locks on the county car. Bonita really meant well. "How about joining me for lunch later on?"

Two birds with one stone.

Bonita seemed pleasantly surprised and accepted the invitation as I darted off to Chico.

ଛ ✝ ଓ

I moved Grace from the hospital, only to have the door slammed in my face at the SAFE (Stop Abuse for Everyone) House shelter for battered women.

"What's the problem here?" I asked Erika, who had been the shelter director forever and now stood in the doorway.

"Can't we talk about this?" I asked.

Erika relented, smiling sweetly as she opened the door to let us in. She turned to one of the women behind her, who eyed us curiously, and asked, "Casey, would you mind making some hot chocolate for our guests." Erika motioned for Casey to take Grace with her to the kitchen, and I gave Grace an encouraging nod.

Grace followed Casey, walking as though she were in a lot of pain. I assumed the doctor had treated her physical issues accordingly. My part was to make sure that she was safe.

"We can talk in here," Erika said as she led me into a private room on the bottom floor of the two-story house. "Please Sunny, have a seat." She gestured to a chair opposite her desk.

"Grace has been a victim of domestic violence. She needs a safe place." I had tried before to get Grace into this safe house, without success.

"I know that Grace is also a survivor of ritual abuse," said Erika, "and I understand that she needs help." She propped her elbows on the desk, templing her arms and clasping her hands. "Mental Health might be a more appropriate resource for your client."

I scowled in the face of her smile. "My client doesn't need to be locked up. She needs rest. She needs to feel safe."

"Let me remind you," said Erika, "that managing a shelter is hard work. We have regularly scheduled group sessions in which women get together and talk about being victims of violence. And let me tell you—that can be very stressful even under ideal circumstances. It doesn't help to have an RA survivor add to the discussion by telling the group she has 'Bride of Satan' carved into her back."

"What do you expect? She's been tortured. Her psyche is damaged."

"Exactly. That is why RA victims are exempt from shelters. Believe me when I say that our policy is consistent with that of most domestic violence shelters. RA survivors are too disruptive. We are trying to stabilize and empower women here, but your client is . . . is . . ." Erika searched for a politically correct term.

"A victim. That's the word you're looking for—victim." I positioned my arms on her desk to mirror hers. "I'll tell you what. How about keeping Grace here for a couple of days while I work on a relocation plan. Then she'll be gone—out of the county—for good. I promise."

Erika relented, probably because I worked for the district attorney and because it was in her program's best interest to maintain good relationships within the criminal justice system.

I explained to Grace that I would develop a relocation plan, and she nodded but remained mute.

Stroking her face softly with my fingertips, I said good-bye, then hugged her and let her know that I would call the shelter as soon as I had something in place. Grace nodded once more and moved away, her eyes tightening with every step. She shuffled across the living room, hunched over, walking slowly with a severe limp, ascending the stairs one painful step at a time to a room that the shelter had prepared for her, as far as possible from the general population.

ℬ✟ℛ

Duncan frowned when Bonita got out of the car with me at "our" restaurant, Tong Fong Low's, aka Chow Mein Charlie's. I didn't appreciate Duncan's reference to "our" restaurant. In my mind, the story of Chow Mein Charlie's restaurant, with its rich, colorful—real or imagined—history, belonged to Travis and me.

The food arrived, and I noticed in my peripheral vision that Duncan had bowed his head along with mine. "Good Lord," I said irreverently, my head popping up, "You did it. You're wearing real ear gauges, aren't you?" I was staring at modest round earrings called *gauges* that looked like giant black grommets embedded in his thick lobes. "Duncan, are you having a midlife crisis?"

Duncan lit up with a shy nod. "I liked the fake ones, so I thought, *what the heck*, and had them done for real."

Bonita gave him an appreciative look, saying, "I've got a girlfriend who wears those. I like them. She looks hot."

I scrambled to regroup. I knew that "gay" was supposed to be the new normal, but seriously, putting a dog in a cat suit and teaching it to meow still didn't make it a cat.

Duncan all but wriggled like a St. Bernard puppy under my appraisal as I nodded in agreement with Bonita. "You do look hot, big guy." And he did. Duncan looked great, but the thing I admired most of all was the courage behind his transformation. I liked that he was willing to put his traditional "safe" image on the line and change from Geek to . . . What is he changing into? GQ? Metrosexual? Gangsta? Punk?

We shared the various dishes as I steered the conversation away from Duncan.

"So, Bonita, I heard Narcotics borrowed you for a major bust yesterday. We want details."

Bonita's chow mein dangled from her chopsticks. "It was a mega bust. We got the owners of the Card Room on possession and sales so far. Can you believe it? We found a whopping 300 grams of meth all packaged into 8-Balls and stashed inside of some antique soy sauce pots down in the basement." Bonita took her bite, chewed, and swallowed. "The soy sauce pots were really cool."

"How much is an 8-Ball and what's a soy sauce pot?" asked Duncan.

"An 8-Ball is three and a half grams . . . so we're talking around three-quarters of a pound." A woman of many talents, Bonita chewed her food, talked, and tipped her head as the numbers rolled through her brain like a slot machine. "That would be . . . let me see, about forty thousand dollars in street value." She shrugged dismissively and then got excited about the soy sauce pots. "Now the pots are really amazing. They are this beautiful patina blue-green hexagon-shaped clay pot." She held up her hands as if holding something the size of a grapefruit. "Probably holds about a quart of soy sauce."

"Umm," I said, "now that you've been in a downtown basement, do you really think it was just a basement and not part of the Chinese tunnels?" The tunnels were a myth to everyone but the locals.

"It looked like a basement to me. Are there really secret tunnels?" Bonita asked.

"It depends on who you ask," I said with an air of mystery. "The official answer is maybe. We learned in school how the Chinese came here in the 1850s and 60s and became part of the gold rush to escape oppression in Canton. Only, when they got here, they found out that foreigners couldn't buy property because they weren't American citizens—which meant they couldn't own gold claims."

I looked up from my plate and noticed that Duncan had stopped eating and was staring at me in fascination. "Why didn't they become Americans?" he asked.

"People came from all over the world during the gold rush. That doesn't mean they gave up their native citizenship. Most of them, like the Chinese, planned on getting rich and going back to their native lands. Have you seen the Chinese temple?"

Duncan and Bonita each shook their head. "It's unprecedented in history because it embraced all the different religions that people brought with them from China. It's a historical landmark. You should check it out," I said, taking another bite of lunch.

"Anyhow, back to your question. The temple was built on a bluff above the river. Rumor has it that the Chinese tunneled under the temple toward the river where they illegally mined for gold. That's what we learned in school," I said with a maestro jab of my chopstick. "There has never been official 'proof' of other tunnels or activity. I doubt if the guards they kept posted at each corner of the Moon Temple—upstairs with a 360-degree view—were there for the church social."

"So what did you learn outside of school?" asked Duncan.

I gave Duncan a nod of approval. "What we learned after school is a whole different story. I knew kids who said they'd been inside the tunnels—partied in them and lost their virginity in them." I laughed with a shrug and cleared my throat. "The kids said several tunnels run under the shops downtown."

"Which shops?" asked Bonita.

"I don't know. I was a teenager. That wasn't the part of the stories I cared about. Besides, most of the tunnels were flooded and are under the dam now."

Duncan looked infatuated with the idea. "But you think they still exist?"

"I agree with the conspiracy theorist." I glanced around and lowered my voice. "I think local government calls it 'myth' to keep treasure hunters and ghost trackers from ripping up the streets."

Everyone laughed, and we returned to the business of eating.

Bonita, who probably didn't have a life outside of investigating—or getting into other people's business—returned to the unwelcome topic of phone threats, asking me for the millionth time, "Any new thoughts?"

"Probably my ex," I repeated for the millionth and one time. "He's doing time on some gun charges up at High Desert."

Duncan's eyes popped. I gave them no more information than what was publically available.

Bonita deftly attacked the last of her chow mein and then paused to speculate. "You know, Sunny, I can see why ATF was investigating you. Most people would welcome, probably even be demanding, protection from law enforcement, and yet you fight it every step of the way. What's up with that?" she asked with practiced ease.

Bonita's face had taken on the warm, inviting expression of friendship that investigators use to gain information from suspects. A glint of insincerity flicked through her brown eyes, giving her away. It always did. Not that Bonita was wrong. I looked as guilty as hell.

I pushed the rest of my lunch away with deliberate care and reached for a fortune cookie as I weighed my past against my future.

The truth was as close as the paper I pulled from the cookie. "In everything, there is a piece of truth. But only a piece."

CHAPTER 15

ೞ✟ಚ

Screams bounced off every window throughout the complex when a hairy black and brown tarantula the size of my hand jumped from my in-box onto my face. No one was laughing as I knocked it across the room, sending it skittering across the floor. Chairs and files scattered before the storm of frantic secretaries stampeding for the door. Paige almost gave birth as the giant spider up on its back legs and advanced, charging at her with forelegs waving high in the air.

It was a new week—a new prank and a new threat. This time the creature was not made of nylon and rubber, but lived and moved, causing mass hysteria in the intake room. It took an armed investigator standing guard over the tarantula before the maintenance man finally removed it using a shovel and a Hefty trash bag.

Jack demanded answers—there were none. The assault made me want to cut and run. The secretaries got over their shock and grew incensed, as if the latest prank had been my fault. Glares and stares followed me throughout the department. Being an outcast added hurt to my fright, and I couldn't dismiss the possibility that one of the secretaries might have been a part of, or working in cooperation with a cult. I had read that followers actively recruit members in the law enforcement community.

The incident left me frightened, embarrassed, and emotionally hemorrhaging from old wounds that I had acquired growing up as a social reject. I was only twelve hours away from San Diego, Chance, and the promise of a new life minus the insanity. But of all the mixed emotions that threatened to overwhelm, anger was the strongest. I was furious that anyone thought they had the right to destroy my career. Correct that. Someone thought they could make me surrender my future without firing a shot.

No one is going to run me off.

Jack stood in the intake room, ramrod straight, flushed, and breathing fire. He told Bonita to investigate "what the hell is going on around here," probably hoping it was a prank, but contemplating the possibility of serious threat. Then he directed me, in front of God and all the secretaries, to continue my work with survivors of ritual abuse. Suddenly, spending the rest of my life in Southern California didn't seem so bad.

಼ ✝ ಞ

Following directives, I trudged over to Mental Health to meet with Dano.

According to Taylor—Dano's patient with multiple personalities—tonight would issue in that rare cosmic event known as a blood moon—a prophetic moon, according to the Jewish faith. I imagined Satanists the world over doing whatever it was they did to desecrate that which others celebrated.

This was the third time I had sat in on sessions with Dano and Taylor, who shape-shifted her way like a jungle shaman through the various personalities that inhabited her being. It was "Pat'" who primarily communicated with me and proved to be the most informative of the two personas that shared Taylor's body. I asked Pat if an event was scheduled for tonight's blood moon and if she had ever attended such a ceremony before.

Pat rolled her eyes and took a tone of exasperation." Of course there will be a ceremony. I wouldn't miss it." Pat raised her voice. "I told you. I've attended many gatherings and High Holidays. And Mass, naturally." She toned down. "I don't recall a blood moon exactly, although blood was a part of every meeting." She narrowed her brows, lifting them into an A-frame above her piercing brown eyes. "Why? Are you looking for an invitation?"

My heart pounded in my ears. It was hard to hold her gaze with war drums thrumming in my head. It was the breakthrough I had been waiting for—praying for. If Taylor's stories were true about animal sacrifice and sexual abuse of children during these events, then arrests could be made and the local cult taken down.

Or perhaps it was a ploy to discredit me with law enforcement. Everyone already thought I was a little weird. It would only take just one time of convincing law enforcement to respond to such a bizarre threat to my credibility to be blown from now to forever, leaving me with a reputation like Witch-Hunting Wally if it turned out to be a false alarm.

"No," I hastened to advise Pat. "That would be against my religion. I am a good Catholic." I wasn't a good Catholic. I wasn't a good anything at the moment, but since Satanism was always the antithesis of Christian tradition, mocking Catholic rituals, she nodded with understanding.

Under Dano's guidance, Pat handed the reins back to Taylor, who retained no knowledge of anything her alter personality had told me.

I pondered my options throughout the day. If I gave this information to the sheriff's office and it turned out to be a setup, my professional life would be zilch. Instead of being respected, I would be ridiculed out of my job, if not out of the county. But if I didn't notify authorities and the lead turned out to be a trap, I could be . . . what? Sacrificed?

People around the world would be watching with curiosity and fascination to see the full pale-yellow moon transition through a lunar eclipse into total darkness and then emerge like a hatched dragon set free from its shell, all dressed in flaming red, the color of spilled blood.

Sunk low in my Volkswagen, I peered over the dash and watched the sky as ragged strips of clouds reached out to pinch the sun, like dark fingers snuffing a candle, extinguishing the last light of day. The street was dark and hours passed. Pat, the stronger of the two personalities, had yet to emerge from the house where she lived, safely ensconced in the body she shared with Taylor.

And here I sat, spying on Taylor-Pat, and, for all I knew, a couple of other undeclared alters all happily cohabitating in one body—or not. I reconsidered, imagining what it would be like to be trapped in a tiny cell as years dragged by, shoulder to shoulder with people I despised, all fighting for control of the claustrophobic space. I recoiled and sat, fixated at length on the dark house filled with darker secrets. Poor Taylor, I thought with fresh compassion. Her life must be a living hell. I didn't have a plan beyond my determination to prove that satanic cults existed and to find out where they held their meetings.

Fingering the wooden cross around my neck, I wondered if I should have brought a Bible for backup. I had left Chance a message before leaving the house, saying that I was going to follow a client named Taylor Jarreau to a possible cult gathering. I told him not to worry, and I would call him back later with the details. Then I turned off my phone.

My stomach rumbled. I yawned and stretched, and began to wonder if perhaps Dano had been wrong and Taylor really was delusional when I noticed a shadow wearing a hooded sweatshirt slipping along the fence line heading toward Taylor's darkened doorstep. The figure knocked, then stepped back as Taylor exited the house dressed in a dark skirt and a hooded cape. She followed the shadow figure back along the fence until darkness swallowed them. I got out of my car and ducked low, determined to follow.

៛ ☥ ៛

The house where Taylor lived was located in a tired outlying area at the edge of Oroville's city limits, just below the dam, where rural city abutted brushy foothills dotted with digger pines and valley oaks. The wild inhabitants included coyotes and bobcats that dined on deer and raccoons, and rabbits, squirrels, and skunks that served as take-out for foxes. Predators like bears and mountain lions rarely came down this low, so I wasn't afraid of being eaten by wildlife. It was people, not wild animals that frightened me.

I followed Taylor and her cloaked escort along a series of tangled trails that descended into a steep, jagged ravine until arriving at some brush-covered half-hidden railroad tracks. The night was cold, but my teeth would have chattered regardless. The full moon rose, a cold pale orb that slowly crested the ridgetop.

Taylor and her escort had made the descent without talking. Now they turned and followed the rails, the crunch of gravel beneath their heels masking the sound of my pursuit. And then, they vanished. Nothing remained but silence.

Long fingers of cold wind crept under my collar and down my spine. I had almost given up searching for them, when the breeze brought the sound of voices, talking low with intermittent laughter. All I could do was back away from the tracks and lie flat in a thicket of scrub brush, and pray that God would make me invisible.

Six people came into view—four adults and one child, who was around seven or so. The woman who led the way held a flashlight in one hand and a baby in the other.

"Over there!" the first woman exclaimed, using the light to reveal a trail of white rocks. The beam illuminated a row of white crystal-bearing quartz that pointed the way as clearly as a white line down the center of a highway reminding me of Hansel and Gretel who had followed a trail of white rocks straight to a witch's lair.

I burrowed deeper into the brush that scratched and tore, keeping out of sight as people continued to pass in groups of six.

Six groups; each made up of six people, each group with at least one child in tow, had passed. I was beginning to wonder if the procession would ever end, and then, the night was deathly silent. Up in the sky, the eclipse was beginning. Instinct told me to bolt back up the trail, but it was pigheaded determination that anchored me to the spot and burning curiosity that propelled me forward. The trail dipped and turned one more time and then vanished—this time under a shelf of rock exposing a gaping tunnel that looked and felt like a wormhole leading to Gehenna.

Going back was not an option. Shivering with cold anxiety, I looked for courage and found none. The next step was a literal leap of faith. Or stupidity. Or both.

Cold, rough walls bit into my fingertips as I trailed down the tunnel, using my fingers like a blind man's cane. Step by painfully cautious step, deeper and deeper into utter darkness, until at last a light shone at the proverbial end of the tunnel—except this light was not a light of hope but a light that could expose my presence to people worshiping evil. The tunnel ended, and just beyond, a glowing bonfire flickered and danced. I crouched low, hardly daring to breathe as I watched in fascination from a kind of twilight zone.

Candles. Lots of candles. A convocation of robed people had gathered in a crescent shape in front of an altar, and what appeared to be a priest and a priestess. The priestess was almost as black as the cloak she wore, and the priest standing next to her looked as pale and cold as death. A ram was tethered to one side of the altar, bleating in nervous agitation. The priestess chanted in what sounded like French, or maybe Latin. The convocation intoned in unison, responding to her invocations as the tempo increased. My breathing quickened with mounting terror. No more doubting—it was time to get the hell out of there.

Rising, I started to turn—when a powerful arm grabbed me from behind and clamped a hand across my mouth, muffling my cries. Kicking and struggling, I completed the turn, biting the hand and scratching at my assailant's face as a man's body pressed tightly into mine, slamming me hard against the tunnel wall, pinning me until the only movement I could make was the violent trembling beyond my control.

He pressed in even tighter and hissed in my ear.

"Don't move. Don't scream."

CHAPTER 16

ෂ ✦ ෂ

I didn't. And slowly, too slowly, the pressure relented, and the hand that had almost strangled me loosened. Free at last, I swung around, slapping Travis across the face.

Hours later, I sat glaring at Travis through swollen eyes, trying not to grimace as the doctor injected me with a shot of cortisone. My face looked like I had been dragged by a car face down on a graveled road.

"A severe reaction to poison oak," said the doctor.

A network of blisters already covered the back of my hands, going deep between my fingers, probably preventing me from pulling a trigger—if I only had my gun. Angry and humiliated, I wanted to cry. Badly. It was probably a combination of everything: from being itchy and miserable to totally embarrassed and humiliated. I was fully prepared to shoot myself—or Travis, before I would cry in front of him. Travis, who sat in the ER looking as pained as I felt.

Travis had guided me out of the ravine, taking a much more direct route back to the highway than I had used to follow Taylor. He practically dragged me up the hill in silence, and I had let him because it was easier than hauling myself and the extra pounds I had put on since Thanksgiving.

We paused to catch our breath. Then Travis took my face in his hand and tipped my chin up to meet his lips—lips that were pressed into a hard tight line—and abruptly told me to get in the car. Travis drove in his usual steely silence straight to the ER. He didn't need to say anything.

This wasn't the first time I'd had allergic reactions to either poison oak or Travis. If I opened the floodgate with so much as a single word, the dam was sure to burst, and I would go crazy on him. I saved my fury for the ride home. Apparently, he did too.

"What the hell were you thinking?"

"My thoughts exactly!"

Nice to know we are on the same page.

"You . . ."

"I . . ."

". . . could-have-been . . ."

". . . gotten us killed."

Our words tangled, fighting for first place, and then dissolved into a stress-busting absurd burst of laughter.

I searched Travis's statuesque face. "I was afraid," I confessed.

"I was afraid for you," he replied.

We drove on in silent agreement back to my house, even as the first fingers of dawn caressed the horizon. There we sat, parked in the driveway like a pair of love-struck teenagers, gazing at each other stupidly until Travis broke the silence.

"Sunny. You look like shit."

I slammed the car door first, and the house door second. Undeterred, Travis followed, making himself at home in the kitchen. He went to work without a word, finding a pot and brewing a smelly concoction of oatmeal, baking soda, and green tea. The mixture smelled disgusting. I watched in silence, wriggling my nose, and then headed for bed when I saw him add ice cubes. Healthy has its limits; I would die before taking a bite.

Sometime later Travis entered my bedroom where I lay, wrapped in a blanket of pain and misery. Gruel in hand, he sat on the bed next to me and proceeded to gently, tenderly, bathe my tortured face with the cool, soothing potion he had made. Closing tired eyes, I slept.

ຄ✞ຌ

Paige's baby shower was scheduled for today, and I was thinking how I could justifiably excuse myself, when Ashley called chatting as gaily as a flock of squirrels, if squirrels flocked, which of course they don't. Still, she chattered on, and my next thought was that talking to twins was going to come naturally for her.

The swelling was gone, Travis was gone, and apparently my excuses were gone too. I peered into the bathroom mirror as Ashley carried on about a velvet sheet cake, wondering whether or not I thought she had bought enough. All the while, I was pitying the stranger in the mirror who looked sunburned and acne riddled with dark circles under her eyes. I heaved a major sigh. Since the party had been my idea, I felt obligated to at least make an appearance.

I didn't need to bring a gift. Shane had already helped me haul an ornate crib up to their home for the big event a couple of days ago. It would serve to hold gifts as well as being a gift in itself from both Chance and me.

Ashley was glowing like the New Orleans Superdome on game night. She paused to tell me how bad I looked and offered a dozen home remedies before hurrying off with her new friends to plan some kind of game or other that had to do with clothespins and dirty diapers. It didn't sound all that appealing.

Oma was there, and I wondered what she would say if she knew about Baby Russian Roulette—the real-life game that has everyone guessing which dad in Paige's arsenal had fired the fateful bullet. God only knew. I was tired of the game and confused by the pang that I felt as my thoughts of Paige turned to thoughts of Travis, wondering if he had spent the night with her.

Shaking my head to clear it, my mind returned to Oma and all the rotten things I had said about her. She stood in a corner looking lost and out of place. As an act of contrition, I grabbed a couple of mini muffins and a cup of coffee and headed her way.

"Hi, Oma. Nice to see you. You're looking a little lost."

"I'm fine," she said with a half smile as she idly fingered her cup of hot chocolate. "I guess I do feel a little lost," she added. "If you don't mind my asking—what happened to your face?"

"Poison oak." I hurried to change the subject. "And if you don't mind my asking—how did you come by such an unusual name?"

Color rose in Oma's cheeks. "It's a Hebrew baby name," she said. "The word means cedar tree."

"How precious. Your father must have thought your life would be upright and enduring."

Oma blushed harder. "If you knew my dad, you'd think it was a reference to his manhood." We laughed together like good friends.

"I haven't seen you in church for a while. Are you still seeing Mac?"

She dropped her eyes, and a soft shade of pastel pink crept across her cheeks. "We date once in a while," she said. "It's a little awkward dating a pastor. I'm not really sure what all it involves, or if I'm really cut out for it."

I laughed at that and rolled my eyes. "Don't say that! My husband is in seminary school, and I'm counting on you for advice."

The gray in her eyes deepened in color, looking as sadly out of place as two dark little clouds in a brilliant blue sky. "I've tried to fit in," Oma said, with obvious disappointment. "It's just . . . the church women are pleasant enough, but sometimes, they seem so—"

"Pastor possessive? Disdainfully distant? Closed cliques? Reminds you of high school?"

Oma leaned back against the wall and crossed her arms. She shrugged with a short huff that made her curls dance. "Maybe little bits of all that." She lowered her voice to confide in me. "If you can believe it, Sunny, they think I'm . . . I was . . . a prostitute." She gave another huff. "Why would someone say anything so despicable? So hateful? So hurtful?"

The muffin caught in my throat, making my eyes water as I coughed a chunk into my napkin. Kindhearted Oma thumped me gently between the shoulder blades—right where she should have been plunging a stiletto.

"Ughm." I cleared my throat, swallowed some coffee, and sniffed. "I wouldn't worry about it if I were you," I said with a slight cough. I scrambled to undo some of the damage I had helped to create. "They aren't the people who matter the most. They won't be the ones to share your dreams or your hopes . . . or your fears." I coughed again; another crumb of truth had caught in my throat. "Just focus on Mac." I tried to encourage her. "He's a good man. Whatever is going on with everyone else is their problem, not yours."

A ray of hope peeked out from between her clouds. "You must be the counselor—the advocate from the district attorney's office. And your husband must be Chance?"

A powerful engine that sounded like Paige's ride drowned out our conversation. Pulling the gauzy curtain aside, we looked out the living room window at the candy-apple-red Beemer as the driver wheeled into an open space.

It was Paige all right, and my mouth dropped when a crisp-looking Travis pulled in behind her and got out, walked to the Beemer, and opened the car doors. First came Paige, and then a very elegantly dressed platinum-haired woman stepped out and walked around, laying an affectionate arm across Paige's shoulders as she shepherded her toward the house.

I opened the door to let them in. Paige was in full bloom. She looked like a child from the Make a Wish Foundation whose big dream had come true. We hugged, and the wondrous, joyful look of appreciation that Paige gave me melted the polar ice cap that gripped my heart.

"Sunny, this is my mother, Cali. Mom, this is my . . . good friend, Sunny."

It was easy to see where Paige had gotten her good looks. If a pre-pregnant Paige could have been the cover girl for Seventeen magazine, her mother could be a cover model for More, a glamour magazine for mature women of style and substance. Cali was as gracious as she was beautiful.

"So this is Sunny. I have heard so much about you. I can't thank you enough for throwing this party for my daughter. It means so much to her and to me." I looked down, wondering if she could see the rags of guilt that covered my party clothes. I didn't deserve her praise. New guests arrived, and I slipped out.

"Good morning, Sunshine!" Travis threw me a dazzling smile that reached all the way up to his Oakley's. Dressed in casual denim pants, topped with a dark-green shirt under his russet-colored suede jacket, Travis was more appetizing than the stirring smells of breakfast buffet that drifted from the house.

I growled, and his smile broadened.

"I take it that's your first cup?" Travis asked, gazing pointedly at the coffee in my hand. Then he reached out with unexpected tenderness and caressed my inflamed cheek while clicking his tongue in sympathy. "Come on, help me bring in gifts." He took my cup and set it aside, then circled the car and popped the trunk open.

"I didn't know you and Paige were talking, much less . . ." I waved my arm at the car.

"Chauffeuring? It's for Cali. She's a good woman." He lowered his voice as another guest walked past. "Not at all like her daughter."

I tried to read Travis's mind. Never an easy task, and was now even more complicated. Until very recently, Cali had been Travis's mother-in-law.

"Do you think Cali can get Paige to disclose who baby's father is?"

Travis shrugged. "If she can't, no one can."

ଛ ☥ ଓ

It was with reluctance that I dragged myself to church the next morning. It wasn't just what Oma had said at the party but the growing understanding that I also felt outside the group. I was the zebra in a herd of horses, a pair of mismatched shoes, a lone kite on the end of a string. Always trying to fit in but destined to fly alone.

I missed Chance and resented his absence for about the millionth time.

I could be a pastor's wife—if the pastor would only come home.

Ashley was volunteering at the Sunday school nursery these days, and while I was certain she made the Lord smile, she made me pout. I missed her sitting next to me. Shane volunteered on Wednesdays to work with the teenagers and was enjoying rock star success. All the girls had a crush on him, and the boys were awed by the reformed outlaw biker.

My bottom remained on the bench, but my mind drifted to Travis. He had been distant at the party, which would be normal for any man attending something as goofy as a baby shower. But there was more—a lot more. Maybe it was the softness in his face, in his entire body, as he relaxed against the doorjamb watching Paige shriek with delight, giggling with childlike abandon as she opened pastel bags—pink, blue, yellow, and green, decorated with duckies, rattles, and lambs. Everyone ooo'd and aah'd over the baby crib, but the Ninja Man completely disarmed me when he gave me a haunting look of appreciation and mouthed the words, "Thank you."

Only Travis, Cali, and I knew about Paige's tragic and traumatic childhood. There were reasons that she sometimes acted like a little girl. Typical of trauma survivors, a part of Paige would always be trapped in time. For her—a child of thirteen.

Unnoticed, I slipped out the back door and cut through the woods bound for the road home. I ran, legs flying, heart pumping. I hated life and could not move fast enough to escape the myriad of feelings that nipped at my heels as I fled down the road.

Safe at home, still panting, I shut the door behind me as the phone rang. It was Chance. No breaks.

"You've been running." Chance's voice was full of concern.

"I jogged back from the baby shower," I said between gasps. "I thought I would run off the Death-by-Triple-Chocolate cake and chocolate ice cream."

Chance chuckled. "You know I love you, hon. You really are amazing." His voice warmed. "Thank you for all you're doing for Paige . . . and the little one."

I let the undeserved compliments slide.

"Was Travis there?" Chance asked.

"Of course." I couldn't resist, "You sent him, didn't you? You know—a little detour to Oakland on your way to San Diego?"

Silence reigned for a couple of heartbeats, followed by the guy-grunt, throat- clearing noise that men make when buying time.

"I know I can trust Travis to look out for you," said Chance with slow deliberation. "The question is, can I trust the two of you beyond that?'"

Another long pause as I considered his remark—after all we had been through. I resented the implication that I needed help but accepted that Chance having my old lover watch out for me had to be an act of love.

"Trust is a two-way street," I replied, "and I am pretty sure it's not called Easy Street. The good news is, we are still walking it. Right?"

"Right."

Alone, at last, I picked up Kissme and snuggled into the comfort of her warm body and soft fur. Then I climbed into my sanctuary, the recliner, and spent the evening looking out through the French doors, across the valley to the Coastal Range. Evening approached with open arms. It was a time that invited reflection and contemplation regarding the men in my life.

California sunsets rivaled anyplace in the world for beauty and magnificence. Tonight, dramatic colors blazed across the western skies, throwing flaming streaks of liquid gold and burning orange as far as the eye could see. The great globe slipped toward the crest line of the dark-purple Coastal Range and spilled over into the floodplain below.

The central valley, filled with lakes and rice fields and vast miles of standing water, waited expectantly. I could feel the presence of a mighty God and trembled in awe as the water splashed with color, resplendent with flames that mirrored the fiery sky. Slowly, with great deliberation, the massive ball of fire began to merge, sinking into itself, as the sun swallowed its own reflection. The two became one. It was . . . majestic. And somehow ominous.

CHAPTER 17

෩ ☦ ෨

Four large cardboard boxes sat stacked in the corner of my office, filled with pictures, reports, and taped interviews taken by the sheriff's office over the past five years. I sorted out the animal cases—photos depicting dozens of mutilated animals. The six birds had been racing pigeons. Someone had broken their necks and plucked the feathers, then hung them up from the rafters inside the coop. The cat's legs had been had been zip tied before they were beheaded. One poor dog had been found hanging upside down in a tree, and another had a pentagram carved on its head. There was livestock in addition to pets—pictures of dead chickens, goats, and cows.

Chewing thoughtfully on the top of my pen, I pondered why it was easier for me to work with battered women than look at tortured animals.

Maybe I thought I could change social behavior regarding domestic violence but felt powerless to affect ritual abuse. I hated feeling helpless, and I could still hear the pitiful cries of the ram at the blood moon fest.

Travis walked in accompanied by a good-looking young man wearing a cowboy hat, jeans and boots, striding with the natural gait of a cowboy whose horse was parked outside. And maybe it was. This was Butte County—cowboy country. Travis was also attired in casual outdoor clothing.

"Sunny, I'd like you to meet Forrest Woods, Butte County's brand inspector," said Travis.

It seemed as if everyone under the age of forty in California had a name as colorful as the state itself. "Hello, Forrest. Welcome to the trendy name club," I said, taking a weak stab at humor.

"A pleasure to meet you, ma'am," he said, removing his hat. "It was my Grandpa's name."

Open Mouth "A." Insert Foot "B."

I pointed to the chairs. "Please, sit down," I said, noting that his denim-blue eyes matched his jeans and work shirt.

"We hiked down to the ceremonial site this morning," said Travis as their attention shifted to the pictures spread out before me.

"Did you find anything?"

"Oh yes, ma'am," said Forrest. "The remains of the ram you reported seeing was there"—he glanced meaningfully at Travis, who nodded—"um, minus its horns, eyes, tongue, and male parts. It was all very surgical, not from predators. I've seen similar patterns of animal mutilation throughout the region. It isn't really new to people in my field. I'm thinkin' you might also want to talk to Animal Control. They see a lot of that stuff too. It just doesn't make headlines, if you know what I mean."

I knew exactly what he meant. YouTube had recently blacked out several videos taken at the Chinese Dog Meat Festival for the horror they depicted. By contrast, traditional American news stations seemed to prefer sensational entertainment over uncomfortable truths—and findings of ritual sacrifice were definitely out of people's comfort zones.

"Anything else?"

"Someone brushed away footprints. Even the quartz rocks that you followed were gone. Not scattered—gone. Nothing else in the way of evidence . . . except . . . maybe this." Forrest held up a tiny silver heart that gleamed and flashed like a fishing lure. I took it from him, turning it over in my hand for a closer look. Etched on the back was a little pair of footprints.

§Ω♀☙

Lunchtime found Travis in a familiar place, sitting across from me over bowls of won ton soup at Chow Mein Charlie's. I had kept my composure and suspicions when handing the charm back to Forrest. After all, millions of them had been sold. Just because it looked like the one I gave Paige didn't prove anything. There was no way she could have hiked down that hill in her condition, and she would have needed a four track to haul her back out. Only a total paranoid would jump to such a conclusion without further proof. Still . . .

Travis was saying that he had to pick up Cali for the trip home when Duncan and Bonita walked in. My face must have registered surprise. I paused mid-wave. It was hard to believe the metamorphosis taking place in Duncan. Today he wore a leather coat and a pair of sunglasses in spite of the fact it was raining outside. But a much bigger surprise was not the clothes and accessories but the scathing look he gave Travis even as Bonita pulled up a chair to join us.

I knew that look—Duncan's look. I knew it all too well, from Logan. The jealous, possessive look that Duncan the newbie gangster fired at Travis.

Travis put out the fire with the simple narrowing of his eyes. Just one look from Travis and Duncan reverted back to an insecure, oversized little boy. I felt sorry for Duncan, and to Travis's amazement, I sat the big guy down between us and patted his arm.

"I got your things ready back at the office, dear," said Duncan. "Shall I go with you?"

Travis raised his brows at me, and Bonita volunteered, "Sunny has a meeting with a high school counselor and a probation officer. They're doing a room search on a kid busted for selling pot at the high school. Not all that exciting, really."

"Why would they ask you?" Travis asked me.

I shrugged. "The kid is a self-proclaimed warlock, and I'm the new resident cult expert. His roommate down at juvie said the guy keeps a book of secrets detailing gatherings, attendance, activities, and such. His PO thought I might want to be there if the book shows up. Anyhow, the boy is only sixteen. Not exactly leadership material."

"Let me know if there are any references to the blood moon gathering," said Travis.

Duncan tore his eyes from the menu to look at me with his mouth hanging open. Bonita answered "okay" for me.

"You should take Mercy with you," Travis suggested. "It's a safe bet he hides his dope wherever he hides the book. I'll call the SO and see if Mark can get away."

Like my life, it was complicated. Mark Anderson had been a good friend of Chance's and one of Paige's many lovers. He had been captain over Chance at the sheriff's office, and through that agency, they had worked together in Search and Rescue. Our German shepherd, Mercy, had had extensive training from both the military and law enforcement. With Chance gone, Mark had become Mercy's foster handler.

It was time to go. I skipped the fortune cookie, thinking maybe it was time to write my own.

Travis and I stood on the sidewalk under the overhang of the restaurant close enough that I could smell the strong, masculine fragrance that he wore mingling with the freshness of the rain-washed air. "Listen," said Travis, "I am going to find out what's going on. The items from your inbox, the CD in the car, and the message on the phone—they are probably all related."

I rolled my eyes. "And you got your Super-Agent badge, where? At the Dollar Store?"

Travis shook it off. "I'm in touch with Lieutenant Barcus from Special Investigations up at High Desert regarding the phone message. He'll be giving me updates on Logan. We'll find out if he called your work number, or, for that matter, if any inmate in the state has ever called any of your numbers." Travis wet his lips and moved closer. "Just remember—even if it comes back negative, there is still no guarantee that Logan didn't have someone on the outside working for him. Are you still packing your gun?"

My gaze dropped in reply, and he took me by the shoulders with a firm tug. "Start carrying it." And then he drew me to him and kissed me. Long. Deep. Passionate. The taste of him melting in my mouth was like a rich, tempting appetizer.

"I'll be in touch." And, like Chance—like Starla—he was gone, leaving behind the lingering, tantalizing taste of love that first excites the palate, then quickly fades into memory.

𝕊𝕠 ♱ 𝕔𝕤

Black on black on black. How could any parent let a child paint his room black? Ceiling black, curtains black, sheets, bedspread—everything black-black-black. The only color in the room came from posters of rock stars: Marilyn Manson and the rock bands Behemoth and Nattefrost. Over his bed was another of the tarot death card.

I wondered who was sicker—the child or the parents that consented to such decor. How hard was it to say no?

The probation officer led the way past a fashionably dressed irate mother who insisted, "It's just a passing fad—a trend. It's called Gothic. Don't you guys know anything?"

Warren Aldrich had had years of experience with juvenile offenders, and Mark and Mercy wasted no time getting a hit over the mother's continued protests. Warren whipped out his Wunder Bar and went to work prying the baseboard from the wall as I tried in vain to calm the mother.

"You can't help your son with wishful thinking," I said. "Don't you want to know the truth?" She didn't. She wanted the wall fixed and us to mind our own business—when in fact, this was our business.

"Your son seems to have a passionate interest in the occult," I said. "Does he belong to any . . . er . . . clubs or groups that share his passion?"

"His girlfriend is a witch. A white witch," the mother clarified.

Is she serious?

The mother's green eyes snapped.

Yup. She was.

I looked her in the eye. "While witchcraft and Satanism aren't the same, you might like to know that Antone LaVey, author of the Satanic Bible, says that white witches and black magic are. He says that every practitioner believes they are doing the right thing."

She stared at me as if I was from Mars.

Warren had replaced the baseboard after removing a black leather-bound book the size of a diary and a small bag of marijuana as evidence.

"Mrs. Blackstone," began Warren, "your son, Chase—"

"Charles," she interrupted. "His given name is Charles."

"Charles may be involved with some very bad people."

"He isn't doing anything his friends don't do. Is Harry Potter a criminal, for Christ's sake?"

Warren paused so Mom could catch her breath. "Ma'am, I would say that thirty to forty percent of the kids in high school are caught up in some form of the occult."

"Exactly!" said the mother triumphantly.

"And seventeen percent of those kids get involved in criminal activity because of it."

"You mean that little bag of pot? Even the president of the United States smokes pot. Mr. Aldrich, please don't put my son back in Juvenile Hall. He's all I have."

First logic, now tears.

Warren looked sympathetically at the young man's mother. "Ma'am," he said, "I am telling you this because it sounds to me that you love your son very much. You should know that out of that seventeen percent, ten percent will become repeat offenders and go to jail, and from that group, some will end up in prison."

She shifted gears from pathetic to angry. "Not my son! You have what you came for, Mr. Aldrich. Now you and your associates get the hell out of my home."

Out by the vehicles, Mark puckered his lips and pinched his fingers, snapping them as if to cool them off. "Ouch! She's got teeth! Too bad Mercy didn't bite her back."

Warren shrugged. "She's partly right. Listening to death metal music and dressing Goth doesn't make a person a Satanist. Neither does doing drugs or being a fan of demon and zombie movies. But one thing is sure."

"What's that?" I asked.

"They may not all end up Satanists, but dabbling is exactly how they all started. I'll let you know about the book."

Chapter 18

စာ ⊕ ಛ

"Duncan. We need to talk."

"Do we ever! You bet!" The big guy picked me up and gave me a bear hug, then blushed as he sat me down. "Come on, Sunny. You gotta see this! Come on! Come on!" He grabbed my hand and headed for the door.

How could I refuse this gentle giant who looked for all the world like . . . like a ? Wait—I caught myself. The St. Bernard look was definitely gone. Somehow Duncan had transformed into a bull mastiff.

Stunned and amazed, I let him lead me by the hand downstairs to the parking lot.

There it sat in all its glory.

No way!

War horses were for knights and Harleys were for bikers. Yet Duncan, the introverted computer tech, was showing me a beast of a ride: 1800 CCs of black paint, chrome, and raw power. He, Duncan, stood there, his face as radiant as the sun on your best day ever.

My eyes widened in amazement and lips bowed into a tight, crooked smile. "Okay. I give up," I said. "Whose is it?"

"Mine! All mine! Ours!"

"Whoa! Duncan. You have to stop. Enough with the 'dear, ours, and us' thing." His face fell, looking like last week's party balloon, so I squeezed his hand. "Whose bike is it, really?"

"Mine." Duncan lowered his head and lowered his voice, tightening his expression to repress the tremble that flicked across his features. What little neck he had disappeared. "Didn't you tell me I should live the dream?"

It sounded vaguely familiar. I probably had said something like that. "But Duncan, dear . . ." Awkward ". . . friend. You can get killed on this machine. It's an animal. I don't want you to get hurt."

Love and hope rekindled in his eyes. "I'm taking lessons. Don't you like it?"

I weighed the possible outcomes between encouraging and discouraging his dream: broken heart or broken bones. "It's . . . awesome. Magnificent."

His chest swelled.

Bonita strode by on her way back from the sheriff's office. Her eyes gleamed as she took in the bike. "Well, well, well. What do we have here?" she asked with a look of appreciation.

"It's my new bike." Duncan dropped his gaze again, making his answer sound more like an apology.

"Way to go. It suits you, big guy. I like it. Definitely, like it."

"He could get hurt," I said defensively.

She laughed it off. "I know women that ride 'em. He'll learn."

I recalled the biker woman Bonita had been cuddling with that looked like a road captain for Dykes on Bikes and couldn't argue her point. I wanted to choke her but had to beg off and hurry to court.

It was trial day against a man who had tried to kill his girlfriend—chain-sawing through the roof of her car as she sat screaming, trapped inside until she lost her voice from traumatic shock. There were no guarantees that she would ever get her voice back, but today, I would speak for her.

૭ ♀ ൦

I supposed most everyone had a highlight in their career, and I was blessed to have had many. There was the case of which my testimony persuaded the judge to enhance a sentence from one hundred and eleven years to one hundred and thirty-six years against the man who had kidnapped his girlfriend and kept her tied up in his trailer for days while he injected her with drugs. Then there were additional victims in a perpetrator's past that I managed to locate and persuade to testify on behalf of the current one—a twenty-three-year-old blind girl who was engaged to be married and then raped by the best man on the night of the bachelor party. Ah yes, but those were triumphs of a different kind.

NOVA was a different kind of highlight, and there was no more prestigious honor for an advocate than to be invited to speak at the National Organization for Victim Assistance. After all my years as an advocate and expert witness on the topic of domestic violence and sexual assault, it seemed ludicrous that I should have been invited to speak on, of all things, ritual abuse. However, turning down an invitation from NOVA is like turning down an invitation to the Academy Awards.

It was a crapshoot, but I was determined not waste the opportunity. I would make my presentation the best, most comprehensive training ever compiled on the subject. So spotlighted, I would either succeed in restoring national awareness or become an object of derision. The realization made me wonder if this was how historical figures of old felt when going public—when they expressed such radical ideas as the earth being round, simple hygiene helping prevent disease, and all people having a right to freedom and equality—radical stuff back in the day.

Bonita stopped by my office to talk about a pending domestic violence case, and we started talking about the upcoming conference. "Ever been to Florida?" she asked.

"No, I haven't." Florida was my NOVA conference destination. "Any advice?"

"Sí. Two major tips: sunblock and leave the hairspray at home. The humidity will leave your hair as sticky as a spider's web. And speaking of spider webs, any new surprises in your inbox? I noticed you're picking up your mail before the secretaries arrive."

I leaned back in my chair and eyed her curiously. "Are you spying on me?"

Bonita tipped her head and smiled her reply. "Absolutamente."

It was a losing battle. "I don't need everyone freaking out again if some new weird thing shows up in my box. Did you see Jack last time? I thought he was going to have the 'big one' right in front of us."

"It's true, chica," Bonita speculated. "You could be the death of him. But to be honest, Jack didn't exactly ask me to watch you. He asked me to watch out for you. So how's the presentation going?"

I sighed and returned to my burgeoning PowerPoint presentation. "I decided to expand on the one I already had—a little something for everyone—using national cases this time to illustrate my points. It's a real pain. I thought I'd begin by introducing myself and why I can speak on this topic. Then throw in some disclaimers, so progressive liberals don't burn me at the stake for a beach bonfire. God forbid I should say anything pro-Christian or anti-Wiccan." I felt the familiar taste of my foot in my mouth as I noticed that Bonita was wearing an ornate rainbow-colored star on her shoulder.

Her brown eyes tracked my gaze, and she laughed. "I may be liberal, but I am broad-minded enough to put up with you narrow-minded Christians." Bonita winked. "What else do you have?"

"Ahh . . . good. Big of you. So, I'll start with mental health issues: multiple personalities and delusions, followed by a short discussion on social trends and the progression of cult involvement, such as curious kids with their games, music, movies, parties, and such, to radical participants, like serial killers. Then I thought I would wrap it up with a segment for advocates: recognition, response, and referrals." I threw her a look of self-satisfaction. "Did I miss anything?"

"Humph!" Bonita eased her bulk onto the corner of my desk and rubbed her chin. "Will law enforcement be attending?"

"Sure. A lot of police departments have in-house advocates these days."

"Okay, so you probably want to add something about investigation and evidence"—she pointed to herself—"and talk to Amanda about prosecution. And I'm sure Wally gave you enough cases to reference for the rest of your career."

Which could be shorter than I planned. "Okay. Thanks."

Bonita was heading out then paused and turned. "And Sunny, you will tell me if any new threats pop up or fall down. Correcto?"

"Sí." I nodded yes, having already decided not to tell her about the baby charm that Forrest had found at the ceremonial site. I would check out Paige's bracelet for myself first.

I didn't have long to wait. I saw Paige from my office window rolling my way, looking like a bowling ball bearing down on the kingpin.

"Oh, Sunny," Paige gushed. She got a strike. "How can I ever thank you enough? I had so much fun at the shower"—her blue eyes sparkled and gleamed—"and I got sooo many presents. This kid won't want for anything."

"Mmmhmm . . . except . . . one itty bitty thing . . ."

Paige waited expectantly, in every sense of the word.

"A dad. You could give your baby that, you know."

She considered this for a nanosecond before ditching the thought. "Get serious. Why would I do that? Dads aren't good for anything except sperm donors."

I thought back on Lefty and all the love and priceless fatherly wisdom that he had imparted.

ॐ ☥ ॐ

"Dad. Where's Mom? Where does she go when she leaves us?"

Lefty was polishing his motorcycle, lovingly shining each chrome spoke as I sat on a stump watching him work. I had been afraid to ask this very adult question, and now I was sorry I had. The question made my dad sad.

"Your mama is one of a kind." He grimaced, looking up and looking around. "She's not like that flock of birds eating all the cherries out in the orchard. She's more like . . ." Lefty paused. ". . . that osprey nesting down at the lake. You can safely say your mother is an endangered species." He laughed at his own joke.

"I don't understand."

"Well now. You don't need to know everything, but understand this: your mama loves you as much as she is able to."

He saw me frown and continued. "I remember the day you were born. We were camping up on Silver Creek when her water broke—under a full moon, just like she said it would."

"Mom told me she'd wanted an abortion."

"Oh yeah, Starla said a lot of things. It's true, she didn't want kids. But she did want to know what it felt like to have a baby grow inside her and what it was like to give birth. She had you at home, you know. She wanted you to be born naturally." He stopped shining chrome, momentarily lost in a different kind of reflection. "Your mama was about the most beautiful thing I had ever seen in my life—until I saw you." He gave me a sly wink and shook his head.

"Ah, heck. You wouldn't understand." He glanced around again. "Maybe she's more like that hummingbird over there." Lefty pointed to a ruby-throated hummingbird that flashed and darted from flower to flower along the rail fence that bordered our little front yard. We watched the bird as it eagerly sipped sweet nectar from the heart of each flower. "That'd be Starla. She never could stay put," Lefty mused.

"But where does she go? Where does she stay?" I wanted to know.

I noticed that my father's hair was turning gray. It was starting to look like the chrome on his Harley. "She goes from flower to flower, little girl. Sucking the life out of every man she meets. She can't help it. It's just the way she is."

I was never as understanding or forgiving as my father. I didn't feel that a child should be a fashion statement—something to be tried on and cast off later when she was no longer a good fit.

ℰ ☥ ℜ

I shook my head clear of my childhood memory with renewed amazement at the similarities between young Paige and my mother. Then I wondered what Paige's father was like. Travis really liked the man, but I could only guess at the resentment Paige must have harbored. She was only twelve or thirteen years old when she had been snatched from in front of a cigar lounge in Mexico. Her father, Perry Atchison, had lamented, "I only wanted some genuine Cubans." Maybe Paige had gone from holding on to hope and faith that her dad would rescue her to hating him and blaming him as months in captivity slipped away.

I wished Paige a "Merry Christmas. Just in case you have the baby before I get back from Florida." I produced the trademark Pandora black bag, topped with a red satin ribbon.

"Another charm?" Within minutes, Paige was dangling a tiny silver and gold baby carriage. "Oooooh, you shouldn't have."

Oh yes. I should.

"Where's your bracelet? I'll put it on for you," I offered.

Paige's blue eyes flashed as she held the charm, rolling it over and over in her hands. "It's so cute!" I don't know why you are so kind to me. I don't deserve it," said Paige with a wistful sigh.

No. You really don't.

"My wrists and my ankles look like water wings. I've been too swollen to wear anything on my wrists or hands. She shook her ankle in front of me, saying, "Even the butterfly on my ankle looks like a nightmare from The Mothman Prophecies.

Another forty-five dollars out the window, I thought ruefully. "What does your doctor say?"

She thought for a moment as she rubbed her ankle. "He says the problem will be going away in a couple of weeks."

ℬ ✚ ℛ

The warmth of the pillows felt seductive. I reached . . . moving, moving . . . to wake, finding myself fiercely clutching Chance's pillow . . . between my knees. Okay, I was sort of humping Chance's pillow between my knees. I felt like a dog. So strong was the power of lust at that point, if there had been a pile of my husband's clothes on the floor, I would have scratched around and rolled in them.

I groaned. It was so unfair that a man could have a sexual dream culminating in completion, but I always came up short, waking in a bundle of frustrated knots until my husband could untangle them, one delicious knot at a time. This morning the ache was so consuming, so long and so intense, that I either needed help or I'd have been tackling the job myself. I put Kissme on the floor and reached for the phone.

"Chance." It came out as a whisper, or maybe a prayer.

"Good morning, beautiful."

"Ask me what I'm wearing."

"Umm . . . you're wearing . . . nothing."

I smiled. "How do you know?"

"I can smell you."

"Ooh," I moaned.

"What do I smell like?"

"You smell naked."

"Naked?"

"You smell like the last day of summer, when we made love on the lawn under the jacaranda tree. Your skin was bronze like the sunset . . . except for the parts that were like . . . ripe plums."

"What did I smell like?"

"Summer. Dusky. Earthy. Like ripe fruit . . . almost exploding out of its skin. Begging to be picked. Tasted. Savored. Enjoyed."

My breath came faster. My pulse raced. "And . . . ?"

"Flowers. You smelled like the flower I picked. The one I used to tickle and kiss every inch of your body—until you begged for more."

I gasped. "Where did it kiss me? Where did it touch me?"

And my husband made love to me. Slowly. Restraining his own needs as we relived the dizzy, breathless passion of that night under the stars. The night that God and all his angels had smiled down on our love—until at last our passion was spent and we lay in our beds, a world apart, wrapped in the memory of each other's arms.

Deeply in love. Completely spent. Totally fulfilled. Almost.

I still missed his touch.

CHAPTER 19

The early morning sun had crested over the rim of the distant Sierra Nevadas, spilling golden rays into the valley and filling it with a pale winter light on the two-hour trip to the Sacramento airport. Traffic had been light, and I was looking forward to some warm Miami sunshine.

The flight from Sacramento to Miami would take six hours. I sat on the plane next to Serena with one Ativan melting under my tongue and another tucked in my shirt pocket. It was my alternative to admitting to Serena that I had never been on an airplane before.

Serena was going to NOVA as an attendee. Aside from being the executive director for Rape Crisis, she was a friend of mine and a pastor's wife. Today she was dressed in white, and with that silver halo-colored hair of hers, she looked like a shorter, thinner version of Della Reese in Touched by an Angel.

The flight attendant interrupted our chatter to present the safety features on the airplane, pointing out the seat belts, overhead oxygen mask, flotation devices, and exits.

I had myself lashed in and gasped when I saw the oxygen mask dangling from her hand, and committed the exit doors to memory. I didn't think that the flotation device would do me much good if we crash-landed in a cornfield. Perhaps a little more Ativan wasn't a bad idea. The bottle said I could take two a day. It didn't say anything about two at a time. So I took another one. I smiled and sucked on it as if it were a breath mint.

Around noon our conversation turned to the conference. "That's a heavy topic you're speaking on. Is your church praying for you?" asked Serena.

"I haven't told anyone outside of work, and Chance, of course, and my neighbor, Ashley. And I only told Ashley because she's babysitting Kissme. I sure as heck didn't tell my pastor."

Serena cocked her head with the poised look of a bird considering a juicy bug. "Why all the secrecy? The topic must have merit, or NOVA would never have invited you. And the district attorney's office sure as heck wouldn't be footing the bill. Everyone in Victim Services knows about RA survivors. That's part of the problem. Everyone is too embarrassed to talk about it."

I sighed. "I give my church enough to talk about. If I tell my friend Ashley, she will feed the information through the gossip chain. Besides, it's hard enough getting laughed at when I'm at work without the church making fun of me also. And, no, I haven't told my pastor because I'm not talking to him."

"Poor baby. People are making fun of you?" Serena mocked sympathy.

Fired up, I gave her a scathing look. "You don't know what it's like."

"You don't know what I know. For one thing, I know that God's work is not a popularity contest. And don't think for a minute that you are not doing God's work." Serena tipped her head. "What is a 'gossip chain'?"

"It's another term I use for 'prayer chain'—where everybody talks about everybody else's personal business. I never asked for this caseload, and it wasn't part of the job description either."

"A prayer chain," said Serena "is only as good as the hearts that participate in it. If people abuse it, you have an obligation to speak with them and pray for them."

Serena continued. "Now, Sunny, you know we all have duties and responsibilities in life that we didn't sign on for. For that matter, we didn't 'sign on' for anything. Life is a gift from our Creator, and we are here to do His will, not ours. Now tell me, what's going on between you and that wonderful man, Pastor Mac?"

I squirmed in my seat, relieved that the third seat in our row was empty. I couldn't lie to Serena and knew it was useless to try. I knew this because I'd tried in the past and she always saw through me. And besides, I was starting to feel very relaxed.

"Mac has this new girlfriend and . . . well . . . I guess I might have started some rumors about her."

"What kind of rumors?" Serena's eyes narrowed, her right brow arched like a door into a cathedral.

I raised my hand to the passing flight attendant and ordered a glass of wine.

Yes. I was feeling very relaxed indeed. "Nothing much. Something about her son being in prison."

Serena's eyes widened. "Is it true? Your work is confidential. Are you jealous of her?"

My eyes shifted back and forth as I considered her questions. "Yes. No. It's not that simple. I walked in on a group of church women gossiping about her. I guess . . . okay, I know—what I did was wrong. I just wanted the women to like me. So I made up some stories about the pastor's new girlfriend."

The wine was delivered. It was cold, clear, and sweet.

"What stories?"

I started to feel as if I could tell Serena anything . . . everything. "Umm . . . that she used to be an alcoholic."

Serena's black skin paled fifty shades of gray. "Good Lord, Sunny. Have you told the new girlfriend yet?"

"Not exactly." I sipped on my wine.

"That is why you're avoiding your pastor?"

"Yes."

Serena reclined in her seat and released the drop-down tray in front of her to receive her juice and bag of pretzels from the flight attendant. Munching thoughtfully on a pretzel, she continued.

"Anything else?"

"I said she was a prostitute."

Serena sputtered, set her juice aside, and called to a passing flight attendant.

"Ma'am! Ma'am! A glass of wine, please."

ॐ ✟ ☪

It couldn't have just disappeared, and there was no possible way it was an accident. It was a complicated process to delete a file from a computer. First, you had to delete it from your active file which always gave a warning prompt: Are you sure you want to delete this? If you accidentally deleted it, the file would go into the Recycle Bin which served as a kind of backup. Deleting the file from the Recycle Bin would initiate a warning prompt a second time.

You would have click "Yes" in order to permanently remove it. So deleting files was a deliberate four-step process.

My presentation was MIA. I had reviewed it no less than ten times since arriving in Miami. Always second-guessing myself, I had continued making changes in my presentation for greater impact. I wanted my delivery to be awesome. No—I want it to be exemplary. I was scheduled to speak at one o'clock. The last time the laptop was open was just before breakfast. And now the laptop was sitting on the desk grinning at me, and the presentation was gone.

I glanced around the room, heart racing, stomach threatening. Overwhelmed with shock and disbelief, nausea threatened to send me racing for the toilet. This can't be happening. It's just not possible. And yet I rushed to blame myself because the alternative was unacceptable.

It was noon when I made the discovery—and the clock was ticking. My options were few with just one hour to go, so I went with the obvious, option number one: I cried in frustration, burying my face into the hotel pillow, bunching the bedspread in my hands as I sobbed hysterically, "Why me? Why? Why is it always me?"

I was such a wimp. Frightened and horribly embarrassed. I would have to cancel my session.

What could I say—I have a headache? I picked up the wrong suitcase at the airport? There's been a death in the family? I guess none of it was far from the truth since I felt sick and wanted to die.

"What am I supposed to do, God? If I really am doing your work, then why is this happening to me?" A whispered prayer of desperation tumbled from my mouth.

Have faith, Sunny. God whispered to my heart. I will give you words, and I will give you strength.

The prayer led to option number two: I called Duncan, still in tears.

"My computers crashing," I cried. What else could it be?

"Let's hope it's just a fender bender." Duncan tried to sooth my fears as best he could. "Stay strong, sweetheart."

I asked if there was a backup copy at work. There wasn't, but Duncan had an idea. He called back five minutes later to say that he had located a copy of my outline and would fax it to me at the hotel's business center. I called the front desk, and they said that business center was located "outside the lobby, just across the valet parking ramp, beneath the palm tree with the Christmas lights, down the hall, third door to your right." I had twenty minutes to go.

I slammed the lid shut on my laptop, shoved it across the desk, and threw my briefcase across the room. I'd have thrown the laptop too, but I was angry, not stupid. I hadn't put in all those hours, all that work, and all my hopes to quit now! No way was I going to let the Devil have his way with me.

Divine insight arrived in a second heavenly message. Toughen up, baby girl.

I slipped into my running shoes and jogged to the business center, kicking myself all the way while Serena's words reverberated in my head. "Is your church praying for you?" Quickly, I whipped my cell out of my pocket and speed-dialed Serena's number.

"Serena? Start praying!"

I decided I would rather be a fool for God than a trophy for the Devil. Nothing mattered now except that I show up and give it my best shot. Truth be told, I supposed that was all God ever asks from any of us.

The Bible arms us with a sword of truth. It was time to draw my rusty blade. Heart knocking, pulse-pounding, not a minute to spare, walked into the conference room like I knew what I was doing, stunned to see every seat filled and the walls lined with overflow. Standing-room only—and barely any of that was left. People wanted to hear about ritual abuse.

A person once told me that the definition of a great speaker is someone whose computer crashes and is forced to wing it. So I opened with the truth—apologizing for technological malfunctions—then winged it. I guess I passed the test. At the end of three long hours, with a ten-minute break given to attendees to either use the bathroom or make a graceful permanent exit, people returned, still standing along the walls and asking questions.

Later on, I ordered a bottle of wine up to my room. The reviews had been copied, and I casually picked them up at the hotel's business office with an air of nonchalance, as if it really wasn't the most important thing in the world at that moment.

Back in my room, I shook as I prayed. "Dear Lord, tell me I wasn't a complete idiot. That I didn't totally embarrass and humiliate myself." So praying, I opened the wine, poured a glass, and started at the top of the pile.

From a New York VIP: "I gave the speaker one star only because there were no minus stars to choose from. I am shocked that NOVA has lowered the bar on its standards of excellence to allow for theatrics. This speaker should be blacklisted from public speaking."

Tears brimmed. I scrunched my face, refusing to blink and let them fall.

Next. From the New Yorker's female counterpart in Philadelphia: "I found this speaker to be highly unprofessional, whose cases in point read like cheap tabloids in a checkout line. This speaker should be removed from law enforcement and barred from public speaking."

My expression fell, the restrained tears fell, and the papers spiraled on white wings as they dropped to the floor. I lay back on the bed and searched the ceiling for answers—longing to crawl back to a simpler time.

ഔ ✝ ൙

The sharp smell of gasoline filled the bathhouse. I pulled the choke. One-two-three yanks on the little Briggs and Stratton. The engine fired up with the familiar throb that signaled laundry day. A green garden hose connected to the faucet mounted over the claw-foot bathtub and arched up into the tub of the Maytag wringer washing machine.

I smiled, happy with the latest upgrades. The claw-foot bathtub that Starla had acquired from a thrift store was so deep that I could sink my entire body under the water—at least until later years when I got pregnant. Then my belly had looked like an island popping up in the middle of a lake. On-demand hot water was a miracle—no more building a fire under the redwood Japanese bath. Now I could wash the family clothes in hot water.

I pulled the lever to On, and the beaters were as steady as a heartbeat as they swished the dirty clothes back and forth. And in some ways maybe the washing machine really was the heartbeat of the cabin. There were always dirty clothes to wash, and the sound filled the empty spaces. The only other sounds were me calling Frito, who liked to play keep-away with the dirty socks; an occasional urgent high-pitched squawk of a hen as she labored to deliver an egg; and the shifting of the wind as it rustled through the trees.

Lefty had replaced the old wringer on-off switch with a bulbous foot-powered air pedal. I only had to step on it to make the wringers start and stop. He didn't want me running my hand through the wringers and breaking fingers when there was no one home to drive me to a doctor.

A heavy black hose drained the gray water through a hole in the floor and out back into a drainage ditch watering the marijuana plants that Lefty grew behind the bathhouse. Wash, wring, rinse, wring, repeat.

I liked laundry day. It gave purpose to my life.

$$\wp \; \maltese \; \wr$$

It seemed as though hours had passed. I didn't want to return to the present. I ached for the kind of simplicity that had once given me positive feelings of self-worth. Even my mother liked that I did the laundry.

I fought the urge to keep reading the reviews. It seemed like a weird form of self-abuse to continue. Did I really want to beat myself up some more? But then, curiosity is one of my great weaknesses, so I read on, and everything changed.

Nearly everyone else that attended my workshop thanked me for "bringing this important topic back to the forefront" and saying that it was "long overdue." I was surprised at the number of people who offered prayerful support. And, of course, they all wished that pictures and handouts had been available. But there were no more hate reviews. Not one. And it seemed more than a coincidence both hostile reviews had been placed on top of the stack.

It was a humbling moment—perhaps an epiphany—as I looked at the pile of reviews. When it came to the topic of ritual abuse, I had been like most people: disinterested and uncaring. I had been going through the motions, like faking the big "O" without any real passion. A little care, but no real dedication—just enough to please the boss. I had spent more hours resenting my victims than caring about them.

I genuinely cared about my domestic violence and rape victims. Having been a victim of both crimes, I could relate to their pain. By contrast, the injuries and stories that accompanied ritual abuse victims tended to feel surreal. Their claims were so far beyond the average person's comfort zone, they made acts like rape with a foreign object and setting your girlfriend on fire seem normal by comparison.

Setting the positive reviews to one side, I slipped the two hostile ones in my back pocket and put a pair of flip-flops on my feet. The soft slap of shoes echoed down the marble halls that led to the beach.

The revolving glass door that propelled people out of the hotel was like stepping through Alice's looking glass into another world—God's world. Nature always had that effect on me. The outdoors had always been my refuge, my place of peace and healing. It was good just to stand and breathe. The warm salt air was an instant balm to my spirit, and the rhythm of the waves sang a sweet lullaby to my soul. It had always been there, beneath the din of laughing children and adult chatter. One just needed to stand and listen.

A familiar form was standing in the water. Her gauzy white wrap caught in the breeze and looked like angel wings. "You must be ready to tell me what happened today," said Serena, whose arched eyebrows magnified her oversized sunglasses. We stood side by side in the vast Atlantic Ocean, silent but for the sound of waves that reminded me for a brief moment of the swish of the old wringer washing machine as I allowed the startling blue water to wash away the stress of the day.

I told Serena everything about the missing presentation, my desperation, and my petition to the Lord. "Thank you for praying for me," I said to Serena. "It must've worked because I somehow pulled it off without any props. I can hardly believe that people stayed for the duration, especially those poor people standing along the walls."

I pulled the two hateful reviews from my pocket and handed them to Serena.

White-capped clouds swooped across the bright blue sky looking like a flock of gulls in flight. The air cleared my senses, leaving the tang of salt on my tongue, and the sun that warmed my face seemed to brighten my insides as well.

By contrast, Serena's look was as dark and deep as the ocean floor as she studied the reviews. "You know they're here, don't you?"

"Who's here?" I asked.

"The Satanists. Honey, that's who wrote these reviews," she said, shaking them in her hand. "They're intended to discourage you and keep NOVA from inviting you back." Serena pulled down her sunglasses, making direct eye contact. "They—the Satanists—come to these conferences. They're watching you, child, to see what kind of impact you make. Sunny, believe me, they are the ones who deleted the program from your computer."

Did she really just say that? It never occurred to me that administrators might actually harbor personal opinions that would include such radical beliefs in this age of political correctness. "I don't understand," I said. "How could anyone get in my room? The only time I'd left my room was for a quick breakfast. I wasn't even gone that long—I had been too nervous to eat. The only other person who came in my room was the maid."

Serena looked at me sympathetically. "Oh, child, you don't know who you're dealing with, do you?"

Serena's comment was deeply disturbing. It wasn't the first time I had been asked that question. "You want to enlighten me?" I asked, half curious and half defensive.

"They are the richest and most powerful people in the world," said Serena. "Have you ever heard of global elitist? Does the word Bilderberg mean anything to you?"

The wind ruffled my hair as I shook my head. Goose bumps popped up on the back of my arms in spite of the intense heat.

Serena continued. "The name Bilderberg comes from a little hotel in the Netherlands, where the wealthiest people in the world first gathered over fifty years ago. They came together to determine how they could unite to control our world." A shadow passed like a dark cloud across her face. She gave a sage nod. "They were highly successful and have continued to meet every year since. They run the world we live in, Sunny. They make and break countries. And they are active Satanists."

Shocked and amazed, I did a double take of Serena, shaking my head in wonder. "You? You're a conspiracy theorist?"

Serena's eyes narrowed, and her tone deepened. "No, my dear friend, I am a realist. And you know me better than that," she scolded. "You don't have to be a conspiracy theorist to see the truth. That maid was either paid by the cult or is part of one. Either way, she did her job cleaning out your program along with your room."

Serena took me gently by the arm, turning both of us to stand face-to-face. "Look at me, Sunny. I'm telling you something, and I want you to hear this and hear it well: never take someone else's word for anything. Do your homework. Take a hard look at crime bosses and politicians and try to look past their obvious criminal and financial activities. Take a good look at their personal activities and beliefs. You should know who the real enemy is. Power and money are the fuel that keeps hell's furnace burning.

CHAPTER 20

꧁ ☥ ꧂

The morning broke—cold and clear, rain-washed bright, filled with the promise of a beautiful day. The promise turned out to be a lie. The day proved to be a disaster.

Walking into my office humming a little tune from K-LOVE, a popular Christian rock station, I looked up to see a wounded buffalo shambling toward me. Except the buffalo turned out to be Duncan, and Duncan was on crutches with a cast covering most of his right leg.

"Oh my gosh! Duncan! What happened? Are you okay?" I rushed down the hall of the atrium to meet him as he stumped his way from the elevator and turned into the long corridor.

Duncan was ghost white, his pursed lips looking like a mouthpiece slashed across the sheet of a child's Halloween costume as he attempted a weak smile.

Bonita was the next person to step out of the elevator, taking in the scene before her; she paused to perform damage assessment and control.

"What the hell happened to you?" asked Bonita.

"Broke my leg and got a couple of hairline cracks on a few ribs. Nothing prescription painkillers, three hours in surgery, and a half-dozen titanium screws couldn't fix." Duncan winced as he tried to joke. "In answer to your question, my dear," he said, looking at me, "I took the Harley for a spin—or maybe I should say the Harley took me for a spin."

"Well, Duncan"—Bonita let her observation roll off of her tongue—"I've always suspected you were screwed up. Now I know it's a fact!" Bonita seemed to be in a jovial mood.

"Poor Duncan," I sympathized. "I'm sorry I ever encouraged you to get a motorcycle. I feel responsible, like this is my fault."

"Oh, now, Sunny, don't feel bad." Duncan reached out to touch me with tender compassion. "I was having a great time before the accident."

"You should be home using your sick days," I said.

"I used them up when I had food poisoning last month," said Duncan. "Three days on the toilet."

I grimaced. Too much information.

"Man up, big guy," said Bonita. "It's just a broken leg. It's not like you took a bullet or anything."

Bonita turned to me. "How was the conference? You look like you got a tan."

"Duncan saved the day. Did he tell you what happened?"

"Yeah, he told me, and there's something you might like to hear about your missing presentation." We talked as we walked toward our offices. "I've heard of presentations getting stolen before. I once worked with a guy who had that happen to him. This guy, Marcus, spent almost a year researching and preparing a presentation that had to do with corporate investments, and then it went missing on the morning of his delivery. It showed up about nine months later in Australia being presented by someone else." Bonita paused in my doorway to shoot me a pointed look. "Not that anyone would want to promote your topic. They would probably just delete it."

ᏏᏜ ♀ ᏟᏧ

"I have to agree with Serena and Bonita," said Chance. "Files and evidence have been known to disappear from the sheriff's office, especially when investigating anything that smacked of ritual abuse. We always suspected that cult members existed inside the department, but it wasn't something we talked about at briefings."

"It must've been pretty scary, knowing that someone came into your room. How are you handling it?"

Chance and I were having dinner together as we Skyped.

"Good days and bad. At first I was really depressed over the two hate reviews, but later on, I thought it was incredible that people actually stood for three hours without a slide show to hear what I had to say. That says something, doesn't it?"

"It means everything," said Chance. "The people were looking for information, not entertainment. They could've stayed in their rooms if they wanted that."

That sounded right.

"Several advocates came up afterward to talk with me. One really nice woman told me that she had been raised in Mexico and that the local police found a huge pit full of dead bodies in her village back in the 1980s. It turned out that an old lady and her sons were practicing Santeria, a religion similar to voodoo. They were drug dealers making human sacrifices through ritual killings because they believed it gave them power over rival gangs." The woman's story got me thinking.

"Chance . . . do you think the drug cartels are run by Satanists?"

Chance took a sharp intake of breath, then puckered and blew. "Ever heard of La Santa Muerte—the Holy Death? It's the fastest growing crime cult in Mexico. You could say it's a newer version of the one that lady told you about, and a lot more intense."

"Yeah, as a matter of fact, I have heard of it. Dr. Shelton mentioned it when I was in San Jose. He called them 'Holy Death' cults."

"Uh-huh, that's right, and the drug lords love it. Their logo is sort of a bad girl version of the Virgin Mary—a skeleton dressed up in the traditional image of Mary, only this one blesses things like rape, prostitution, and crime. People come from all over the country, crawling on the ground in front of the statue, worshiping death. They pile sacrifices on an altar—everything from money to drugs. Pretty amazing stuff. I guess they think it's their ticket out of hell, not into it."

"Hmm. Sounds kind of like the Aztecs," I said.

Chance nodded in agreement. "Yeah, pretty much the same thing. You know, it's all about power and control. It's all over Southern California and in the prison system, thanks to the illegals."

"Here's another one I heard at the conference. Ready for this? Did you know that the US Supreme Court ruled that animal sacrifice is religious freedom? We are talking lambs, pigs, chickens, goats—Animal Control even found cow tongues hanging in trees up in Virginia. Crazy, huh? They say that city workers in Florida pick up hundreds of dead animals from the parks every week."

"Some people call it religious freedom," said Chance.

"Well, I call it sick, and it gets worse, a lot worse. I got a quote from a chief deputy in Florida who told me that Satanists had been caught stealing fetuses from abortion clinics for use in their rituals."

Silence.

"Do you think that's true? Do you really believe that happens? I hate thinking about it, but now I can't stop."

"Everybody feels that way about it, hon. No one wants to think about anything that atrocious because no one wants it to be true. But things like that do happen—whether people believe it or not. There are plenty of cases and mountains of evidence for what you are saying, and you know more than most that there's an endless stream of victims. It's rampant—and no one cares."

Silence.

"I care."

ଞ ✝ ଔ

"Sunny," Gayle called from reception, "it's Warren Aldrich on the line from probation regarding a . . . a . . . uh, warlock?"

"I'll explain later," I said, slumping at my desk. "Please pass him through."

"Hello, Sunny, this is Warren. I'm getting back to you about that little black book that we found at the Blackstone residence."

"Hey, Warren, what did you find? I'm guessing it wasn't a book of spells, huh?"

"It reads more like a diary. The names of attendees and the locations of their meetings are all in code. Of course, our little Charles isn't talking about that. But he did say something you might be interested in. He bragged about having unlimited access to drugs, booze, and sex since the first party he attended back in seventh grade. He made it sound like a dream come true, and basically, he thinks that we are a joke. I asked the kid why he thought that, and he implied that his group has powerful friends."

"How powerful? Did he give you names?"

"No. But he did use some pretty big titles."

"Such as?"

"Members of Congress, program directors, cops—big stuff like that. No names. I made a copy of the book. I didn't find anything criminal, so I'm dropping the original off at his mom's this afternoon. I'll let you know if we crack the codes or the kid—whichever happens first."

No wonder there is such a powerful attraction, I thought. What teenager is going to say no to that kind of party—especially teens who have no moral guideposts? People always talk about the freedom of living without boundaries, and yet this child was already a slave to all the vices. I got to thinking that Charles was a perfect example of what happened when people got whatever they wanted.

ॐ ☥ ॐ

I had finished giving my testimony in court. The victim was a man whose wife had broken his collarbone when she hit him with a wine bottle. Such a waste of good wine and a good husband—both were rare and usually improve over time.

My appointment with Dano was in ten minutes. I hadn't seen her since the morning of the blood moon incident, but I had called her the next morning and updated her on everything that had transpired. She told me that I could question Taylor on her next appointment.

Travis wanted Taylor's name, but I held back, claiming that she was my client, and the information was confidential. It was such a stretch of the truth that I could only hope the backlash wouldn't rip my head off.

Taylor was already in her usual seat, tenderly hugging herself, rocking back and forth when I arrived. Dano gestured for me to take a chair and asked Taylor if it was okay with her to speak to me.

Taylor nodded her head up and down vigorously. "Hi, Sunny," she said shyly.

"Hello, Taylor," I said. "I'm going to ask you some questions about things that happened after our last meeting here."

Taylor repeatedly denied any knowledge of attending a blood moon gathering. We were getting nowhere, when Dano interjected, "Perhaps you know someone else who was there?"

A couple of minutes passed. A clock ticked from somewhere in the background.

A fragile high-pitched little girl's voice quavered, "Can I have a cookie if I tell?"

Dano set up straight with renewed interest in her client. "What is your name, little girl?"

"My name is Tinka. Tinkabell. My daddy loves Tinkabell." Taylor blushed with a little giggle and wriggled deeper into her chair.

I threw Dano a questioning look, and she replied with a pair of raised eyebrows and a shrug. "Tinkabell" was the emergence of a new personality.

Dano spoke, "Hello, Tinkerbell. Did you go with Mommy and Daddy to the gathering?"

"I went with Mommy and Daddy to the moon party. Can I have a cookie now?"

"What is your mommy's name?" I asked.

Taylor's features had grown soft and childlike. Her eyes were big and round. "De-da. She's a queen."

"What is your daddy's name?"

"Me-ma." She giggled. "He's a king."

I thought she had their names backward—whatever. "What did you do at the party?" I asked.

Taylor tipped her head, pressing her index finger to her bottom lip as she scrunched her face. "We sang and played games."

"What kind of games?" I asked.

Her answer brought a wave of nausea, which swept over me like a rogue wave that threatened to rip me from my foundation, sucking the life out of me as it dragged me out to sea.

The little child inside of Taylor continued to provide graphic details of how the adults had sexually used her. It seemed like a safe guess that the cookies and punch had been laced with Ecstasy and painkillers, or perhaps Rohypnol, the date rape drug.

Dano had Taylor drug-tested before she left the building. The results were inconclusive. Rohypnol did not stay in the system. She tested positive for opiates, but, then, Taylor had a valid prescription for Oxycodone to help her manage the pain she still suffered from numerous childhood injuries.

CHAPTER 21

ଛ ☥ ଓ

It was going to be easy to keep "Christ" in Christmas this year, especially since I would be spending it alone. I admit, I wasn't particularly happy with His decision to keep my husband in His service instead of mine, but I accepted it. And while I had never been able to get into the commercial aspect of Christmas, the annual office Christmas party had arrived, whether I liked it or not.

Office parties were a great opportunity to unload last year's gift—those notorious white elephants taking up space in the back of the closet and collecting dust for the past year. Traditionally, everybody brought a gift and dropped it off in the break room. After work, some lucky person played Santa and drew names from a bowl, one at a time. The person whose name was drawn got to pick out a gift bag.

Paige looked exceedingly pleased to be chosen as Santa's helper this year. She certainly looked the part with a sprig of mistletoe in her hair and her nails striped like candy canes and wearing a red velvet jumper over her prodigious belly.

I made sure, with Paige's help, that Duncan would be the first name drawn so he could go home early. He was delighted when I offered to pick out a gift for him so he wouldn't have to get up from his chair. Of course, I went straight to the bag wrapped with Harley paper and a red bow. It was next year's calendar, with every month depicting a different motorcycle. No sex-starved calendar girls draped over the machines—just Harleys—and Duncan's eyes sparkled like the tinsel on the tree.

I was third from last, and a lot of the people who already had their gifts made polite excuses and headed out. My choice was an obvious one, pulled from back behind the tree. The bag had a team of Chihuahuas pulling a sleigh, and inside was a small box wrapped in white tissue paper with red paw prints. Hugging my gift, I returned to my office to savor the moment. I was having fun in spite of myself when Bonita and Amanda popped in to say good night.

"Open it, open it." We all wanted to see the toy.

I opened the box to find a Magic 8 Ball. A Magic 8 Ball was a fortune-telling ball that looked like an oversized cue ball, or an undersized bowling ball, depending on your perspective. The ball had a little window, and when you shook the ball, a little message appeared in the window with the answer to your question.

"I need one of those for court," said Amanda. "Go ahead, ask it a question."

Exaggerating big-eyed excitement, I asked, "Will next year be better than this year?" and swished the ball back and forth. The message read: "Outlook not so good." Everyone laughed.

"Try it again," said Bonita.

"Are these people ever going to go home?" We all laughed.

Same message: "Outlook not so good." I didn't feel like trying my luck a third time.

"Huh! Maybe I don't need one after all, unless the message says 'Guilty' every time," Amanda said. Then she wished us a merry Christmas and left, taking the spirit of fun with her.

Bonita remained behind. "Try it again, chica." She was serious.

"I don't think so."

"Let me try." Bonita reached out for the eight ball, and I hesitated, reluctant to hand it over. She inspected the ball, then gently swished it. "Hmph. It looks like my 'outlook isn't so good' either." She started examining the box and paper. "Any ideas where this came from?"

"The office party?"

Bonita gave me a look of disgust. "Does any part of this have a personal message for you?"

My heart pounded at the memory of my best friend Frito, the little one-eyed Chihuahua mutt that my dad always claimed was part gopher. There were nights when I still woke, teared up as dreams forced me to relive the awful day I found the "gift" my ex had left me.

I stared at Bonita.

"Tell me about it," she said, leaning in and placing a reassuring hand on my arm. "It's okay."

I swallowed hard, fighting back the tears, and somehow found my voice to tell her. "Logan, my ex-husband, the one doing time up at High Desert. He mutilated my dog—a Chihuahua—and left his body in a shoe box. Wrapped in duct tape . . . sitting on my car seat."

"I see," mused Bonita. "And you think he might have sent you this?"

"I don't know what to think anymore," I said. "Not a damn thing."

℘ ⚕ ℆

Santa's helper stopped by my office to say good-bye. "Have a nice vacation," said Paige.

"Are you sure you're okay holding down the office? I know you're not due for another week or two, but it seems to me you should be taking time off."

"I'll be okay," said Paige. "I'd rather save my maternity days for after the baby comes. What are you going to do with your vacation? Going to see Chance?"

I arched an eyebrow the way a cat arches his back. "Probably not. I have some ideas, but I haven't decided. I hope you have a merry Christmas, Paige. I should be back before the baby arrives. Are you going to your mom's house?"

Paige frowned for a moment and rubbed her belly like a Magic 8 Ball, then relented. "Yeah, maybe. Sure, probably. Why not?" Her head and shoulders slumped, sending the message: "Outlook not so good."

"Okay . . . well, have fun having the baby. I can't wait to see it."

"Really?" Her face looked so young in contrast to the dark circles under her sad searching eyes. "You really want to see it, or just inspect it?"

I paused to consider her remark, and then reached out and hugged her in a burst of benevolent holiday compassion. "Of course I want to see your baby. I love children, and you're going to make a wonderful mother." I smiled reassuringly and gave her another hug. It was the best gift I could give under the circumstances.

℘ ⚕ ℆

If it was possible for someone to fade from pale to ghastly gray, Duncan had done so. He appeared to be in extreme pain as he haltingly stumped his way toward the elevator. I thought he would have left by now.

"Duncan! Duncan . . . hey! If I don't see you, have a merry—"

Duncan spun in my direction, his round face lighting up like a Christmas tree behind a frosted window pane as the elevator doors opened. He gave a feeble wave with a crutch and then turned as the elevator door slid open. The second crutch must have stuck in the door guide, toppling Duncan out of control, launching him headfirst into the elevator—with a cry that ripped through the atrium, out the doors, possibly reaching as far as the North Pole.

"Ahhhhhhhhhhh . . . hhhhhh . . . hhhhh . . ."

I followed the ambulance to Oroville Hospital. The flashing red lights on the crossbar failed to restore my holiday spirit. I felt responsible for breaking Duncan's arm. It's not like I pushed him or anything, but I still felt guilty.

Six hours that felt like ten, aging in the waiting room, I was finally allowed to see Duncan fresh out of surgery. He looked pathetic, like a third-rate character from a low-budget horror movie. His right leg was still in its cast, and now he had a matching left arm and a gauze bandage on a corner of his forehead. Duncan groaned softly in his sleep, making me wince. I leaned over and kissed his cheek, patting his arm in encouragement when something caught my eye.

What the heck is that?

I angled around the bed, moving his IV line for closer inspection. Sure enough, tattooed on his arm in old English script were the words BORN TO RIDE.

ဆာ ♱ ରୟ

I stared at our wedding picture as I sat next to the phone thinking about the Bride of Frankenstein, seeing myself as both desirable and abhorrent. I wanted to hold the precious picture next to my heart, and I also wanted to throw it across the room and watch it explode against the wall. It occurred to me that I could do both. But I didn't. I picked up the phone instead.

I told Chance about the office party and the eight ball.

"I can't do this anymore, Chance. I'm scared, and I want you to come home. I'm begging you. Please. Come back."

More than the expected sigh, Chance jettisoned his frustration in an expletive of air. "You have to be kidding. Listen to yourself! You've been in danger for the past two years and hated me every day for my interference. Now I'm down here in San Diego— respecting your need for space and your insistence that you can take care of yourself. You seriously expect me to drop everything and rush home? Honey, I'm leaving for Mexico in the morning."

"I can't believe you're leaving me. Logan mutilated my dog, and now he's going to kill me."

"Kissme is dead?"

"Frito."

Another sigh. "Listen. The eight ball is just another work prank, like the bat and the tarantula in your inbox. It probably isn't related to Logan."

I raised my voice and clenched my fist. "Rat! It was a rat in my box—not a bat. You never listen to me!"

"Calm down. I'm listening. To be on the safe side, I think you should call Travis. He has the latest updates on Logan. I'm sorry that you're afraid, but I really don't believe that you're in danger."

"What about the chicken nailed to the front door of the cabin? Huh? What about that? You thought that was important once."

"Call Travis. Okay? Promise me you'll call him?"

"I can't believe you!"

"I said call him, not go to bed with him."

I bristled but did not respond. How could I, with the memory of Travis's kiss still lingering on my lips?

Chance and I had come close to divorcing last summer. The paperwork had sat on my desk for months, but I never filed it. It wasn't just hope and love, although hope and love were a part of it. And it wasn't because church doctrine said divorce was wrong. I didn't file for divorce because my faith said it was wrong. I loved Chance, and I would never leave him.

My stomach growled in need of comfort food. Done moralizing and rationalizing, I made sandwiches for dinner and sat across from Kissme who ate her own BLT; Bacon Less Tomato.

I should have been packing for my vacation instead of calling Travis. Just because Travis and I had a past, didn't mean we had a future. But a promise was a promise, and I had promised Chance that I would make the call.

"What you think, Kissme?" The little dog whined and turned in a circle, probably more concerned with bacon than Travis. I picked up the phone and dialed his number. The same woman answered as last time. And like last time, I hung up. I guess I had been hoping she was a one-night stand.

Like last time, Travis called me back within minutes.

"I don't want to talk to you," I said.

"You just called me, Sunny."

Awkward.

My eyes rolled toward heaven looking for an answer. "I dialed the wrong number."

Stupid.

There was a pause fraught with tension.

"She's a friend of mine," said Travis.

He's lying.

I cut him off. "I don't care who you see." We both knew that I cared, but I sped on like a drunken driver in a getaway car. "I talked to Chance a little while ago, and he made me promise to call you."

"He's already called me because he figured you wouldn't. He told me about the gift you got it at your office party. A Magic 8 Ball with a single message. What was the message?"

"The message said 'Google it.'"

"Seriously?"

"No. It said 'Outlook not so good.'"

"Did you handle the ball?"

"Yeah. I took it to the bowling alley."

"Did you give Bonita the ball and the wrapping for follow-up investigation?"

"No. I gave her a Spanish-English dictionary."

I heard what sounded like a locomotive blowing steam through clenched teeth.

This is so stupid. I wanted my husband, not a babysitter. "I'll talk with you after Christmas."

I cut him off and disconnected. Then I pulled the cord from the jack, got up, and turned off my cell.

"I am going home for Christmas," I declared to Kissme, who perked up, wagged her tail, and predictably turned in a circle. "You are going to the babysitter's."

Mercy the Magnificent had been at Mark's house for the past two weeks. It was important to Chance that Mercy stayed on a training schedule and Mark clearly loved having her, so her temporary care worked out for everyone.

Chance and I went to the cabin every year for Christmas, and while I wished he were here to keep up the tradition, I imagined him busy—drinking mojitos and serving beans to the poor. I could handle the being alone part. After all, I'd spent most of my life alone in the cabin. A few days more or less, depending on the weather, would be nice.

Genesis 22:7
Isaac said
"… where is the lamb for the burnt offering?"

CHAPTER 22

Patches of ice crunched and cracked underfoot as I made a final trip to the car. The air was sharp and biting with the promise of snow. The back of my Volkswagen held several good books and a suitcase with extra clothing. The front held my old Bible, Kissme wearing a red doggie sweater with white poinsettias, her bed, and a bag of canine cookies for her and her friends.

"You're going to Shane and Ashley's house," I told Kissme. "Be a good girl and have fun with the boys," Kissme whined and looked doubtful.

Shane and Ashley had invited me for Christmas dinner. I declined with a hug and asked Ashley for a favor instead. I almost lost Kissme last Christmas. She was just a little thing, and she had literally disappeared beneath two feet of fresh snow at a rest stop. This year, she was going to the babysitter. Ashley was dependably gracious, and in the holiday spirit, went so far as to carve out an exception in her new germ-a-phobic rules that would allow Kissme to stay indoors.

Ashley greeted me at the door with open arms. She looked enormous, her eyes almost as round as her belly, radiating warmth as genuine as the rock fireplace that heated their home. Poor Ashley! She looked as large as Paige, although Paige was due any day now and Ashley's kidlets weren't due to hatch until February.

"You're not going to believe what I heard," said Ashley as I wiped my feet on the doormat. "I heard that Pastor Mac has called off his engagement with Kinsey." Ashley quickly closed the door behind us with a wistful sigh. "Poor Mac," she sympathized. "Oma seemed like such a nice person. I guess you just never know."

Yeah, but we're not clueless. I flinched and made a mental note to talk to Mac when I came back. I owed him that, and so much more.

"Hey, Ashley, your dogs are back in the house. Aren't you afraid they'll infect the unborn?"

Ashley rolled her eyes. "It's Shane," she said. "He can't stand the idea of the dogs freezing outside, so we compromised. I trained the dogs to stay in the kitchen."

"What about Kissme?"

"Oh, don't worry. Little dog, little germs. She'll be fine."

I didn't ask what that meant, but it wouldn't kill Kissme to spend the next few nights in Ashley's kitchen. At least she would have company.

Back in the car, I turned on the radio. I was leaving my problems behind—a kind of sabbatical. I was going home.

℘ ♀ ℭ

Olive Highway went past Oroville Hospital on the way to Feather Falls. I pulled in for a quick check on Duncan. Not knowing if it was inappropriate to bring a man flowers, I bought him a coffee mug from the gift shop printed with OUT OF SICK DAYS — CALLING IN DEAD.

The BORN TO RIDE tattoo on Duncan's arm made me uneasy. In some ways it was charming, but then, ink always implied a contract, a legal relationship, and Duncan wasn't exactly biker material.

Duncan was mostly asleep, although he appeared to be coming off his meds when his eyes fluttered. He moaned, softly tugging against the IV attached to his good arm. His complexion was whiter than the bleached sheets around him. Poor Duncan! I felt responsible—with him first buying a motorcycle, and then falling into the elevator. He now had his left arm, in addition to the existing right leg, in a cast, not to mention a thick gauze pad on a corner of his forehead. Damp hair framed his childlike face. I leaned over him and gently brushed it back.

Moved with compassion, I took a red Sharpie from my purse and drew a heart on his cast and wrote: "Get well soon, love, Sunny." I gave him a little kiss on the cheek and whispered in his ear, "I'm sorry, sweetie. I know all about wrecks," I said, vividly recalling my own motorcycle accident and lengthy recovery. "I'll make it up to you."

Two more stops; gas and Raley's Supermarket before the one-hour drive to the cabin. Raley's was bounded by a couple of department stores presently filled with women toting gifts and men milling out on the sidewalk looking like sad reindeer that hadn't made the cut during the rut. The grocery store reminded me of driving on a highway with no lines and all the lights green. But I bought my game hen, my stovetop stuffing, a packet of instant potatoes, eggnog, and frozen pumpkin pie—all the trappings of Christmas dinner—checking out with a giant ache in my heart. I almost drove back for Kissme.

Overhead, the sky looked as gray as the pavement. Black clouds pushed up against the Sierras, creating a dark towering mountain chain that soared high into the heavens, mirroring the earthly one below. I thought they looked majestic, although some people might use the word foreboding. It held the promise of an early snowfall that called to me, ringing in the season.

So many reasons to go to the cabin, but mostly I needed some time to get back in touch with the One who was the reason for the season.

Leaving the valley behind, I began my ascent up the narrow winding road to the town of Feather Falls. Of course, the town was long gone. The sleepy little logging village with its rustic company houses had gone the way of the mill—demolished by environmental regulations and the slow death of the timber industry—leaving behind a few scattered residents and the grade school.

∽ ⚹ ∾

The cabin was the center of my universe. It was home. The one place, the one thing, my parents had agreed on. Slanting walls covered with aged cedar shakes, a roof that had sometimes leaked. Add on rooms that rambled, a large kitchen whose walls had been lined with felt paper resting on a bare plywood floor. That was before Chance and I fixed it up. We still cooked on the propane cook stove, and the propane refrigerator still chugged along. It hadn't been pretty then, but it was cozy now—always looking out on a garden full of promise, an orchard rich with produce, and mountains that echoed with freedom.

Home.

Home was the place where Starla had meticulously embroidered vines dotted with colorful flowers and butterflies on clothing that she had made on her treadle sewing machine. Where she did yoga standing on one leg, arms clasped above her head as if reaching for the rising sun. Where songs were sung as we worked in the garden and canned fruit. Those remembrances remained alive, lingering and fragrant in my mind.

It was the place where the tired framework of the cabin hugged the living room window where I had stood, enchanted, watching my mother dance under a full moon to music that only she could hear, marveling at her beauty and her mysticism. The cabin was her true north. The compass of her heart would always guide her back, regardless of how long she was gone or how far she strayed. Eventually, this is the place where my mother would return.

Home also is where Lefty rode in like a king with his entourage, heralded by the deep-throated roar of his Harley, dressed in black leather patched with his red Hell's Angels death head. My father would scoop me into his strong arms and laugh and tickle and tease, teach and guide.

People, including his biker friends, had all feared my father and his metal hook. Lefty had not embraced life, but neither had he feared death. So strong and so powerful was my dad, that the feeling of safety still permeated the little cabin, long after he was gone—long after his death. If my father could return from the grave, he would surely come to the cabin.

Visits to the cabin always rekindled pleasant childhood memories. Chance had a hard time understanding that, what with all the violence that had transpired there—my father beating Starla and Logan beating me.

"Why not sell the cabin?" Chance had once suggested.

The thought was inconceivable. The outside world would always be more intimidating than the cabin. It was true that dark memories of Logan's abuse and my mother's abandonment inhabited the domain. But treasured remembrances of my father, Frito, and the happy years with just the three of us would always be the sunshine that chased the clouds away. A part of me would always feel like a wild creature trapped in a domesticated world.

"I'd sooner sell a kidney," I had replied. "It's part of who I am."

Chance had laughed and shaken his head. We did some major repairs and went on to make memories of our own.

ৡ ⚲ ৵

"I'm dreaming of a white Christmas . . ." My spirits soared, rising on the wings of elevation. Up and up, past the manzanita, whose silvery leaves flashed and danced like schools of fish when it rained, and mighty valley oaks—those loan sentinels standing guard over golden rolling hills. ". . . just like the ones I used to know . . ." The valley vegetation gave way to gnarly ancient black oaks and their neighboring tall, rangy digger pines. "May your days be merry and bright . . ." I knew I was almost to the cabin when I saw the crowning glory of the Sierra Nevadas—those majestic towering sugar pines with cones nearly two feet long, and their beautiful queens, the soaring cedars—both of which stood guard over the little cabin. ". . . and may all your Christmases be white."

No tweakers, no break-ins, squatters, or dead animals nailed to the door. After a quick cursory check around the house, I hurried to unlock the front door and padlock on the propane tank, cranking it on to power the stove and refrigerator.

"Stuffy" was a good sign, but the place begged for freshness. The sweet winter air seemed to knock on the living room windows, asking to be let in. A few tugs on the single-pane windows were all that was needed—a healthy alternative to pine-scented aerosols.

Another trip to the car and back. I hauled the suitcase upstairs. Each step groaned like a stooped grandpa picking up a grandchild that has grown too big to carry. I paused before the bedroom that had once embraced my parents, calling out in spontaneous, joyful silliness, "Hi, Mom. Hi, Dad. Hey, Frito love."

No greetings in my heart for Logan. Later memories of Logan in the bedroom completely obscured any earlier, romantic ones.

I hurried to the woodpile and warmed to the job of splitting kindling. "Thank you, Lord, for dry wood," I said, tugging on the old canvas tarp that the wind had tossed up, exposing cord wood that looked like a stack of knobby legs poking out from beneath a giant blanket. Balancing an armload of firewood, I headed indoors just as the first flakes of snow kissed my face.

ৡ ⚲ ৵

Secure in my cocoon, wrapped in a soft fleece throw and an even softer sense of peace, I curled up next to the heater to sip hot chocolate and read my old friend, the Bible. It seemed the perfect place and the perfect season to learn about the birth of Christ. However, it seemed horribly ironic that I had finally escaped the clutches of Ishtar—the apparent fertility goddess of Butte County—only to find myself reading about another pregnancy and birth. I winced to think that God had even thrown Mary a surprise baby shower with the arrival of wise men and their camels loaded with gifts. Apparently, there was no getting away from the pregnancy-childbirth thing.

The new day arrived bringing the first soft puffs of snow, filling the world with a sense of wonder that something so delicate could come from something as cold and miserable as freezing rain. The snowfall quickened, twirling around like a feathery dust devil, every inch deepening the sense of tranquility.

Feelings of safety always wrapped around me when I was snowed in—or the summertime equivalent of drowsing on a rock in the middle of a stream. Snow and rushing water always felt like the arms of Mother Nature wrapping around me and keeping me safe from predators. By nightfall, the snow was three inches deep.

I didn't need a weatherman to tell me that this storm was going to be a big one. My only regret was not having brought Kissme and Mercy. Still, I thought, this is how a retreat is supposed to be—a time for thoughtful meditation. It didn't matter at this point. Volkswagens were not designed for snow chains. I wasn't going anywhere.

Stretching across my bed, cradled under a goose-down comforter, I indulged in a nap and a dream.

ၟ ♀ ℛ

Logan's eyes were dark and dreamy, full of passion and promise. His hair was black, shiny as polished onyx, hanging in waves to his shoulders. His skin was the color of oiled patina that glistened in the moonlight that splashed across our bed.

"I can't believe you're mine. I can't believe I got Lefty's daughter. Umm, sweet!" Logan whispered in my ear. His words made me feel like a priceless treasure as his hands wandered, exploring, brushing, teasing, and arousing my young body to unimaginable heights.

"Don't hurt me," I gasped, trembling. The first time had been so painful that I had begged him to stop. The following morning we were "married," and pretty soon I didn't want him to stop.

"Never, baby. Never. Trust me." And I had—until the violence began.

The first year had been a thrill ride—a roller coaster of wild romantic highs followed by increasingly deeper, more unstable lows. I was in love with a dangerous man.

The heart of an advocate had beat inside of me long before I became one. I was always excusing and defending Logan's behavior, even when I was the victim. I wanted to rescue him, to make him happy, to set him free from his childhood abuse.

Motorcycles and outlaw gangs were Logan's heritage. His father had stabbed a guy from a rival gang and had been doing life in prison before Logan was out of diapers. Mom's new boyfriend was also a biker—a vicious man who beat both him and his mother on occasion. She was dependent on his drugs, and Logan was dependent on his mother.

Everything has a breaking point, and Logan was no exception. As a teenager, he defended his mother by taking a baseball bat first to her boyfriend's motorcycle and later to the boyfriend. That was when Logan became a national statistic. He was one of the "majority of boys" in prison between the ages of eleven to eighteen, there for killing his mother's abuser.

A part of me, a small part, still remembered and pitied Logan.

CHAPTER 23

ಐ ✟ ಜ

The aroma of hot oatmeal and cinnamon lingered long after the last dish was put away. My heart felt lighter than the puffs of snow that continued to fall. The Cornish game hen sat thawing, resting on the counter next to the pumpkin pie. Humming a favorite Christmas carol, I picked up a wicker basket and headed outdoors. It was time to decorate the cabin, and I headed out in search of sugar pine cones and branches of the holiday-red toyon berries that grew down by the Indian grinding stones.

Tomorrow I planned to visit my neighbors, Joyce and Kenny. But tonight was Christmas Eve, and that meant family. Although my family was either dead or far away, I could feel their presence.

By the end of the day, the halls were decked, and kerosene lamps lit. It was time to bring in wood and start dinner. It was going to be a "silent night." I stuck out my tongue to catch fresh falling flakes of snow and chanted a mantra of thanks with a grateful heart as I walked to the woodpile.

"Thank you, God. Thank you for the snow, the good memories, and the firewood. Thank you for—" I did a double take, unsure if I had prayed too soon—or too late.

An intruder puffed and staggered down the driveway, looking like a drunken sailor trying to keep his footing on a rolling deck.

I wasn't afraid. Clearly, the person was in distress and in need of help.

I hurried toward the ghostly specter as the form slowly took shape through the whirling curtain of falling snow.

"Good God! Paige, what are you doing here?" The words exploded in angry white puffs. "Where's your car?"

Paige was sweating profusely; her red face looked hot in spite of the freezing temperature. She practically collapsed onto the chopping block.

"Car . . . up on the road," she huffed, referring to the paved road about a half mile away. "Water broke. Help me."

My scolding turned to ranting as I helped her up. "Why aren't you in a hospital? Or with your parents? What would make you come up here in your condition? You must be out of your mind.

"Come on," I growled with finality. "Let's get you indoors."

Clucking like a hen, I eased her onto the sofa and continued to rebuke her even as I flew around the cabin trying to make her comfortable. She wasn't going anywhere soon, so I brought a pillow and bedding down from upstairs and added wood to the old Franklin heater.

"Thirsty," she croaked. I hurried to get fresh water to quench her thirst and then made tea from the kettle that I kept on the heater.

Dismayed, I rambled on about how hard it was snowing as I squeezed the tea bag. Although Paige had been to my home in Yankee Hill and worked alongside me at the district attorney's office, even sharing my husband for a time, she had never been to the cabin. More than intruding on my privacy, she was invading my sanctuary.

"You want honey or sugar in your—" I pulled up short to study the once beautiful young woman, who was now gaunt in the face with dark circles under her eyes, curled up on the sofa sound asleep. There was nothing I could do. She probably just needed to rest, and then we would go.

I looked out the window.

No way could my car make it up the driveway.

I pinched my lips.

When she wakes up, we'll walk out to her car and drive to the hospital.

There was no phone, no electricity, and no cell service, or I'd have dialed 911. Once we got out of here and down the road about eight miles into a good cell area, I would call an ambulance. One thing was certain—the baby was on its way.

Paige woke with a yelp that triggered a panic attack in me.

"Paige. Can you make it up the driveway? Out to your car?"

I was pretty sure I could pack Paige up the driveway on my back if necessary. They say that women in crisis have been known to lift a car, freeing their child trapped beneath its wheels, and this felt like a similar kind of crisis.

Paige started to rise and then sank back onto the couch. "I am right where I need to be," she said with conviction. She surveyed the cabin.

"So this is where Logan—"

"We need to go. I am getting you out of here."

"I'm not going to a hospital, so you can stop with all the hospital talk. It's not going to happen." Paige was adamant.

"That's what you think," I said, raising my voice. "You have no say. We are leaving— now. Think of the baby!"

Paige sighed. "I am thinking of the baby, and I'm not going anywhere. I think about the baby all the time. You can't know. You'll never understand. Not really. Besides . . . you'd never forgive me."

Anger battled with curiosity, the two emotions using me as a punching bag. I struggled with the truth—she really was having Chance's baby. The certainty pierced like a sword through the heart, although axe in the back might have been more accurate. I couldn't think about that now. I needed to stuff my emotions, knowing they would wait, lurking like fearful shadows in a dark corner of my mind. More urgent thoughts pressed in.

"You can apologize later," I said. "We have to go."

Paige fell back, lying on the sofa, talking to the ceiling. "If I go to the hospital, they will find me. They will find us. They'll take my baby . . . and I am not going to let that happen." Her face was set, her voice grim. "This is the only safe place, and you're going to have to help me, like it or not."

I was pretty sure my jaw bounced off my knees. I couldn't possibly have heard right. I needed to stick my fingers in my ears and shake them until they unplugged.

Or shake Paige until her teeth rattle and the baby falls out. Not really. But almost.

"Don't freak out on me," said Paige. "Women have been having kids forever. How hard can it be?" She lifted her brows dismissively, then scrunched her face and curled upward, clutching her belly and crying out as if in answer to her own question. Falling back, Paige breathed heavily as her eyes took on a glassy, otherworld look.

"Mexico," she said in a voice as soft as the falling snow and just as chilling. "It was so bad that it kind of blurs . . . one man after another. It never stopped." Paige's eyes darted back and forth as if she were flipping through a picture book of horror stories.

"At first, I fought to live because I knew my dad would rescue me. I kept thinking; *if I can just make it through today.*"

A single tear formed at the edge of her eye, as bright and hard as a diamond stud shimmering in the light of the kerosene lamp. "The next day came . . . but my dad never did . . . not for a really long time." She sniffed and the cloud lifted. Her expression hardened. "They won't find me here."

"Nobody wants you, Paige." I winced. "Sorry. That's not exactly what I meant. I meant to say the cartel wants me, not you. They want the guns and money that Logan stole from them. Listen, I need to go get help." I could make it to Joyce and Kenny's house before dark if I ran.

I had a plan. "My neighbor—my friend—Joyce has given birth nine times. She can help you while Kenny and I drive out to the road and call an ambulance."

Paige moaned—louder this time. I glanced at the clock. Her contractions were about ten minutes apart. I considered Search and Rescue and rolled my eyes. Where is Chance when I need him? "I'll go get help. Maybe they can medevac you out of here."

"No, don't leave me," Paige pleaded as she grabbed my arm. "Promise me." Her grip was tighter than a sadistic nurse pumping relentlessly on a blood pressure cuff. "Promise me. Promise!"

"Okay, okay," I promised, rubbing my arm. Paige left me no choice as she succumbed to another, stronger contraction.

"You need to calm down and take a deep breath—count one, two, three, four," I said.

I was not a midwife. I was an advocate, and I had never given birth. Since this was the only breathing technique I knew, I offered up a silent prayer and instructed Paige in the way Chance had taught me.

"Breathe in, one, two, three, four. Hold, one, two, three, four. Breathe out, one, two, three, four. Hold, one, two, three, four. Let's do it together."

Okay, this isn't exactly in the Lamaze handbook. It was designed to prevent heart failure, so if it doesn't help you, maybe it will help me.

Paige let loose with a yelp that caused my heart to skip a beat—or maybe two or three.

I helped Paige undress between contractions and wrapped her in my bathrobe, grabbed scissors from the junk drawer in the kitchen, put a pot of water on the stove to boil, and brought some towels down from upstairs—because that was what they always did in the movies.

Maybe Paige is right. Maybe I can do this. My mother gave birth to me right here. I was born in this cabin. My father had caught me with one hand and a hook.

The single-pane windows almost shattered with Paige's next contraction. Her cries echoed through the mountains sounding more like the death throes of a wounded animal than the ushering in of new life.

Throwing another log in the heater, I paused at the door to look up the road—searching for a miracle, when I saw . . . something.

Probably snow sliding off a tree. Maybe a deer.

I dared to hope, but I didn't budge.

Something darker than the encroaching night bolted from behind a tree and disappeared behind another.

Paige struggled to sit up. "What's wrong?" Paige panted, her hair hung loose, like a blond cotton mop wrung with fear and pain. Strands clung to her face with long wet fingers that magnified her look of terror.

"I think something. . . or someone is out there."

"Ohmygod!" Paige sobbed.

"Shut up, Paige! I can't think," I said, clenching my teeth and spinning from the door. "You brought this on yourself. On both of us! You should be in a hospital with security, not here."

"I'm sorry. I'm sorry, Sunny. I am so sorry!"

"Too late for sorry," I tossed the words over my shoulder, crouched, and continued my surveillance. Nothing happened. I crept back to Paige. "What's really going on?"

"He's here," she gasped, hanging on my arm. I pushed her back down and pulled up the blanket. "He's here . . . oh God . . . I am so sorry . . . sorry for everything." Paige fell back in exhaustion, heaving and sobbing.

CHAPTER 24

᰾ ✚ ᰻

I stared at her with an open mouth and ever-widening eyes. "Good God Almighty! What have you done? Who the hell is out there?" I pressed Paige, mad enough to choke her. "Who. Is. It?"

Paige's scream recalibrated and then dropped, from brain-piercing shrill to a series of determined grunts from behind clenched teeth. Her eyes bulged, mirroring her swollen belly as she pushed against the armrests with her hands and feet. The baby was coming regardless of our wishes, regrets, or fears.

I glanced at Paige, then the front door, and then the upstairs bedroom. "Fuck!" My obscenity trailed me through the house as I raced for the stairs, taking them two at a time. Frantically digging through my closet, I tossed sheets from the shelf and kicked shoes and boots across the floor. Logan's ghost probably laughed as my heart thudded in my ears.

There! There it was—in the furthest corner. A furry brown teddy bear dressed in black leathers, wearing a happy smile beneath a Harley Davidson cap and a black leather vest with little silver chain extenders. The bear had been a Christmas gift from my father when I was ten. Right now, it was the best gift of all.

With a shout of triumph, I hastened back down the narrow stairs, clutching the bear to my breast.

᰾ ✚ ᰻

"Wake up, Daddy! It's Christmas! Get up!" I bounced on my father's bed with all the exuberance of a Labrador puppy.

Lefty yawned and rolled over in his otherwise empty bed. "It's too early, girl! Christmas isn't until next weekend."

"Da-deee!" I exclaimed in exaggerated distress.

"Merry Christmas, baby girl." He laughed, sweeping me into his bear hug, planting a big sloppy kiss on my cheek and tickling me before advising, "Now, you scoot downstairs before I get out of bed and you see something you shouldn't," he warned.

Screaming a little girl's shrill scream of ecstatic joy, I flew down the stairs to let Frito outside while Lefty got into his trousers and headed down to join me. Then I tugged the sliding glass door open, letting Frito back in and the heat out as he yapped and barked and danced around us. We all gathered dutifully around a scrawny Christmas tree that I had cut myself and strung with dried cranberries, popcorn, pine cones, and chicken feathers. I thought it was beautiful.

Lefty held a package behind his back in his good right hand, scratching his beard with the hook on his left. It was good to see my father smile. He'd hardly ever smiled since Starla had left us on the Fourth of July. I supposed that had been her way of declaring her independence. Lefty planted another kiss on my forehead, and I hugged and kissed him back. Starla would have rolled her eyes and told me I was too old for such nonsense if she had been there. There were times like this when I was glad she was gone. We don't need her, I told myself, although I secretly hoped that she might come home for Christmas, of all days.

"What did you get me, Daddy?" Excitement flashed from my father's eyes, like the morning sun off the snow after a hard night's freeze.

Lefty produced a dark-brown biker teddy bear, dressed in black leathers and a black vest, wearing a Harley Davidson biker cap. My father had modified the bear with a little metal hook where his left paw should have been. Squealing with joy, I threw my arms around his neck. "Oh, Daddy, I love it! It looks just like you." I held it to my heart.

Lefty roared with laughter. "So where's my gift?" he asked.

I shyly brought out the school project I had worked so hard on and hidden last night beneath a pillow on the sofa. It was my school picture, trimmed and glued onto a papier-mâché sun with red and orange glitter flames fanning out around it and a braided yellow yarn loop to hang it up.

I had never seen my father cry before. He was a tough man. Sometimes a violent man. My dad had been feared with good reason. Yet tears that I would always treasure twinkled like jewels in the corner of his eyes. "It's perfect," he said. "This is the best gift any dad could ask for." He wiped his eyes. "Time to stoke the fire and get us some breakfast. I love you, Sunny girl."

"I love you, Daddy. Merry Christmas."

❧ ✝ ☙

Grabbing the scissors from the end table, I attacked the teddy bear, repeatedly stabbing it in the back until a gaping wound allowed me to reach inside and pull out the small .22 caliber pistol that now lay in my hand like a troubled heart waiting for defibrillation.

Looking around, I stuffed a small flashlight into the waistband of my pants and blew out the lanterns, sending the oily scent of kerosene into the air. We were out of time. Moving back into the living room, I studied the area up near the gate. Deer don't hide behind trees, and neither do honest people. The old window rattled in protest as I raised it a few inches. Only six bullets. I knew I had to make each one count.

Taking careful aim, I waited. And waited. The metal was cold against my sweating palm. It had been a while since I'd shot a gun, but told myself that it was like riding a bicycle; I just needed to keep my balance, keep my head, and focus on where I wanted it to go.

The shadow darted from behind a distant Ponderosa, sprinting forward. I squeezed the trigger; the sound magnified in the little room, bouncing off the walls and causing Paige to cry out in fear. The shadow froze for a heartbeat and then stumbled forward through the snow, throwing itself behind a thick cedar. The odds of hitting my target in the failing light, through a curtain of snow at that distance with a little .22, were zilch. I could only hope to slow his progress and buy some time. Let him know that I was armed and dangerous.

"I can't do this." Paige gasped, falling back on the couch. "I'm going to die. I brought this on myself. It's him. It's my—my—eee . . . uhhh . . ."

Spotlighting Paige with the flashlight, she cried out with a deafening bellow of fierce determination as she curled her upper body, gripping a pillow between her hands while pushing her feet against the armrest. I saw with mounting horror a red stain blooming on the sheet beneath her.

So much blood.

I crept over and lifted the corner of her robe, and as I did, a tiny face emerged from Paige's body. Without a thought, I reached for the baby as it slid from a warm, safe world into a cold, dangerous one, right into my outstretched hands.

I had never seen anything born. Breathless, trembling with the awesomeness of the moment, I was torn between the exquisite freshness of new life and the utter terror of the threat lurking just outside. Worse still, I was terrified of accidentally killing the baby through ignorance.

Time stopped for a few beats—and then, it was as if a divine shot of adrenaline coursed through my body, jump-starting my heart once more. Letting go with one hand, I reached tentatively to touch the little wrinkled face—its first contact with the outside world—protesting, batting tiny fists furiously in the air. A feeble wail followed—as thin and fragile as a snowflake, but piercing enough to unleash an avalanche of events, sending out vibrations of new life—created life—life born with a purpose.

"Oh, Paige!" My voice shook as I set the baby on the sheet between her legs and reached for the scissors on the end table. Still shaking, I cut the end of my finger as I severed the umbilical cord, watching in amazement as blood from my finger dripped onto the baby's forehead, as if sealing our destiny.

"Paige… it's a . . ."

Paige laid silent, motionless, eyes closed, semiconscious. I thought she was dead. Quickly, I wrapped the infant in a towel and placed it next to her. I pressed my fingers to Paige's neck, silently cursing Chance. Alive, I thought, although I wouldn't know a weak pulse from a strong one. Chance was the one with EMT skills, not me.

Paige released a deep sigh of relief—the kind of sigh a laborer gives marking the end of a hard day—as the placenta slithered onto the sheet beneath her. Another gush of blood.

Too much blood. I knew "bad" when I saw it. No time. I simply wadded the extra towel and snugged it between her legs, pulled the robe down and blankets up, expecting the door to be kicked open at any moment.

"I'm sorry, Paige. It wasn't supposed to happen like this. I've got to go. It's me they want me, not you."

Paige cast about with her eyes as if searching for an answer, finally nodding. She whispered, "Take the baby."

"They don't want you or the baby." I assured her.

Precious seconds were slipping away.

Armed with the .22, I crept back through the living room, crouching below the window. Scanning the forest through the dim snow-lit night, I studied the scene with the instincts of a hunter until; at last, a movement caught my eye. I spotted the figure, who was dressed in black that was two shades darker than the encroaching twilight. He had continued his forward motion, closing half the distance from the bottom of the driveway to the cabin since I'd first spotted him. I had about two minutes left to make life-or-death decisions. Doing nothing was not an option. I pulled the trigger, firing a second shot.

Paige didn't scream this time, but the baby wailed. Pulling on my coat, I stuffed the flashlight in my pocket. Giving the gun to Paige, I kissed her on the forehead. "I'll bring back help. I promise. If anyone comes through that door, shoot him—and don't stop until you're out of bullets. You understand? You guys will be okay."

Paige's voice garnered strength as she did the unthinkable. Pressing the .22 to the side of her head, she snarled in fierce determination, "You will take my baby, or I will pull this trigger."

CHAPTER 25

෯ ✚ ෫

"Okay, okay. Don't do anything crazy. Put down the gun. For God's sake, put it down. Save the frickin' bullets for whoever is coming through that door."

I picked up the baby with trepidation. God, it's so little. A deep breath to steady myself, "I'll do it, but I'm not responsible," I said as I swaddled the mysterious creature within my fleece throw.

The kitchen door opened with hardly a sound as I stepped onto the raised porch and then dropped down. We fled through the orchard, where the last shades of twilight faded the snow to dingy lavender, plunging toward the dark purple shadows that pooled beneath the forest canopy. Past the bomb shelter and down past the Maidu grinding stones, into the steep dry wash that ran along the backside of the property—leaving a trail as plain as a freeway exit.

The baby whimpered softly from deep within the bundle as I loped, heading away from the paved road, into the woods and toward the safety of Joyce and Kenny's home. It was labor-intensive. Plowing my way through the half foot of snow was like trying to run through sand. I couldn't move fast enough.

Pop!

A single shot cracked the night.

Tripping, stumbling, catching myself, breathing hard, I turned to look back, uncertain, swiping my face with the back of my hand, then stumbled on to the end of the wash.

A branch snapped somewhere behind, cracking like a hot streak of lightning, splitting the muffled hush of the falling snow and sparking terror another degree. Veering sharply from the wash was a steep bank that led to the crest. Not far, but steep.

A deadly silence reigned, only broken by an occasional swish and thump of snow sliding from laden branches. Then a crunch. The sound propelled me forward as I struggled up the bank.

Freezing air tore at my lungs as the sting of sweat trickled into my eyes.

Constant praying, "Oh God, tell me I'm not smothering the baby, not killing the baby, not hurting the baby . . . please don't let the baby cry."

Almost there.

These were my woods, and I knew where I was. My playhouse wasn't far now. Launching over the top of the ridge, fiercely clutching the tiny bundle, I planted my butt in the snow, scooting and sliding down the steep embankment on the other side until coming to an abrupt stop against an ancient oak. Not just any old oak. This tree held a secret within its heart, a heart that had been slashed by lightning, burned by fire, and hollowed by time. The keeper of secrets—where Frito and I had played and whiled away many happy hours of imaginative fun—was now my refuge. My temple. I crawled inside the heart of the oak and prayed.

"Fuck!" A man's voice uttered a string of curses from above. Angry. Very angry. And close. So close. Probably deciding whether to pursue me down the steep incline or not.

I prayed between gasps of air, rocking back and forth, silently and mindlessly repeating "Oh God, oh God, oh God" in holy supplication. The child whimpered and struggled, but the tree kept our secret.

"Bitch! You fucking bitch." There was something final in his tone as if he had reached some kind of conclusion, followed by the soft crunch of footsteps that faded into the night.

I would have stayed inside the tree until daylight if not for Paige, if not for the baby. Instead, I waited until deeper shades of nightfall blanketed the woods.

Leaving the safety of the tree required what scant courage I had left, and then some. What courage I lacked, I faked, and it was enough to propel me from old oak's ancient womb. Paige would die if she didn't get help.

The baby renewed its whimpering from deep within the throw. Peeking in I saw the little shape move its head back and forth like a baby bird, reaching out for a mother that was not there. I empathized with the child, instinctively kissing its little head.

So warm and soft.

"You," I admonished, "are a pack of trouble."

Rewrapping the baby into a tighter bundle, pressing it close to my chest, I began the ascent, slipping, sliding, and crawling forward on hands and knees to the top. I dared not risk the flashlight. Darkness hid beneath the trees, but moonlight filtered through the clouds, casting a pale, diffused glow out in the open. I followed the ridge line that led to the backside of Joyce and Kenny's home.

A pair of black-and-tan hounds came out of the dark to announce my arrival. Kenny opened the door holding his hunting rifle, calling out in a gruff voice, "Who's there?"

"Kenny—it's me, Sunny. Help me."

True to his culture, my Native American friend never wasted time on useless questions. It was enough that I had arrived with a child in my arms, asking for help. There would be time for questions later.

"Come inside. Quickly."

I hurried indoors; fairly falling into Joyce's loving arms.

"Oh, Joyce." I sobbed, shaking with relief and clinging to her as if she were a life preserver before she gently pried the baby from my arms. "Her mother's at the cabin. I think she's dying. She's bleeding badly."

"There's a man with a gun out there somewhere. Logan's sent him for me."

Kenny turned to Joyce. "I'll get the chains on the truck. Get them ready," he said with a nod, and then vanished into the night.

Joyce took the baby to a chair near the wood stove. Setting the bundle down, she opened the package with her strong brown hands. "A girl," Joyce observed as she went about the business of cleaning the protesting child. "Tell me about the mother's condition."

I felt awkward and incompetent as I described the child's birth. My thoughts had been focused on the intruder more than the delivery. Wrapping the baby back in the blanket, Joyce handed her to me.

"Watch the baby, Sunny," said Joyce as she pulled on her boots.

Holding the baby, I rocked her back and forth in an attempt to comfort both of us. God forgive me. I could not help myself— holding the baby up to the light—searching for Chance's sky-blue eyes and Travis's sandy-colored hair. This felt wrong; shallow and calloused under the life-and-death circumstances of the moment, but continued to search for clues and signs—answers to the question I had long held in my heart.

The roar of Kenny's truck pulled me back into the world. All I found, all I could see, was a child with undeclared slate-blue eyes and mouse-colored hair, knowing that both would likely change over time. Joyce shouldered her way into a warm coat and hat. "Let's go," said Joyce, taking the baby.

Kenny opened the door to the truck and boosted me in. Joyce handed the baby up and climbed in next to me. Kenny got in the driver's seat, and the old truck groaned as he put it in gear.

"Leave me at the top of Sunny's road," Joyce said to Kenny. "I'll take the baby and go down and tend to the mother. You and Sunny go get help."

"No—you can't," I cut in. "Paige has my gun. I told her to shoot the next person that comes through the door. She . . . she isn't thinking straight. She put the gun to her head and said she would shoot herself if I didn't take the baby with me."

Joyce frowned as we bounced and lurched along the road. "Keep the baby then and go to someone's house and call for help. I'll try to help the mother."

Kenny nodded. Minutes later we stopped at the top of the driveway to the cabin. There were tracks; a vehicle with chains had come in, turned around at the top, and left, heading back toward the pavement. Kenny reached behind me to place a hand on Joyce's shoulder. Their eyes met and lingered as they exchanged volumes of unspoken words and unexpressed emotion. Joyce gave a reassuring smile as she gazed into his eyes. "I'll be careful. You be careful too. Hurry." I gave Joyce my flashlight, and she climbed out of the truck. The light bobbed from side to side as she strode down the driveway, finally fading into the distance.

Putting the truck into gear, we drove away into the night. Kenny pulled his rifle from the rack behind my head and cradled it in his arms. An angel must have whispered a warning because I turned to Kenny and said, "Turn off your lights." Kenny killed the lights; moonlight was enough. He slowed his speed to a quiet crawl, inching forward until our tires finally touched the pavement of Lumpkin Road. I looked over my shoulder out the side window. Down there. I could barely make it out—parked to one side of the pavement, a dark-colored SUV with a single person sitting inside. Waiting.

Kenny saw it too, and we nodded to each other in silent acknowledgment. He patted my leg and gave a confident squeeze. "We must take to the mountains while there is still time. If we hurry, we can make it to La Porte."

I looked at him in astonishment. "We can't do that. It's snowing. The road will be closed."

"Not yet. Not if we hurry."

"But he'll see us."

"No, he won't." Kenny put the truck in Reverse, backing up a hundred yards before turning sharply off the road onto an old path, my old shortcut that ran along the apple orchard behind the school. The trail came out near the playground, far above the assailant's line of sight.

"What about Joyce and Paige?"

"My wife is wise," said Kenny. "Your friend is in good hands." He nodded in conclusion. "We cannot get past this hit man. We will go around him. There will be help in La Porte."

I had looked to Kenny for help, and now I needed to trust him in spite of my doubt. He was older and wiser and had saved me many times from Logan's wrath. I needed to trust someone, and I wasn't ready to trust myself. We stopped at the end of the trail and looked both ways, up the road and down. Both felt like certain death. Clutching the baby, I took a sharp intake of breath as Kenny pulled out and turned the truck uphill.

The front tires bumped along; the chains on back tires chattered on the pavement. Less than a mile above town the pavement would end and branch off into a network of dirt roads through the high country. Tonight, the roads would be a white maze. The glare of the headlights reflected off the snow, bouncing into our eyes as we drove.

God, I hope he knows what he's doing.

CHAPTER 26

The road was defined by a velvety flatness bordered on either side—a berm of snow on the downslope, and a steep incline on the other. Ghostly trees bent beneath the weight of fresh snow and seemed to reach out, stretching their arms as if to snatch us from the road. On a sunlit morning, the landscape might have resembled a Norman Rockwell Christmas card. Tonight it was reminiscent of Dickens's Specter of Death.

Kenny has always been like a father to me, but this night I wanted my daddy, I wanted my husband, I wanted Travis to show up with the cavalry. I wanted to be home with my dog, drinking hot chocolate and sitting next to a Christmas tree. This is the last place on earth I wanted to be.

The road wound on and on, climbing higher and higher with every turn. I felt the baby moving and wriggling in my arms and heard her fragile cry for her mother. I commiserated with her, wanting my mother too, when the truck suddenly fishtailed to a stop in front of a fallen tree.

"Crap." Once again, true to his heritage, Kenny summarized the situation in one word.

"What now?" I looked to Kenny for answers, hoping he would say "go back."

Kenny sat in silence and then said, "We turn around." He nosed the truck, first right and forward up the slope, then rolling back as he cranked the wheel to the left, repeating the maneuver on the narrow road three times—back and forth, back and forth. The third time, the truck slid, and the front tires groped for the road, and the truck shimmied for a moment as if surprised by the change, as the rear wheels spun freely in the air.

We slid—backward—angling downward. Then the sickening realization washed over me—of slipping off the road, plunging and bucking downhill to the tortured sound of shrieking metal as we plummeted, ripping and tearing through the foliage. Our piercing screams of fear amplified, sucking the oxygen from the cab as we continued to fall back and down for an eternity; ending at last with a resounding crunch as we slammed abruptly and upended, with the tailgate wrapped around a tree.

Perfect silence followed, except for the thrum of the engine, the beating of hearts, and heavy breathing. We reclined in the front seat, staring out over the hood with the headlights illuminating the slope and road high above.

"Are you okay?" Kenny croaked, his voice tight.

"Yeah." My voice broke, quavering with fright. "You?"

"Not so good." He gave a little gasp. "My back . . . I think. . . something is broken." He paused. "The baby?" he asked.

The baby was crying plaintively from within the blanketed bundle that I still clutched to my chest. Pulling back a corner of her blanket, I peered inside at the squalling baby. I didn't know what to look for. "Hey, kid. You okay?" She wailed louder, sounding more angry than hurt. "Yeah, she says she's okay. At least I hope she's okay. What should I do?"

"Don't move. Stay warm and still, and let me think." The engine was still running and the heater working. "See if you can open your window a little."

We sat for what felt like hours. The baby quieted down. Puffs of snow continued to fall, blotting the view as they stuck, accumulating on the windshield and shutting out the sky as if a gravedigger were burying us alive. Kenny turned off the headlights. His breathing was ragged, the sound punctuated by an occasional gasp. And then, the motor died.

"Kenny?" I called out in fear.

"Sunny," Kenny said, his soothing voice firm, as if he had reached a decision. "It will be light soon. The hunter will find us. You must take the baby and go."

His words were more frightening than the accident had been. "I'm not leaving you. I'll never leave you. You would never leave me."

"Come close," said Kenny, and I responded, unbuckling the seat belt and carefully sliding next to him, curling beneath the shelter of his arm.

"I remember when you were just a little fox—a wild, shy thing that would hide behind the trees on the road to our houses."

I gave a little laugh. "I know. My dad always told me to hide from strangers, although you and Joyce weren't exactly strangers."

"And then you became a woman. Our children moved away, and some moved on to the Great Journey in their afterlife." Kenny groaned and drew us close as I shivered. "Like a daughter, you have been to me. You brightened our old age with your youth and your pregnancy."

His unexpected words twisted like a knife in my gut. Why would Kenny talk now, of all times, about the most painful moment of my life? I didn't want to think about Logan or my pregnancy, or how he had pushed me from the upper deck, killing our unborn child.

"You were a gift," Kenny continued, "just as this little one is a gift to you. Children don't always come from our bodies. Sometimes they are a gift from God. I have loved you like a daughter"—he paused to catch his breath—"and now, you have a daughter of your own."

I wrinkled my nose unconsciously. "This isn't my daughter. She belongs to another woman."

"She belongs to whoever has her in their care."

Kenny hugged us both. The night was as silent as death, broken only by Kenny, who softly chanted one of his native songs.

"What are you singing . . . Father?" I asked, returning his love.

"I am going home, Sunny. And you will cross the mountains in the morning, taking your daughter with you."

"No. I can't. I won't. I don't want to."

"Nonsense. You are not a child anymore. You're a woman. We're not that far from La Porte, and there is only death behind us. You can send for help." He gave me another reassuring hug. "Sleep now. I will wake you with the first light."

I was cold—bone-chilling, bone-aching cold. In spite of my chattering teeth, I unzipped my coat to tuck the bundled baby closer to my body. I wondered if she would live. I wondered if I would care. I was so cold. All I wanted was to be warm. To feel safe. To go home.

It was Christmas morning. My eyes fluttered. Most Christmases brought back happy childhood memories. But there had been a couple of Christmas days that were bad. Really bad. And I feared that today was going to be another one.

℘ ☿ ℧

Blaming my mother was easy. She was not a nice person. In spite of her lifelong quest for peace and love, she'd had little of either.

 Few people understood how I, an advocate and expert witness on felony domestic cases, could possibly have loved my father—a man who sometimes beat my flower-child mother.

 It was Christmas vacation, so-called before the school system robbed the holiday of its true intent, and the snow had fallen nonstop, much like today. Every few years a big storm would roll in and park on top of the cabin, dumping a couple of feet of snow that would last for weeks.

 That was the Christmas of the big one. My socks were wet. My toes blue with cold. Pajamas from Second Time Around thrift store were thin and short, barely containing my seven-year-old body. I shivered—hard enough to make the butterflies on my pajamas take flight as I pounded on the door, hugging Frito who had been tossed out behind me.

 "It's your dog. If you can't take care of him inside, you can both go outside where you belong. You can come back in when you say you're sorry," Starla yelled from the other side of the door.

 "I'm sorry. We're sorry. It will never happen again. Mama, please. We'll be good. Don't leave me out here." My tears left tracks as cold as a pair of ice skates sketched across the face of a winter pond.

 Frito had crapped behind the wood stacked next to the heater, hoping to stay warm and that no one would catch him. But Starla found it. She always did. And now we were freezing our butts off.

 Hours passed while we sheltered in the Japanese bathhouse. That was before my dad put in the hot water tank and the claw foot bathtub. It was more of a hippy bathhouse back then, located about fifty yards from the cabin. It was freezing out there. If you wanted a hot bath, you had to build a fire under the redwood tub. I had tried to start a fire, but the only thing that ignited was the entire matchbook. I tried clutching a snowball to cool my scorched fingers, but they still hurt.

The only thing colder than that Christmas Eve was my mother's heart. Frito and I repeatedly beat a path from the bathhouse to the cabin door to beg and plead for forgiveness from Queen Mother. All in vain. It was a safe bet that she was either passed out on Valium or tripping on "shrooms."

Santa never found our cabin that year, but Lefty did. In spite of the icy roads, my dad arrived from Oakland in the van, slip-sliding down the driveway. Headlights swept across us as he swooshed to a stop, the door cracking with cold when he popped it open.

"Sunny," Lefty called. It wasn't a question but more like a statement of disbelief. "What the f—" He scooped me up in his big strong arms, his beard brushing my icy cheeks as he covered them with kisses, holding me tight and rubbing my back to warm me. He had been drinking.

Lefty didn't bother with a key. He just leaned back and kicked the door open with his heavy boots, cracking the door frame, sending splinters flying.

Starla fled upstairs.

After wrapping me in his Hell's Angels coat, Lefty paused to add wood to the heater. Then he turned his attention upstairs. I clung to Frito. Music drifted down from the radio upstairs. Credence Clearwater wasn't the only one who saw a "Bad Moon Rising" that night. Frito trembled in my arms as I sang along to the sound of my mother's screams.

හ ✞ ଓ

"Wake up, little fox." Kenny had somehow taken off his coat and removed his shoes and socks. He took the baby and added his jacket over the blanket. Then, in spite of my protests, he had me help him replace his shoes, then put his socks over my hands. The effort left him exhausted, visibly sweating and shaking. "It's time for you to go."

"I can't leave you." Tears welled up. "You'll freeze."

"I have everything I need," said Kenny, patting the rifle in his lap. The muscles in his face tightened with pain as he spoke. His breathing was labored, his words forced. "Your tracker is coming. You must hurry. Don't go back uphill. Go down first . . . cut along the hillside . . . then go up. He must think you're . . . still in the truck. You know the way. Now—obey me . . . like a good daughter. No more words. Go. Now. The Holy Spirit . . . will guide you."

The old truck shuddered with each bone-jarring shove of my shoulder before the door gave way. First a crack, then a small wedge, and finally daylight and powdered snow spilled in as the door broke free from its icy grip. More powder loosened and slid down the hill with a whoosh and a thump and a cracking noise on the brush beneath the vertical truck. I looked down through the wedge. No earth below—only a smile of daylight for a footstool, grinning like a hungry animal waiting for its breakfast. I swallowed, guessing that the nearest branch was a full body length away, with no certainty that it would hold my weight.

I looked back at Kenny, who gave me a wordless nod and set the baby on the seat.

"I'll send help. I promise." Rolling onto my stomach, I slid feet first across the seat and out the door. Halfway out, I tucked the bundle under one arm. "I love you," I said to Kenny, and slid free from the truck.

The branch I aimed for bent beneath our weight and gave way. The baby howled, and smaller branches slapped my face as we fell through, hitting the ground and tumbling down the hill. When we finally stopped, I was looking up, staring at the tailpipe of the truck.

"Don't fall. Don't fall." Turning to the baby. "Shhh. Hey— you're okay, right? Shhh-shhh." There was nothing to do but follow Kenny's directions; cutting across the bottom of the hill and then the long climb back to the road on hands and knees, emerging above the truck and far up the road.

I sat on the road, gasping, sweating, scared. How could I be so exhausted before starting this impossible journey? The road home beckoned.

The first fingers of sunlight slanted down, poking between the trees, followed by another whoosh and whump that signaled a reminder that I had a predator on my heels. There was no turning back. The way home was blocked in every way.

Hitching the baby higher in my arms, I turned to face the mountains, and then took the first step up the road that carved its way through the heart of the forest.

CHAPTER 27

ℰᴼ ⊕ ᴼℛ

I walked and sang to comfort myself. Mostly I sang Christian rock—not to drown out external chaos but to lift me and strengthen me from the inside. Today cried out for sturdier, more traditional music, like "A Closer Walk with Thee," and "Blessed Assurance." The tunes began as a wordless hum and faded to a whisper. Today my songs were muffled beneath the weight of responsibility, and yet somehow infused me with the courage to take another step.

I felt the presence of Kenny walking with me, and occasionally I felt the presence of my dad. "Keep going, little fox! Toughen up, baby girl!" They seemed to whisper in my ear above the rush and bluster of the icy wind. I was trying to be a good daughter but found myself doubting the wisdom of my surrogate father. It was crazy to think that I could cross the Sierra Nevadas with a newborn infant at the onset of winter, just miles from where the Donner Party had once faced the same elements—and ended up snowbound and cannibalizing one another to stay alive. It was ludicrous when I thought about it.

And the Donner party had guns and horses, oxen and a wagon. I have . . . I took a breath and took a step.

A resounding boom echoed up the slopes, and my thoughts froze in their tracks, sweat turning to ice as I turned to look back, shivering. Something was wrong. Terribly wrong. I couldn't see it, but I had heard it, signaling a new level of danger.

Fear mingled with billowing plumes of air as I struggled to catch my breath, my eyes darting about like a rabbit that senses the presence of a predator it cannot see. There was no choice, no grand decision, just a turning back to the road before me and taking another step. And another. And another.

Precious rays of sunlight were stolen by new waves of clouds that flew overhead on the wings of the wind. The sky steadily darkened as the wind dropped, kicking and tossing the fallen snow high into the air, then falling back to earth in swirling whirlwinds that shadow danced across the road. Icy crystals built up, sticking to the jacket I had pulled it over my nose, now white and crisp as a surgeon's mask. I cursed the storm and welcomed it, stumbling on as my feet broke through the top crust, sinking into the powder. Every step felt like two.

To stop was to die. The baby had not moved or cried since leaving Kenny, and I shuddered to think I might be carrying a corpse. The thought strengthened my determination, yet I dared not open her blanket for fear of losing heat—or finding none. Better not to know.

Familiar with the ways of nature, I was sure I could survive if not for the heavy burden in my arms. The responsibility weighed me down as much as the effort. Snow quenched my thirst, but my stomach growled for food to fuel my dwindling energy. My legs ached, my back ached, my head ached. God knew, my heart ached too. Blowing powder felt like needles, pricking and stinging, burning the skin around my eyes—not so with my fingers and toes, which were already numb.

My bones cried out. My voice cried out. When my body was too weary to take another step, the promise of safety kept me moving. Somewhere ahead is a person and a phone. Visions of saving Kenny and Paige, a roaring fire, and a hot meal kept me plodding along, one shaky step after another, until the last one that launched me face down into the snow. Muscles burning, legs throbbing, I rolled over and stretched out like a snow angel, when I saw it—a shadow among shadows gliding along the ridge.

There were only three things I feared in the mountains—from smallest to largest: black widows, rattlesnakes, and mountain lions. Black widows predictably hid in dark places. Rattlers usually gave warning. But now, bogged down in the snow, spent, I felt like a rib eye steak being eyed by a hungry lion. Today, at least, I was too tired and too angry to be afraid—or perhaps, I had nothing left to lose. Either way, I wasn't going down without a fight or at least without having the last word.

"Hey, Lord. Here I am." I breathed a hasty prayer before rolling the silent bundle off my chest and onto a drift. Standing tall,

I removed my coat and surveyed the hill. Moments later, a flash of gold crouched down. Pure adrenaline, possibly the most ancient and powerful drug in human history, coursed through my body like a hotshot. My body became a living arsenal.

Holding tight to one sleeve, I slung the coat like David's sling that took down Goliath, whipping it about in wild gyrations and screaming a warning in a performance that would have made my mother proud.

"Fuck you!" I screamed. "You can't have me! Get out of here! Go on—git. You come near me I will beat the crap out of you. You hear? I. Will. Eat. You!"

Where did that come from? I had no idea. But I liked to imagine it was the Holy Spirit, if God sanctions such language. The big cat hesitated, studied me a little longer; ears up, head shifting side to side, and then retreated.

I could have slept. It was the post-adrenaline crash. I could have lain down and taken the Big One right then and there—if not for fear of being back on the takeout menu for the Road Kill Café. The cat wasn't likely to permanently abandon such a promising meal.

A reassuring squall came from within the bundle, and this time I tunneled through the blanket and peeked inside to a red, wrinkled howling face and a smell that only a mother could love. "Oh, baby, you stink. I'm sorry. We're almost there. If your mom's not dead . . . I'll kill her myself."

Who is that stranger talking in my head?

A different person seemed to inhabit my body. Where was the compassionate advocate that rescued people for a living? What happened to the woman who esteemed the noble salmon that ran upriver to die in the name of self-sacrifice? Had she died in the truck with Kenny? Had she been consumed by rage toward Paige, Travis, and Chance? Irrational as it seemed, the blame fell on them. Gone was my sense of Christian forgiveness. Maybe it had chilled along with my fingers and toes. I had no answers—only anger, resentment, and bitterness to power me up the hill. Which it did, with the wind shrieking curses as I went. I guessed self-sacrifice implied that you had something left to give . . . and I was running on fumes. My emotional fumes were probably as foul in the nostrils of God as the smell that exuded from the baby's blanket. What a pair we made, this child and I.

With that thought, I picked up the child, bundled her in Kenny's coat, and took another step. And then another. Sometime during the day, the wind had died down, and the snow showers stopped. Clouds broke just enough for the sun to slice through with a blinding light that alternated with dark shadows, painting the forest in stark shades of black and white. Tree boughs seemed to hold their breath beneath their burden of fresh snow.

It was late afternoon when we finally crested yet another bend in the road to emerge above Little Grass Valley Lake. This had been the first major snow of the season, and the storm left a silvery strand of slush that blended into the sparkling blue water. The scene was worthy of a postcard, but today its beauty eluded me.

Hope blossomed with arrival at the lake. Only a couple miles to the south lay the tiny mountain community of La Porte. Thirty miles and a couple of snowcapped peaks north lay the larger town of Quincy.

I turned south. "We made it." Words broke the stillness with the clarity of glass shattering on tile. Words that hung in the air, only to be swallowed by a greater sound—the faint, distant sound of an engine, a baritone bellowing through the forest.

"Thank God."

Maybe it was absurd, giving thanks while still trapped in the wilderness, but my circumstances were the result of my decisions, not God's, and the sound that blessed my ears was like a miracle. It was a truck with chains, or perhaps a snow cat.

Rescue was on the way!

The Bible says the joy of the Lord is my strength, and it must have been so because I plunged on toward La Porte and the sound of safety. Even as despair had drained my energy, joy now fueled my steps. "We're going to make it, little girl," I exclaimed to the infant, laughing and jogging my way down the road. "We're really going to make it."

From out of the shrubs, a small rabbit bolted at the commotion, racing first to the left and then abruptly doubling back, darting to the right in a wild frenzy of flight. A small gray fox popped up from the shadows to give chase. It didn't take long. Within seconds the shrill death cries that erupted from the rabbit were cut short, sharp as a knife, ending in silence. I froze, horrified. The fox rose from its kill, the rabbit dangling from his jaws, poinsettia-red blood dripping across alabaster snow. The fox considered me with a piercing gaze. Then turning, he took the rabbit and trotted away into the forest.

The sound of the vehicle had reached the campground below. I paused to consider the dark-blue Jeep that rattled along to the sound of chains whirring and chattering until it pulled into the parking lot next to the lake and turned off its engine. The Jeep door swung open, and a pale, long-legged man got out, his skin and hair around his face as white as sunlit snow against his black clothing.

It was the fox and plight of the rabbit that caused me to reconsider and exercise caution when I might have run, waving my arms and shouting for joy. So I waited and watched.

Leaning back against the Jeep, the man pulled a pack of cigarettes from his pocket, shook out a smoke, and threw the empty wrapper on the ground. Fishing around for a lighter, he lit up, drew deeply, and exhaled as he scanned the area from horizon to horizon, cigarette smoke mingling with his breath in the frigid air.

This was no nature lover or sportsman taking in the view. Neither was he a rescue worker driving a service vehicle. More than his casual disregard for the environment was his clothing. Black on black—cap, sunglasses, pants, and leather coat—he looked like every biker I had ever known. He couldn't see me, but I was certain if he listened, he would hear the hammering of my heart.

Ducking down and moving back onto the trail, I turned, contemplating the possibility of making it to the town of Quincy. La Porte was no longer safe.

Baptist Camp. Maybe I can make it before dark.

It was highly unlikely that this guy, whoever he was, had ever heard of Baptist Camp.

Baptist Camp was a private retreat high up in the mountains, not far from where we were. Summer invited young people to the camp to meditate, hike, pray, and generally enjoy God's creation. Winter ensured the return of the annual bear fest. Local residents laughed at the church administrators who continued to stock the camp with canned goods every fall, knowing that the bears would return to break down the doors, pop open the cans, and party hearty every winter.

CHAPTER 28

🙰 ☩ ☙

The sun dipped behind the mountains, slathering them in shades of gray that reflected my spirit. Deathly gray. Ash gray. Faded gray. Gunmetal gray.

Yeah, I feel like all that. And lead. Don't forget: lead gray.

The steps in front of Baptist Camp required superhuman effort. Or die . . . It was so tempting to just collapse on the bottom step and die . . . or not.

I can do this . . . since the door is open.

There was no need to break into the lodge. The bears hadn't wasted any time. Snow fell weeks ago in the high country, and the bears had kindly opened the door for me, snapping the dead bolt, breaking the chain, and ripping a large chunk of the frame from the front door as if the sturdy structure were little more than a child's playhouse. A couple of shuttered cabins stood off to one side of the building, chained and padlocked—as secure as Fort Knox. Behind the great house stood a solitary weary-looking outhouse that I doubted either owner had secured or bears cared to disturb.

The lodge was a humble weathered building with a steep shake roof, and a wraparound deck that might have been quaint and picturesque if not for the damage. Working my way through the wreckage, careful not to impale myself on the jagged spears of wood that protruded from the door frame, I stepped inside.

The room appeared to be a huge conference room—large, cold and bare—and probably doubled as a dining room from the looks of a couple of large hand trucks stacked with folding tables and dozens of folding metal chairs. My eyes swept the room. The furnishings were simple but elegant. A far corner showcased a sturdy wooden roll-top desk with an oversized leather-bound Bible on top. The opposite corner entertained a worn black piano, graced by an Aladdin kerosene lamp with a pale green shade with a ring of pink roses painted in a circlet around the middle. Standing next to the piano, reminding me of a whiskered and weathered miner with his thumbs in his jeans, was a tall, lanky-legged wood heater that had probably been around since the gold rush. And on the wall behind the heater, Thank you, Jesus, hung another antique: a pair of heavy-duty wooden cross-country skis.

The air had a bite; the sharp tang of fermented garbage emanating from where I guessed was the kitchen, back behind the wall with a door and a sliding panel to a service bar.

The only sound was my breathing—breaths that came out in frosty plumes that hung in the air, then slowly dissipated. Hours had passed since the baby had last moved. Her pitiful cries had leeched at my reserves and drained my strength. Later, her cries had dwindled to whimpers, and finally silence. Or perhaps I had blocked them out.

The Bible says there is a time to every season, and this sure as heck wasn't the time or season for compassion and pity—emotional shackles that would have brought me to a halt. Perhaps I had abandoned compassion on the trail along with other emotional baggage, like fear and worry—the antitheses of faith and hope. They were all a waste of energy. It was rage and resentment that had fueled every step and kept the engine turning. Some people caught a second wind, and I was on my sixth or seventh.

If she is sleeping, there is no sense in waking her, I thought. If she is dead . . . well, I would think about that later.

If I die, we both die. Right now, I just needed to survive.

Setting one burden down, I picked up another. I needed wood. Within minutes I was at work, ripping pages from the Bible on top of the wooden desk and piling kindling from the shattered doorjamb into the woodstove. Staggering to the side of the porch, I found a woodpile, picked up an armload, and made the long trek back inside.

Next, the kitchen.

The kitchen was chaos—as if a gang of riotous looters had torn through the place, smashing cans and vandalizing everything in sight. Cupboard doors were ripped from their hinges, drawers pulled out, silverware, pots, and pans flung about the room. The bears had opened the pantry and squeezed cans of food between their huge paws, then punctured and gnawed them open with razor-sharp teeth, glutting and slobbering, leaving splashes of bright red spaghetti sauce and chunks of canned fruit tossed about as if creating a macabre form of art.

For all the mess, the bears hadn't destroyed everything. The back door looked solid, the chain and padlock secure. There was still food and more: cans of milk and beans, boxes of institutional food, jars of peanut butter, condiments, and . . . matches.

After building a fire, I returned to the kitchen to find some towels and dishcloths, a couple of small pots, and a turkey baster. Milk went into one pot, and I filled the other with snow. I set them on the wood heater and hurried over to the silent bundle. Peeling back the layers of Kenny's coat and my fleece blanket, I peered down at the silent infant burrowed deep within her sour-smelling cocoon.

"Baby? Hey there—are you still with me? Hey. Don't be checking out on me . . . Don't leave me alone. I . . . I need you," I pleaded. The struggle was over for the moment. I lay down my weapons. I didn't have to be strong. Warm tears slid across cold skin as I massaged her back with an aching heart. She was so small. So fragile. No movement, and then—a soft mewing, a weak nuzzle.

Who knew what possessed me. What force, other than God, could have moved me to lift my shirt and hold a dying child to my breast? It felt surreal, yet perfectly natural. Shock rippled through my body as her warm, soft skin touched mine—tiny fingers grabbing at my nipple, rosebud lips eagerly grasping the tip of the baster, then batting at the hard plastic fraud in frustration. I almost drowned her by squeezing the bulb too hard, and then . . . we had it. Rhythm. Hope. Rhythm and hope, she sucked and sucked.

Curled next to the heater that gave off more smoke than heat, the realization hit me again—today was Christmas Day—and I responded appropriately by crooning "Away in a Manger" as best I could, voice faltering, breaking, my tears seeming to harmonize in a chorus of emotion. It was the perfect song for our plight; a traditional song about the harsh circumstances surrounding the birth of Jesus, who had also been homeless and short on provisions. And like Christ, this little one had no crib.

"At least Jesus had a mom and stepdad," I said. And then it came to me in my spirit that God was her father and I was her stepmother, and maybe, perhaps, everything would be okay.

When milk began to dribble from the sides of her infant's mouth, I cleaned her up using a kitchen towel dipped in warm water and took a couple more to use later as diapers. Rewrapping her, I did the pat-on-the-back-burp-thing that all women seemed to know, and rocked her in my aching arms until she slept.

My turn. When I was done heating and eating, I packed a few necessities: more milk, the baster, a box of matches, and a couple of cans of food. Everything was rolled into the dishtowels and stuffed into a plastic trash bag. After adding some wood to the fire, I lay down, utterly spent. Using the bag for a pillow, I huddled next to Paige's baby beneath the blessing of Kenny's coat.

Only then did I laugh in derision at the irony of life as I hugged the sleeping child.

I can't believe I just breastfed you your first meal.

Who would have thought?

 හ ⚕ ඥ

Bump! The building shuddered. Wide awake, I leaped to my feet and snatched the baby in an all-in-one motion.

Thump! The sound of scrabbling and a sharp crack followed. The remains of the broken door went flying.

Baby in one hand, a bag of food in the other, I shoved them both under the desk.

I had not been idle, and I was not unprepared. The kerosene lamp was lit, the bag of food was ready to go, and I had managed to wheel the carts full of furniture in front of the broken door before falling asleep. After all I had been through, I planned on making it through the night.

A snuffling and a whuff.

There was just enough light to make out an enormous bear pushing its way through the door and into the building, casting and splashing massive shadows across the walls as it rocked back and forth.

Don't panic! I knew what I needed to do. No screaming, no crying, no throwing up, no messing my pants, and definitely no running. Deep breath. Look big. This was always the hard part. It required courage that I didn't really have. I would have to fake it.

I could do that.

Standing tall, I grabbed the two large pans I had taken from the kitchen and banged them together over my head, percussion instruments on my field of war, followed by a battle cry comprising of a series of four-letter words. The rule is not to make eye contact, but there was no way in hell I was taking my eyes off that bear.

The beast roared, and the heart-stopping sound boomed and echoed throughout the empty room. I had a few words for Ranger Rick—and none of them were kind. I was going to die.

Not without a fight.

I raced to open the heater and fell to my knees, covering my ears at the deafening reverberations and agonizing scream of twisting metal that rent the air. The room rocked with the clamor of cascading tables and flying chairs as the bear gained purchase.

I was ready, if not steady. Two logs the size and shape of baseball bats were waiting near the heater, their ends wrapped in towels and soaked with kerosene. Yanking wide the door to the wood stove, I thrust them into the fire. The bear broke free of the wreckage as the firebrands caught and burst into flames.

Wheeling around, I froze, and not from cold this time. Instinctively letting go of one brand, I gripped the other, drawing back like a batter and hitting a line drive into the bear's face that made him pull back with a squall. Rearing up, the bear cut loose with a savage growl. I roared. Nothing heroic—purely reactive, repeating swings and jabs that continued to drive the bear back toward the door. Canines popped from his jaws—three-inch daggers whose blades dripped saliva. Shadows on the wall multiplied, looking like a dozen bears gyrating erratically in an insane shadow dance.

A whoosh of claws blew past, pushing me back, the tips slicing as neatly as prongs on a pitchfork down the side of my face. I fell back on a metal chair that folded and snapped like teeth on a steel trap around my leg. The room tipped sideways as I twisted and fell. The remaining burning brand skittered across the hardwood floor. The bear moved in, and I could feel the heat of his breath as he took another swipe, this one to the shoulder, knocking me deeper into the tangled wreckage of furniture.

What a crazy way to die.

The room fairly trembled with the roar that followed. Not rage, not anger, but agony—or a blend of all three—that made me cover my head with my arms and wait for death.

Smells churned in the air; the torrid smell of burning wood, burning fur, and burning flesh. The building shuddered again with another roar as the pain-crazed bear charged out the door.

The world was on fire.

ဢ ♀ ၛ

A massive crack shook the building—followed by a thunderous whump as the roof collapsed and a whoosh of air was sucked from the building and hurled into the sky, the oxygen in the air feeding hungry flames that climbed up the walls to feast on the remains of the roof. Sparks filled the air, violently propelling themselves upward like whirling dervishes of flaming dust moats.

Natural instincts screamed, every cell demanding that I save myself, run, follow the bear out the door. We would both die if I tried to cross the room to the baby—the baby that had brought all this on me. In a world where women disposed of unwanted babies like so much trash, it was the ultimate irony that I should risk my life to save this child that I hated. No time to philosophize or rationalize, only the decision to act.

Stooping as I plunged ahead, I fought my way through the carnage to the baby and bag of supplies. Fire dripped down the walls like melted candle wax igniting the skis over the fireplace. Mounted on pegs, the skis were an easy grab—the tip of one burst into flames. Tucking the baby under my arm like a football, clutching the food bag in the same hand, skis, clunky and awkward tucked under the other arm, I scrambled back through the tangle of the wreckage for the door. The baby blanket was burning as we squeezed through, plunging, tripping, falling down the stairs and onto the snow.

Snow. On my knees, I frantically rolled the bundled baby, the blanket hissing, smoking, stinking as I rubbed snow into the smoldering remnant until at last the last ember was extinguished.

I sat in the snow. Sat there, hugging the baby, rocking and crying, as the building continued to burn. Outside was bitter cold. Icy gusts of wind tossed the blanket around us, sending it flapping like a stranded sailor signaling a ship. The stars above looked like crushed ice sailing across a blue galaxy as I searched the heavens, sitting and searching for the constellations that my father had taught me.

 conoco

The stars always seem brightest in the winter, and Lefty loved the stars, even as he had loved me. Coming down from the hills after a joyous day spent plodding up hills and then sliding down in the sled he had given me for Christmas, my father pulled off the road, wrapped me in a warm blanket, and set me on the hood of our old pickup truck. We shared cold cheese sandwiches and a hot thermos of coffee. My dad never worried about little things, like giving coffee to a kid. He probably figured there were worse addictions, and he was right, although those sweet memories were probably stirred into my lifelong passion for the brew.

Proud of his knowledge, Lefty hugged me and laughed as he pointed out the various constellations. "That one there—the one with five points pointing to the Milky Way? That is called Cannabis Sativa. It looks just like a giant pot leaf, doesn't it? And those two bright ones over there, off the tip of that tall Ponderosa. Yeah, those. That's the Harley sign. The two stars are the wheels, and the three in a row just above them—those are the handlebars." I laughed and shivered, and he gave me a squeeze. "Look over there, baby girl. That red star with the three crooked ones at the bottom? That's the one-eyed Chihuahua constellation called Frito Trublito." I laughed so hard that I rolled back, deep into my father's arms, and stared straight up into the heavens above.

"Daddy," I asked, pointing. "What's that one?"

Lefty paused for a moment, as he always did when he grew serious. "I call that one the God star."

I frowned, puzzled. I didn't think my father believed in God. "What is the God star?" I asked.

Lefty sighed wistfully. "It's the one that never changes."

conoco

It looked like a blood moon, the way the smoke painted it red as it roiled through the night sky, softly lighting the scene with a morbid kind of beauty, as though it were a campfire for friends to gather around instead of a source of hopeless destruction.

Paige's child continued to cry, and for a time I joined in. She was alive and okay, except that part of her arm had burned where the blanket had caught fire. Reaching up, I cupped my face that also burned, but mine burned from the lash of the bear's claw. We were hurting, inside and out.

There was nothing to do but hug the last shivering flames and wait as night slowly crept toward dawn. I shook with anger—anger at the men who might have fathered this child, anger at Paige for forcing her responsibility on me, anger with Kenny for sending me into the mountains.

Angry, angry, angry.

Overwhelmed, I lamented into the night, "Hey, God—where the hell are you?"

But I was like Elijah in the Bible, who looked for God in the storm and in the earthquake and in the fire and did not find him.

God was not in the fire—not even when the propane tank exploded. Not in the freezing snow that numbed my hands and feet. And not in the moon that seemed to bleed for the tragedy playing out below. God was finally found by Elijah, and by me, and would always be found by the seeker in that still small voice within the human heart.

I am here. I will never leave you or forsake you. God seemed to speak to my spirit. Or maybe I had just memorized that verse and was now regurgitating it like so much undigested soul food.

"Yeah, God? Well, then, do something! How about a rescue, huh? How about a roof over our head or a set of bolt cutters to get into the other buildings?" I fingered the ski with the charred tip with hurt and anger. No longer a ski, it was just a burnt board with a clamp. "How about a whole ski, God? Is that too much to ask for?" A new wave of tears rose and fell. The egregious kind of tears born of betrayal that well up and issue from a broken heart. One would think that I should have been used to it by now.

A washboard of pale-pink clouds rippled across the sky. Sunrise found me digging through the smoldering rubble, hoping to find something useful—like a cell phone, or a flare gun, or a snowmobile—but none of those things appeared. Just a tiny flutter of white in an ocean of black that happened to catch my eye. Picking it up and blowing off the ash, I discovered a fragment from a page in a Bible. Only a couple of uncharred inches were readable, but the message was clear. "We went through fire and through water, yet you brought us out into a place of abundance."

Sure you did. Real freaking abundant. Bitterness was so strong; I could taste it in my mouth. I wadded the page and threw it across the snow, where it bounced and rolled, coming to rest against a piece of blackened stovepipe—a bent section of pipe designed to join two straight pieces when the woodstove and the vent didn't line up.

And then, I saw it in my mind.

CHAPTER 29

୪୦ ☦ ୪୦

It takes a lot of courage to cross the backside of Pilot Peak when hiking in the summer as the mountain is both high and steep and draped with a blanket of slippery blue shale. Now the mountain and shale were covered in white. While it as possible in the dead of winter to cut across the backside of the peak using good skis that cut into the hard-packed snow, only an insane person—or an exceedingly desperate one—would plod along on a pair of heavy antique wooden skis—one ski operational, and the other rigged with a makeshift tip from the elbow of an old stovepipe rammed on the ski and pounded flat with a rock. It looked like an elf shoe with a curled-up toe.

The first snows had given over to a hard freeze that gave good footing, but fresh snow in sunlight is a recipe for an avalanche. Ideally, we should have waited at least two days before attempting to cross, but the situation was anything but ideal. We were midpoint on our journey, and going back was not an option. I inched along one cautious step at a time, shivering and shaking, exposed to icy wind gusts that could easily reach seventy to eighty mph, threatening to snatch us from the slope and hurl us eight hundred feet to the forest floor.

Paige's baby was anchored to my back, swaddled in strips that I had ripped and knotted from the now-soiled throw and topped off with Kenny's coat, tied at the bottom with sleeves serving as straps. Trash bags full of provisions dangled from my waist, and I felt like a garbage collector using litter sticks for ski poles.

Looking north from the top of Pilot Peak were the active volcanoes, Mount Lassen and Mount Shasta. Looking east, I could see all the way to Nevada. Today, I only had eyes for the small town of Quincy and the desperate hope of reaching there before dark.

Cutting across the peak was like jogging along a beach that sloped down to the ocean—slow, painful, and out of balance, causing jolts of electric pain to shoot through my injured shoulder and back. The gripping cold magnified the pain of every step. My breath condensed and froze along with the blood that oozed from the claw marks on my face, sticking to the kitchen towel wrapped around my neck and pulled high over my nose. Every step was an ordeal. Step—glide—step—glide—step—glide; the forward motion was agonizingly slow.

Maybe it was instinct that caused me to look back. There on the side of a steep slope, in the midst of freezing, raging wind in the middle of absolutely nowhere, I looked back to study the terrain with prickling fear, searching for the man in black.

What I saw was a lion in gold—and laughed. "It's . . . just a cat." I barked out a tight laugh and adjusted my backpack, somehow overwhelmed with relief that it was neither human nor bear. Thousands of big cats now roamed these mountains ever since hunting them became illegal. They were so overpopulated that they had recently been seen hunting in packs. Seeing only one lion gave me an absurd sense of relief.

Probably the same one I chased off before. I can do it again. I hoped.

I was fresh out of weapons, balanced on a dangerous slope, and not about to risk an avalanche or fall by yelling and jumping. I could only return to the task at hand: step—glide—step—glide—step—glide, a little faster.

Made it. Shivering and shaking, exhausted and numb, I sheltered beneath an outcropping of rock and let the baby suck on my finger before moving on. Only the subtle movement of the sun signaled the passing of time before reentering the tree line. There, we stopped again while I drank a can of chicken noodle soup and fed the baby cold milk with the turkey baster. She fought it, and I tried not to drown her. It was only her third meal ever, and I thought she should be more grateful. Regretting the delay, I moved on, the squalling baby signaling our location to every predator in the forest.

"Girl," I advised her, "we were born in these mountains, and if you don't shut up, we are going to die in them." She studied me, her expression serious as her gray eyes searched mine. And then, to my utter amazement, she laughed, and her laughter echoed in the hollow places of my heart, bouncing around until, at last, the sound took wing, flying from my own lips like a new song into the light. Wrapped in Kenny's jacketed embrace, I hefted my "daughter" back onto my back, and we started our decent to Nelson Creek and Quincy.

The sun had crawled across the sky from behind Pilot Peak to hover above the rim of the western horizon when next I stopped, too shaky to take another step. Everything and everyone has limits, and I had reached and overstepped mine. My gas tank tipped to empty somewhere above Nelson Creek Crossing, just a few miles from civilization and the outskirts of Quincy. The first distant lights of the town were winking on in the fading light.

A distinct sound, the sharp snap of a branch breaking beneath living weight, caused me to jump, twisting about in time to see the tail end of a cat. Instinct told me it was lining up for the kill. Crouched low and moving forward.

God, forgive me. The first thought to flash through my tired brain was to put the baby on the road and run for the bridge. The cat would surely go for the easy target. Nevertheless, I bent and pushed off, sailing down the slope until the swish of the skis joined its voice with the steady rumble of the creek below.

It was just a glance—a nanosecond of glancing back—when the stovepipe tip hit a rock with the force of a car driving into a brick wall, snapping the ski and catapulting us down the snowy slope toward Nelson Creek.

Icy waters, cold as death, opened hungry jaws and then constricted, swallowing me whole and cutting me off from the frozen world above.

ॐ ☥ ☪

It wasn't like I hadn't been cold before. I knew all about the cold. I sometimes thought that if I were to carve a statue in memory of my mother, I would choose ice as a medium. Starla was a coldhearted woman, although there were times when she burned with inexplicable fire.

The proof lay in her fiery fingerprints still burning on my cheek.

"I hate you!" I screamed. "I hate you, I hate you, I hate you."

"Yeah, yeah, I got it. You don't know me!" Starla's eyes narrowed, panting from the heat of battle. "You think you're the first person to tell me that? You think I haven't heard it all my life? Who the hell are you to judge me?"

Hand to cheek I drew back, cringing against the wall. "I will never be like you. You're a heartless, mean, self-centered bitch. I wish you were dead!"

Starla laughed and rolled her eyes. "Honey, you don't know the meaning of a heartless bitch. You have no idea what you're talking about. Give yourself time. You'll learn."

My mother never talked much about her childhood. I only knew that when Starla was my age, she had been taken from her mother by the county and railroaded through several foster care homes before finally running away to Haight-Ashbury in San Francisco.

Starla grew soft and distant, as if remembering a more innocent time. "I was going to be different too," she said. "Save the world. Peace, love and all that bullshit." Her face hardened as she came back to the present. "Good luck with that one, baby girl."

Later, I asked my father about Starla's remark.

Lefty had stopped what he was doing and gave me a long, searching look. Then with a deep sigh, he took my hand and sat me down next to him on the couch. Wrapping his right arm around my shoulders, he stroked my hair thoughtfully.

"Your mom didn't have it easy. In fact, she had it pretty bad when she was a kid. Her mother was a"—Lefty paused, his fingers tightening on my hair—"troubled woman. It was good that the county took Starla from her mother, but it was sad that they placed her in homes where men used her. She was just a kid when that happened—just like you." Lefty seemed to have tears in his voice, his heart clearly aching for my mother. Again, Lefty searched for the right words. "Your mom's been hurt. A lot." He swallowed and then sniffed. "I guess you could say . . . your mama—she has a lot of scar tissue around her heart."

I didn't know what all that meant at the time, but I would think about it many times over the years that flowed through my life like troubled waters.

ಶಿ ✝ ಞ

The baby screamed like a banshee from the bank, announcing to the cat that dinner was served, even as the icy current pulled me under. The metal clamp on the binding of my broken ski was sucked down by the force of the creek and wedged itself beneath a submerged boulder. The other ski whipped about in the turbulent water, threatening to break my leg as I fought to gain purchase. I was a prisoner—held captive by my boot.

The world went black, but through the darkness, I felt the rhythmic smack of a limb banging against my thigh. Twisting around, I grabbed ahold of the branch and pulled, hand over hand, following it up until at last, I exploded through the surface, gasping for air. A desperate wild-eyed glance for the baby revealed the cat, eyes glittering as it crouched low, making its way down the slope.

Frigid fingers tightened their grip; the cold was as deadly as the water itself. Fighting for breath, time slowed, and for a moment, the world seemed to fade.

Hypothermia.

Chance was shouting in the distance over the constant throb of the creek, calling out to me, "Unlace your boot."

Then I was back, and the situation was all too real. Unbuckling my belt, I let the dead weight of supplies tumble down the creek and took a deep breath. Plunging back into the watery course with fingers so numb I could barely feel the swollen laces, I tugged and jerked in the darkness until panic set in, and I turned once more to grab the branch, pulling and climbing my way up to air and life.

The big cat was close, crouched against the snow, tail snapping, head subtly shifting left and right as it scrutinized the bundle whose voice now echoed the timeless plight of the ages—the final cries of the weak and helpless that signaled victory to the predator.

It could only be a near-death experience. It was Travis this time, Travis whispering in my ear, "Close your eyes."

A final breath. Closing my eyes, focused and determined, I sank beneath the river, forcing my free leg—still clamped in its own ski—down with me. Pushing my free leg against the offending boulder to act as a counterbalance, I gripped the boot and began the methodical process of unlacing, one X at a time. With a final tug, my foot was free—only to feel the current pulling me from my lifeline.

Breaking through the surface, thrashing, screaming, claiming another breath, I bent as if to touch my toes, and with the flick of the lever, released my other foot from the binding.

The water was steady and forceful, running less than a foot over my head, allowing me to dive down and push off, surging upward, exploding through the surface with a roar, hurling the remaining ski toward the bank as I did.

The big cat hissed and backed up to reassess the new threat. The ski clattered and slid back into the creek, where it was promptly claimed by the current and sent bobbing downstream. Life was only a few strokes away. Thoroughly chilled and weighted down with wet clothes, every stroke felt like a mile. And then . . . I felt rock.

The life-and-death drama was out of sight as I struggled up from the edge of the creek. The bank was steep and slushy as I crawled, threatening to give me back to the river as I fought my way up. Hand and foot I crawled, grasping at loose rocks that continually threatened to give way. When at last I could stand, I was armed and dangerous.

The cat had its claws hooked in the baby's blanket, pulling it across the snow, unwinding the morsel within.

"HAAAAA! YAAAAA!" I threw rock after rock, barely missing the baby, but close enough to intimidate the cat.

Flattening its ears, hissing in defiance, the hungry lion relinquished its prey and turned away at last. Back on the road it glanced back with a final hiss and flicked the tip of its tail angrily before fading into the woods.

Tears gushed as I reached the helpless child whose cries echoed my own. Dropping to my knees, I clutched the shrieking bundle as though she were a life preserver, shaking and shivering violently as I rocked back and forth, hunched in inconsolable grief and shame.

"I'm sorry—sorry—so sorry . . ." It wasn't the first time I had almost abandoned the child to save myself. I rocked and realized that all we had, all we may ever have had for what time we had left, was each other . . . and I had almost sacrificed her to save myself, more than once: on the road, at Baptist camp, and here at the river.

Racked with sobs and tears of remorse, in some wild, inexplicable way, under these—the most bizarre and extreme of circumstances—I was overwhelmed with self-condemnation and the certainty that I had finally become as cold and heartless as my mother.

"Forgive me. Please, forgive me," I begged as I rocked. "I love you, baby. I need you. Don't leave me. Please—don't leave me. I promise—I won't leave you. Not ever again."

Freezing winds and darkness swept down from the peaks. The steady babble of the creek seemed to sing a song of sleep. Time passed.

It is such a relief to finally be warm, I thought, as I peeled off my hat and coat. You can have them, kid. I am hot. Hot and tired. I just want to sleep . . . forever.

And I almost did—until my father's voice woke me.

"Baby—wake up! Look! Over there. See? Lights. Wake up."

Opening my eyes, I searched through the fog of my mind, and there on the horizon, down toward the bridge that crossed the creek, a light was growing. With it came a buzz that sounded like a nest of wild honeybees. Louder now. Brighter. Closer.

I am dreaming.

A second light bobbed up and down, and then a third and a fourth. The buzz now reverberating, amplified, as if the beehive had been cracked open and was under attack.

This is no dream.

Crawling forward on hands and knees, slipping once, and then twice, eventually reaching the road, we waited for either rescue or death. It no longer mattered. I was good with either one.

CHAPTER 30

శా ♱ ఌ

Red light. Diffused. The translucent kind of light that filters through eyelids, illuminating your head with a meaty glow. Nausea battled with fatigue as I swam through the red cloud, surfacing to find a stranger's face hovering just inches from mine. A red face, brimming with fury and hatred so palpable that I flinched, jerking my head back, deeper into the pillow.

"You killed my daughter—and you damn near killed my granddaughter!" Tears glistened in the corners of Cali's eyes, her chin quivering with restraint.

"Cali! Knock it off. What are you thinking?" Chance rushed to her side and placed an arm around her shoulder, gently turning her away from my bed.

"You know damned well what I'm thinking." Her venomous words slipped out.

"You have to leave. Now. This won't change anything. Besides . . . your granddaughter and husband need you," I heard Chance advising Cali as he guided her toward the door.

Paige's mother resisted, pausing to look back with one more piercing glance before turning to look into Chance's eyes. Her face visibly softened as she reached up, touching his face tenderly before relenting. "Okay . . . but I meant what I said. I understand you—but I will never forgive her for killing my daughter. I feel sorry for you, Chance," she added, and then Cali turned away. The sound of her heels tapped a retreat as she left the room.

Chance moved back to the bedside, his blue eyes as rich as the heart of a topaz glowing under a jeweler's lamp, a love light that shone through his haggard expression.

"Sunny . . . I . . . you're . . ." He choked, his words breaking and scattering like a wave casting his emotions along a desolate beach.

"How? Where . . . ?" I asked, with words so weak I could barely form them.

"You're in the hospital. In Quincy. You're going to be . . . okay." Chance's eyebrows pinched, scrambling for the right words as he placed his warm, reassuring hand over mine. "And the baby—she's alive."

"Paige. She's . . . needs . . ." The words croaked from my throat that burned hotter than the flames of Baptist Camp.

Oh, that's right, I remember now . . . she's dead.

My mouth was parched, lip swollen and cracked. So hard to think. So taxing to try.

"Kenny . . ." Exhausted, I fell back as the room faded and narrowed to just the stubble on Chance's chin and the slight ripple that quivered beneath his jaw when he swallowed. My eyes wandered, lost, as if they didn't know I was rescued, traveling up to his soft lips, pressed together in a tight line as a single glistening tear slid into the crease. Chance sniffled as my gaze followed the wet track past his nose and up to his eyes that shimmered in brimmed with tears, answering my questions without uttering a single word.

Chance went in and out of focus. I tried again. "Paige . . ."

He cut me off with a determined, "Shhhh." A cloud of sadness swept over him as he gave a reassuring squeeze to my hand. "Don't worry about Paige, and try not to think about Kenny. There's time for that later. Right now, you need to get well. You've been through a lot. You need to rest."

Chance let go of my hand and reached over the bed, pressing the alert button for the nurse's station as he spoke. Only, it wasn't a nurse that hurried in; it was a doctor.

After what seemed like only a cursory glance at my condition, the Dr. concurred with Chance, confirming my need for rest. He held my gaze and gave a one-word directive: "Sleep," before reaching up and doing something with my IV.

The room tipped and swirled as another wave of nausea swept in, carrying me out on a tide of pain, out to a dark and restless sea.

Memories swept in plunging me beneath the river until I couldn't breathe. Then I was dragged to the surface only to be plunged again, and again and again. I was caught in a maelstrom of memories that swirled through my mind like shadows beneath the raging water. The memories pictures flashed in sequence, like snapshots of a horror movie: The man that followed Paige to the cabin, Paige, oh my God, it's a baby, he's coming, "Kenny, help" . . . help Kenny, I can't do this, not another step, so cold, I'm dying, burning-swirling hungry flames, bears and mountain lions are chasing me, I can't breathe, help—help me! Sucked to the bottom of the river, I fought my way to the surface and woke to find tears surfacing with me . . . running down my cheeks . . . over a thick gauze pad.

ಐ ✇ ಚ

There sat Chance, next to my bed with his arms resting on the blanketed edge, sad eyes searching mine. From the looks of his haggard expression, I expect he had been there the entire time I slept. A short, heavyset woman stood behind him who looked like a nurse or lab technician. Chance turned to her asking, "Would you please tell the doctor she's awake?"

"Of course," said the woman, who nodded and quickly left the room.

"Paige. . . " I breathed her name, and the word seemed to soar on the wings of a soft sigh. Then I took a deeper breath and managed a few more words. "Paige and Kenny?"

Chance shook his head in a slow and deliberate no and opened his mouth to speak even as the Dr. entered the room, immediately usurping Chance's place next to the bed.

The doctor's eyes did a quick body scan before looking into mine. The young doctor looked very uncomfortable, hugging his clipboard as tight as a child clutching a teddy bear. His Adam's apple bobbed up and down as he spoke.

"Hello, Ms. McLane. My name is Dr. Bauman. You must be frightened and a little confused, so I will bring you up to speed. You were found by some snowmobilers in an advanced state of hypothermia, and very near death. You have suffered severe frostbite to your left foot. As soon as you are stable, we will medevac you to Feather River Hospital for surgery. I am sorry to have to tell you this, but your condition may necessitate removal of some toes and the damaged portion of your foot.

"I know this is a difficult decision for you and your husband right now, but with your permission, we would like to move you as soon as possible. The next step after surgery will be rehab. You will walk again; prosthetics have come a long way. This is a process, and I'm sure you are having a flood of emotions and questions. I will answer all your questions to the best of my ability, and we have counselors who can help you manage your feelings."

The doctor paused to catch his breath. "So now it's your turn. Do you have any questions for me?"

I blinked and managed to ask, "Do you have any . . . hooks?"

Chance gave a slight smile as the doctor tipped his head in confusion. "Her father wore a prosthetic hook on his left arm," Chance explained to the doctor who in turn, who gave us a deadpan look before launching into a lecture on amputations and prosthetics.

"It was a joke. Not serious." I interrupted his discourse.

The good doctor's face went blank as he cleared his throat. "Of course you weren't," he said, his eyes shifting from me to Chance. "Well, don't overtire her. She needs rest. I'll contact Feather River Hospital and schedule an afternoon flight. Butte County Sheriffs have established jurisdiction and will want to speak to you when you get there.

"Good luck Mrs. McLane," said the doctor and hurried out the door.

ॐ ♀ ॐ

"Everything. I want to know everything." I picked up with Chance where we had left off before the doctor had interrupted. But another intrusion came before he could reply.

Breakfast arrived with a bump, and a rattle as someone from food services wheeled it in on a metal cart. A cheerful young woman delivered my tray and uncovered the various dishes to reveal what seemed like a banquet of eggs, oatmeal, fruit, toast, milk, and decaf coffee.

"I'll tell you everything—but you must eat," Chance said as he handed me a spoon.

"You are helping. Where would I be without you?" I tried to smile, but let the spoon slide from my fingers back to the tray. "What I am starving for is answers. I want to know everything." The cart rattled from the room and down the hall. "Paige was murdered, wasn't she?" The words came out, ghostlike and distant. "Tell me."

The moment was mocked by a laugh track from someone's TV that slipped in through the open door. Chance rose to close the door before returning to his chair. Taking his seat, he leaned forward, tightening his hold on my hand as if tethering me to what he was about to say. "It's not your fault, Sunny. We both knew Paige. She was a determined woman who made her own choices, and lived . . . and died . . . as a consequence." He leaned forward another couple of inches, bringing his face closer to mine. I could see tears pooling in his eyes. "Joyce said there were no signs of forced entry when she got there. She had to break the glass in the front door to get in. Paige was already dead. She . . . Paige . . . had shot herself."

The privacy curtain around the bed seemed to move on its own as if Paige herself had somehow drawn near. I thought I might blackout again. "Not possible," I gasped. "Paige was alive when I left. I left her my .22. There was a man outside, coming for me —he must have killed her and then staged it to look like a suicide.

"She begged me—no—she threatened me. Said she would shoot herself if I didn't take the baby and go. And now . . . now you're telling me she killed herself anyhow?" Trembling, my heart twisted, wringing tears from a pool of regret that never seemed to run dry.

Chance handed me a box of tissues and helped to dry my face along the bandage that ran from eyebrow to chin, covering the wounds where the bear had swiped my face.

Closing my eyes, as if in doing so I could somehow simultaneously close my ears, I asked; "And Kenny?" I already knew the answer, but I needed to hear it from Chance.

"Your neighbor at the cabin, Joyce—she called the sheriff's department and told them that Kenny was driving you to La Porte. She told them Paige was dead." Chance sniffed and swallowed to control his emotions. "Mark called me from the SO, and I chartered a flight to Oroville. By the time I arrived, the rescue team had found Kenny, but there was no sign of you."

"What did they find? Kenny—what happened after I left?"

Still hanging his head, I could see his eyes tightening and muscles working along his jaw as he grappled for the right words. "Someone stuffed a rag down the gas tank and blew it."

Kenny. "Was he already dead?"

"I don't know. I doubt there will be conclusive evidence one way or the other. The explosion—" Chance shored himself up with a breath, "There wasn't much left."

Tears rained as I felt the loss of my friend all over again while Chance sat in respectful silence as I mourned.

"Tell me everything that happened," Chance gently prodded. "Why was Paige at the cabin?"

I didn't hold back. I told him everything I could remember. Between waves of grief and rills of tears, the words rolled like pebbles, triggering stones and boulders that slid recklessly and without regard like an avalanche pouring from my mouth.

"She said she was afraid of being found at the hospital. She said 'they' would kidnap her baby. I asked her who. Paige must have been talking about the cartel because she kept talking about her captivity in Mexico, and how she'd waited for her dad to rescue her, and it took so long that she gave up hope."

"Anything else? Any last words before you left her?"

"Just a lot of mumbling when she was in labor. After the baby was born, I gave her the gun to protect herself and the baby from whoever was going to come through the door. She got angry—crazy—started threatening to kill herself if I didn't take the baby with me. I kept telling her that the cartel was after me and Logan's money and guns—that no one was after her. I guess . . . she must have thought they wanted her child for sex trafficking." I cradled my head in my hands. "If only she had listened. But she wouldn't. There wasn't time. I had to run or risk a shoot-out in the house and all of us being murdered."

Chance ran his fingers through my hair with long gentle strokes with one hand, lifting my chin with the other to meet my gaze. "You did the right thing, sweetheart. You did the only thing. You did good. Really good."

Somehow the clock on the wall kept moving forward. The second hand swept around and around. It felt so impossible, so unfair that my life should go on while people had died. All because I had left a gun in the hands of a suicidal woman.

The heavyset nurse returned to ask me how I was doing. I had no words, just a quivering jaw supporting a tear streaked face. She smiled sympathetically, reached up and adjusted the IV, giving me the gift of sleep.

ဆ ♀ ର

The delicious smell of food drew me back to the real world.

"You must be starving," Chance said with a smile as he reached for a spoon and stirred a bowl of vegetable soup. "Here, take a bite. Just one." He shoved the spoon in my mouth and then caught the dribble, scooping it from my chin and putting it back as if he were feeding a toddler.

I snatched the linen napkin before Chance could wipe my face and did it myself. "Hon, it's my foot that doesn't work, not my hands. I can do that."

"Sorry, I just want to help." Chance looked awkward as he apologized. "You will keep eating, won't you?"

He didn't need to ask me twice. I dove into the food, savoring every bite as we talked.

"I'm just so thankful." Chance's eyes glistened as he spoke. "You know, it was a miracle you were found. Some passing snowmobilers – being in the right place at the right time. I heard that one of their group hit a rock and broke a fuel line. By the time they figured out the problem and siphoned gas from one of the other machines, it was almost dark. Any earlier or later and they might have missed you." He paused, and then reached out to pat my leg as if reassuring himself I was really there. "I wish I had been the one to find you," he said.

"Oh, Chance. I prayed that you would find me when I was up on the mountain, even though I knew you were in Mexico. And then"—the memory came flooding back—"I was drowning in the river . . . and I heard you calling my name. Seriously, I know it sounds crazy, but I heard you telling me to untie my boot when it was wedged between some rocks in the river. I would have died if I hadn't." I reached for Chance. "Did you? Did you have a premonition?"

Chance reached over and took my hand, stretching the IV tube, making me wince when it tugged on the needle in my vein. "I don't know what to say. I guess you were either hallucinating from hypothermia or else God was speaking to you."

"Sorry to interrupt." We turned our eyes to the floor nurse as she made her way past the privacy curtain. "I just wanted to let you know that the helicopter has been dispatched from Paradise. We will be prepping you for your departure in..." she glanced at her watch, "about a half-hour." And then she left, with a smile as sweet as the pudding on my tray.

I turned to Chance. "I'd like to see the baby first if it's okay." I wasn't sure.

Chance bent over the bed to plant a quick, reassuring kiss next to the bandages. "Of course it's okay. I'll make it happen." And he did. As soon as I had finished eating and dressed for the trip to Paradise, two orderlies appeared with a gurney.

Chance hummed a little tune of satisfaction as he wheeled me to the nursery. The wheels on the gurney made a soft whooshing sound like that of skis skimming across the surface of a frozen world.

The drugs were powerful and my pain minimal. My mind was hazy but my emotions almost tactile, with a vibrant need to touch the baby and confirm that she was really alive. That *we* were really alive.

"You'll need these," said the pediatric nurse, who gave me a curious look as she slipped a surgical mask over the derisive smirk on my face.

She's protecting the baby—from me. I thought. Me—the one who saved her.

We bumped through the doors of the neonatal intensive care and headed toward an isolette, where a stout-looking gray-haired nurse adjusted her glasses as she straightened from bending over her little patient. She said something to two people who were seated on the other side of her and then smiled kindly as she stepped aside.

"What is she doing here?" Cali rose from her chair as if to run interference, her expression colder than the ice on Nelson Creek. She started toward me, when the man who had been sitting next to her, took her by the arm and gently restrained her. White-haired, handsome, with a clean, strong jaw—it wasn't hard to guess that he was Paige's father, Perry Atchison.

"Cali." His voice had depth and authority. One word spoke volumes. Cali froze, then relented and sat back down, clamping her jaws and pressing her lips into a tight line.

I didn't dwell on the grandparents. My eyes reached for the child with an ache and a longing that words could not define. Turning to catch the watchful gaze of the matronly nurse, I pleaded, first with my eyes and then with my voice, "Can I? Please?"

Cali almost knocked her chair over as she jumped up again. "Absolutely not. Don't you dare touch that child. You've done enough harm." Cali reminded me of the cougar, smelling weakness, with claws extended, ready to pounce.

"Do you have any idea what I went through to keep her alive?" I asked.

Chance and Paige's father exchanged looks, and then Paige's father rose to take a sputtering Cali by the elbow and guided her from the room over her protests.

The nurse smiled apologetically and gave me a curious look before turning to Chance. "Are you the father?" she asked.

Chance stopped short, looked at me and then at the nurse, and then back at me. "Yes. I am Chance McLane."

I silently wondered if Chance was making a claim or staking his claim. Couples often race to the courthouse when filing for child custody as the law seems to favor the winner. And we both knew that there is nothing like misfiled paperwork to jam up the legal system.

The nurse smiled and picked up the child, admonishing Chance to "be careful now" as she handed him the baby. His leather-tough outdoor features softened as he embraced his daughter, nuzzling her and making cooing noises.

"You sound like a pigeon," I observed.

Chance smiled an awkward boyish smile. "Here. Hold your baby, Sundance," and he laid the wriggling bundle, tenderly as a gift on an altar and into my waiting arms.

I raised my brows, shooting Chance a questioning look as I reached out to accept her, but all I could hear was Kenny's words ringing in my memory; and now you have a daughter of your own.

"Hello, baby girl," I whispered with a tear in my throat. "We made it, didn't we?" My heart swelled with happiness as it drummed a celebration of life. And then I realized—her mother is dead—and I was the one responsible. Regardless of Paige's ridiculous decision to hike into a cabin during a snowstorm in her condition, she might still be alive if I had not left my gun behind. Nothing could ever alter the fact that it was my gun that Paige had used to take her life. The lump in my throat continued to grow.

The little one smelled fresh, sweet and new; aromatherapy that triggered a flood of emotions. Trembling, I loosened her blanket and let my fingers explore. Soft, incredibly soft silken down crowned her pale-pink skin. I inhaled her essence and drank in her perfect beauty, getting lost in her dark lashes that fluttered like butterfly wings above her intense gaze, tracing her rosebud lips with my fingers, over her chin, across her shoulder, and down her arm . . . then bumped. She jerked, howling, balling tiny fists and waving them in the air like a shadow boxer, kicking her way free of the blanket to reveal thick pads of gauze wrapped around her forearm and hand, and one foot entirely dressed in bandages.

Quincy wailed pitifully.

"What's this?" I looked at Chance, and he shrugged to minimize.

"Some burns on her arm and frostbite on her foot," Chance explained, stroking my arm and giving me a tight smile. "You're not the only one losing some toes." I knew he was trying to be supportive. "She'll be okay—you'll both be fine. I'm just so thankful that you're both alive."

The shock of her injuries came as a blow. "I'm so sorry," I whispered in her tiny ear, rocking her as well as I could. She slowly calmed as a song welled up, breaking from my lips like the first flower of spring, I sang the only child's song I knew. "Little ones to Him belong. They are weak, but He is strong . . ." Her gaze steadied, fixed and trusting. I had spent most of the journey through the wilderness resenting the helpless infant that now lay in my arms. It seemed a great mystery that this child, a baby I had begrudged and sometimes even hated, would suddenly feel like a blessing.

The nurse cut into our reverie to retrieve the baby, whose renewed cries tugged at my heart as she was returned to the isolette. "Don't leave yet," the nurse admonished. "I have some paperwork. It will just take a minute." She gave an apologetic smile and picked up a clipboard and jotted some notes. "Okay, I have the father's name. What's the baby's name?"

Chance and I looked long into each other's eyes. So much had happened. I wasn't surprised when Chance claimed to be the father of Paige's baby, but I was stunned when he turned to me and asked, "Honey, have you decided on a name?"

Again, that long searching look, and I think Chance was trying to tell me something that I should have understood, but didn't. I wished the nurse would go away and give us some privacy, but she waited, hugging her clipboard. I dropped my gaze a couple of inches from Chance's eyes to his neck where my particleboard cross, removed no doubt by the hospital, was hanging. As I stared, an inexplicable peace washed over me.

Quincy. "Her name is Quincy. Quincy McLane."

Chance gave me a chaste kiss on the forehead and signed the papers. Just like that, in spite of the mountain of misgivings that kept piling up, we became parents of a baby girl.

The momentous occasion was interrupted by Paige's father, knocking on the door and motioning to Chance. "I'll be right back," said Chance.

"I'll be right with you Perry," Chance called to Perry before turning to the nurse and taking her by the elbow. He lowered his voice, but I heard every word.

"My child," Chance affirmed to the nurse. "I am the father, her biological mother is dead. As Quincy's legal father, I want you to write this down regarding my daughter's medical treatment. I hereby authorize this hospital to continue her care and treatment as prescribed by the treating pediatrician. Furthermore—and I want this in writing—no paternity test is to be taken, regardless of who requests it."

The nurse's jaw dropped, and eyes widened in shock and dismay even as Chance gave her a reassuring pat on the arm and turned away, leaving the room to join Perry in the hall.

I managed a weak smile. My husband had just become a shaft jammed into the wheels of justice. I hoped that the kindly nurse would not lose her job and then I gave in to exhaustion, dropping deeper into the arms of the gurney.

There was nothing left to hold. Chance had vanished through the door, and all that remained of Quincy was the plaintive sound of her cries that continued to fill the room.

I must be crazy. It's got to be the morphine. Me, pretending to be Quincy's mother.

My foot and face were madly throbbing, making me fidget. Tears quickened. It was all too much; the pain, the fight for survival, Paige's suicide and Kenny's death, Cali's hatred, the baby's amputation, my pending amputation—and now this churning mass of hope and doubt. I could almost hear the sound of my heart snapping in two as I motioned to the nurse. "Please get my husband."

"Good-bye, Quincy," I whispered in farewell.

The steady thwack-thwack-thwack of the chopper blades thrummed as we headed down a hall toward the EchoStar 130, the newest helicopter of its kind waiting to transport me to Feather River Hospital and my friend and surgeon Dr. Lance.

Cali's voice thundered through the hospital and echoed down the hall as I was lifted from the gurney and placed onto a backboard.

"He what?" Cali shouted. "He is not the father of that child . . . they have no right . . . baby (something-something) with us . . . I won't . . . " Her voice trailed and faded beneath the reassuring words of the flight crew as we rounded the corner, heading for the exit that led to the helipad.

CHAPTER 31

☙ ✠ ☗

I woke to a set of three smiling faces and minus three toes—
including a portion of my left foot and a small section of the top rim
of my ear. I had no idea it would hurt so bad. At least the faces
around me looked reassuring; a soothing balm to my mental and
emotional state.

Chance spoke first as he tenderly stroked my cheek with the
back of his hand. "Hello, sweetheart. How's my girl?" He looked
more rested and less stressed than he had looked in Quincy. He
gave me a little wink, and the corners of his mouth turned up,
making his mustache smile with him.

Standing next to him was Dr. Lance with his usual charming,
teasing ways. "Miss Sunny," he began, "how many fingers am I
holding up?" He held up five as if to give me a high-five.

"You're about to get one finger," I said, my head pounding and
spinning all at the same time.

"Ouch!" Dr. Lance exclaimed, shaking his hand as if stung by
my words. "You're on the fast track to recovery, always the fighter.
If you don't mind"—he smiled—"I'll just take a quick look at your
foot."

"And if I do mind?" I asked as Dr. Lance who went about the
business of pulling back a sheet and inspecting my ankle and leg for
swelling, purple streaks, and whatever other alien life forms might
invade a surgical site.

"I'll wheel you back in and remove some vocal chords," he said.

Dr. Lance left after giving me the status on my foot and ear,
assuring me that I could go home in a week and probably start
rehab and be back to work with a special shoe in a month. At the
moment, I didn't know how I was going to make it to dinner. My
foot hurt, my stomach ached, and if my head could throw up, it
would.

"Anything else?" asked the doctor.

"I want my dog."

"If you promise to be good and not throw things this time, you can have your dog at the end of the week when you go home." My doctor was referring to a previous stay in the hospital. With a wink and a reassuring flash of his laughing eyes, he left with a promise to return later.

The third face had been silent, sitting patiently in the background, all soft and round and red-cheeked, with round gauges that reminded me of a second pair of eyes staring from his earlobes. It belonged to Duncan. He was sitting in a wheelchair with a hard cast on one leg, a soft cast on his arm, and the smile of a kid who has just got his first-bicycle-ever from Santa. You had to love a face like that.

Chance completely ignored Duncan as he talked with me about the surgery, my recovery, and my scheduled physical therapy. He told me that he had quit school and would be staying home to take care of me. Every now and then Chance would glance at Duncan, seemingly irritated by his presence. It seemed odd that Chance would not be more gracious toward my invalid guest.

Ignoring Chance, I motioned to Duncan, who sometimes reminded me of myself back when I was in high school—a shy wallflower, different from everyone else. Duncan's smile broke out like sunshine from behind a lone, dismal cloud as he wheeled his way toward me. I smiled at the duck-foot cast on his leg with more signatures than a guest book from a celebrity wedding.

"Chance, hon, would you do something for me?" I looked at Chance and squeezed his hand. "Would you get me something unhealthy from the cafeteria? Chips, ice cream, candy?" Chance frowned and then shrugged.

"Sure. Be right back." Chance left the room with his thumbs hooked in the front pockets of his Levi's, nodding a silent acknowledgment to Duncan as they passed.

"Hey, buddy, don't be shy. Roll closer. Come sit by me and tell me what's been going on," I said as Duncan rolled up next to my bed.

"Hi. How are you?" Duncan's face radiated genuine affection. "We all heard something about you being lost up in the mountains and then being rescued. I hacked into the system and found out you were life-flighted here. I'm glad you're okay. I've been worried about you."

"Yeah? I think I'll make it. How about yourself? How long will you be in a wheelchair?"

"Me? You know me—I'll be okay—strong as an ox and sometimes as dumb as one too."

"You shouldn't talk like that." I rested my hand on his arm. "I don't think you're dumb at all. You are one of the smartest people I know."

Duncan blushed. "I don't think your husband likes me."

"What makes you say that?"

He looked down. "No reason."

I moved past his discomfort. "So, what's going on at the office?"

"Nothing exciting—now that you and Paige are gone. Just the usual shoot-outs, drug busts, robberies, and such." He laughed into my eyes, then shifted his gaze and wet his lips. He was holding tight to something that needed go.

"What aren't you telling me, buddy?" I gave his arm a little squeeze of encouragement. I was starting to nod.

Duncan squirmed in his chair as his eyes roamed the room. He seemed to reach a decision. Leaning close, he pulled something from his pocket, lowered his voice, and whispered, "I found this in your in-box."

I frowned. "What were you doing in my box?"

"Looking for stuff . . . making sure no one put another trap in it. I didn't want you to come back and prick your finger on a poisoned dart or stick it into an open light socket or anything weird like that. I was looking out for you," he said.

I squinted for a moment trying to figure him out. "You and who else?" I asked. "And stop squirming. Just answer my question, please," I added as an afterthought.

"Bonita." He said. "We've been on the lookout for the person who was sneaking things into your box. This is the only thing I've found. I thought you should see it before Bonita."

"Yeah? What is it?"

Duncan handed me what appeared to be a playing card, and in a way, that's just what it was. My mother had owned a similar set of cards when I was young, claiming that she could read her future. The tarot card that Duncan gave me was a familiar-looking card called the High Priestess—a female sorcerer, robed and sitting on a throne with her left foot resting on a crescent moon. Only, this card has been modified. In place of the high priestess was the traditional portrait of the Virgin Mary—but Mary's sweet, compassionate face had been replaced by a bleached skull.

I turned the card over and over in my hand. Duncan continued to squirm like a little boy needing to use the bathroom. He was holding tight to something that needed releasing.

"You're still holding something back. What else?" I asked. I was ready to squeeze his neck instead of his arm this time.

"Guess what I got us for Christmas?" asked Duncan.

"Us?"

"Yeah, check this out." To my amazement, Duncan almost blinded me when he pulled a snowy white arm from his long-sleeved shirt, exposing a bare Santa belly topped with a thatch of curly brown hobbit hair on his chest. Turning in his chair to give me a shoulder pose, he flexed his arm. Beneath his large tattooed banner proclaiming BORN TO RIDE, scripted in Old English and couched in a bed of roses was the word Sunny.

Stunned and amazed, I was pretty sure my jaw hit the hospital bed.

No wonder Chance is mad.

"You like?" Duncan's brown eyes shone with anticipation, his features filled with joyful expectation.

"Uh . . . nice tattoo. In fact . . . it's . . . beautiful. But, Duncan—you know I'm a married woman."

"That's okay," said Duncan as he shrugged back into his shirt. "I don't mind. I can keep our secret." I lay there with peaked eyebrows and a weak smile, puzzling as I shoveled through the mountain of recent traumatic events, trying to remember what I might have said to Duncan when he was in the hospital that he would consider secret. My memory blurred.

"Our secret? I don't understand."

A heated shade of fire-engine red shot from beneath Duncan's collar all the way to the silly grin plastered across his face. Dropping his eyes, he stammered, "You know . . . remember? You told me that you 'know all about sex.'"

Oh yeah. The throbbing tempo in my head escalated into a pounding bass drum in a marching band—accompanied by a set of cymbals clashing behind my eyes as the memory came back to me. I was pretty sure I had said that I knew all about wrecks—not all about sex.

Chance walked in carrying a cup of coffee in one hand and a bag of tortilla chips in the other, his eyes briefly crossing swords with Duncan's.

I tried to analyze the look. Anger? Jealousy? Maybe contempt? Duncan dropped his gaze in defeat, mumbling, "Well, I hope you feel better soon," and turned to beat a hasty retreat.

"Good-bye, Duncan. Thank you for coming," I said.

"I'll see you soon," he said, tossing the words over his shoulder as he wheeled out the door.

My head was killing me.

"Chance, what does it mean, for us, that we signed those papers for the baby—um, for Quincy?" I corrected myself.

Chance's hopeful expression was at odds with the pain in his eyes. "It means we have a baby to raise, honey. Just like we always wanted. We're going to be a family."

Closing my eyes, I shook my head in disbelief. "Now who is the crazy one? We must be out of our minds. What were we thinking?" I needed time to process all that had happened—Paige's death and the aftermath. Now talk about raising her baby. "I guess Travis and Cali will have something to say about that . . . and I kind of doubt it's going to be 'Good luck.'"

"Umm, well." Chance chewed his bottom lip thoughtfully, his blue eyes sifting through mental notes. "I don't think Paige's mother will have a problem with us raising Quincy."

A short, derisive laugh escaped. "Really? I must have missed that part when she was screaming at me. What about Travis?"

Chance shrugged. "We both know Travis isn't exactly the family type," he said with certainty.

Stung, I scowled. "You think you have it all figured out, don't you? You always do that. You never consider anyone else."

"Actually, you're wrong. I have thought about everyone else . . . which is why I said I was Quincy's father."

"But why? There was plenty of time to do a paternity test. Don't you want to know the truth?"

"No. I don't." Chance squared his shoulders and took a wide stance, positioning himself for battle.

I stared in stunned in disbelief. "You are . . ."

Things were heating up into a familiar pattern when Dr. Lance walked into the room and into the crosshairs of our remarks. His eyes shifted rapidly between us.

"Now what?" he asked, extending his arms and lifting his hands with his palms turned out. "Can't we all just play nicely?"

We groaned, and he smiled. "You both should be counting your blessings instead of arguing." He turned his eyes back to me in invitation. "Morphine?" he asked.

ഔ ✞ ര

Mark Anderson was in the room talking with Chance when I woke. Bonita was arranging flowers she had brought with her, a get-well gift from the office. They were there in an official capacity to take a written report regarding the "incident." They were compassionate and sympathetic. Chance and I had a longtime relationship with Mark. More than sheriff of Butte County, Mark was a dear friend who'd had an amorous relationship with Paige.

But then, who didn't? I wondered.

"Hello sweetheart," said Mark with a kiss on my forehead. "How are you doing?"

"Hey Chica," Bonita joined in. "¿Cómo estás?"

Mark seemed to be holding up well, but I noticed that he had brought Bonita in on the investigation. She would probably be the one to ask the painful questions. And they were—horribly painful—hurting in places and causing emotional pain that morphine could not numb.

The week blurred. Chance came at least twice a day.

Duncan returned several times with Bonita, whose endless questions forced me to relive the nightmare again and again.

"Just one man at the cabin, right?" Bonita had already asked me several times.

"That's what I said."

"And just one man standing by the car out on the main road, Lumpkin Road?"

Sigh. "Yes. Did you not hear me the first six times?"

"Sí. Just double checking. And at the lake? It was the same man you saw approaching the house?"

"The same."

"You are certain?"

"Unless there's a pack of albinos chasing me. Yes."

Bonita smiled tolerantly. "Just making sure he was acting on his own. He filled up with gas in La Porte."

"Alone?" I asked.

"Solamente. What about . . . ?"

"Adios. Please, Bonita. I can't do this anymore. I'm tired."

Bonita put away her notes and gave me a gentle hug before leaving. "Get well, my friend. Some of us have to get back to work while others of us take naps."

Duncan had sat staring at me with supportive puppy dog eyes. If he had a tail, he would have wagged it in adoration. I made a mental note to talk with Duncan the next time we were alone.

Ashley rolled in, looking like two bodies with one head, or perhaps more accurately, three bodies with one head. My dear friend assured me that Kissme was being pampered and counting the days until her mama could come home.

Shane and Pastor Mac visited a couple of times to encourage and pray for me.

Then Chance arrived one evening with fresh flowers and a box of chocolates, talking about his day as he sat down and turned on a football game. I had spent the day mentally replaying a previous conversation between us, and the unasked question that resulted was driving me crazy.

"Chance, honey, I don't think I understood you. Something you said when we were in Quincy. You told me that you chartered a flight to Oroville. You chartered a flight from Mexico?"

Chance quietly reached for the remote and turned off the TV. He sat up, thoughtfully chewing on his lip, with only the soft whirring of the electronic monitors that tracked my vitals filling the distance between us. "I wasn't in Mexico," Chance said at last. "I was in Sausalito."

"I . . . I don't get it. You were supposed to be in Mexico. What were you doing in Sausalito?"

Chance raised his head, turning up the intensity of his gaze. He seemed to be garnering strength, like a soldier who's been waiting for the order to attack. Sitting tall, Chance said, "I was staying with Paige's parents. Paige's father works in Oakland, but they live in Sausalito."

I could feel furrows deepening between my eyes as I processed his words, from puzzling, to concern, to suspicion. Closing my eyes,

I shook my head back and forth. Trying to unscramble my thoughts was like trying to sort out a pan full of beaten eggs; it wasn't going to happen.

"You what?"

The fire was lit, burning up the fuse for a solid sixty seconds.

"Don't make me pry it out of you," I warned.

Chance cleared his throat, running his index finger back and forth along his thumb in a nervous tic. "It isn't anything new. It never stopped. It's just a continuation of where things left off when Logan went to prison." He took a deep breath, squinting as he exhaled. "I've been working undercover for ATF."

More morphine please—preferably an overdose. I squeezed my eyes shut and slowly opened them. Chance was still there. It wasn't a nightmare.

"Are you telling me you haven't been in San Diego . . . all this time?"

Chance exhaled again, this time with a long, drawn-out sigh that answered the question more clearly than words. "I spent some time in San Diego, between school and work. Old job—fresh eyes, tracking the cartel that kidnapped Paige. They're the same people that bought guns from Logan."

In a flash, my brain was in the ultimate to-the-death cage fight with my heart, each trying to pulverize and eliminate the other forever. It was a good thing that I was more than just brain and heart. I was also spirit.

"Okay." Been here, done that. I took a deep cleansing breath. "Let's agree to put the whole lying thing on hold for now," I said, knowing the subject should wait until I was stronger, less vulnerable, and less likely to be sabotaged by my emotions. It was one of those defining moments that spoke to the unshakable core of my faith: that God can make good things come out of bad for those who believe.

Not that I believed it was God's role to rescue me. I don't think that God puts people through fiery tests and trials. I think he brings his people out of them and then shames evil by turning it to good.

In this moment of crisis, I clung to my conviction that what some people called crisis could be an opportunity for God. I didn't always believe that, but I'd learned it, one crisis at a time.

So I dealt with what I could and tabled the rest in faith for later.

"Why you? Paige's father is a director at ATF. Why would he need you when he has a whole fleet of agents?"

Chance looked down and to the left as he continued to nervously rub his thumb. The tic told me he was stressed, but his eyes said that he was truthful.

"I volunteered to work undercover, working in the mission field and traveling to Mexico. When my job took me back to headquarters, I would stay with Perry and Cali."

My heart twisted, and the word love knot came to mind—or was it love not?

"Were you planning on them being your future in-laws? You and Paige, planning to raise your child together?"

"No, honest! Nothing like that." Chance sat up straight and looked me in the eye. "I didn't see Paige once, and I have never thought about leaving you. Not ever. You're my wife," he exclaimed. "More than that"—Chance lowered his voice—"you are my life."

I gazed into his face, a face that I loved: blond hair and mustache over turned-down lips, a strong jaw covered with a slight stubble, his skin bronzed from the outdoors and the light of truth shining through him.

About time.

"I've gotten close to Cali. She has a lot of guilt over what happened to her daughter, and she's not well. When I found out that she was sick . . . terminal, well . . . I've been able to talk to her about death and God and his promise of an afterlife."

"Sure." My tone had teeth. "You never talked about Paige or the baby, right?"

Again, Chance looked down and repositioned himself. "Of course we did. She knows that the father of her grandchild is either Travis or me, but since neither of us could do anything about it, we mostly just talked about Paige and what happened to her in Mexico."

I was pretty sure that Chance and I were both thinking the same thing. "Nothing is standing in the way now," I said. "So why did you really sign papers prohibiting a paternity test?"

"Because, in a way—but for different reasons—I've come to agree with Paige. It doesn't matter anymore who the father is.

What is important, is who is willing to be a father, and of course who would make the best father. I've known lots of bio dads who weren't fit to own a dog, much less raise a child. Nothing is more important to God than the love of a family." Chance's brows pinched in earnestness. "Sunny, you and I can give this child a family. It's an answer to our prayers. It's what we always talked about—God making something good come out of something terrible."

I felt like a rabbit in a trap. Nothing like being snared with your own words. Give me enough rope, and I would usually hang myself.

"It's too sudden. I can't think straight." A little groan escaped. "I'm in too much pain. I need time."

"It's okay," Chance hastened to reassure me. "We don't need to know all the answers right now. All we need is for you and Quincy to get well."

A twinge of jealousy sparked and smoldered, how *we* had become *us* before the spark was smothered under a blanket of guilt. Paige had died because I left her behind, knowing that she was unstable and that danger coming through the door at any minute. And now, here I was, hesitating over the correctness of raising her child as Cali's words rang in my ears: "Haven't you already done enough?"

CHAPTER 32

ဢ ✚ ಞ

Pale pink and yellow fingers of light waved seductively from the rising sun, beckoning and calling to me as they flash-danced through the treetops. Blazing through nature's strobe lights, I soared up the canyon on my Harley Fat Boy, completely elated—exhilarated. I leaned with my machine as I rounded the bend.

In the road stood a tall man, legs apart in a shooter's stance, two hands on his pistol grip, arms thrust forward as he took careful aim. As fast as I could process the scene, the trigger was pulled, and my world exploded.

When I opened my eyes, I was lying in the wreckage, my foot—torn from my body—still twitching inside the boot that lay just out of reach. The killer walked with a confident air as he stalked through the twisted metal to where I lay, broken and bleeding, writhing in agony. His leathers were black—his skin as pale as death—and he had come for me. Laughing. Laughing.

"Help! Help me! Someone . . . anyone . . . help . . ."

"Sunny. Sunny. I'm here." A familiar voice slashed through the veil of the nightmare that held me like a trash bag pressed into my face, leaving me fighting and screaming as I wrestled the apparition.

"Help! Can someone please help in here?" the familiar voice called out.

Nurses rushed in, taking over the job of alternately ordering me to wake up and calm down. I was okay.

Fresh air rushed in to soothe my burning lungs and sweep the dark images from my mind. When I had finally quieted, sinking back into the half-sleep of medication, I looked around to see that Chance was gone. His startling blue eyes had been replaced by a pair of solemn brown ones.

Joyce? Joyce. The brain fog started to lift, and memories returned. Joyce. I had killed her husband. I had killed her precious Kenny—the always patient, always kind, always giving Kenny. Joyce had lost her husband. Her children had lost a father and grandfather. The guilt was unbearable. I could not face one more truth. I could not face her.

Twisting the top half of my body to face the wall, I turned my back to Joyce and wept in secret. The consequences of my decisions were piling up like rocks on my grave, weighing me down and burying me alive.

"Turn over, Sunny. Don't you turn your back on me or on Kenny's memory." Joyce's voice was X-Acto sharp, slicing through my defenses. "Turn over and look at me. Talk to me." A poignant pause followed. "You owe me."

"Please go away." My shoulders quivered, words trembled. "I can't. Don't make me. I can't change what I have done."

The tension in Joyce's voice ratcheted tighter. "You will turn over and look at me and not shame the memory of my husband."

I gritted my teeth and swallowed hard as I struggled to obey. I turned over, but I still couldn't look into Joyce's eyes.

So this is hell.

Fiery pain shot like a flamethrower up my leg, and yet the agony paled before the emotional inferno that consumed me.

"Sunny . . ." Joyce's voice softened. "Daughter—look at your stepmother."

Kenny had called me that. He had called me his daughter. Ashamed, I raised streaming eyes and looked into Joyce's brown wizened face. She sat, crowned with pure white hair that shone with an angelic glow beneath the ambient overhead light. Her eyes were sad but there was strength in them. Joyce was a survivor. She had birthed nine children and buried five of them. Now Kenny would be laid to rest near the five.

Joyce studied me in silence, searching long and hard. And then her back stiffened, her shoulders squared, her chin lifted. She was Maidu royalty—proud and brave and beautiful as if she were sculpted from the heart of an ancient oak.

Joyce leaned in close and laid a leathery hand against my wet cheek, her eyes only inches from mine.

"Don't you dare do this!" Her voice was stern and authoritative. "Don't you dare blame yourself." Joyce drew back. "My husband was a wise man, and I have never known Kenny to make foolish decisions. He knew exactly what he was doing when he took the road to La Porte." Joyce nodded to herself. "The accident was unforeseeable because we are just people, not God. We live and die by our choices, but choices are ours to make."

That sounded a lot like something Chance had said.

Joyce drew herself up. Her voice remained steady as her features softened.

"You will not diminish your stepfather's honor and integrity with this foolish self-pity. He loved you, and so do I. When you are well, you will tell me Kenny's last words. But for now, you must rest." Joyce reached out and lovingly brushed the hair from my face. "Get well, Sunny. We will have the memorial in two weeks, and Kenny would want you there."

Then she kissed me softly on the forehead, lingering as she continued to hold my cheek. Pulling away, she gazed lovingly into my eyes, imparting her great strength with a long reassuring look. Such was the Maidu way.

ℴ✝ℛ

The sounds of silence told me it was the middle of the night when I woke. No TVs, just soft voices from down the hall. No other sounds of life beyond the soft whir and click of the monitors that continued to track my vitals. And yet, I sensed the presence of another person. There—silhouetted by the dim glow at the foot of my bed. I sighed with relief. Just an orderly dressed in scrubs, wearing a surgical mask.

I was halfway back to being fully submerged in a pool of sleep, when my eyes shot open, warning bells jangling in my head with a familiar rush of adrenaline coursing through me, strong enough to back up into the IV. I bolted upright as the figure jumped. We wrestled, and his mask slipped.

The specter of death had found me—a thin face with white hair and smooth, translucent skin. His lashless eyes were so pale, they looked corpse gray, and his breath smelled of decay. A knife glinted and flashed in the dim light. He grabbed my hair, yanking my face up and pressing the knife against my throat, sharp and intentional. Bloodless lips pulled back into a cruel sneer revealing crooked teeth as pale as his skin.

"The baby," he rasped into my ear. "Where is the baby?" He seemed to breathe the words rather than speak them. "Baabee. Tell me where she is—or I. Will. Cut. Your. Throat. Unless"—he hissed—"unless you'd rather tell me where Logan hid the money he made from our guns. You decide but make it fast. The baby or the money."

My heart jack-hammered in my chest loud enough to set off security alarms. I didn't know it could beat so fast. My mind went crazy, scrambling for options when there were none.

"Trying to be brave, are we? How noble. How very . . . Christian. And that, after you murdered her mother." He clicked his tongue in a tsk, tsk. "How about I open your morphine drip and let you sleep while I do some additional amputation? Maybe your thumbs, huh? Or maybe your nose?" He reached for the IV, and I shook my head no from beneath the blade.

"What's that you say?" He asked, leaning his dreadful face even closer.

I gasped, drenched with terror, shaking violently. I croaked out some strangled noises, and the pressure of the knife backed off my throat as he tipped his hideous head, putting his ear next to my face.

I bit, and he cut my throat.

Screams bounced off the walls, but there was no power on earth that could unclench my jaws. He did the damage to himself— yanking and jerking in his violent effort to disengage, leaving me with a mouthful of ear and blood dribbling down my chin as he fled, screaming a stream of curse words that trailed him down the hall, not caring if he was seen or heard. An alarm went off in the background, and I heard voices shouting and feet running.

℠✝℞

No smiling faces to greet me this time. Dr. Lance, Chance, Mark, and—really? Was that really Travis? They seemed to be waiting, poised for the moment I woke up. They look tired, stressed, and strained—quite possibly worse than I felt, in spite of being pumped full of drugs.

I wanted to sleep forever.

"The baby or the money." The memory snaked its way in. "Oh God—he wants the baby! Quincy!" Hysteria clutched me with fingers that squeezed with a smirking grin. The men looked at each other, and Travis bolted from the room.

I tried to pull myself up, but Dr. Lance gently pushed me back and used the electric lift to raise the head of the bed instead. The bed whined as my fingers explored the newest bandage, wrapped like a priest's collar about my neck. I looked to my doctor for an answer.

"Dull knife," said Dr. Lance in his usual glib manner. "Superficial cut. You'll be fine." He gave me an encouraging, compassionate look and a reassuring squeeze to my arm.

"What else?" Mark persisted, with Chance standing anxiously next to him. Always more questions. My mind spun like a washing machine trying to wring words from a muddy memory. Dr. Lance gave me something to relax, and within minutes, answers to questions trickled in.

No—I do not know the man. Yes—I have seen him before. He may have even followed me to Fresno. It might have been him outside the cabin. I'm sure I saw him at Little Grass Valley Lake.

"Money. He said something about . . . me having a choice. Something about . . . either the baby or"—my words broke with a sob—"or the money."

Mark had assured me before he left that an armed guard would be posted outside my room until I was discharged from the hospital. Chance immediately volunteered for the job, but Mark declined, saying, "You're on sabbatical," and then looked from one of us to the other. "Okay. Fine. I will arrange for the hospital to let you stay here at night—in addition to one of my deputies."

And then, it was just Chance and me. He lay down next to me and wrapped his strong arms around me. Just held me, nuzzled me, in much the same way I had held and comforted Quincy. Held me. Supported me. Loved me. His head resting on mine, our hearts clinging desperately to one another as he breathed into my ear, "It's okay. Okay. Everything's going to be okay. I love you."

There was peace in surrender. I no longer wanted to keep score: my lies—his lies, his betrayal—my betrayal. At this moment, there was only love. I knew that we were both strong people—not always making the best choices but always choosing to do our best, sometimes with blessed results, sometimes with catastrophic results. But we were people of action, Chance and me, and for the most part, we acted and reacted out of love. We made our choice when we said "I do," for now and forever. We would talk about everything when I was stronger, but in the end—there would be no end. We would continue on, for better or for worse.

৪১ ✦ ৫১

Travis hustled back into the room and pulled up short at the sight of our embrace. His features were tight; he was in full cop mode. "The baby—she's gone. The night nurse is dead. We don't know how. No one knows how long she's been missing, but things are in motion. Security is searching the parking lot, and investigators are scrambling to the hospital to review the security cameras. With luck, we'll be able to issue an APB and an Amber Alert within the hour."

"Quincy? Oh, my God. Chance, they have Quincy." The words swelled in my throat.

Travis raised his brows and shot me a questioning look. "Quincy?"

Chance boldly met his gaze. "Sunny named the baby. We're her legal parents now," said Chance, sitting up and putting his feet on the floor.

"Yeah, Perry told me," said Travis, his body rigid and green eyes slanting as they fixed on Chance. "But that doesn't make it so. The word isn't father; it's fraud, but I doubt the Atchison's will press charges." Travis shifted his eyes to meet mine, and the tension was temporarily defused. "I know I won't press charges if we agree to work together and agree to find the truth. Quincy deserves to know who her real father is. But we can all talk after we recover the baby."

Travis left, and I could see that Chance was anxious, torn in two, afraid to leave me yet eager to join in the search for Quincy. It felt as if hours had passed when Travis returned to say they had a lead from the hospital's video.

"Here's what we have: a large, middle-aged, dark-skinned African-American woman entered the nursery, and after talking to the charge nurse, she did something—probably injected her with something, because the nurse collapsed on the floor, and there weren't any visible injuries. Then the perp put . . . uh, Quincy . . . under the shawl she was wearing and walked out. She kept her head down to avoid the cameras. Also, Plumas Hospital doesn't have cameras in the parking lot. The bad news is, we don't have any clear face shots."

A deputy arrived to take up his position, standing guard outside of my room. I told Chance he should go.

ॐ ♁ ℃

The days that followed were a blur of faces: pain, morphine, sleep—and deepening depression. I didn't want to talk or visit with anyone. I wanted to be alone, back in the mountains, on the backside of Pilot Peak. Or maybe on the moon. Far from everyone and everything. Far from my past and my present. No questions, no I'm sorry, no pain, no guilt that continued to eat at me with greater ferocity than the amputation.

Tick-tick-tick. I was alive, and Kenny was dead. Tick-tick-tick. I was alive, and Paige was dead. Tick-tick-tick. I was alive, and Quincy was missing. Somewhere a family was mourning the loss of the nurse—a mother, sister, daughter, friend. My face was scarred. Three toes and a missing chunk of my left foot keep cramping, the pain shooting up my leg. Nightmares haunted my sleep. Nightmares when I was awake. Tick-tick-tick. If only, if only, if only . . . tick-tick-tick . . . my fault, my fault—All. My. Fault.

Guilt threatened to crush the life out of me. Had everything happened for nothing? God may not have been keeping a scorecard, but self-imposed hash marks kept cutting away.

The days had flown with no further leads as to the whereabouts of Quincy or the woman who had taken her.

Dr. Lance dropped in to say that I was going home tomorrow. Tomorrow is New Year's Eve, and although I would be home to usher in the New Year, there would be no celebration. I could only think of those who would not share in its arrival.

Chance was home, sleeping. He usually arrived around eight p.m. When he did, we talked, but rarely communicated. The focus was mosty about Paige's death and the child abduction. Details, always more details.

Details were the very thing I wanted to forget. My eyes trailed around the hospital room for the millionth time, having memorized every inch: the number of squares on the ceiling, the slight overlap where the curtains met at the top of the window, a wood knot on the bathroom door that looked like the Madonna, the faint stain on the back of the chair next to my bed and . . .

"Travis?" It was good to see him. "I didn't hear you come in." But then, I had rarely ever heard Travis enter or leave a room. The man lived in perpetual stealth mode.

The warmth of his smile echoed in his voice. "Sunny." He said that word as if it were a complete sentence. He was incredibly handsome as he stood there; his green shirt perfectly matched his forest-green eyes. Brown pants and shoes offset his sandy-colored hair. He moved next to my bed, and I breathed deeply, taking in the familiar spicy scent that always moved with him. We were like two old lovers who were alone at last. And in a way, the thought was true.

"I've missed you." His voice was soft, and his fingers slid down my arm to clasp my hand. Without thinking, without a clue how it happened, we found ourselves wrapped in each other's arms, holding each other so tightly that we could feel the beating of the other's heart. When we separated, Travis cupped his hand over the bandage on my face and softly stroked it with his thumb.

"I've kept up with you—your work, the cabin, the rescue, your health. I'll never stop caring about you."

I disengaged and lay back on the bed, pulling a curtain of sadness between us.

"Then I guess you know how badly I messed up. Paige . . ." My chin quivered, and Travis moved closer, completely disregarding the space I had just put between us.

"Later, babe. You don't have to relive it again. You've been through it enough. Now isn't the time." He let go of my cheek, gently running his fingers through my hair. "I've taken care of everything. It wasn't your fault." A sad smile crossed his face. "Everyone knows how hardheaded Paige could be." The muscles along his jaw flexed, his mouth tightened into a straight line, and I noticed his lashes batting at tears he fought to rein in.

"I set a date for Paige's funeral—two days after Kenny's. Are you okay with that? I figured you would want to attend both and then put them both behind you." He continued to stroke my face. "It won't be easy for you, but there's no sense in dragging it out. Your doctor said you should be strong enough if it's okay with you."

I nodded wordlessly and wondered how I could possibly survive attending Kenny's and Paige's funerals when they should have been attending mine.

CHAPTER 33

Home for New Year's Day and the dogs went crazy with joy as Chance helped me from the car. Mercy beat a path, racing back and forth and up and down her long pen. Kissme spun like a whirling dervish until I scooped her into my arms and we swapped kisses.

The sky had aged to a hoary gray. Clouds dangled and trailed like beards sweeping across a sooty sky, draping over the lavender mountains that silhouette the skyline. The air smelled like rain, and the first drops fell as we unlocked the door.

The following week was dedicated to healing—both physically and relationally.

"For you, sweetheart," said Chance, holding up a pair of JW Stannard wind chimes, appropriately named First Light and Moonrise. He hung them at either end of our deck, adding, "You are the music that flows between them." I loved my husband beyond words.

In bed, our arms tangled, fitting together like the last two pieces of a three-dimensional puzzle. Kissme snuggled next to my feet, and I felt safe and content. The feeling didn't last.

Chance grew restless in the days that followed, always pacing and fidgety. He finished unpacking and moving in, and while I welcomed his presence, it was frustrating to have his things piling up on top of mine. There was a time when we were first married that all our things fit side by side. Somehow the house had shrunk, or things had spread out during our separation, and now they overflowed. The tension wasn't about love. Love didn't have anything to do with the dirty underwear I picked up off the floor and had nothing to do with commitment. I was committed but not particularly happy—especially when I tripped with my partial foot over the boot Chance had left under a bath towel, nearly landing me in the toilet—and he had left the seat up.

Things literally reached the breaking point on the following day when I whacked my foot on his tackle box. The same tackle box I had asked him to move more than several times. Real world stuff. I howled, and we squared off like a couple of gunmen at high noon, both shouting, frustrated, something about not being able to take it anymore. At least we agreed on something.

It was time to talk the talk, and we spent the day talking about everything from recent events to dirty underwear. I encouraged Chance to join in the investigation and search for Quincy. He knew better than to argue when I assured him, "I have a gun, and I can take care of myself."

Ashley stopped by to tell me that she heard Pastor Mac was shacking up with his new girlfriend, Oma.

"I thought they broke up," I said, smiling at her gossip because she was my friend. I didn't embellish it this time, but I didn't end it either.

Ashley frowned in thought. "I haven't seen her in church. It's just something I heard."

And of course, Ashley had questions. Always more questions. Ashley wanted the details of "everything" that had happened.

How could I tell her without reliving it? Isn't it enough that I relive it every minute of every day? So I minimized everything and skipped the part about signing paternity papers. Quincy was gone, and I told Ashley, "If it weren't for my foot and face, none of this would seem real."

"Maybe that's why God allowed you to lose your toes," said Ashley, "so you'll never forget who brought you through it."

Ashley put my hand on her belly, and I could feel the soccer game going on inside her. Must be boys, I think, although Ashley and Shane were adamant about not wanting to know the sex of their children in advance of their birth.

"We want it to be like our wedding night," said Ashley with a slight blush. "We want it to be a surprise—unknown and exciting. There aren't that many opportunities for those kinds of surprises in life, and we don't intend to miss out on this one just for the sake of color coordination."

I thought their decision was beautiful beyond words. Just beautiful. I sighed, thinking of Quincy, and I wanted to hold her in my arms once again. I laughed as I imagined us with mother-daughter matching casts on our feet, covered with silly decorations and loving words—and then I hastened to ask God to forgive me for being so shallow when no one knew if she was alive. And here I was, making jokes about an amputation that was my fault.

Mac stopped by too. We did not talk about Oma. We talked about guilt. Mine.

"Quincy had some toes on her right foot amputated," I told Mac, "and they were watching her burns and possible damage to her fingers when she was taken." I choked up as I spoke, but at least I didn't break down into a sobbing mess again.

Mac and I spent a pleasant hour drinking coffee and sitting in front of the fireplace. It was nice to finally be with someone who didn't ask me to recap events but chose instead to listen attentively and offer an occasional comment.

"Mac," I said, "I feel as though God has given me a burden that I cannot bear."

Mac reached out in sympathy and replied, "God will never give you more than you can bear. Have you ever thought that maybe you alone were chosen for this burden because you alone can carry it? In fact, when I think about it, I would have to say that the entire incident sounds like a major miracle to me. It seems like that baby, Quincy, was incredibly fortunate to have you rescue her." Mac's mustache turned up at the corners, and his warm smile reached to his eyes that lit with admiration. "Really, Sunny—you are one of the strongest, most courageous women I have ever known."

Rescue? Courageous? Seriously . . .

Mac continued, "You did what the child's mother asked you to do. That sounds to me as if you were honoring her choice, and a mother usually knows what is best for her child. Just because her decision ended badly, doesn't mean it couldn't have ended worse: like a homicide-suicide, killing the baby along with herself. It happens." Mac rose and bent over, giving me a warm, compassionate hug. "Quincy may have lost some toes, but she gained her life. She owes that to you. It took a lot of faith for you to cross those mountains. Don't stop now. Her kidnapping is just another mountain. Keep the faith, my sister." Then we prayed, asking God to make a way for Quincy's safe return.

At some point, I realized that the visitors continually dropping by were mostly compassionate, exceedingly kind, and brutally curious. I also realized that they were babysitting me while Chance was off on business. I was never alone. Even our almost-two-hundred-pound German shepherd, Mercy the Magnificent, had somehow become a house dog, shedding, knocking things over with her tail, and tormenting Kissme whenever she grew bored.

I really wanted time alone to process my feelings instead of the daily repeating of details. I needed to fit together the missing pieces of the big picture. Instead, my focus had narrowed to endless cups of coffee, the state of my missing toes, and a messy house.

What Chance and I had not talked about was the deceit that continued to taint our relationship. I was not sure at what point outright lies—the lies of omission and evasion—had become our norm again, but we had yet to talk about his so-called missionary trips to Mexico. It was hard to accuse Chance of being a liar when I was one. I hadn't told him about the bracelet charm found at the ritual gathering site that looked like the one I gave Paige, or the tarot card that Duncan found in my in-box, or, for that matter, the kiss I had exchanged with Travis outside Chow Mein Charlie's. Perhaps by excusing Chance, I thought I was justifying myself. This didn't feel like a fresh start. It felt more like a continuation of the same problems that drove us to separation. We had stopped demanding truth from each other. After all, how could either of us believe what the other one was saying?

Sometimes I thought those partial truths would be the death of us.

ॐ ♀ ☌

"You lied to me, knowing that deceit is what drove us apart before, and yet you did it again. You lied about Mexico. A mission trip? Honestly, Chance. It's practically sacrilegious. And all that time you were playing secret agent."

It was time for the talk.

Pillow talk. Heart talk, from deep beneath the down comforter.

"You." Chance's answer was as straightforward and direct as the man himself. He stretched out next to me staring at the ceiling, his fingers woven together under his head. "You will always be more important to me than us." Chance glanced at me, then cast his eyes down in disappointment.

"What?"

He sighed and shook his head. "God, Sunny, don't you know that I love you? The core of our faith is that there is 'no greater love' than laying your life down for someone. I've told you before, and I'll say it again, I am your husband, and it is my duty to protect you."

"Yeah, well—how's that going to work for you if we end up divorced?" I was only half kidding. We had come close to the Big "D" before.

Chance rolled over to face me, propping himself up on one arm. "Divorce wouldn't stop me. You're stuck with me, hon"—he reached out and let his fingers trail up and down my arm—"till death do us part."

I arched an eyebrow at him. "And here I had my heart set on happily ever after. How long can we go on like this? It's the lies."

"As long as necessary. As long as you're in danger—and you will always be in danger as long as Logan's alive or until the money's found."

"It seems to me that I would have been a whole lot safer with you here instead of in Mexico."

Chance frowned and eased back on his pillow. "Have you ever heard the story of the Three Sisters?"

Chance and his stories. "You're going to tell me, right?"

Chance reached over and took my hand. "Three sisters left their village to take a walk. When they got to the river, they saw dozens of babies floating downstream. The first sister jumped in the river and started grabbing the babies and throwing them up to the second sister, who was waiting on the bank. The second sister caught the babies and laid them safely on the shore. When the third sister took off running upstream, the other two called out, 'Sister, where are you going?'

"Sister number three never stopped running, but she yelled as she ran, 'I'm going to find out where the babies are falling in.'"

Silence.

"Sunny," said Chance, "you, and apparently Quincy will never be safe until we solve this puzzle."

My feelings warred. Outrage punched appreciation in the nose. Appreciation hugged outrage in return.

"Okay." I hesitated, sat up, and turned on the lamp by the bed so I could look at Chance. I needed to see him and gauge him. I loved him as much as he loved me. I had tried to protect him also. I thought Chance had no idea how vicious and extensive outlaw bikers and their clubs could be—they had killed my father, and I had no intention of letting them bury my husband. Now, this. Now the cartel put his life at risk as he worked to protect me.

It was a losing battle, and I knew in my heart that neither of us would ever surrender. We would both do whatever it took to protect the other.

"Will you tell me everything? No more secrets?" I asked, and Chance readily nodded.

"You'll let me help you?" Chance asked eagerly as he leaned forward, looking expectant and hopeful.

I nodded in assent. I loved this man more than anything short of God Almighty, and I didn't intend to lose him—not to a gang, not to a bullet, not to Logan. Not even to Travis.

"What happened in Mexico—besides mojitos?"

There was a slight twitch at the corner of his mouth, and he pulled himself up to sit next to me. For a moment, I was distracted and disarmed at the sight of his body. He was so manly; my eyes trailed up rippling muscles and stopped at his midnight-blue eyes.

His eyes widened. "I actually did serve food to the homeless and do ministry."

"Then . . . ?"

"Then business as usual. You want the long version or the short?"

My lips pressed into a tight line. "I'll take the full meal deal."

"Okay," Our eyes locked, and his narrowed as he drew his knees up and leaned forward. "The same cartel that kidnapped Paige has expanded their business. Every day they're moving guns and drugs and people across the border. We're talking about hundreds of people—some for human trafficking—a shitload of drugs, and tens of thousands of dollars, daily."

"Yeah, I watch the news." Sometimes. "I know the cartel thinks I'm sitting on Fort Knox. I wish I did have their damned money," I said wistfully "Then I'd tip them off, and when they came to get it, I'd blow them up with it."

Chance smiled with appreciation. "That's my girl! But you know they aren't looking for the truth; they're looking for their cash. The real danger is what they believe—and as long as they think you might know the location, they'll keep coming."

Chance ran his fingers along his jaw. "I keep thinking that maybe, perhaps, you do know something—only, you don't know that you know it."

I shrugged. I had chewed on that thought for so long that it had fossilized before I buried it.

Chance tugged thoughtfully at the end of his mustache, his eyes running back and forth like a hound looking for a track. "Maybe, in the beginning, they thought ATF would locate the rest of their cache. And if they had Paige, they could blackmail Perry into compromising the location of the money before the real bust came down—in exchange for getting his daughter back. If so, then Perry screwed their plans royally when he got Paige back through diplomatic channels."

"But that was over ten years ago."

Chance nodded and said, "The connection to us is bikers. Outlaw gangs are right up there with the the leading purchasers and distributors of the contraband we're talking about. One gang in particular—not new, but you wouldn't believe how fast it's growing—calls themselves Discípulos de Muerte, or Disciples of Death. They are based out of Santa Muerte, Mexico. Figures, right? They've taken over California and the Southwest worse than AIDs in Africa. That town, Santa Muerte? It literally means 'Saint Death.' It's very real."

"Yeah, Dr. Shelton said that followers were coming over the border with the illegals. But I didn't know they were in Northern California. I had never heard of them. I guess they haven't made it up here—to our little redneck corner of the woods."

Chance drew his eyebrows together and gave his mustache another twist. "Actually, I think they are here—maybe the person who nailed the chicken to the front door in Feather Falls is part of that gang, and it's possible that a member might have tailed you to Fresno.

"These guys are very scary, babe. They are outlaw bikers who actually work with both Nortenos and Surenos, meaning they control both Northern and Southern Mexico, not to mention Northern and Southern California. Think about it—that's the equivalent of a third party selling weapons to both Sunnis and Shiites in the Middle East. These Disciples have taken over both the streets and prisons. That makes them extremely dangerous."

"Phew." It was a lot to absorb.

Chance's gaze ignited. "They aren't just another biker gang with a crazy name. People have this outdated idea when they think of Satanists. They think back to the 1970s and 80s Satanic Panic,

Church of Satan, and all that stuff. These guys are the real Satanists of our age. They love death." He blinked. "That's why I asked Travis to keep an eye on you."

"New Age Satanists." I mulled it over and breathed a sigh of relief. "I haven't had any biker-related cases—just the old-fashioned kind, and I get more all the time as people find out I do this stuff. Everyone wants to dump their cases on me."

"I'm sure of it. I just want you to understand what's going on with the Mexico connection."

"They are really that big, huh?" The night was growing colder. I shivered and pulled up the comforter.

"These guys from Santa Muerte—they have literally taken over lots of churches in Mexico, especially those along the border. They worship this figure that looks like the Virgin Mary, except she has a skeleton face, and they believe heart and soul that she blesses their businesses—including drugs, guns, prostitution, and human trafficking. They literally worship death."

Oh crap.

"And, Sunny." Chance's voice took on a sense of urgency. "They are swarming over the border by the hundreds every night. People watch the news and think they are safe because ATF and border patrol make some busts. What they don't get—which is more dangerous than contraband—is the mindset they bring with them. They love death, and they engage in ritual sacrifice. They are Satanists on steroids."

Rough questions tumbled around my mind, like raw material in a rock polisher, slowly smoothing and taking shape. "I've always understood why they were after me. But is it possible they still wanted Paige? Maybe they do . . . um . . . did still want her. She said she was trying to hide from them when she showed up at the cabin. What's the connection? And why . . . why would she kill herself?"

Chance turned off the lamp and scooted over, sliding down under the covers next to me, holding me close. "It's just a hunch I have," said Chance, "but maybe it is the same reason they wanted her the first time they kidnapped her—to control her father. ATF will never close the case until the cache of money is found. All the cartel needs are tips in advance of a bust, and they can get there first and recover their money. If they had Paige, or Quincy— Perry's new granddaughter . . ." Chance let the thought hang between us. "Maybe Paige was terrified at the prospect of her and her child being taken back to Mexico as hostages and forced back into prostitution. Maybe she figured death was a better option."

Ghostlike tears slipped unseen through the dark. "That guy who attacked me at the hospital—he said he wanted the baby. Newborns are a little young for prostitution, aren't they?"

Chance tensed in the bed. "Too young for prostitution, but not too young to sell. You can buy a slave on the world market for around ninety dollars." Chance shifted uncomfortably. "Let's not go there—I don't know anything for certain. I'm just trying to sort it out. It has to go back to Paige's father. Or maybe even Travis."

That got my attention. My eyes popped open. "How does Travis figure into it?"

"Travis could be . . . Quincy's father. And he's also a part of the ATF investigation. That means the cartel could be attempting a repeat performance—using a child to blackmail a father who works inside ATF." Chance lowered his voice. "We are talking about a lot of money here—a lot more than we initially thought. Maybe millions of dollars. They'll do anything to get it. And I mean anything."

The wheels kept tumbling in my mind. "It's time," I whispered.

"What's that?"

I snuggled deeper into Chance's arms. "Nobody else has said it, but I will. We can at least solve one mystery. There has to be DNA somewhere. It's time for a paternity test. Don't you think?"

Outside I heard the sound of wind chimes kissing in the night. Dawn on the left and Moonrise on the right. It is said that the Holy Spirit moves like the wind, wherever it pleases. You hear its sound, but you cannot tell where it comes from or where it is going. So it is with everyone born of the Spirit. Tonight, spirit and the music resonated as I lay somewhere between the two chimes, listening, and feeling the touch as I fell asleep.

Chapter 34

ଚ ⚷ ଓ

"Are you ready?" asked Chance.

No. How could I be ready? How does one prepare for a funeral except through the power of disassociation? And that's where I had been all morning, trying not to think about the present or the future. Unfortunately, looking back didn't turn out to be such a good idea either.

ଚ ⚷ ଓ

The smell of exhaust, leather, and testosterone filled the air, filled the city. Harleys as far as the eye could see, men had come to pay homage to my father who had been murdered at the Laughlin shoot-out. These were hard men, like my dad, battle-scarred and tough. They had respected my dad.

Logan and I rode out in front, just behind the president of the Oakland Chapter of Hell's Angels. I had not ridden with Logan since the fateful trip to Sturgis. The parade could have taken the short route, directly from Oakland across the Bay Bridge to the cemetery, but my father would get the full circuit tour. The cavalcade would travel north to Richmond, across the Richmond–San Rafael Bridge, and then south on Redwood Highway before the last leg, crossing the magnificent Golden Gate Bridge to enter the cemetery just beyond.

I reluctantly held on to Logan as we led off. A long black hearse trailed behind us, pulling a longer black trailer. My father was in the hearse; his bike was mounted on the trailer, draped with a million red roses. Our destination was the San Francisco National Cemetery for veterans. The cemetery was filled to capacity when my father died. In order to get a space in this prestigious cemetery, where fallen soldiers now guarded the city like silent sentinels looking out where the ocean meets the bay, somebody had to disinter—which was a fancy way of saying a dead guy needed to vacate the premises. This rarely happened, but somehow a prime spot miraculously became available in the days that followed Lefty's death.

On the morning of the funeral, Logan had been particularly amorous—in spite of the fact that I was in mourning and sex was the last thing on my mind.

"Come on, baby—we're celebrating life here." He covered me with kisses; his body felt warm and hard. He was feeling playful, but I knew how quickly his moods could change. "Give me a little honey, Sunny. You owe me."

"I owe you?" Skeptical but curious, I asked, "How do you figure?"

"Umm." He nibbled on my body and murmured, "I got your daddy the best seat in the house."

"What's that supposed to mean?"

"It means roll over and be nice. Give me a little bit of Lefty. It's payday."

Logan was always talking like that, so I didn't give it a lot of thought at the time.

Experience had taught me there was no denying Logan when he wanted sex. I could give it nice, or he would take it with violence. It was all the same to him. I was his. Signed. Sealed. Delivered.

ဆ ♀ ର

"I guess I'm ready," I shrugged. Chance helped me into the Dodge.

January was always a strange month for California weather. Some days it snows, and other days will find people dressed in shorts and tank tops. Californians usually economize; heavy jackets over shorts and socks with their Birkenstocks. Today, ragged clouds scudded across the foothills, sunshine occasionally popping out between them, offering shimmering rays of hope.

Kenny's daughter arranged for his memorial to be held in the administrative buildings of Feather Falls Casino, far from the brassy business of taking money. His surviving sons and daughters sat near Joyce, who stood up when I walked in. Head held high,

Joyce boldly crossed the room, daring anyone to give me hostile looks or murmur accusations.

"Sunny. Chance." Joyce welcomed us. "Come. Sit with me." Joyce was an amazing woman. How was it possible that she could be thinking of me and my feelings on this day, of all days, with anything other than blame or rage?

The service was simple. Kenny would have liked that. Friends and family took turns standing up and sharing memories. Some funny stories, some generous stories—all a testament to the wonderful man that Kenny had been. Typical of the Maidu people, the tables along the walls were overflowing with homemade food: platters of carved meat, tempting casseroles, baskets with warm bread, steaming vegetables, and bright-colored desserts. The delicious smells were intoxicating as they drifted silently around the room, inviting life and stirring appetites on this sad occasion.

After the storytelling came the feasting. After the feasting, the drumming. Outdoors the drummers gathered in a circle, the circle of life, blessed by the warmth of the pale winter sun that came to say good-bye. With the drumming came the songs. Songs that invited the Maidu ancestors to come and sing and guide Kenny home.

ℴ♀ℛ

Saturday was spent packing and making the three-hour drive to the Bay Area for Paige's funeral.

"I don't want to stay with the Atchisons," I said with a scowl. "Cali hates me."

And I don't need Paige's ghost tiptoeing into my room.

"We need to." Chance was insisting as much as I was resisting, and things were tense. "It's the best way to talk with Cali and Perry about the baby."

There was something incredibly attractive, yet unbelievably foolish—possibly even stupid—about Chance's obsession. My thoughts swirled south like the spin cycle inside of a toilet.

What baby? Chance needed to get a clue. Ridiculous, but I held my tongue for love's sake. Who is he kidding? We both worked in law enforcement and knew that the odds of recovering Quincy significantly decrease day by day. It had been weeks now, and the odds were still slipping, landing somewhere between slim and none.

Yet Chance talked as if Quincy were at Grandma's house. Oh well . . . I let him hope for the both of us. For me, I had none.

Rain clouds wrung every drop, and we were not only grateful but sorry to see it slacken as we neared the Bay Area. Another year of drought, I thought as I gazed at the windshield, watching the rain turn to a drizzle, then a mist, then looking like glistening cheeks after the tears.

We finally arrived in beautiful Sausalito, where I gawked like the country bumpkin that I was.

"Wow. What you think these homes cost?"

Chance snorted. "Probably somewhere between a half-million and multimillion."

We took a narrow road that wound to the top of a hill and turned into the driveway of a sleek modern two-story home with a commanding view of the ocean. We got out of the car, and I breathed deep in the rain-washed salt tang of the air, admiring the house as I stumped my way up the drive. Their home was breathtaking; the front of the house, mostly glass, was framed in white and bounded by a pair of gnarled cypress trees that grew from an outcropping of serpentine. The trimmed lawn hugged sweeping stairs of flowers and shrubs and vines that defied the winter weather.

I gripped my crutches, already feeling awkward and out of my element.

Paige's mother greeted us at the door with an assistant guiding her wheelchair. She looked one step away from being next in line for a funeral. I shook her hand, thinking, I hope they bought a family plot, before turning red and mentally making the sign of the cross.

Everything was formal. Her greeting was formal, the decor formal, the hired help formal, and the conversation stilted and formal. I found myself squirming inside my bandages.

"It was hard to find shoes to match my outfit," I joked, feeling underdressed in my pants and unflattering shoe with a thick rubber tread. The last thing I needed was to do "a Duncan" and slip on the Atchison's polished wooden floor and break a leg.

I had to hand it to the Atchison's—they didn't serve wine from a box. The wine came with corks, and it came in abundance. There was a pop and a sigh when they uncorked; wine flowed and appetizers arrived, served by one of those ageless Asian women who wore an apron and a smile that lit up the room.

A little while later, there was a knock on the door.

"Please, come in." There was some friendly bantering between the staff when a familiar voice made me gasp and inhale a brioche-and-crème-fraiche tidbit into my lungs. My eyes watered as I coughed and sputtered as Travis entered the room. "Need a drink?" Travis asked, looking amused as he snatched a glass of wine from a tray and handed it to me.

Chagrined, I gulped the wine and held out the empty glass. "More?" Travis's back was to everyone. I was the only one who saw his dimples deepen and green eyes dance as he nodded to the hired help for more wine.

Travis was all business when he turned back to the group. Everyone did the meet-and-greet thing as if they had not seen each other in years. Travis kissed Cali on the cheek and shook hands with Perry and Chance.

The domestic help brought me another glass of wine that I nursed through their discussion regarding Quincy. Everyone acknowledged that there were no updates and then proceeded to talk about her as if she were in the next room. I sat there, biting my tongue and wagging my finger whenever my glass ran dry.

Admittedly, I had never sat in the company of so many idiots gathered under one roof to debate an issue that had no possible solution. But then, I have never engaged in politics. I listened to their conversation in amazement. First, Chance argued that he and I would make the best parents, then Travis countered by saying, "You don't know that." An hour later Cali said, "The child is all I have to remember my daughter by . . ." with a surreptitious glance in my direction. Finally, everyone agreed that Cali would keep Quincy until bio dad could be determined.

It was a good thing that no one attempted to engage me in their stupid conversation. The floors were starting to move, when the help finally announced, "Dinner is ready," and Cali turned to ask, "Is that agreeable to you, my dear?"

I looked at her, dumbfounded. "No. It is not agreeable," I said, mimicking her tone and snooty expression. "What the hell is wrong with you guys?" I was sloshed but not slurring. Woozy, but I could stand and probably walk in an almost straight line considering the condition of my foot. I held my head high. "I think you are all stupid beyond belief. You're all sitting here acting as if Quincy is alive—when we all know she's as dead as her mother." Turning away, I made my way to the nearest exit; through the door that led to a balcony overlooking the ocean and threw up.

I wiped my mouth with the back of my hand and then looked out at a sky the color of bruised plums and a restless sea of angry blue-black waves that crashed along the shore. The wind was fresh, and the cold helped to clear my head. I blamed the salt air for making my eyes water.

Chance followed, furious. "Is this how you show the Atchisons that you can be a good mother? By getting drunk and being rude and profane and . . . did you throw up? Dammit, Sunny."

"I'll do what I want and say what I think," I told Chance. "And I'm not hungry—go have dinner with your friends and leave me alone."

Chance stormed back in, and Travis drifted out. After a short period of silence, he said, "They have a great cook here. They planned tonight's menu with you in mind."

My eyes narrowed with suspicion. "Oh really, and what is that? Crème de Bologna?"

Travis's laughter was as light and refreshing as the breeze. "Salmon."

We stared at each other in silence. Travis knew that the wild salmon were symbolic for me, that their lifecycle reflected my own spirit: dedicated, self-sacrificing, expending their lives for the benefit of their species. They were nature's advocates.

Nothing more needed to be said. Travis took me by the elbow and guided me to the table. He was right. The salmon was delicious. I ate in unapologetic silence while the others made small talk and went to bed early without saying good night.

When Chance finally came to bed, he was holding a thick leather-bound book. "What's that?" I asked as he placed it on the table next to the bed.

"Cali gave it to me," he said, his voice low and tight. "She told me that she knows she is dying and believes that the baby is . . . should be . . . ours." He sat on the edge of the bed staring at his feet. "Even if Quincy turns out to be Travis's child, Cali hopes he will give her to us to raise."

The words slid through clenched teeth. "Are you guys for real?"

The soft light from the nightstand was just enough to see Chance's face darken a couple of shades. His eyes blazed in the half-light as he worked the muscles along his jaw. "Cali wanted me to have Paige's personal effects: her scrapbook and some keepsakes. She hopes that one day we will give them to her daughter."

There was the daughter thing again. I couldn't take it any longer.

"Why do you guys persist in believing Quincy is alive?"

Chance took offense and returned my glare. "Why do you have to insist she isn't?"

Another losing battle.

"What did Perry have to say about you getting the scrapbook and the baby?"

"Cali told me in private. She says that Perry acts tough, but he'll be as lost as yesterday when all his girls are gone. She figures that when she dies, Perry will probably have some cleaning service come in and throw everything away and that he is too set in his ways to raise a child alone."

Chance paused and then added, "I gave them your apologies."

My face tightened, and I held my pillow in a chokehold. "Never, never, apologize for me again. If I want to apologize to someone, I will. My choice. Not yours."

Chance drew back. He looked stricken for a moment and then agreed. "Of course. You're right. I'm sorry." With that, I rolled over, and Chance laid our fight to rest. I think he knew that different people coped with grief differently and attributed my outrageous behavior to the fact that I had been through hell.

This was true, but he still missed the point.

ഇ ☥ ൠ

We were the first to arrive at the funeral home, having traveled with Cali and Perry after a light breakfast. The sun sent pink threads that wove their way through a gray-blue sky above the horizon. The ever-present tang of salt seasoned the morning breeze. The white mortuary with a red tiled roof reminded me of Tara in Gone with the Wind, with high marble columns on the portico and a sweeping emerald lawn and circle drive, perched on the side of a hill with a view of the ocean. Inside, the anteroom led to an elegant atrium that reached up to the second floor and was filled with the scent of exotic flowers and a delicate mist from a cascading waterfall.

Perry stood well away from Cali, who was clinging to Chance, her shoulders heaving like a pair of angel wings taking flight, her tears deepening the charcoal black of his suit as she wept on his shoulder.

Paige's funeral was nothing like Kenny's. Instead of pickup trucks and used cars, the funeral home looked like a car lot for the rich and famous—shoulder-to-shoulder Cadillacs, Lexuses, Mercedes-Benz, and BMWs. Congressmen and senators arrived via their private jets from Washington, DC. And of course, with money came the press with microphones and cameramen in tow.

Perry shook hands with Senator Keeler and Director Sanger from Homeland Security. They had not come to pay respects to Paige but to Perry. Travis was standing behind Perry and off to one side, wearing a black suit and a pair of Oakleys, looking more like a mobster's bodyguard than a mourner.

I was shocked to see Jack Savage shaking hands and talking to Perry at the front door, but then, Paige and Travis had both worked undercover within our district attorney office. The bust in Feather Falls that led to Logan's imprisonment had been a coordinated effort between Butte County Sheriff's Office and ATF. Besides, Jack would never have missed the free drinks and the photo op that was sure to follow.

Perhaps even more surprising was the sight of Duncan hobbling in with a cane and Bonita trailing behind. Duncan and Bonita are not here for me, I told myself. They're here for Paige, their friend, and coworker. Well, coworker, anyhow. And maybe Duncan really was here for me. Hard to say.

Unlike Joyce, I had no support coming from Cali. I didn't blame her. Not at all. Cali Atchison and her sisters and in-laws withdrew, sequestered in a privacy room with a one-way window. I would've thought a person of Cali's caliber would have had the grace to invite me into her sanctuary to protect me from the family's hostile, grieving friends, much as Joyce had done. Instead, she threw me to the sharks.

They say that San Francisco Bay is one of the most shark-infested waters in the world. I can tell you that the funeral home contained even more; the waters fairly chummed with beautiful young women with killer eyes and an instinct for blood. Their words—polished white—were razor sharp and cut deep. Oh, you're the one. Oh yes, I saw you on the news. I've heard so much about you. And, of course, Paige told me all about you. I would have left, but Chance tightened his grasp on my hand and kept me anchored to the seat.

Travis joined the peons sitting in the nave, and I was shocked to see him arm in arm with a tall dark-haired woman wearing an elegant black dress and a sweeping black hat. Our eyes briefly touched from across the room, when an usher intercepted them and attempted to guide them to the front seats. Travis declined, giving their seats to an elderly couple, and took a seat further back.

Something tugged at my heart as I pondered my feelings for Travis. Once you have given someone a piece of your heart, you can't just take it back. It can wither and die, but you can't take it back and pretend that you are whole again—not any more than you could donate a kidney and get it back and pretend nothing had changed. It is bound to incur some damage.

I considered any traces of love I might still have for Logan. Like residue in a burned-out building, I mused, as soft background music filled the air. People often wonder why a victim of abuse would return to their abuser. They don't understand that men like Logan weren't always abusive. People can't imagine that soft, seductive words were whispered long before the cruel, damaging ones. Caresses and touches that once culminated in orgasmic ecstasy came long before his fist ever blackened my eye. I had given Logan my heart and could not take it completely back either. I had lived for years on the hope that one day Logan, the charming man I had so glibly given my heart to, would return. He did not.

Some last-minute flower arrangements were delivered by a couple as colorful as the flowers themselves; she was as black as night, and he was an albino, and they placed large silver and black urns on either side of Paige's casket as the music began.

Is it possible? Warning bells went off in the back of my mind.

"Chance . . ." I tugged his sleeve, whispering into his ear as the pastor stepped up to the pulpit followed by silence.

Chance patted my hand absentmindedly.

"Chance!" I cried out as I rose from my seat.

There was a flash—a bang—and all hell broke loose. The smell of smoke roiled through the room like a thick black fog as people screamed, pushing and shoving their way toward the exit. Panic reigned—but my husband instinctively covered me with his body while assessing the situation, then swept me into his arms and carried me to safety.

ɛᴑ ♀ ᴄʀ

Please, God, give me another rape case. Another domestic violence case. Anything—anything at all, except another ritual abuse case.

I was the first one to arrive at work in the morning and the last one to go home at night. I hid in my office behind my door and dined on salty tears for lunch. I didn't want to remember. I didn't want to go home. Home had become an emotional cauldron, simmering, steaming, and occasionally boiling over.

"I tried to tell you," I told Chance. "The albino—it was him at the cabin, at the lake. My God, he's the one that cut my throat."

"If we had just known sooner," Chance said.

But we hadn't. Poor Paige had never made it to the cemetery. Her remains were incinerated along with her mother and several other members of the Atchison family. Not Perry. Perry was in front of the mortuary greeting the governor, whose limousine had been delayed in traffic.

There'd been no other fatalities. The bomb seemed to have been set to do the maximum damage to the family sitting in the privacy room. The guests, including Travis and my coworkers, were not seriously harmed. The investigation revealed that pipe bombs had been planted inside of the two urns that bordered either end of the casket, and the casket had been snugged up beneath the viewing room window.

Cali was dead. Leave it to Chance to say that it was a mercy, sparing her from a prolonged and painful death. For myself, I remained numb and disassociated. I was not going to one more funeral. Ever. Not even Cali's.

Chance played the guilt card. "But she's the grandmother of our child."

I completely lost it. "Shut up, Chance! Just shut up! You're insane—listen to yourself. There is no our child. Quincy is gone—dead, just like her mother and grandmother. Get over it already!"

Chance went to her funeral, and I went to work.

ഇ ✝ �

"Sunny, are you awake?" Chance whispered softly in the dark. He was back from Cali's memorial. I was facing the wall, pretending I hadn't spent the past six hours waiting and worrying . . . wondering when he would come home.

"Umph." I made a stupid little grunting noise to let him know he was disturbing my sleep and continued to lie still with my eyes closed. I heard the muffled sound of his shirt being unbuttoned, followed by noise of a zipper and the soft thump of pants dropping to the floor. I felt cool air as the sheets were pulled back and breathed in his masculine, woodland scent as he slid into bed, careful not to touch me.

I lay there waiting for I don't know what—probably waiting for the sound of his breathing to lull the both of us to sleep. Instead, I felt him curl into a ball—his back to me as soft vibrations hummed through the mattress. Chance was crying, and my charade crumbled in the wake of his tears. I was out of words. I had nothing left to give but my heart and my body.

I reached out for my husband, drew him in, and gave both.

PART THREE

Ephesians 6:12
We wrestle not against flesh and blood…
but against rulers of the darkness of this world.

CHAPTER 35

ℰℭ ☦ ℭℛ

"Help me! Sunny, you gotta help me. They're here. Oh God . . . Oh shit," came the desperate whisper, fearful and shaky as a rattle in a dying man's chest, her anxious words crept through the phone.

"Don't hang up! Stay on the line," I said, automatically beginning the process for tracing calls in case we became disconnected. "Is this Grace? Hello? Grace—is that you?"

"They're at the front door. Listen—"

Background sounds of heavy pounding and muffled curses could be heard without pressing my ear to the phone. I hoped a neighbor was dialing 9-1-1.

"I've locked myself in the bathroom," Grace panted. "What do I do?" Panic escalated in her voice. "Oh God—they're in the house."

"Is there a window? Get out—run to the nearest shopping mall and call me from there. Go!"

Leaving the phone connected, I hurried to my door and yelled at Bonita, who was just leaving Amanda Cross's office. Bonita let loose with her "Tengo este," ("I got this") and came running. Within seconds, she had control of the tactical parts of contacting emergency responders and was dispatching them to Grace's location from the address that I pulled from my files and handed to her. I used Amanda's phone to contact Mia at Victim Witness in Shasta County.

Mia was familiar with Grace's case. When it comes to work, an advocate's closest ally is always another advocate—someone you can actually talk to about ritual abuse cases when you think you are going crazy. Additionally, Mia was the go-to woman for relocating victims.

Mia called her contact from The Women's Refuge, who agreed to respond to the Top of the Hill shopping mall out by the interstate. The responder would be on standby to pick Grace up when she called.

Bonita wanted more details about Grace and the perp and was not happy when I refused to give them. Victims were my priority, which was opposite of the perp-priority business of prosecution.

Bonita turned surly, pointing her finger at me and saying, "If we catch the perp, there won't be another victim!"

"Put the gun down," I said. "Never aim a loaded finger at me again. I know you're doing your job and I promise that I will do my best to help you—as soon as I have done my job and relocated the victim."

"We can do both," Bonita argued. "We can arrest these guys and have Victim Witness relocate her later."

I hadn't told Bonita—and I never would—about the doctor's call regarding the "basement" cesarean, or about Grace's amazing personality transformation as she morphed from fully impaired to completely capable. Bonita didn't understand the fragile relationship that existed between victim and advocate. Grace and I didn't start off with a pouring-your-heart-out relationship. It had been a long, slow process of building trust. Our last day together was the crowning moment as we waited for the ride that would relocate her to Redding. That was the day that Grace shared her darkest secret.

We had sat in the cold winter sun on the little lawn behind the SAFE house in Chico, side by side idly picking blades of grass, twisting them and flicking them away with the same apparent randomness that she herself had been selected, used, and now apparently was to be disposed of.

Tears glistened, looking like bits of frozen sunlight against her pale skin. "They killed my baby." She choked on the words. "I was impregnated by the warlock. He told me that I was Satan's bride, and it was my duty and a great privilege to bear his child." She swiped the tears from her face and then absently wiped her nose on the back of her sleeve and sniffed. "I ran away. I didn't want them to take my baby. One of the other women in our 'church' told me that her child had gone to be with Satan, and I wasn't going to let that happen to mine."

Grace's silence lasted so long that I finally prompted, "What happened next?"

Her words came out on tiptoes, although there was no one else around to hear. Just me . . . and God.

"They found me. They always find me." Her face was sad, her eyes haunted, lost in memory. "They took my baby—"

The doctor was right. I hadn't wanted to believe it. Now those butchers were after her again.

I clicked my fingernail against the face on my watch and checked it against the clock on the wall. Could time go any slower? My head jerked at the sound of the phone. It was Mia, confirming that Grace had been picked up at the mall and was in the process of being transported to the women's shelter in Chico.

The paper trail stops here. I made the decision regardless of Bonita. With Mia's help, Grace would continue to be relocated. Within the week she would be in a different state. Her circuitous journey would include multiple layovers at various shelters using a different name at each location until reaching her final destination on the East Coast.

Grace's rescue would be the result of a coordinated network of response executed by dedicated advocates. Such networks have historically been an invaluable resource for victims of domestic violence. They worked in the same fashion as the Underground Railway during the Civil War, where a network of Quakers coordinated with an African American Union spy named Harriet Tubman to move runaway slaves from the South and quietly dispersed them throughout the North.

"Good-bye my friend," I said as Grace and I hugged each other, gently swaying back and forth as if our bodies were waving farewell.

The car engine idled in the alley behind the SAFE house, a cloud of smoke puffing from the tailpipe into the chilled morning air as Mia packed Grace's bag into the car.

"Will I ever see you again?" Grace whispered.

"No. You mustn't try to contact me or anyone else from your family, in any way. Not a call, a text, e-mail—"

Grace tried to smile, but it failed to reach her eyes. "No carrier pigeon? No smoke signal?"

"No. Not even that. Think of this as the Witness Protection Program without ever having to be a witness. A new start," I said, with an encouraging look. Squeezing her shoulders, I stepped back.

The car door shut resolutely. Mia nodded through the window as they pulled away.

"Godspeed," I called out with a wave.

ഔ ✝ ര

"Dano, we need to talk."

"You bet we do. I've got some news about Taylor."

"No—no ritual abuse cases. Not this time. It's me. I need to talk with you about me. I . . . I can't do this anymore."

"Oh my gosh, Sunny. I'm sorry. How could I have forgotten? I heard about Paige and something about an explosion at her funeral. That must have been a nightmare. I'll clear my calendar for you. Give me a half hour to reschedule my patients and then come over. I'm here for you, as a friend and as a mental health counselor. However, you need me."

The walk to Mental Health seemed unusually long as I hobbled along thinking about all the insanity I had been through: Paige killing herself, Kenny sacrificing his life for me, the trip over the mountains, the bear, the river, the amputation, Quincy missing, and then bombs at the funeral home. I couldn't take anymore. Perhaps a part of me was coming to understand Paige in a whole new light. There comes a time when you are so overwhelmed by life that death doesn't seem all that bad. Not that I was suicidal, mind you. I didn't have a plan to die. I just didn't know how to go on living.

I spent the next two hours recapping the events for Dano. I told her truthfully that I couldn't take it anymore. I couldn't handle the responsibility of another life and possible death.

"Latte?" Dano leaned back in her chair and high-beamed love lights from her eyes, then she walked around her desk to hold me while I cried—and cried—and cried some more. That how some people handle crisis. When the dam finally breaks, everything comes out. I could finally grieve for Paige, Kenny, and Quincy. Dano made us a pair of lattes while I wiped zebra stripes of mascara from my cheeks.

"None of it was your fault, Sunny. You know that. You just forgot. You're an advocate who gets some of the worst cases there are, and you can handle them well because you know that whatever happens to the victims is not your fault. You're overwhelmed right now and in shock. Let's break it down into pieces the same way you do for your clients. Okay?"

"Ready." The familiar smell of sweetened lattes crept through the room, the warmth of the cup and Dano's voice were comforting.

"Correct me if I'm wrong. It sounds like Paige made the decision to come to the cabin and later take her life, without consulting you."

I nodded in agreement.

"That's called self-determination." Dano paused to sip her coffee and to let me absorb her point.

"It sounds like Kenny was a remarkable man who dearly loved you. He thought of you as his daughter. Tell me, Sunny—what father wouldn't give his life for a beloved daughter?"

I thought about Perry Atchison, who would gladly give his life to get his daughter back. And I thought of Chance and Travis, who would do anything to find Quincy. Then, I thought about my own father, who had devoted his life to me. I knew that my dad would have died to protect me.

"Yes," I nodded in agreement. "You're right."

"Sunny, your trip over the mountains was nothing short of heroic. You are the most amazing, courageous woman I have ever met, and I am proud to be your friend. I would trust you with my life any day. That baby is alive because of you. What happens to her now is out of your hands and in God's. You know that."

Dano's words sent a pang echoing through the hollow passages of my heart, awakening a poignant longing for Quincy—a profound desire to hold and protect her once again. God—just to see her, smell her, touch her. I shook my head in resignation and then gave Dano a curious look.

"I didn't know you were a believer," I said.

"You never asked me." We exchanged a knowing look reserved for kindred spirits. "Now . . . about the funeral home. You have obviously stumbled onto something that is very threatening to some very powerful, very evil people. You didn't ask for it, and it's not your fault."

"In a way, I guess I did ask for it. I married Logan and the fact remains that I've brought horrible consequences on those around me."

"You deserve nothing of the kind. You deserve your amazing husband, a little house with a white picket fence, 2.5 children chasing Kissme around the house, a hefty mortgage, drowning in credit card debt, dental bills for the kids' braces—you know—the American Dream."

One short bark of laughter sent my grief flying like a wet dog shedding his burden.

Maybe laughter really is the best medicine.

Dano gave an encouraging smile. "The bombing at the funeral home? You know that was the work of crazies, not you. You're not crazy. You are strong and capable. And this"—Dano paused to write on the back of her business card—"is my home number. You call me anytime, day or night."

"How do I thank you?"

Dano rolled her eyes. "The next latte is on you—and I'll take a hot apple turnover to go with it." We stood and hugged as she whispered in my ear, "That's what friends are for."

I made it to the door before turning around, one hand on the knob, remembering. "You said something about Taylor that I needed to know?"

Dano's face lit up even as she shook her head in amazement. "My point, Sunny. You just made my point. Look at you," she said, slapping her hand on top of her desk. "You are an advocate to the core, and you are really good at what you do." Dano showered me with praise that I soaked up like a ShamWow infomercial.

"My last session with Taylor—she told me something I thought you would want to know."

"What's that?"

"She said she was worried about her little sister."

"Little sister? Is she referring to her alter personality, Tinkerbelle?"

"I don't think so. Not Tinkerbelle. She says she has a little sister that is going to be baptized at the next gathering."

"Baptized? Like—dunked in water?"

"No. Like, "passed through fire."

Understanding dawned, like throwing back a set of blackout curtains on a summer afternoon. I clearly saw how satanic cults continued to thrive in this age. Their security lay in perspective and social disbelief.

Rapes, robberies, shootings, beatings, kidnappings, and serial killings were considered atrocious but not extrodinary crimes. Then there were victims of satanic cults—victims whose injuries were so heinous that they became questionable. Crimes so bizarre as to generate disbelief and therefore attributed to psychopaths.

Denial is a cult's best friend, and the primary ways of diverting the truth is to lead people down the paths of mental health and sitcoms—prompting one to believe that allegations of ritual abuse must be delusional because everyone knows that Satanism is a joke.

When you laugh at anything, it loses its power over you.

Dano continued, "The cops won't listen to anything she says. They see her history of §5150 and send her back to me. I thought maybe you might have more influence with law enforcement than I do."

"When is this baptism supposed to happen?"

"February second. Candlemas—the day Jesus was brought to the temple after his birth and Mary was purified. Oh—and Sunny, one more thing. Please, don't follow her again. Why not let your husband and your friend Travis take care of it? After all, they're trained for that kind of work." She gave me that encouraging look again with the parting admonition: "Have faith."

A brisk wind swept down from the Sierras, painting startling white clouds with long brushstrokes across an azure sky. A pale winter sun, the color of the moon, was at its zenith. It was a perfect winter day. The kind of day my mother had chosen to take her life.

Taking a deep breath of the oxygen-enriched air, I cast aside the depressive thoughts that had skirted the fantasy of suicide. I guess God still has a plan and a purpose for my life.

I hobbled back to my office in my special boot, with slow, painful determination, reflecting on the deeper meaning of the Bible verse "Faith without works is dead." I guessed the best way I could thank God for me not killing myself was to stay alive and use the gifts he gave me.

But that was only half of the picture. Even as Dano had finished pumping me full of high-octane optimism, her parting comments had unknowingly dredged up reminders of how tenacious I could be. There was a difference between determined and pigheaded. The difference lay somewhere between wisdom and stupidity.

৪০ ✞ ০৪

"No—you're not getting a damn bike. Motorcycles are for men. Your job is to shut up, wrap your arms and legs around me, and hold on." It was late, about half-past drunk, and Logan was hammered, head nodding as he scowled through a pair of rheumy brown eyes.

"You know I can ride as good as any man. I still ride the trail bike Daddy gave me in seventh grade." I had my battle plan in place. "Besides, it's my money. I saved it up. It won't cost you anything, and I'll have a way to get around while you're gone. Come on, Logan. Please? I really want my own motorcycle."

Logan barked, hooting like a jackal. His black eyes narrowed, and lips curled back into a sneer. "Any money you have, you got from me, so technically it's my money." He lip-locked a bottle of Jack Daniels and took another hit. "You got no business riding anything but me." Again, he laughed. "You—on a bike. Now that there is seriously funny. Your job is to stay home and guard the house."

His words had lit my fuse, and I was fit to blow. Insulted and enraged, I stalked from the room. I didn't have long to wait. A few more swigs and Logan was out.

Taking the key from his pocket, I fired up his Harley and hit the road for the best twelve hours I had enjoyed in years. Soaring up the canyon along the Feather River, taking all the back roads, breathing the sweet air of freedom, I rode with the wind, feeling independent and complete—until coasting home at the end of the day with the gas tank on empty.

Unfortunately, those twelve magical hours translated into the same number of weeks to fully heal from the black eyes and fractured ribs that Logan delivered when I finally returned his bike. I went to sleep that night smiling to myself through swollen lips. I won! Logan could beat me, but he would never break me. The only thing that Logan could do that I couldn't—yet—was commit murder. But I was getting there.

ॐ ✝ ☪

Dano's remark had done more than rekindle an old flame. Her words also lit the lamp that illuminated my path. Between the visit with Dano and flashback to the day I'd taken Logan's Harley, I started to accept that maybe I really was smart and brave and capable.

If what Taylor told Dano was true, then urgent legal intervention was needed. But Taylor had been relegated to the "invisible" caseload: those cases that cops and crisis centers all have but rarely acknowledge—victims of ritual abuse. Law enforcement would not respond to Taylor's allegations. An advocate was her only means of defense.

If I don't help her, who will?

I knew the answer. I didn't want to know the answer, but I knew it nonetheless. The truth is like that—inescapable. Truth can be filed but not deleted. Just an hour ago I had hobbled into Mental Health wanting to be the problem instead of the solution. I wanted Dano to prescribe a pill that would take away the pain of my circumstances. I had longed to lay it all down. No more trials. No more guilt. No more death. No more insanity.

But now, on the even longer walk back to my office, came a great realization. Conviction left no room for doubt that I was born to be—and I will always be—an advocate. I could no more alter this fact than a wild salmon could sprout wings. Some things were simply written into our DNA. I smiled and embraced God's plan and purpose for my life.

Not only was I Taylor's advocate, but there was Quincy to consider. I had turned my back on Quincy while Chance and Travis had both held to hope, frequently alluding to those men of faith as "Dumb and Dumber." Now was my time—time to grab onto faith, accept the gifts God gave me, and start thinking for myself.

By the time I reached my office, I was footsore but vibrantly alive, analyzing instead of disassociating.

The question still begged to be answered: Why would Paige kill herself, with a heavy emphasis on the word *why*. After all, I mused, suicide is a permanent solution to a temporary problem. I asked myself again: What was so terrible for Paige that death was preferable?

Bonita dropped by to press me for information about Grace. Good as my word, I provided Bonita with Grace's new address in Connecticut. If she wanted to subpoena Grace for a trial, she could. Whoever was after Grace was really only guilty of breaking and entering. Without Grace's cooperation, it would be impossible to prove that Grace was in fear for her life.

I tried to make it up to Bonita by giving her another SRA case, the latest information on Taylor. Within hours, Bonita confirmed what Dano had already told me—that Taylor had been picked up under Code §5150—a code that provided a legal means of detaining a person who has not committed a crime, for up to seventy-two hours of mental health observation. The criteria for §5150 detention is that the detainee is believed to be homicidal, suicidal, or unable to meet her basic needs. Like most victims of ritual abuse, because Taylor had a long history with mental health, she now lacked credibility with law enforcement.

"Bonita," I asked, "why do you think Paige killed herself?"

Bonita eased her large frame onto the sofa and studied me as if trying to read between the lines. "What do you think?" she asked. "You knew her better than anyone." Her answer gave meaning to the term "cop-out."

"Thanks, Sherlock."

"Que es Sherlock? Why d'you keep calling me Sherlock?"

"It's a compliment. You're an investigator, and he was the best," I fibbed. "I'm asking you because I want your opinion."

Bonita cupped her chin and ran her thumb along her jaw. "Amanda told me about Paige—the kidnapping and prostitution. Maybe she never got over it. She seemed depressed to me. Distant. Maybe more so as her time drew near. She seemed that way to me anyhow." Bonita shrugged. "That's my guess. I'm no shrink."

I asked Duncan the same question when he came waltzing in, no longer on crutches and the cast off of his arm. His sleeves were rolled up, revealing my name tattooed on his forearm. "Duncan, we need to talk about that tattoo. But first I need to ask you a question."

"Fire away."

"Did you do something different to your hair?" I cocked an eyebrow. That wasn't what I had intended to ask, but something about Duncan had changed. Instead of 1950's buzz cut, his hair had grown out and was finger-styled with gel on the top. Extremely attractive.

He got that shiny-faced little-boy glow. "You like it?"

"Very much." I shook my head to clear it and get back to where I started. "It looks great on you. But that's not the question I wanted to ask. The question I want to ask you is, why do you think Paige killed herself?"

Duncan sat in the same spot that Bonita had, and his hunches weren't a whole lot different from hers. "Paige seemed really sad. It must've been tough carrying a child and not knowing who the father was. Maybe she felt abandoned all over again."

I couldn't sympathize with the unknown father theory. "She could have bought a paternity test kit at Walmart any day of the week."

"Oh." Duncan's thoughtful frown gave way to a look of elation as he leaned forward. "Maybe she was running from something. Or . . . or someone. Why else would someone blow up the funeral home?" His eyebrows danced in animated excitement. "Maybe it was the baby's father that blew the place up. You know—domestic violence?"

Yes, I know domestic violence.

Duncan's cell phone rang, and he reluctantly excused himself before we could talk about the tattoo.

I was going to keep asking until I figured out the answer. Kenny had taught me about the power of observation. He told me about a group of elders who sat in a circle inside a lodge, with an eagle feather placed in the center of the circle. Each person took a turn describing the feather as they went around the circle. While their descriptions were similar, no two people saw the same thing. Although the feather was one object, it had many sides. Each viewpoint was unique and yet a part of the whole.

Perhaps everybody was a little bit right, and eventually, I would get the whole picture.

I continued to mull it over as I cooked a special dinner for Chance and me. The house came alive with savory smell of pot roast with all the trimmings. I then took a break and pulled up my e-mail.

My stomach did a slow roll.

CHAPTER 36

ഇൻ ✠ ൙

"WHAT?! What? Fuc . . . fuc . . . fu . . . fff." I tried not to curse, but the shock was the emotional equivalent of having my fingers slammed in a car door, and something bad was going to come out of my mouth. The stream of half-curses fizzled as I banged my fist on the desk. The water in my glass sloshed as if rocked by an earthquake, the computer shuddered as if attacked by a virus, and the mouse jumped in terror.

One of the beautiful things about the church I attended was the faithfulness of the congregation to pray for one another. Whenever a person had a need, they simply sent an e-mail to one of the church ministries, and it would be promptly forwarded to caring church members. I had always felt it a joy and a privilege to pray for my church family, but I was furious over the outrageous e-mail in front of me.

Please pray for Sunny McLane—healing from her friend's suicide, her amputated fingers and toes, the dead child, and restoration for her troubled marriage.

The prayer chain had become a gossip chain, leaving me so upset that I had to dial Ashley's number four times before getting it right.

Ashley stood at the door looking like Mauna Kea, the world's biggest mountain—on the verge of eruption. I hugged all three of her and realized with a pang how much I missed the times we had once shared before we literally grew apart. Gone were the carefree activities, back when we rode bikes, kayaked, and jogged. The only thing we seemed to exercise now was our mouths, and the only "secrets" we shared was gossip.

My hug was followed by my scowl as I reached for her arm and hauled her over to my computer, pointing a righteous finger of indignation at the message on the screen.

"Did you do this?" My voice was high and tight with suspicion. Ashley's eyes widened as she read the message, her brows bouncing up and down like a bobber with a trout on the line. Trained to observe and assess people, I determined her innocence before she opened her mouth.

"Wow Sunny, you didn't lose any fingers!"

"Brilliant deduction, my dear Watson."

She should team up with Sherlock at work.

"So who the heck wrote it?"

"Not me. I didn't do it," she said, her eyes as round as a pair of communion wafers, "but you know I'm praying for you."

"Who would do this to me? This is the most embarrassing thing that has ever happened to me."

"Really?" She looked dubious. "I would've thought it was the time you—"

"Ashley. Stay on topic. Why would someone write this horrible stuff about me? This is private—personal. How am I supposed to ever go back to church?"

"I don't know. A lot of people have been dropping out of church lately. Oma is one of them."

"Oma dropped out of church? How is that possible? I thought that she had something going with Mac."

"Yeah, I think that was the problem."

"The problem?"

"Yeah . . . she had something going on with Mac."

"That wasn't exactly a secret."

Ashley rolled her eyes and then rubbed her belly suggestively and restated, "She had something going on with Mac."

I was learning a lot this week about how a sentence could change its meaning simply by having its emphasis changed. One minute the implication was that Oma was sweet on Mac, and the next minute I had visions of Oma bouncing between the sheets with Mac. My eyes popped, and Ashley confirmed my suspicions with a sage nod of her head.

Then I picked up my scowl where it had left off. "I intend to find out who sent this e-mail, and when I do, I'm going to make sure that they are the next ones to drop out of church instead of people like Oma and me."

ℰ ☥ ℬ

Hands on my hips, I showed the offending e-mail to Chance. All he did was shake his head and say, "Delete it."

"That's it? Don't you care that we are being slandered by the church? You don't want answers?"

"Yes, I do want answers, but not to this. This means nothing to me."

"How can you say that? Did you skim through it, or did you actually read it?"

Chance shrugged it off. "I don't believe in karma, but I do believe in the law of sowing and reaping. Plant seeds of kindness, and reap a harvest back. Plants seeds of gossip, and one day you'll be on the end of the ugly stick."

Ouch! That hurt. But then, the truth always does.

"They will get theirs," said Chance with an air of confidence. "What I want now is some of mine."

Kneeling next to my chair, Chance placed a hand on my thigh. His smile spread and blue eyes kindled, inviting me to soar with him as he brushed my hair back from the angry red scars that marred my face. Reaching up, he lovingly kissed each claw mark, pausing to linger a bit longer and kissing a bit deeper with each one, breathing the words "I love you" each time he came up for air. The passion was unexpected and long overdue. He worked his way to the top of my ear, which was significantly shorter than it had been before frostbite, tugging gently with soft lips as he breathed warmth into my ear. We had not made love since my rescue and subsequent surgeries.

Chance rose to his feet and said, "Does this look like we're having problems with our marriage?"

The glaring e-mail that had so raptly held my attention began to dissolve and fade into indifference under the warm glow of growing passion. Embers ignited, ready to be consumed. I didn't want to go there in my mind, but since Chance had been unfaithful to me before I was maimed and scarred, I felt a kind of quiet desperation to know that he still desired me, wanting me in the way a man longs for a beautiful woman.

I shook my head no, answering his question about the negative state of our marriage and wrapped my arms around his neck. Chance quickly lifted me from the chair and carried me through the house to our bed—where Kissme lay curled in a ball, indulging in her sixteen-hour-a-day beauty sleep. Raising a reluctant head, she growled at the prospect of being tossed off the bed.

What is it about not having sex in front of my dog? Kissme was not only booted off the bed, but Chance also locked her out of the bedroom as well.

Our laughter didn't diminish the mood, if anything it refreshed our passion for life in the way an unexpected summer shower gladdens the earth, teasing it to create.

One kiss at a time, one button at a time, we undressed each other for the first time, again.

☙ ♀ ❧

"Chance?"

We lay beneath the sheets in a lover's repose, enjoying the closeness, the softness, and the warmth of each other's bodies.

"Um-hum?"

"Why do you think Paige killed herself?"

Chance rolled his head back on his pillow with a weary sigh, sounding like a man whose burden had returned to his tired shoulders.

"I'm sorry. I shouldn't have asked you. At least not now. We can talk about it later."

We were more than interrelational; we were interdependent. We had, as our faith instructed us, become one person. I didn't think either of us could exist without the other.

"Hey, you don't have to be sorry for sharing what's in your heart. That's what I'm here for." Chance held me close, stroking my skin in the same familiar pattern that I sometimes used to calm Kissme. "I may not always have the answers, but I will always listen," Chance said, his voice as soft and inviting as the pillow beneath my head.

"I keep trying to figure out why—why"—I emphasized—"would Paige kill herself? I don't get it. I should have asked Danielle."

"I doubt that Danielle would have your answer. They didn't know each other."

"But Paige had everything to live for." The words tumbled out of my mouth. "She was young. She had my gun to protect herself from whoever was after us. She had a brand-new baby to love and raise. I can't figure out why she would kill herself. Are you positive it was suicide? Not staged to look like a suicide?"

"Absolutely," said Chance, pausing to collect his thoughts. "Maybe it wasn't any one single thing. Maybe it was a combination of things. You told me that right after Paige found out she was pregnant, she asked you to raise her baby. She certainly seemed depressed. Cali said that Paige wasn't eating or sleeping properly and that she never could verify whether she was under a doctor's care. I'm with you, sweetheart—trying to fit the pieces together. There's so much we don't know about her past."

"Long past, or when she was held by the cartel?"

Chance shrugged. "Maybe both. I keep thinking the truth lies somewhere along the line that connects her past to the present." I could hear the gears of his mind whirring in the silence between us. "The heart of the matter, the big question for me—and I don't mean to sound hard-hearted—is why this . . . this hit man . . . would want a baby. Maybe Quincy is the key."

The darkness of the night seemed to deepen. The gloomy thoughts were burdensome. It was as though our down comforter had suddenly been transformed into a dozen woolen quilts.

We lay in silence for a while, and then, reaching for Chance's hand and taking it in mine, I moved it upward to the soft swell of the curves that covered my beating heart. Chance's eyes kindled blue-hot, and once again we surrendered dark thoughts of death to a pleasurable erotic celebration of life.

CHAPTER 37

༄ ✚ ༃

Duncan strolled into my office with his smile stretching from one large ear to the other. "Notice anything new?" He wagged his eyebrows suggestively and did a pirouette that resembled a St. Bernard chasing its tail more than a ballet dancer. The newest Duncan looked rugged and handsome—nothing like the geeky nerd that had walked through the door only a couple of months ago.

"You lost weight, and you've been working out." Those were two wild guesses that I knew were safe bets.

"How did you know? Can you tell? Ah . . . I bet Bonita told you."

"You got me, tiger. I confess—it was Bonita. She said you guys have been lifting weights over at the gym, and that you're really glad to be done wearing splints and bandages. Better take it slow though. I'd hate to see you reinjure yourself."

Duncan lit up and nodded his head. I had to resist an urge to scratch him behind the ears.

"You wouldn't believe how much that woman can lift," said Duncan. "I swear, I think Bonita could hold my Harley over her head if she wanted to."

I nodded politely, having no problem at all imagining Bonita weightlifting a Harley, even a Harley with her girlfriend straddling it.

Tapping my pen against the desk, I asked, "So, what's up?"

The façade dropped as seriousness hijacked the joy from his face.

My features melted with his. "What is it? What's wrong?"

Duncan glanced back over his shoulder and shut the door with an apologetic look. "I'm sorry, Sunny. It's just that I . . . I found another one. Another weird thing in your in-box." He fished around in the pocket of his sport coat and pulled out a baby charm. A charm that looked exactly like the one I had given Paige. The same shiny silver heart with a little footprint etching that was identical to the one Forrest had found when investigating the blood moon animal sacrifice.

My mouth opened, silently forming the word where. I searched Duncan's gentle brown eyes and was surprised to see them retreat before my gaze.

Duncan wet his lips, pulled a chair close to me, and sat down. Reaching over, he took my hand and pressed the charm into my palm.

"It was in your in-box," he whispered. "You think it means something? Do you want me to put it back?"

"No. No . . . thank you. I'll keep it."

"Who do you think . . ." Duncan leaned forward and dropped his voice to a conspiratorial tone. Too late. My mind had already taken flight, backward in time.

෴ ☥ ෴

High school was a trial, both from the pretty girls in their makeup and the football players who liked to show off for the pretty made-up girls.

The kids were calling me names while playing keep-away with my backpack—part of the usual high school bullying activities while waiting for the bus.

I had gained some respect back in grade school, after shoving a girl into a patch of wild blackberries. But that felt like a long time ago. High school was worse. I didn't know how to fight against "pretty" or fight against "boys." That is—until the day Logan pulled up to the bus stop on his Harley wearing Hell's Angels colors.

Logan revved his engine until it roared like a hungry beast, making kids step back. Then he slowly scrutinized each trembling teen with his piercing black eyes as if searching out his prey, and they froze, mesmerized under his spell. He revved his engine again, making it scream, and laughed when they all jumped back another step.

Then Logan looked coolly at me and said, "Get on, girl." I walked up to the boy who still clutched my backpack to his chest and didn't say a word—just yanked it from his grasp and put it on before climbing up behind Logan and wrapping my arms and legs around him. Logan sneered at them, laughed again, and spit on the ground. He cracked the throttle, and we peeled out, leaving them open-mouthed and eating our dust.

I became the most talked-about girl in school, but the kids kept it to themselves, and it was the last time they ever made fun of me. Me—the little hippie-dippy mountain freak turned biker. It was my first taste of personal power in the adult world, and, I admit—it was exquisite.

Logan became my hero second only to my father. I desperately loved him because he made me feel safe and because he was my husband. I did everything he asked because I thought that's what a good woman did. But Logan became increasingly obsessed, trying to control my every move and thought. He cycled through his highs and lows, and I came to understand the meaning of the word bipolar.

Sex. Logan always wanted more and progressively kinkier sex. At first, it was okay—even adventurous—but over time he grew angry when I didn't, or wouldn't, perform to his expectation. Sex was often awkward and embarrassing; his friends downstairs would laugh and joke as Logan barked directions and howled pleasurable obscenities at my expense from our doorless upstairs bedroom.

Things started to change when Logan gave me a fat lip for refusing to repeat lines from a porn movie. Then there was the weekend Logan rode in with another woman and was infuriated when I refused to do a threesome.

The harder Logan pushed, the harder I pushed back. He grew increasingly violent, and being stronger than I was, he soon took what I would not give. Surrender became a form of victory. I learned that the pain of giving in was a lot easier than the pain of healing from black eyes, bloody lips, and sexual assault. And so we parlayed through the ever-escalating cycle of violence. But he never controlled my thoughts, and what was left of my heart would always belong to me.

ဆာ ✞ ର

"I'm sorry, Duncan. What did you say?"

Duncan paused for several beats, wrinkling his brows. "I said . . . my bike should be out of the shop soon. Maybe we could go for a ride." He paused again. "Are you okay, dear?"

I shook my head, trying to clear my thoughts the same way that Kissme shakes off sleep when she gets up in the morning. "I'm fine. And Duncan, you know, you are very dear to me also and . . ."

My words scattered and then took flight along with youthful memories as I looked past Duncan into the emerald eyes of Travis, whose silent presence suddenly dominated the room.

Duncan turned to look over his shoulder, starting with a sharp glare that quickly melted like an icicle before a furnace. Dropping his head and shoulders, Duncan politely excused himself and carefully squeezed past Travis, who refused to budge.

Men are so strange.

"Hello Sunny."

It was one of those awkward moments that continued to fall somewhere between agonizing temptation and steadfast commitment. For a moment, I allowed myself to swan dive into his eyes and let my mind run amok;—running my fingers through bronze hair, imagining rough hints of whiskers raking and tickling my face. I could feel him. I could smell him. Lord help me, I could practically taste him.

It's a good thing you didn't show up when I was looking to Dano for help.

Or maybe it was a God thing.

I recalled the night that I had begged Travis to "make me forget" my heartache, and forgive me Lord, but Travis had done it better than any drug Dano could have prescribed.

I just wanted to forget.

But I couldn't, and he knew it. It didn't work like that. Good memories are as elusive and fleeting as a beautiful dream, while bad memories are as cloying as a nightmare, impossible to forget.

Reality returned. Clearing my throat, I pushed back from my desk and invited him in.

Travis held my gaze a moment longer. Although his eyes darkened, his features remained smooth and expressionless. The first hint as to the reason for his visit came as he closed the door and slipped his hands in his pockets—a simple gesture that spoke volumes from "Iron Man." Travis was bearing bad news. He sat on the sofa and clasped his knees. Another bad sign.

My words trembled. "What's wrong? What's happened? It's Quincy, isn't it? She's . . . she's . . ." Something was going on inside. I could feel it. My words gave light to a darkness that I had secreted from myself, and I drew back in surprise, taken aback by the revelation. Something inside me was breaking open, hatching, birthing from something as rare and exquisite as a Faberge egg. A new kind of love was being exposed, naked and vulnerable. I understood for the first time that I longed for Quincy as fiercely as any mother would long for her lost child.

Travis reached out and gently pressed his fingers to my lips, hushing me with a "Shhh, shh . . . it's okay, babe. It's not Quincy." The eyes that had been soft only moments ago now ducked behind a protective wall. "It's Logan."

I closed my eyes and swallowed hard. Logan's name almost always triggered the process of disassociation. It was as though I was wired with a voice-activated mechanism to implode at the sound of his name.

"Logan?" My lips formed the words.

Travis's countenance hardened. "He's escaped."

Silence reached out like a thick glove, covering my mouth and pinching off my air as

Travis's voice faded somewhere in the distance.

"Sunny—don't! Don't you dare space out. Pull yourself together. I need you focused and alert." He took my trembling hands into his warm ones and pulled me to my feet. "Get up. We're getting out of here."

Ten silent minutes later—that might just as easily have been ten hours or ten days—found us at a familiar spot we once shared: the spillway beneath the fish hatchery. The wind sliced through my defenses, cold and invigorating as it chased the thundering river downstream. My breath caught, taken hostage by the magnificent scene. The frigid air felt alive, throbbing from the intense surge of whitewater that shot over the spillway, hurtling into space and cascading in a frenzied freefall to the river's lower level, where it foamed and churned and gathered strength before continuing its mad race to the ocean.

Travis brought me here because he understood the forces that shaped me. He didn't need to say, "I love you." Just bringing me here was evidence that he cared. He knew that this place was a fountain of strength for me, whether in the vibrant life cycle of the faithful and courageous salmon or in the force of the river focused on its mission. Travis knew that I was a product of the mountains and it was my nature to absorb strength from the world around me. It was through creation that I was in touch with my Creator.

We stood in silence on the brink of the lookout, holding hands to stay grounded in the face of such turbulence. Then I shouted out, above the tumult of the wind and river, "How? It's not possible. Nobody escapes from prison. Not even Logan."

"He wasn't interned at High Desert. He was relocated to the correctional center for minimum-security inmates. He was part of a hand crew, clearing debris from some roads that flooded. He walked away. They're doing a search now, but . . . he's gone."

"Have you told Chance?"

"I didn't need to. A BOLO went out over the wires the minute he was discovered missing. Chance called me. "

I shivered. "How come Chance isn't the one telling me?"

"He's on a chopper with Mercy. I told Chance that I would let you know."

My teeth were chattering, and I blinked hard to hold back the flood of emotion. Travis took off his coat and wrapped it around me, drawing me close until we stood face-to-face.

Our eyes locked, and Travis's expression remained impassive. His words came slow, even, and deliberate, "I'm gonna kill that guy."

Trembling from fear as much as cold, I tipped my face up to meet his. "Promise?"

We carefully weighed each other's words as we both nodded our assent and agreement.

We turned to walk back to the shelter of the car, the noise and intensity fading to a dull roar as we walked. "What are you doing up here anyhow? Why aren't you in Oakland?"

"Major drug bust coming down . . . but don't tell anyone, or I'll have to . . ." He let it hang in the air and winked.

I gave a short, hard chuckle. "I know, I know—you'll have to kill me."

"Killing you wasn't exactly what I had in mind," said Travis.

My smile was back. This time for real. If only for a little while.

CHAPTER 38

᭐ ✟ ᭜

Chance called home from Susanville to repeat the news that Logan had escaped. He assured me that a special agent from the Office of Correctional Safety would be watching the house while he continued to participate in the search. There were no significant clues, just the probability that Logan had walked out to a paved road where a car was waiting to pick him up.

I locked the doors and loaded my Glock, tuned Enya in on the iPod, poured a glass of wine, and curled up on the sofa with Kissme. It didn't work. I turned off the music so I could tune in every sound and found myself gripping the gun at every noise. The glass of wine remained untouched because I was afraid to lose my edge. Tired and wired, the hours ticked away until shadowy fingers of fatigue pulled me down to the depths of sleep.

᭐ ✟ ᭜

In my dream, I saw Starla, my mother. Not the hardened tattooed drug-addicted woman who took her own life, but there—rocking back and forth in a high-back antique rocker, wrapped in the glow of a kerosene lamp—was the young woman that I loved to remember; soft as a rose petal, bright as a star, my mother, the beautiful flower child. She held a newborn baby tucked in a handmade quilt. Her sweet lyrical voice filled the air as she rocked and sang to the child nestled in her arms:

> Don't it always seem to go
> that you don't know what you've got till it's gone,
> They paved Paradise
> and put up a parking lot.

My father worked close by, intently carving a bear from a chunk of manzanita, holding the block with the prosthetic hook on his left arm while selecting from a box of woodworking tools with his right. He was working with surgical precision, patiently carving intricate details.

"Sunny, come see your baby sister," said my mother, followed by a series of soft, silly cooing sounds. "You want to hold her?" She rose to let me sit in her rocking chair, deftly placing the baby in my arms. "There you go, Quincy," said my mother to the infant. "Sunny will take good care of you."

"She's your responsibility now," my mother admonished, then walked away into the kitchen.

I continued the awesome task of rocking and loving the baby, a great responsibility that I took seriously. Slate-blue eyes looked up into mine. A rosebud mouth formed the shape of an O. I placed a single finger on her lip and she responded—a tiny hand with long, delicate fingers that reached up and clasped my mine with all hers. I laughed, and she returned the laughter. For a time, I just enjoyed her sweetness and the newness and purity of the moment.

Lefty stood up and walked over to show us his bear. He mimicked ferocity but growled softly.

I looked at my father with adoration, when the thought seemed to drift in on golden wings; when love is ripped from our grasp against our will—taken by force or by fate—it is as if our Savior has been buried in a tomb, the sun has failed to rise, our heart has been ripped from our chest.

My mother's voice wafted through the house carried on the wings of tantalizing smells from the kitchen.

"Don't it always seem to go
That you don't know what you've got
Till it's gone . . ."

A great truth was revealed that night, and I held tight so as not to lose it on the long journey back from sleep to waking. Nothing is more precious or painful than love that is taken from us against our will.

૬ ♔ ૭

Special Agent Jean Kent arrived from the Department of Corrections. She followed me to and from work and parked outside at night. I tried ignoring her at first because the only agent I wanted following me around was Travis, and since that would be grossly inappropriate, I tried to ignore the one outside my door. By dinnertime on day three of her arrival, I broke down and invited her in to eat, use the shower and whatever else she needed to do. I didn't know if we were breaking the rules by doing so, but she seemed grateful.

Day four found Taylor slowing her steps to match mine as I limped along, traversing the parking lot between Mental Health and the main complex. In light of the upcoming event known as Candlemas, Dano had scheduled a session with Taylor at my request.

Taylor had manifested in her little-girl personality called Tinkerbelle and allowed me to ask her a couple of questions. I admit, I felt stupid talking to anyone named Tinkerbelle; the entire affair had felt as surreal as a trip to Neverland.

Duncan waved. He was standing next to his motorcycle talking bike talk with Bonita's friend. Taylor's car was parked on the far side of the lot, so we paused for quick introductions. Duncan introduced Bonita's girlfriend as "Randy," and I introduced Taylor as "Taylor." We were making jokes about riding motorcycles in the winter when shy Taylor joined in saying, "My dad rides in the winter," then pointed to Duncan's Harley, adding, "on a bike like that."

Chance and Mercy came home, allowing Special Agent Jean Kent to return to Susanville. Chance was moody and depressed.

"Not a single damned lead," said Chance. He tried to apologize as if he had somehow let me down. His promises to "track Logan down and protect me" were no more than empty platitudes coming from a broken man.

I missed the shining spirit and joy that had once characterized my husband; back when his heart was filled with faith and hope.

ഇ ♀ ൠ

Day five, I was at work when the phone rang. Chance's voice exploded through the line. "I've got it! I think I figured it out. I know why they want Quincy!"

Three heartbeats passed. "Oh my God. Why? Who? Talk!"

"I can't. I mean—I'm not a hundred percent certain. I have to wait until you get home."

"Where are you?"

"At home."

"Why are you at home?"

"I promise I'll explain everything when you get here."

I groaned. "Noooo! Just tell me. I have to work late tonight." My brain scrambled for traction. "I have to meet with a victim." I didn't want to tell him that the victim was Taylor, so I threw him a bone to deflect questions; "You're on your own for dinner."

"Not hungry." I could hear a huff of exasperation. "I'm working tonight too. I'm here picking up Mercy." Before I could object to further delay, he explained, "A multiagency drug bust. I can't get out of it. I'm sorry, Sunny. I couldn't hold it in any longer. I had to tell you or explode." His excitement was driving me crazy. "I just can't believe it—all this time."

"You better tell me now if you hope to live to see tomorrow. Tell me already!"

"I can't tell you—I have to show you. I need you to confirm my suspicions." Chance grumbled in frustration at the sound of his cell phone going off in the background. "It's Mark, probably about tonight. Sorry hon, I have to go. Really. It's okay. I love you—bye."

Will this day ever end?

CHAPTER 39

Ꮉ ♁ Ꮌ

It was the night of February second, Candlemas on the satanic calendar, and once again I found myself parked outside Taylor's house. This time I was in the brand inspector's vehicle and in the company of Forrest Woods. If there were animal sacrifices planned for tonight, I had Forrest to make an arrest. And if Taylor really did have a sister in danger, I would have backup. Forrest told me that he had been in combat in Afghanistan, and although he was young and easygoing, he wasn't someone to be messed with.

Forrest was working on a tall can of Red Bull, drumming his fingers as if he were on can number three. We were passing the time, parked along a row of ancient eucalyptus trees planted by the forty-niners—not the football team.

"Isn't your husband a sheriff?" Forrest asked.

"Yes."

"Then, if you don't mind my asking, why isn't he here instead of me?"

"It's complicated."

"Oh."

Forrest just nodded, apparently wise enough in the ways of women not to pop the top on my remark.

"Hey, Forrest, I'm just wondering," I said. "Remember that silver charm that you found at the site of the blood moon gathering? The one with the heart and baby footprints? Did you ever link it to anything?"

Forrest set down the can of Red Bull and thoughtfully tapped a can of Copenhagen. "No. But it's funny you should ask."

"Funny how?"

"Some guy from the DA's office picked it up a couple of days ago."

I put on my best poker face and played my card. "The guy—what did he look like?"

"Really big. Spiky hair, earplugs, Johnny Depp glasses. Kind of strange. Who is he?"

"Top tech for the county. His name is Duncan. Probably going to photograph it or something," I lied, turning the charm over and over between my fingers deep within my coat pocket, all the while wondering what Duncan was up to.

More time passed in amicable silence, when a sleek black Mercedes-Benz pulled up to Taylor's house, looking as misplaced as a bottle of champagne next to a Happy Meal.

We weren't the only ones watching the road. Taylor immediately exited the house clutching a large box. The porch light was off, as was the interior light on the Mercedes. Taylor opened the back door of the car and shoved the box into the backseat, then slid in next to it.

Forest seemed to know his stuff as he carefully tailed the Mercedes from a distance. We didn't have far to go. Their destination was a short hop to downtown Oroville.

The Mercedes pulled up in front of the newest business in the oldest part of town—a motorcycle shop specializing in custom paint detailing and design. A string of very nice cars and expensive motorcycles lined both sides of the street. Oroville usually rolled up the sidewalks by ten p.m., yet there seemed to be a major party going on at the shop. Neon lights were flashing out the door like an 80's disco dance floor, and heavy metal music was thrumming in the night air. We could see through the window as we drove past; people were drinking inside, and a few others were staggering outdoors.

Something was wrong with this picture. There had to be a mistake. This was no ritual gathering in the backwoods under a full moon, speed-dialing Satan with incantations and the blood of a ram. This looked like high society—not necessarily the drug type. More likely to speed-dial their stockbroker as they sipped red wine, which seemed incongruent with the music, to say the least, but times and customs changed.

"Let's park and have a closer look," I said to Forrest.

"I'm on the clock. It's your dollar," he replied with youthful enthusiasm—which wasn't exactly accurate, as he was actually on the county clock and not costing me a cent.

We parked the truck around the corner, out of sight from mainstream traffic, and got out. Pulling my head deep beneath the hood on my coat, Forrest and I strolled down the cobbled sidewalks of Old Town, past numerous little shops with colorful awnings that lined the road toward Bad Boyz Bikes and the sound of voices and music. Forrest jumped when I took his hand.

"We need to look like a couple," I told him, "not like a couple of cops."

His eyebrows bobbed up and down, followed by a sly wink— which was followed by my venomous warning, "Seriously," which was followed by his grin . . . followed by a look of pain as I crushed his fingers in my hand.

Men!

We stopped in front of the Bad Boyz display window that showcased an impressive antique motorcycle. "Do you see what I see?" I asked Forrest.

"Yeah, a 1930 three-cylinder Czechoslovakian motorcycle named Satan," Forrest read from the plaque in front of the bike that went on to identify it as being "extremely rare."

It occurred to me that the bike might be the equivalent of a trail of luminous quartz rocks, like the ones that guided the participants down to the gathering in the woods. It clearly signaled to me that we were in the right place.

I was peering through the windows from every angle looking for Taylor when a tap on my shoulder nearly triggered heart failure.

Shane?

"Shane. What the heck are you doing here?"

"I could ask you the same thing." Shane's eyes drifted pointedly from my face to my hand that was still firmly clasped to Forrest's. I dropped Forrest's hand like a guilty shoplifter caught in the act by security. "I was invited here because this is Ben's grand opening, and in case you forgot, I happen to own a Harley shop," said Shane.

My best friend's husband and I stood there eyeing each other suspiciously.

I took a chance. "I'm working."

Shane took a chance. "I can see that."

I rolled my eyes and took a confused Forrest by the hand once again to prove my point. "I'm looking for someone."

Shane bent forward as if to hug me goodbye and whispered in my ear, "Get out of here, Sunny. You aren't the only one looking for someone tonight."

"Don't tell me what to do," I said, indignant that Shane would still think that Forrest had the hots for me. I pushed my way past Shane, dragging Forrest behind me, and entered the showroom still hoping for a glimpse of Taylor.

"What was that about?" Forrest asked under his breath.

"Nothing. Just keep your eyes open for anything unusual," I said as we strolled from one motorcycle to another, genuinely admiring the precision work while watching for anything out of the ordinary.

"That's unusual," said Forrest, nodding appreciatively toward a heavily tattooed young woman with purple hair. She was wearing a lot of skin under a little black leather dress and purple spiked thigh-high boots.

"You're not in Kansas anymore, Toto."

"What's that supposed to mean?"

It meant I was old. "It means you're in California, and she is normal."

Forrest gave me a pained expression that was not the result of any hand squeezing this time. "Not her—them." He nodded toward two people that were mostly hidden behind shelves in back of the counter. There was a man—a striking albino—standing next to a stunning woman whose skin was as black as the leathers the albino wore.

I hung on to Forrest for a moment as the floor shifted beneath my feet—not a California earthquake but a burst of comprehension that sent me reeling.

It was him—the man from the cabin who had trailed me to the lake high in the mountains.

It was them—the man and woman from Paige's funeral—the ones from the floral shop—just before the bomb went off. The same ones that had been hooded and cloaked, leading the blood moon mass.

It could be her. The African American woman that was seen walking from the nursery the night Quincy disappeared.

Hurrying out to the sidewalk, I sucked in the cold night air, trembling. My missing toes and foot were cramping, but my head and everything else grew crystal clear.

"It's him . . . them," I kept repeating to myself. "God. Why didn't I see it? It's really him." I walked down the street back toward the truck.

Forrest kept repeating "Who?" sounding like an audio loop of an owl as I frantically dialed Chance on my cell phone. Chance had gone dark. His phone was turned off. No time to explain everything to the local police—and I wasn't about to let this opportunity slip past.

"Hey, Sunny." Forrest was clearly annoyed. "Can you stop a minute? I thought we were going after some cult that was going to sacrifice animals?"

"We are. Hang on—" I turned off my phone and put it in my pocket. "As soon as we figure out how to get into the back of the bike shop without getting caught. The action has to be behind the front counter, somewhere in the back of the building."

Forrest frowned in thought and then got a huge smile. "No problem." His eyes danced. "How about we bring a goat to the back door?"

"That is the stupidest thing I've ever heard. Where are we going to get a goat at eleven o'clock at night?"

Forrest grinned. "This is Oroville. Let's go."

Twenty minutes later we were in the alley behind the bike shop with an unhappy goat anchored in the back of the pickup truck. Forrest knew every livestock owner in the county and had no problem "borrowing" a ram from a nearby breeder. Forrest was in his element, clearly enjoying himself as he boldly knocked on the back door of the bike shop while I waited in the alley with the truck.

My heart hammered as an unidentified male opened the back door with a rough, "Whadda ya want?"

"I have it in the back of the truck," said Forrest, gesturing at the goat who was bleating pitifully from the truck bed. "I need your help getting him out."

The man paused to consider. "Miasma didn't say anything about a stinkin' goat," he complained as he followed Forrest to the truck.

"He stinks alright. Grab his chain," said Forrest as he unlatched the tailgate.

The man from the shop jumped up on the step side, leaned over, and reached across the bed. I popped open the door and hit him with Forrest's cattle prod, dropping him to the ground, where I promptly zapped him two more times until he stopped thrashing.

"Did I kill him?" I asked.

"Nah—probably just sterilized him."

Finally, I have earned a Happy Face in the kingdom of heaven.

We shoved the biker up on the front seat of the truck and drove to the lot next door and parked under a low-hanging tree to keep the goat happy. Forrest cuffed the biker to the steering wheel while I slapped a strip of duct tape across his mouth and taped his ankles together. Then Forrest and I stretched our suspect across the front seat, grabbed a pair of flashlights, hurried back to the bike shop and slipped inside.

CHAPTER 40

୫ ✢ ଓ

It was too dark to see without a flashlight, but I was sure we were alone since it was neck-breaking-black when we closed the door. We flicked our flashlights on low. There was a damp warehouse smell and something else that tangled with my senses. Forrest was armed and looked dismayed when I pulled out my Glock. "You got a license for that thing?" he whispered. I nodded my head up and down. The flashlight deepened his frown lines into a scowl. "Uh-huh. You know how to use it?" I nodded yes, but he still worried. "You better not shoot me."

I gave him a dirty look and gestured with my gun to indicate that if he didn't get moving, I might be tempted. He moved.

Shadows seemed to tiptoe on our heels as our narrow beams of light swept back and forth across shelves stacked with boxes of motorcycle stuff that reached to the ceiling. No sign of any people, but there were a few doors to choose from. We eased up on them one at a time.

Softly turning the knob on the largest, most obvious door first, we cracked it open enough to let in the sounds of the party from the showroom and the demonic sounds of Marilyn Manson screaming:

"Erotic sensations tingle my spine.
A dead body lying next to mine.
Smooth blue-black lips
I start salivating as we kiss . . ."

I drew back with the same disgust that I once felt when standing at a victim's meth house, looking at a slimy, oozing life form that had crept over the lip of a frying pan and slithered down from stove to floor.

I shook my head no, and Forrest shut the door. We moved on to the next door, easing it open with the same great care, when a loud rustle and the sound of scurrying made me spin in panic, drawing my flashlight like a lightsaber to face the enemy. I expected Darth Vader but saw nothing more sinister than a hideous black rat with beady eyes that glowed red in my beam. The rat from hell. He paused to bare his teeth and make a hissing noise before scuttling off, holding his gray tail stiff in the air as he ran. I exhaled a stream of relief, and then tensed again as the doorknob to the main room turned on its own.

Forrest and I switched off our lights as we dove, flattening ourselves behind a pallet of boxes where the rat had taken cover. The door swung open to admit a few people and then closed behind them. The warehouse was quiet except for the repeated flicking of a lighter. The room suddenly bloomed above a warm glow of flickering candlelight. More rattling noises came from close by. Too close.

"What's that?" A woman raised her voice in consternation. She lifted her candle, and Forrest and I pressed our bodies to the floor as the sound of her steps cautiously approached. Then the sound of girl shrieks followed by curse words and laughter, as the rat bolted from the pallet and blitzed across the room in front of the woman.

The laughter faded, drifting across the warehouse toward the small remaining door we had yet to open. They passed through and closed the door behind them with a resounding click.

Forrest and I exhaled in unison. The night was cold, but I was sweating. Fear of the rat, fear of getting caught, and fear of whatever lay behind door number three.

"Come on." Forrest switched his flashlight back on and was gesturing for me to follow. He wasn't afraid of hell; he had already been to Afghanistan.

The door led to a small bathroom—the kind one might expect to find in the back of a man's motorcycle shop—small and greasy with the seat up on a disgusting toilet that sat beneath an even more revolting picture of a naked woman. A tall, narrow stall shower stood in the corner. We looked around in dismay. The people seemed to have vanished. We turned our flashlights into each other's eyes looking for answers, temporarily blinding each other before sweeping the room one more time. The floor seemed to hum and vibrate, causing Forrest to step back out of the room and me to open the shower door. I opened it, thankfully looking down before stepping inside.

Immediately inside the shower door was the yawning mouth of a dark tunnel that bent at a steep angle under a low ceiling. A narrow set of wooden stairs led down into even blacker shades of night that quickly absorbed the beam of my light.

Holy . . . wow! I thought, swallowing my fear.

A second beam of light danced across mine, and I knew that Forrest was behind me. He tapped me on the shoulder with his gun, indicating that he would go down first and I was to follow. There was no point in calling the police. The only crimes being committed at the moment were ours: possibly assault, kidnapping, and false imprisonment of the guy we had left in the pickup truck.

The smell I had first noticed upstairs increased with every step down that we took: earthy, dank, and some kind of chemical. The odor wrapped around us like a claustrophobic blanket. Down, down, down. Forrest's beam bounced off the walls, ceiling, and floor, making me feel like a drunken sailor trying to focus on a lighthouse just before a shipwreck.

We were deep within the mysterious Chinese tunnels beneath the city—a reputedly safe place for Chinese gold miners who had engaged in the legal activities of gambling and smoking opium, and the illegal activities of possessing guns and engaging in mining operations. Only American citizens could own gold mines, but legend told the story of clever Chinese who carried out illegal mining operations beneath the city. A legend that local government had vigorously quelled for more than one hundred and fifty years— and yet, here we were.

Eventually, a dirt floor took up where the stairs ended, and we continued along the narrow corridor until it opened into a large cavernous room that could easily hold fifty or more people. Boxes and crates lined the walls—I recognized gun crates—I didn't know what was in the boxes. Machinery of some sort dominated one side of the chamber. Above the equipment were shelves stocked with chemicals. A long work table stood on one side of the machinery with lab equipment tucked beneath. I was pretty sure we had stumbled into a meth lab, and my heart picked up speed, hammering in my chest as though I had just vicariously absorbed large quantities of the drug.

There were entrances to two more tunnels on the other side of the cavern, both dark and narrow, sitting side by side and resembling a vacant stare from a giant skull.

"Which one?" Forrest whispered. We stood shoulder to shoulder, and I could feel him vibrating. Apparently, the meth was affecting him too.

"The left one," I whispered.

"Why?" he whispered back.

"Because Jesus sits on the right."

I didn't wait for his reply but moved forward, the tunnel turning at both right and left angles as we proceeded. There, up ahead, the tunnel opened into another chamber. A pale glow of flickering lights and the murmuring chant of many voices rose and fell in rhythmic, hypnotic incantation. We switched off our lights and inched forward, hidden within the hallowed shadows, and crept down the tunnel and backward in time. A full-blown Satanic High Mass was in progress.

The voices rose in a mounting crescendo as I caught a glimpse.

The room was lit with the luminous blue-white glow of black lights and on the forehead of each robed figure was a glowing pentagram, just as Nina had once tried to tell me—white tattoos that would otherwise be invisible to the naked eye.

The albino stood at the head wrapped in ethereal light, exhorting and crying out unintelligible phrases that excited and escalated the participants into a frenzy. His black female accomplice stood at his right side holding Taylor's box in her arms. The thin wail of a baby pierced the tumult in the room. To the albino's left— unbelievably, impossibly—stood Logan.

Startled, my heart skipped a beat as I turned toward a familiar whine and prod that came from behind.

Mercy? "Mercy, what . . . ?"

"Good God." Chance froze at the sight of me crouched before him with my arms around Mercy's neck. His face paled as white as the albino's. "What are you doing here?" he hissed.

I looked into Chance's eyes as he proclaimed the name of God, and as I did, a bright red splotch flowered and bloomed along his neck, just above the top of his bulletproof vest.

I dropped to my knees and hung on to Mercy as all hell broke loose, shots coming from every direction.

Forrest grabbed Chance who fell to his knees, lifted him from under his arms and dragged him back into the tunnel. Men in SWAT gear swarmed up from behind, calling out directives and pushing us aside as they surged past. More gunshots, followed by the whine of bullets, ricocheted through the chamber as screams and shrieks of panicked participants shattered the night.

A minute later a voice called out, "Hold your fire! Hold your fire!"

I looked up across the cavern to see Travis, who had led a second assault team into the chamber from a different direction. Travis was crouched low, one arm up in the air, the other hand holding his gun up in surrender, his eyes trained on the black woman who now held a wailing baby to her chest with a knife pressed tight against its throat.

Moans and sobs echoed from the wounded. I heard Chance struggling to breathe. Crawling to him, I eased his head onto my lap, crying and begging, "Oh God, oh God, oh God." Forrest pressed his hand tight against Chance's neck to form a compression, but the blood continued to flow, leaking through Forrest's fingers and across my lap.

ဆၣ✝ ☌

Voices receded as the walls of the tunnel fell away. Sunshine streamed through a shimmering white sky. Had we been in the tunnel that long? I thought it only minutes, but judging from the angle of the sun, it must have been the dawn of a new day. All the shouting, screaming people—even Mercy—seemed to have faded away. There was only Chance. Only me.

Looking into the face of my beautiful husband—the love of my life—his ice-blue eyes melted into mine. Chance looked radiant. I had never seen him look so completely happy. He whispered, "I found her. Quincy. We're going . . . ta be . . . a fam . . . ly."

"Yes, you did," I said, shaking my head as I shed tears on Chance's ethereal face. "You did it. You are amazing, Chance. You're the most amazing man I have ever known."

Chance winced and blinked. For a moment, a fleeting shadow from the world flickered over us.

"Remember me . . ." he whispered with ragged breaths. His gaze faltered and faded into sorrow as it grew distant. "You . . . good . . . mom."

"Don't leave me. Don't leave me." Fear ravaged my heart. "I love you, Chance—I need you." I covered his face with kisses that tasted like salt from my tears that had mingled to become one with his—just as our souls had done on our wedding day.

Chance coughed and gasped. His face clenched, and then he smiled and let go, his words trailing from this world into the next. "I . . . You . . . Paige . . ."

Then the sun blinked, and I was swallowed by a great darkness.

CHAPTER 41

ಹ ⊕ ಚ

At last, I understood Paige. I didn't need to keep asking people why she would have killed herself. I popped another pill and considered—*why only one?* If one pill can erase a little pain, then perhaps the entire bottle . . .

There was nothing left for me in the land of the living. My only desire was to be with my husband, my father, and my mother. Life was too painful. It lasted too long.

My last memories were fleeting—shadow dances on a wall in my mind. The chamber filled with tension and fear, sorrow and suffering. I remember four people backing out of the room through a third door. Logan—who got away again. The albino called Miasma. The black woman holding a knife to Quincy's throat. And Quincy . . . whose helpless shrieks still throbbed in my head with terminal velocity.

Would the stain of Chance's blood ever be washed away? I think not. Would the warm breath of his last words be erased from my memory? Not possible. I was soaked in blood and memory.

Strong arms lifted me, pulling me away from that which I could not let go of. Forrest carried me up the tunnel, and at some point, I was no longer looking into his eyes but into the streaming eyes of Travis. I heard mumbled words from a distant world. They had nothing to do with me. Words like *dead*, *shock*, and *hospital*. The paramedics gave me an injection.

ಹ ⊕ ಚ

Evil had triumphed. Law enforcement recovered much more than guns. The bust was considered a major breakthrough—a bust of historic proportions. For along with crates filled with automatic weapons, they did not find nose-candy crank as I had thought but printing presses that cranked out both Mexican and American money. Lots of money. Boxes that totaled nearly a million dollars between the two currencies.

Still, evil had won. Those who worshiped evil and perpetuated the most heinous of crimes against humanity had escaped with their victim. Of what value were guns, drugs, or money when purchased with lives of children?

Mac was there, standing by my bed, and for a moment I thought I was in church. Then I remembered that it was not possible, as I hadn't been to church for the longest time. Mac looked tired. I could read it on his face and in his posture. His steel-blue eyes had faded, or perhaps they were blurred by tears. His or mine, I didn't know. Perhaps Mac was like me and had seen too much death. Nonetheless, he was my friend and pastor.

"Hello, my sister," said Mac. "I've come to take you home."

"Am I dead?" I asked.

Mac squeezed his eyes tight, holding back a torrent of emotion. "No, my dear. Not you." Several heartbeats passed, his and mine drumming in unison. "Chance, you know . . . Chance died from his injuries." Mac took a deep breath and straightened. "Later on, when you are ready, we will talk about the funeral."

I closed my eyes and listened to the sound of my heart. It continued to beat, but I was no longer connected to the force that kept it going.

"No funeral, Mac. I mean it. I'm done with funerals."

An extended, weighted silence hung like a deadfall between us before Mac spoke.

"Many years ago, as I was leaving a patient at the hospital, I walked into the hallway and saw a young man—a boy, really. He was sitting there alone, his face buried in his hands, crying with remorse. It seems he had killed his father's best friend in a hunting accident. He didn't think he would ever get over the guilt. He didn't think that life would go on." Mac reached over to place a gentle hand on my shoulder. "But he did. He went on to be a soldier, and as a soldier he took lives. But he also went on to be a rescue worker. He even studied to be a pastor and dedicated his life to saving that part of man that continues beyond the grave; saving souls." Mac dropped his gaze and gently squeezed my shoulder. "It's not how long we live, but how we use the time we are given."

"You're talking about Chance."

Mac nodded. "That is his legacy." Mac bent over and kissed me, his lips pressed tight against my forehead until the message of love came through, and then he left.

I was relieved not to be burdened with the usual benign platitudes like "He's in a better place now" or "He is with the Lord." As a Christian, I knew my husband was in heaven, but there was nothing in words that could begin to fill the vacuum that Chance's death had left behind.

Ashley wouldn't leave me alone. I woke the next morning to find her sleeping on the recliner. The sofa would no longer hold the three of them. Poor Ashley, I thought, feeling a sad solace in knowing that I would never have to suffer the miseries of pregnancy.

I went through the motions of making breakfast for four; make that five—no, six of us. Kissme and Mercy patiently waited at the entrance to the kitchen. I started the coffee maker and let them outdoors, just as I had done a thousand times before.

How was it possible a new day had arrived? Overhead, the sky was dark and threatening. Somehow I found the impending storm comforting and wrapped my bathrobe more tightly around me. I didn't understand how it was that I was alive and breathing when half of me lay cold and dead in the county morgue.

Mercy's cold nose bumped my hand, and Kissme was standing on her back legs scratching at the back of mine. The air was frigid, and the dogs wanted inside.

Oh—right. Food. I got out the frying pan and cracked eggs, one at a time, and watched them fall.

"Sunny?"

I turned to see Ashley looking like a tired punch ball, round and full, yet sagging from one too many hits.

"Sunny—you're breaking eggs into the sink."

I looked at the sink, and she was right. The frying pan was full of shells, and eggs were staring at me from the bottom of the sink, like sets of watchful eyes waiting to see what I would do next.

The next thing I knew, I was holding a sobbing Ashley. For all her bulk, she was as fragile as the delicate oak leaves on the lawn that were scattering before the storm.

Sometime later over bowls of steaming oatmeal, Ashley rubbed her tired red eyes and sniffled. "At least Chance is in a better place now. He is with the Lord," she said.

ॐ ♀ ॐ

Ashley went home when I told her that I needed some time alone. She left, and sometime in the afternoon, Mark Anderson arrived. He stood at the door looking older than I remembered. Perhaps it was the burden of being sheriff. Only last year Mark had still been an undersheriff. As head of law enforcement, all the glory and all the blame for the events in the tunnel had fallen directly on him.

A chill wind slipped in behind Mark as he entered the house. I trailed him into the living room, still wearing the pajamas I had worn home from the hospital. My hair was snarled, and teeth had not been brushed. I cared not. My face was as dry and desolate as a windswept desert.

Mercy ran past me, jumping on Mark, who knelt down and wrapped his arms around her neck, hugging her the way I thought he might have held me. I was not offended but suspected I was witnessing a secret part of the world of men—men who trusted canines with their hearts because people had disappointed, while their dogs remained steadfast and trustworthy. Mercy frequently stayed with Mark when Chance was away. Perhaps . . . since Chance was gone . . . it would best if she went home with him.

"Sunny." The word came out with great effort. It was all Mark could manage before his voice cracked. I took him by the hand and led him into the living room. Once an advocate, always an advocate. It seemed that it was my life's duty to comfort others.

Turning, I held Mark in my arms while he cried. A big man, a leader, an influential figure who now stood shaking and trembling like a lost child in my arms. My arms were a safe place. When Mark had calmed, I parked him next to a box of tissues and used the excuse of getting him some coffee to give him time to recover.

After the predictable "I am so sorry" and "He was a good man," Mark concluded by saying, "Pastor Mac said he'd stop by later on to help you with the funeral arrangements."

What was not predictable was my reply. "No. No more funerals. I am done with funerals."

Mark stood there, puzzling for a moment as though I had spoken in a foreign language. "I know this is hard for you. That's why I'm sending Mac. He's more than a police chaplain; he's your pastor and friend. He wants to help you."

"I've already seen him and sent him home. You heard me, Mark. No funeral."

Mark ran his hand back and forth over the base of his neck. "I understand." Mark was done crying and back to his role as sheriff. Wetting his lips and nodding, he said, "I got it. You need a little time. These things don't need to happen right away. It's just that I need to notify other agencies across the state. We don't have to have the funeral soon, but I do need to send announcements with a date as soon as possible. Mac and the funeral home can help you with that."

My face froze and hands white-knuckled around the half-empty cup of coffee that I clutched, my attitude growing colder than the plummeting temperatures outside. Drawing a slow, steady breath, I said, "You're not listening. 'No funeral' does not sound like 'later' to me. It sounds like 'no funeral.'"

"Uh, yeah. Well . . ." Mark stood to leave, and I rose with him. He embraced me, awkward, clumsy.

"Take Mercy with you, Mark. Please. Just for a while. I can't look at her without seeing . . . without thinking . . ."

Mark's mouth was drawn down, and his brows pinched in consternation. "No, no. I get it. It's okay. I can do that." He turned to go. "Come on, girl." Mercy jumped to her feet and whined eagerly. Mark seemed relieved to have something that he could control, or at least relate to. "I'll be in touch," he said, kissing me on the cheek on his way out the door.

Mercy turned back expectantly, whining and looking at me with intelligent brown eyes.

Reaching down, I hugged her goodbye and whispered into her thick warm ear, "Don't worry. I'm going to take care of everything."

ℴ✝ℛ

The storm moved in by nightfall. Warmer and kinder, an end-of-winter storm for California, the kind that fed new growth. Still, I am cold, I thought, shivering as I huddled under a warm throw in front of the soapstone heater with a hot cup of tea to warm my hands. There was a time I would have thought it the kind of day that invited memories to come indoors and curl up next to you to pass the time.

Putting the cup aside I petted my dog, not wanting tea, the company of people, or intrusive memories.

I had been so close. So very close that I believed for a time that I had arrived. My big dream had been fully realized—the day Chance stood there, his face shining with love so bright that I was certain his love was unparalleled in the history of love. Our love had been invincible. Nothing in this world could break it, I thought. And I supposed—in the end—it wasn't anything in this world that did. I believed in the spirit world: the Holy Spirit and the Devil. Only great malice, the Devil himself—and not his minions—could have taken my husband from me. That was my belief.

Chance had placed Kissme, our six-week-old surrogate baby into my arms. He had given me a bundle of love, and in so doing had filled a gaping wound from my past. He had given me something to raise, to cherish, guide, and protect. He would never know how much this little creature, a silly little puppy, would mean.

We attended church on Sundays and felt the love of God as powerfully as the love we felt for each other. After church we would return home, satisfied and fulfilled. We had a home; we had a family of sorts; we had faith in each other, in the future, and in God.

Gone. All gone. Or perhaps it had been fading all along, and I had been too blind to see it. I could hear my mother's refrain, "Try not to be stupid, Sunny." Maybe I should have listened to my mother. She was probably right. After all we had been through, Chance had spent his last breathe whispering, "Paige."

Thunder rumbled and boomed overhead, rattling windows as it echoed through the mountains. Through the sliding glass door, lightning flashed, sizzling and searing as it ripped the sky in half. Dusk was approaching and I stared, awestruck, wondering if I had ever really experienced the fullness of life or if I was merely an observer, looking through a window . . . for there was a film, a haze, between what was real and where I sat. And there—a spider lurking in the corner—was waiting to catch me unaware.

A great sadness flooded in. Tears fell. Outside, the sound of rain.

CHAPTER 42

ഇ ✝ ഌ

Kissme barked and launched off the couch at the sound of uninvited knocking on the door. Morning had arrived to spite me, and the only lingering threat of a storm was the one brewing between my ears.

"Go away!" I complained, pulling the pillow over my head.

Why can't people leave me alone?

The knocking paused, then resumed, louder and more insistent. Kissme escalated into a barking frenzy.

"Kissme—quit it!"

The knocking turned to pounding, and my voice went up three notches as I bellowed, "I said 'Go away!'"

The door opened. "I didn't buy all this stuff to eat it by myself." Travis walked in, kicking the door shut behind him, arms loaded with paper bags.

By now Kissme was in a veritable lather.

"Kissme—shut up!" Travis and I shouted in unison. Kissme froze, looking hurt and defeated. She dropped her tail and slunk into the kitchen at Travis's heels.

Travis set bags and cups on the island between the two rooms and bent down to pet the dog, observing, "You look like hell."

My hand flew to my face, and I turned away, aware and embarrassed of my scars.

"What are you doing?" Travis demanded as he walked over to the couch and pushed my hand from the scars. Then he took my face in his hands and looked into my eyes. "I was talking to your dog," he said.

I pulled away, rolling my eyes as I cleared my throat. "She hasn't been to the groomer in a while."

Travis rolled his eyes back at me. "She's not the only one. What is this—the third day? Nope, make that the fourth day, and you're wearing the same clothes you had on in the hospital. No shower, no decent food."

"I ate some oatmeal."

"When?"

"I don't know. What do you want?" I asked, challenging him as I sat upright, putting my feet on the floor for the first time in forever.

"Something healthy. Go take a shower and get dressed while I make breakfast. And, Sunny," Travis said with a pained expression, "do something with your hair."

The man knew how to push my buttons. I threw Travis a dirty look, threw my dirty clothes in the laundry, and threw my dirty body in the shower.

Was that steak? At nine o'clock in the morning? My mouth was watering by the time I dressed and returned to the kitchen, drying my hair with a towel.

"Is that really cow meat? You hardly ever eat meat."

"You'd be surprised at what I eat." Travis winked.

I was both deeply offended and completely relieved that Travis could be his old pain-in-the-butt self. It was reassuring that somewhere in the universe the state of normal still existed. Somewhere, life continued. I was starved.

Seasoned steak, herbed potatoes, and the last of the eggs—it was a feast that I picked at.

I was still clearing the table when Travis announced, "I found the albino."

The room resounded with the sound of shattering dishes and a chair scooting back as Travis rushed to my side. "I'll get that," he said as he bent to pick up the pieces.

"Babe. Sit down. Here." He pulled out a chair, planted me back at the table, and continued to pick up the remains of shattered plates.

"Quincy?"

Travis paused from sweeping up the glass to look up with a searching glance and then shook his head, no. "She was gone. But we found the body of Angelo Ortiz."

"I thought you said you found Miasma, the albino."

"We did. Miasma was his biker name. Angelo, Angel Ortiz, is our albino."

"A Hispanic? Is that possible?"

"Rare alright. But not unheard of. Forensics said it's something like one in over fifteen thousand."

The world seemed to shrink for a moment.

"Sunny. Where's the trash can?"

I pointed without looking, and Travis stopped what he was doing to pull me out of the chair.

"Focus. I need you to help me figure this out."

I stepped back. Unwinding the towel from my hair, I shook my head. Wet hair fell like last night's tears. "I'm sorry."

"Don't apologize," Travis said, in a soft, urgent voice. "Just work with me."

"You said you found him. You didn't say that you arrested him."

"That's my girl." A flicker of relief softened his expression. "I convinced the owner of the bike shop that it was in his best interest to remember what kind of vehicle they drove. 'They,' referring to Angelo and what we now know is his girlfriend, the black woman, Latisha Jarreau. We pulled an address from DMV. The vehicle was still registered to the previous owner living in the Bay Area. The seller said the buyers paid cash for it and described them as 'a very white man and a very dark woman.'"

The shadows of grief receded a little as Travis shed some light on the aftermath.

"We put out an Amber Alert on the vehicle, plus a BOLO to California, Oregon, and Nevada law enforcement." He gave himself a congratulatory smile. "Can't be too careful," he said. "Got a tip two hours later. The vehicle was spotted outside of Guerneville."

I knew Guerneville—a scenic little town north of the Bay Area. "Then what?" I asked.

Travis's dimples deepened, and his smile stretched from ear to ear. "Drones," he said. "The end of free democracy as we know it, but one hell of a tool for law enforcement. We tracked the car to Jenner and made a raid."

"Jenner?" Jenner. And Jarreau. The names were ringing faint bells at the back of my brain when it should have been a blasting bullhorn. The puzzle pieces were all nicely laid out in front of me . . . and they looked familiar. I was just too exhausted to put it together. "What happened at the raid?"

"We found Angelo, executed. Double-tap to the head."

"And the woman . . . Latisha?" Latisha—Latisha—Latisha.

"No sign of her. No sign of Logan either. We figure him for the kill."

"Why would Logan want to kill a business associate?" Stupid question. He had murdered business associates before. I really was tired.

Travis mulled the possibilities and then shrugged. "I can think of a dozen reasons, but I don't know if any of them are right. Bottom line guess would be good business gone bad."

That sounded right—guns, money, double crossings. Logan.

"Sounds like Logan to me too." I agreed. "They have Quincy, don't they?" My voice broke under the weight of the question.

"I hope so," said Travis. "Bad as that sounds, the alternative could be worse."

Travis left me with a clean kitchen and the refrigerator stocked with fresh food. He also left me with a lot of food for thought. Not the least of which were his parting words.

"Chance's funeral will be in ten days. I talked to Mark, and we arranged for his body to be released to the mortuary. I also contacted the Army. He will be receiving full military honors."

Travis had pulled my trigger, and I went crazier than a flash mob at a convenience store. "Oh. No. You. Don't. You can't. You have no right. I am his wife, and you have no authority. I said 'no funeral' and goddammit, I mean no funeral."

Travis's eyes hardened, glittering. His voice lowered. "This isn't about you, Sunny. Chance's friends and associates deserve to say goodbye. And Chance deserves the dignity and honor that is due to a great man."

I stood there, fuming. Speechless. Helpless. Furious.

"The various agencies will be in touch, and so will Chance's pastor. Also, you or Mark need to contact Chance's sister. She has a right to know what's happened and come to the funeral." Travis opened the door and looked back with deliberation, adding, "And, Sunny, you shouldn't use God's name like a dirty word. Chance's funeral will not be damned."

ৡ ♀ ଔ

Rage consumed my every waking minute. I was so upset that I forgot the emptiness of my bed. The vacant space filled with anger and betrayal. The lack of respect was unacceptable. I would never forgive Travis. Not ever. By three a.m. I surrendered to sleep. They can have their stupid funeral, I thought. That doesn't mean I have to attend.

Monday morning found me driving to work—one day short of the mandatory weeklong bereavement leave. Oh well, if Jack chooses not to pay me, its fine by me. Home was making me crazy. Maybe my work as an advocate, easing someone else's pain, would help alleviate my own.

I tried to glide past the dozen or more investigators that worked for the district attorney's office. It must have been their inherent sixth sense that made them top cops. Somehow, they knew I was there, and their internal GPS systems guided them to my office, one at a time, until I swore if I heard "he was a good man" one more time, I would scream until my vocal cords went up in flames.

"Bonita—don't you dare say it! Please. If you care about me, don't say it."

Bonita rolled in, squinting her eyes and squaring her shoulders. "Hey, Chica, all I was going to say is 'it's about time you got your butt back here.' The work is piling up."

I took a stab at a smile, and her face grew serious. "I am sorry for your loss," she said. "Chance was a good man."

Duncan was next. It was unavoidable. The sight of me banging my head on my desk caused him great alarm. "Sunny. Dear. Stop that. You'll hurt yourself."

"If you tell me my husband was 'a good man,'" I threatened, "I am going to quit my job, and I will never see you again."

Duncan frowned and drew himself up, standing tall, sticking his thumbs in his pockets. "Personally, I never cared for the man."

I had to laugh. Good Lord, I had to laugh. Duncan looked at me as if I was crazy, but he smiled.

"Duncan, my friend"—I was about to wreck his day—I need to ask you something."

"Anything. You know that. Anything at all." He looked eager, like I was going to snap on a leash and take him for a walk. But he wasn't getting off that easy.

"Duncan, I have to ask you a hard question. I hope—no, I trust—that you will be honest with me."

"Always. You can trust me."

"Duncan, I need to ask you about those weird things that keep showing up in my in-box. I talked to Forrest Woods, the brand inspector. He told me that you picked up the evidence, the charm he found at a crime scene from his office."

Okay, so the offense turned out to be a poor goat that probably ended up skewered and barbecued, but Duncan doesn't need to know that.

Duncan frowned, reminding me of a schoolboy that had just been caught committing a grade school crime. "There wasn't any crime scene," he corrected me.

I took a deep breath. "It was a violation. A goat was sacrificed down in that canyon."

Duncan lowered his eyes and pursed his lips. "Okay. I'll confess everything," he said, his chin going up as his Adam's apple bobbed down, "even—even if it means losing my job."

You pick a tiny scab, and you never know what is going to come out. Sometimes a lot of bad stuff has been building just below the surface.

"It's all my fault. Everything. It was never Paige. All those things—the spider, the eight ball, the tarot card—I put them there."

I was stunned. Floored. "You what?"

Duncan's story cracked faster than a fat man skating on thin ice.

"Okay." My mouth went dry, and all I could do was swallow, repeatedly. The information was trapped in my esophagus like a bad case of acid reflux. Finally clearing my throat, I asked, "Why? Why would you scare the crap out of me?"

His head drooped, and shoulders slumped. If Duncan had a tail, he would have tucked it between his legs. Any priest would have been thrilled at such a heartfelt show of contrition, but I was not inclined to be so forgiving.

"I did it because . . . because . . . uh . . . because I love you, Sunny."

Okay, I had heard that love is strange, but this was downright freaky-weird. I was no longer seeing a roly-poly St. Bernard puppy. Duncan has morphed into Cujo, Stephen King's dog from hell.

Duncan squirmed as much as the tight-fitting chair allowed. "Paige started it. She started freaking out when she thought you were going to refuse to work ritual abuse cases. She needed a way to make you stay involved. It was her idea, but I did it." A flush crept across his cheeks. "I guess she was right. She had you figured out. But she didn't have me figured out," he added with emphasis.

My brain had come to a screeching halt upon hearing Paige's name, but Duncan was on a roll.

"After Paige died and I almost lost you, I couldn't resist. I don't know why it was important to her that you work those awful cases, but I kept it up because . . . I thought you would like me more. I thought . . . maybe you'd respect me eventually if I protected you and helped you solve the mystery."

The phone rang, and it was Gayle at the front desk. "Good morning, Sunny. Just a heads up to let you know that Mark Anderson is on his way to your office."

Mark was at the door before my phone hit the receiver.

I turned a loaded pair of hostile eyes on Duncan and fired, "We're not done, mister. We will finish this conversation after I talk to Mark."

Duncan looked even more sorrowful as he rose to leave. "I'm sorry. I never meant to hurt you or frighten you. I have to work down in the fraud unit today."

"How appropriate! Now get out."

The men exchanged places, and Mark entered carrying a white file box.

When Duncan closed the door, Mark set the box on my desk and came around to give me a little kiss on the cheek. "How are you doing, sweetheart? You shouldn't have come back to work so soon."

Mark still looked tired, but perhaps that was part of his job description. Maybe it was part of mine too. I tended to avoid self-audits while looking in the mirror.

Mark brought me up to speed on the investigation that followed the events in the tunnel. Basically, he recapped everything Travis had already told me, and then he handed me the box containing Chance's personal belongings.

Mark and I both held the box for a moment, our hands clutching two different sides of treasured memories. We held it in a long embrace and then Mark let go, our eyes connecting through an emotional fog. "The invitations have gone out to law enforcement. Mac is coordinating with the military. Is there anything I can do?" Mark asked.

I sniffled. "Yeah. Keep Mercy for me a little while longer, okay? Chance would like that—his two best friends working together."

Mark gave a silent nod of assent and hugged me, holding me tight. Then he was gone.

I tried to focus on my work but had been completely derailed between Duncan's revelation and the contents of the box on my desk. I stared at the box, captivated by its contents. Our wedding picture rested on top. Chance's eyes were shining with joy—sky blue, crystal clear, and as pure as the water beneath the Tahoe Queen as she steamed her way around Emerald Bay. I looked younger, as radiant as the sun whose warmth reflected off the people around us. The captain of the ship was asking, "Do you promise . . . until death do you part?"

Tears formed in my eyes. We thought we would live forever, Chance and I—or at least grow old together. Fate or destiny or misfortune had intervened. I traced the outline of my husband reliving our special day when I sensed the presence of another person. Duncan had returned and was standing in the doorway, his eyebrows peaked in wonder as he stared in shock and dismay, appearing genuinely hurt.

I looked up at Duncan as if stirred from a dream. "What?"

Duncan seemed to have tears in his eyes too. "You really did love him, didn't you?" he asked, incredulous.

Completely astounded, my eyes widened, and jaw dropped. "What kind of question is that? Of course, I did. He was my husband."

The lines on Duncan's face deepened into a scowl. "He was unfaithful. He cheated on you. You told me he was 'sort of a husband.'"

I couldn't explain it to someone who hadn't been there. I couldn't explain what it means to wholly give your heart to someone only to have it ripped out later. I couldn't account for the love and mercy and grace of God that had performed CPR when he breathed new life into a dying relationship. I couldn't describe that kind of love. There were no words.

"Chance wasn't perfect. No one really is. I guess you could say I loved the good in him." A lame stab at trying to explain the impossible.

Duncan's jaw quivered in anger. "I don't believe you. You didn't love him! You're not even going to his funeral."

His words felt like a hard slap that set me reeling. If Duncan really cared about me as he claimed, he would have understood. He would get that everyone—every single person—has a breaking point. I had just survived birth, death, and dismemberment. Being frozen, mauled, burned, and nearly drowned. Paige, Kenny, Quincy . . . my beloved husband dying in my arms. And there stood Duncan, judging me as if I were no more than a child acting pouty and throwing a temper tantrum.

I lifted my chin, seething. "How dare you?" I snapped. For the second time, I ordered him to "get out."

Duncan didn't move. He stood firm, his gaze and voice unwavering and determined, jaw thrust forward as he nodded. "The truth hurts, doesn't it?" he challenged, squaring his shoulders as he stood tall and resolute. "You really disappoint me," said Duncan. Then he turned and walked away.

CHAPTER 43

ဆ ♁ ര

Morning finally arrived, following the longest night of my life.

Duncan had been right, of course. What was I thinking? By not burying Chance, I could keep him alive? That I could stop death by refusing to acknowledge it? I tossed in the bed, turning over for the millionth time. More likely, I had been teetering on the brink of insanity—one more funeral and I'd go §5150.

Wrapping my arms around Chance's pillow, I held tight and breathed deeply. His essence lingered as I took in the last traces of his physical being. I wanted to lay there forever.

Speak to me Lord, had been the midnight prayer as my body finally surrendered to sleep. And my prayer was answered as dawn slid through the slats of the blinds to wake me. The thought emerged that our days on earth are but a series of funerals—of births and deaths—until we, ourselves, lie down for the last time. Life happens in between.

Today was an in-between day. Time to get up and say goodbye. Another chance, another opportunity to say, "I love you."

I got up and called Mac.

Mac picked me up, and we drove mostly in silence. A small bottle of water and a packet of tissues fit in my purse. I was as ready as I would ever be.

We headed to Harrison Stadium, the perfect location to accommodate a crowd. Fire engines lined both sides of the road facing one another; they stood vigilant, lights quietly flashing, like rows of gleaming angels dressed in red. The parking lot was jammed. Hundreds of people were already there, in the bleachers and on the field. The stars and stripes, the California bear, and US Army flags all snapped in a brisk wind above the stadium. A color guard stood at attention at the entryway to the field, dressed in formal black coats and dress hats with their white-gloved hands wrapped around polished rifles.

Chairs were set up in front of a stage amid an ocean of flowers. Behind the stage sat the Kiowa Search and Rescue helicopter—the same one that had carried my husband to me on the day we met. Today, it would take him away.

A large formal portrait of Chance was mounted on one side of the podium. He was dressed in his sheriff's uniform, looking proud and handsome. The other side of the podium held a double row of chairs filled with VIPs. Jack Savage and Perry Atchison were among them.

All five members of our little church choir stood patiently waiting against the backdrop. For all of their shortcomings—for we were just people, after all—when the chips were down, there were no more selfless, or compassionate, or dependable people than my church family.

Front and center rested the casket, draped with an American flag.

I couldn't breathe. My God, no wonder Cali had hidden behind a privacy window. I can't do this. Too many deaths. Too many funerals. Way too many people.

My heart was racing ahead of my feet. I needed to run—run to the solitude and sanctuary of my beloved mountains. I spun, pulling away from Mac, our arms stretched wide when I was intercepted.

Travis took my hand from Mac, saying, "She's with me." He led me toward the front row of the seating that faced the podium, sparing me from the nightmare spectacle of facing the crowd. "You look beautiful. I'm glad you're here," he whispered as we walked.

Travis directed me to my chair and introduced me to an elegant woman dressed in black seated next to him. I immediately recognized her from Paige's memorial service.

"Sunny, I'd like you to meet my friend—"

She reached out her hand.

The microphone crackled, and the church choir began.

"If You say go
We will go . . .
If You say wait
We will wait . . .

If You say step out on the water
And they say it can't be done,
We'll fix our eyes on You and we will come . . ."

I politely let go of her hand and sat down, feeling somewhat dismayed that Travis would bring his lover to Chance's funeral.

Mac opened with prayer—Isaiah 41:10. "Do not fear, for I am with you. Do not be dismayed, for I am your God. I will strengthen you and help you; I will uphold you with my righteous right hand."

Mark was up next. He brought Mercy up on stage. She sat obediently next to him with her eyes trained on me. Mark detailed Chance's professional life. Army: Special Ops and K-9 unit. Then he recapped Chance's service with Butte County Sheriff's Office—Search and Rescue—and how Chance had mastered the various specialties one by one: K9, air operations, over the edge, search, swift-water rescue, winter, and remote area rescue.

No wonder so many people had come to honor him. I only hoped that my presence would honor him as well. I was trying.

The ceremony went on and on and on. At one point, Travis reminded me to drink some water.

Finally, the piercing squeal of a lone bagpipe broke through my numbness with the haunting tune of "Amazing Grace."

The honor guard snapped to attention. Seven of them took position and fired their guns three times, for the twenty-one-gun salute. Travis prompted me to accept the folded flag from Mark. The tears I had held in check released without my even knowing it. A bitter wind blew, and I could feel their cold tracks as they trailed down my face.

The casket was escorted and loaded onto the Kiowa. Two other helicopters appeared as if by magic, hovering above the stadium right on cue. The Kiowa revved its engine and thundered upward to pause for a moment with the others—forming a perfect triangle. Then, it broke away, taking Chance away from me . . . and home to Yankee Hill Cemetery, forever.

CHAPTER 44

꧁ ✠ ꧂

My bed didn't stay empty for long. Mercy, the Wonder Dog, had become Mercy the Bed Hog. She took up two-thirds of the bed, and Kissme and I competed for what was left. Better the bed too full than too empty. At least I was sleeping at night without the help of prescription meds.

Work was a blessing, and I buried myself in my tasks as January came to a close.

Every day I received new cases of domestic violence, involving battered women who'd had their internal navigators disrupted in much the same way a solar flare can fry the delicate circuitry in satellites, disabling their guidance systems. Domestic violence wounds a woman in her most private emotional place—the place that once harbored the light of trust becomes a black hole of betrayal. Victims of domestic violence needed love, guidance, and protection until they can heal and rediscover their true north.

Sexual assault cases came in too. They were fewer. Victims of rape who had been violated in the most intimate of places—the heart of their sexuality—a place designed by God to experience heights of passion, sometimes culminating in the greatest miracle a human being can experience—the bringing forth of a new life born of love.

The cases set before me broke my heart, but the work was also a blessing. I honored each survivor by giving my very best.

Ritual abuse does not go away. Will never go away. It has been around since Eden. The evil often lies hidden, like the snake in the garden, but if an advocate is willing to look close enough, and if that advocate reads between the lines, she will recognize the truth when she sees it.

This time the RA factor was found "between the lines" of the police report. The charge was domestic violence, but I no longer had to search for the truth. The photographs in the file showed the victim's husband with devil horns tattooed on his forehead, pentagrams on his arms, and the number 666 tattooed across his back. Additional pictures taken at the scene showed the usual black-on-black home decor, stacks of demonic movies, Gothic art on the walls, and sadomasochistic devices in the bedroom.

What am I supposed to do with this?

I chewed thoughtfully on the tip of my pen, keeping time with the restless tap of my foot. I was pretty sure that Victim Witness would not pay for an exorcism.

This particular ritual abuse case had come on the heels of a case out of Alaska that rocked the nation. Miranda Barbour had admitted to being an active participant in a satanic cult and murdering twenty-two people. The fact that it was ritual abuse would soon be swept aside, until the next grisly discovery. No one counted the little RA cases that peppered the news between the classic killers, Richard Ramirez and Sean Sellers. Few people knew, or would even care that RA was a component in the investigations of more recent headliners like Jonbenét Ramsey and Scott Peterson.

Who? I imagined people asking, and to which I would reply, "My point."

Because the latest ritual abuse case had come on the heels of the one making national headlines, Jack decided to send me out to provide more training—this time throwing me to the wolves in San Diego. There was no city in the United States where the topic of ritual abuse was less welcome.

Thanks, Jack.

The conference was not for a couple of weeks, so I tried to stay focused on the case at hand.

"Good morning, is this Elsie?"

"This is Electra."

Of course it is.

"My name is Sunny McLane. I am the advocate with the district attorney office looking to speak with Elsie Rozelle."

"Is Romulus still in jail?"

Romulus aka Ronald Shelton was Devil-boy down at the jail. After I had verified that Elsie was aka Electra, I said "yes," and provided her with legal information regarding bail and arraignment for Romulus.

We talked about her safety, and Electra raged. "What do you know? There. Is. No. Safe. Place. It will never end." She went on to tell me uncomfortable truths in more detail than I wanted to hear, but I knew my job.

An advocate's job is to listen and believe. "How long have you been . . . ?" "You're not crazy . . ." and "I believe you."

Ritual abuse survivors have suffered similar issues as POWs. My father told me about the brainwashing and the physical torture that he'd endured as a prisoner during the Vietnam War. Survivors of ritual abuse have also been held captive; controlled by cults who employ similar tactics of torture and brainwashing.

Electra's voice came on strong and then collapsed under the strain. "They are always watching me. They can tell me what I ate for breakfast, who I talk to on the phone, what color of underwear I put on for God's sake. One time I went to LA to visit my family . . . oh shit." She broke down with a gasp and a sniffle and then lowered her voice as if they would hear us. "They told me everyone I talked to while I was down there, even a stranger on a bus."

I offered hope. "I can help relocate you through Victim Witness. I have a list of therapists that specialize in helping survivors of ritual abuse."

Like my father, whose hand was cut off when he was tortured, Elsie's physical damage had been extensive and ritually inflicted over an extended period of time. She had recently been treated at the ER, but she would need long-term holistic treatment.

I validated her pain: "I can see by this report that you've been a victim of . . ." Today I referred her to Rape Crisis and counselors with the domestic violence program. Elsie had not only suffered physical trauma, she also had severe mental, emotional, and spiritual needs. As Elsie and I grew in trust, I would offer her additional resources. She would need qualified counselors who specialized in long-term abuse. I figured if a counselor is not qualified to treat a prisoner of war, then they probably aren't qualified to treat a survivor of ritual abuse.

"I'm a bad person. They made me . . . Romulus beat me and sodomized me. I have scars . . ."

I reassured. "I believe you are a good person. I'm sorry that happened to you. You didn't deserve that. Are you feeling suicidal?"

I showed her I was informed. "Was this part of a blood ritual for St. Walpurgis Day?"

"Yes, yes." Elsie was astounded at first and then became suspicious. "How did you . . . ? are you one of them?"

I established trust. "No, Electra. I didn't mean to frighten you. It's good that you're cautious. My job is to help you and I can't help you if I'm not familiar with ritual abuse."

I supported. "You have been a victim. I want to help you to become a survivor."

I hung up the phone and sat quietly for a moment, wondering if I was going crazy. These cases unnerved me. Elsie's fear was contagious, and I wondered if I was paranoid. Maybe she was a setup; maybe my phone was tapped. After all, I had a history of being followed.

CHAPTER 45
ജ ♱ ര

Travis was back in town regarding the numerous reports that had been generated by the various agencies involved in the drug bust. I couldn't look him in the eye at first. I was afraid of what he would think.

"Travis." I stared at my desk, looking guilty because I was guilty. I knew that Travis would not be pleased that I had delayed in providing him with this information. "Chance called me."

I glanced at Travis who sat in the chair across from me. He stiffened and leaned in, studying me like a watchmaker looking for a few loose screws.

"Quit it. I'm not crazy. Chance did call me, a few hours before the raid. He told me that he had figured out the why part of whoever wanted Quincy, but he wouldn't give me any details. He said he would explain everything when I got home."

Travis's features tightened as he stood and leaned over the desk. Sure enough, he was not happy.

"What else did he say?" asked Travis.

"That's all. I guess. I forget."

Travis circled my desk. Taking my chin in his hand, he drew my face up until our gazes met. "There has to be more. Think, Sunny. It's important."

Irritated, I slapped his hand away. "I don't know. I guess everything got—blurry—what with the blood and bullets and . . ." I dropped my gaze and shook my head. "He said . . . he had something to show me when I got home."

"What? What did he have to show you?" Travis was so close that I could smell his essence—heated, alive.

"I don't know. He wouldn't say. Mark was calling him on the cell phone, and he said he had to go. He told me he would explain everything later. He thought that I could somehow confirm his suspicions."

"What else did he say?"

My eyes kindled and then blazed. "None of your damned business." My husband's last words belonged to me. Except, they really didn't. Chance's last breath had been a memorial to another woman.

"There's more. You're holding something back from me."

"You don't need to know everything."

Travis narrowed his gaze, looking for all the world like a sleek cat wound up inside, crouched and fixated on its prey. "I know you," he said.

Travis moved closer, his face once again in front of mine. "Babe, I wouldn't ask you if it wasn't important. Trust me. Please, trust me. Chance would never waste his last breath on anything meaningless. What did he say?"

Frustration and hurt threatened from the corners of my eyes. I guess if I had to share Chance's last words with anyone, Travis would be the least judgmental and the most understanding, considering. I knew how Chance's words sounded to me, and I wondered how they would come across to Travis.

"Paige." He said, "I . . . You . . . Paige . . ." And then he died. "He was trying to say, 'I love you, Paige.' I'm sure of it." Tears welled, and my chin trembled, but in a way, it felt good to finally say what I had been thinking, however hurtful.

Travis's countenance softened under a mantle of compassion. "I don't think so, Sunny. He must have meant something else." He walked around and sat on the desk just inches away and lowered his voice, almost as if talking to himself. "If I ever doubted for one moment that Chance loved you . . . well . . . things might have turned out differently for all of us."

"What does that mean?" I looked into Travis's face, lost for a moment in the depth and intensity of his gaze, then tensed at the sound of a door closing and Amanda and Bonita discussing something about a release of evidence as they passed my door.

Travis slipped a hand behind my head and tipped it forward as he leaned in and kissed me on the top of my head. He pressed his cheek and head against mine for a long moment and then drew back. "It means it's time to go," he said.

I gave Travis a few seconds, but no more. He wasn't the only one with questions, and I never knew when I would see him.

"Travis? Don't go yet. I have questions too. Will you answer a question for me? Honestly?"

Dark eyebrows rose above green eyes deep enough to drown in, like vernal pools in a marsh teeming with life.

Focus.

I did a quick intake of air before releasing the question that still loomed. "Why do you think Paige killed herself? Why would the cartel want Quincy?" I raced ahead as if to cross the finish line first with answers to my own questions. "They couldn't be using her as leverage against Paige because they took her after Paige was . . . had . . . died."

Small muscles rippled beneath the perpetual shadow along Travis's jaw. His eyes boldly invaded mine, searching for something—before retreating to his Zen spot, the place where he was at one with himself. Not that Travis found all his answers in his peaceful place. It's just that, unlike me, he didn't put himself through a shredder trying to sort them out.

"Let's put our heads together," said Travis, pulling me close and placing his forehead against mine, his breath warm against my skin. We held each other close for a few moments, and when we drew apart, we both were smiling. I didn't know how he did that—made me feel better in the heart of my grief. Travis hadn't always been a shining light, but sometimes he reminded me of a Christmas tree or a candle on a birthday cake—glowing brightest when things were darkest.

"Let's sort this out together."

I nodded in agreement.

"You said that Chance called you just before the raid. He had figured out why Quincy had been kidnapped, but he needed you to verify that what he had discovered was valid: he needed you to confirm a person, place, or a thing."

"I suppose so. That's what he said."

"That means that you know the answer."

I puzzled as Travis continued.

"Let's move on. First, Paige. There's no denying that she was deeply scarred from her abduction and sexual abuse. Paige liked risky behavior, and she wasn't afraid of death. Always acting tough"—his features continued to soften—"but deep down, she was just a frightened little girl—not the ditzy bimbo she pretended to be." The corners of his eyes crinkled. "I think Paige liked to ask stupid questions just to bring out stupid answers in men." He gave a harsh little chuckle. "It was probably her way of getting even with them."

"Was she suicidal?"

"Frequently. But I'm not sure that she took her own life."

"What do you mean?"

"I mean, maybe it was more like a sacrifice than a suicide."

Lines deepened on Travis's forehead, and for the first time, I noticed a touch of gray intertwined with the sandy-brown hair at his temples. His eyes shifted thoughtfully down and right as he tapped into the creative part of his mind, and then returned to meet mine.

"Try this: the gunman enters the cabin and points a gun at Paige. She is lying on the couch and holding the gun you gave her, but she is not aiming it at him."

"Why would you think that?"

Travis chewed his lip thoughtfully. "Because one of them would have pulled a trigger, and there is nothing to indicate that one person fired at another." Travis's brows continued to knit a thoughtful pattern. "I have to agree with your friend Dano and her notion of self-determination. Let's say that Paige is holding the gun to her head while the armed man is facing her and she makes the decision to pull the trigger." My gaze dropped and Travis shifted to maintain eye contact. "I think . . . I'll bet . . . that she knew him. There has to have been a relationship between her and Mr. Miasma Ortiz. I just don't know what it was."

"But Travis, if Paige thought he was after her child, wouldn't she have shot him instead of herself?"

A soft smile crept across Travis's face. "She must have believed her baby was safe with you. And, as it turned out," he said, lowering his voice and lifting his brows in salute, "she was right."

Visions of a maimed infant formed in my mind, and I quickly dismissed his notion.

"But the front door was locked when Joyce arrived, so he never went inside."

Travis tipped his head and pursed his lips. "Maybe. Or maybe he locked the door behind him when he left."

"That's it? That's all we have to go on?" I wondered if my own frown lines were any deeper than the furrows plowing their way across Travis's forehead. The enigma was adding years to our lives.

"No. Let's work on your other question—why the cartel would want a newborn baby."

I sat with folded hands and shuddered, reluctant to voice my thoughts. "Sex trafficking. Paige told me they never have enough . . . children. Kids grow up and need to be replaced." My fists white-knuckled. "The demand for new children—it never ends."

"That's true." Travis nodded in agreement. "But not newborn babies. Diapers, bottles, teething, toilet training—you hear what I'm saying? Not when newborn white babies pull top dollar on the market for illegal adoption. The worst-case scenario is she is somewhere safe. I feel it in my heart."

Good to know that a human heart beats inside the person I have come to think of as, the man of steel. Travis reached out and placed his hand on mine. We comforted one another for a couple of seconds.

"There has to be more to it," I said. "They—whoever they are—didn't go through all that—hunting me like an animal through the mountains—just to get a new baby, when they could've grabbed one at any hospital. It's like Chance said—they wanted Quincy, and they wanted her for a reason."

ℰ☥ℛ

The meeting was a good idea, and since it was mine, I tried not to be late. I felt a strategic meeting was in order. Amanda, Dano, and I were scheduled to discuss legal proceedings in Amanda's office after court. Shifting from Travis to Taylor wasn't easy. Going to the meeting required mentally shifting gears from a full stop—halfway up a steep hill while hauling a heavy load.

Taylor had been arrested along with nine other cult members. If you included Miasma, Latisha, and dirtbag Logan, the total attendees at the ritual came to the ominous number thirteen.

I stopped breathing when I read in the initial report that Taylor admitted to carrying "her little sister" in a box to the meeting. She later stated that the baby "belonged" to her cult family. When asked her purpose for bringing the child, she said, "To be baptized. I was told to bring her. I didn't want to. I like her."

The investigator noted Taylor's behavioral change during the interrogation, stating that "Ms. Jarreau was initially cooperative and very childlike." Then he wrote that Taylor suddenly "became hostile and aggressive, insisting that her name was Pat." Pat went on to make a lengthy, detailed statement covering years of being victimized and abused at the hands of a satanic cult.

Legal issues were popping up like tips of icebergs in the path of a cruise ship.

Dano arrived, hung her raincoat on the back of her chair, and pulled it up to one side of Amanda's desk. There were two remaining seats. The door opened, and Bonita bounced in looking like a water spaniel fresh from the hunt. I scooted my chair next to Dano with a sick feeling that I was about to be lectured as opposed to being informed.

Amanda dropped in her chair and began emergency repairs. She looked like an exotic bird after a monsoonal rain, or maybe a cat that just had a bath.

She did not extend offers of refreshments. "Grab some chairs, ladies, and make yourselves comfortable. I apologize for being blunt. It's been a long day, so if you don't mind, let's get to it."

Everyone nodded.

Amanda slipped on a pair of round reading glasses and began with a brief summary. "Regarding Ms. Taylor Jarreau, who was arrested, deferred to Mental Health and subsequently released from a seventy-two-hour §5150 hold, we are here today concerning her allegations of child abuse and sexual assault. Ms. Jarreau is currently"—Amanda flipped the report to the cover page—"thirty-seven years old."

She turned to Dano. "It is important that you understand that when I go to trial, the case must be proved beyond a reasonable doubt. The minute I say the word cult, I lose my jury." Amanda shook her head as she tapped her pen. "On top of that, Taylor's allegations go back twenty years—that's a problem right there."

"There is current evidence of abuse," I said. "Taylor has scars."

Amanda pursed her lips. "We don't know how those injuries happened. We only know what the medical records say, and I'm sure they don't include the words ritual abuse."

Dano interjected, "The abuse is still current, and the perpetrators are alive."

Frown lines deepened across Amanda's forehead. "Actually, if you are referring to Taylor's father, Mr. Angelo Ortiz is dead."

Shock registered on Dano's face. "What about her mother, the priestess?"

"When she is arrested, Latisha Jarreau will be charged with kidnapping, forgery, and possession of guns and drugs."

The injustice was outrageous. "You won't tell the jury about the cult? They just get away with everything? Who would think that truth would enable the guilty to go free?" I switched tactics. "I guess that's why I'm just an advocate and not a prosecutor."

Amanda shot me reproving glance. "You know better. Individuals will be charged according to their crimes. But let's cut to the chase regarding Taylor Jarreau." Amanda leaned forward with both elbows on the desk, her gaze targeting Dano. "I have a question for you. Is it possible that a person with multiple personalities can have one personality that is still active in the cult?"

Dano blinked, looking wary. "Yes, that could happen."

Amanda arched her brow. "Knowing that is a possibility begs the question: If you were me, how many subpoenas would you send Taylor—and which personality would appear on the witness stand?"

CHAPTER 46

ജ ✞ ൙

Frito anxiously dogged my heels as I searched the cabin. "Me-ma? Day-Day?" I was seven years old—all grown up and didn't talk baby talk. And yet, my feet traveled the weary, familiar route—first the downstairs, then my parents' bedroom upstairs (the meditation-room-turned-lair), out to the Japanese bathhouse, and finally the garden and orchard, looking for parents that were rarely there— wailing, "Me-maa... Day-Dayy..."

When the echoes died, I squared my little shoulders and stooped down, scooped up my dog, and rocked him like a baby. "Don't be afraid. I won't ever leave you," I crooned, reassuring my ratty little one-eyed friend, "Ever. I will never be like her."

I was rewarded with a grateful lick on the face. And then another and another until I woke to Kissme's tongue in my eye. "Yuck. Kissme. That's disgusting." I looked at the clock and scrunched my face. "That's even more disgusting," I said, relocating her to my chest, where she promptly settled down and went back to sleep, leaving me wide awake. Thinking and remembering.

What a weird dream. Actually, it had been a familiar dream. Just weird, because I had never called my parents by the baby names Me-Ma or Day-Day. Not even in a dream.

And remembering. Remembering.

A hot summer day. Blazing hot. Screaming mad.

"I am your mother. I am your mama. You will not call me Starla."

"You are not my mother—Starla. You don't deserve that name. You just popped me out—like a dog. Even Frito can do that. I will never call you Mama again."

Starla's eyes narrowed to slits. "Well, aren't you perfect?" Her voice was deceptively low. "What do you know about being a mother? You don't know anything." Starla snorted then laughed—

raspy, deep, throaty, from too many cigarettes and too many nights bent over a crack pipe. She was leathered and tattooed, her hair punked. "You're just like me." Starla had spat it out, like a judgment—or a curse.

And then she had paused, her eyes time-traveling to some distant galaxy, sad and wistful as she whispered, "I used to be just like you."

"You were never like me—and I will never be like you. I hate you!" Rage was my armor, and I braced myself for the slap that didn't come.

Tears shimmered in her watery gray eyes. "Give it time, baby girl. You don't know what you will become." Starla blinked. "Probably just like your old lady."

Better than an alarm clock, the memory propelled me out of bed. My greatest fear in life was morphing into my mother. I couldn't shake it. Something about my dream clung, leaving me anxious—like the cloying smell of body odor, I couldn't get away from it. Something. Something beyond the obvious influence of Taylor's Tinkerbell lingered.

Locking the door and saying goodbye to a pair of unhappy dogs that Shane had promised to watch, the dream trailed me as I got in my car and slammed the door.

"I am not like you!" I said in affirmation. The memory paled before the rising sun.

I had a plane to catch, and I still had to pick up my laptop and the stack of handouts, get fuel for the car at the gas station and fuel for me at Starbucks.

"Thanks, Duncan," I would be lost without you," I said in a whirlwind of last minute office activity.

Duncan had packed the laptop and projector into a hand cart. A shadow flickered across his tired expression. "Really? I doubt that."

I had been so wrapped up in my own pain that I had completely forgotten about his. "No. Honestly," I said with an encouraging pat on his cheek. "You are the undisputed techie king."

Duncan shrugged. "That's what friends are for."

ॐ ☥ ॐ

To my relief, the conference was held in an Episcopal Church instead of the state university. Besides divine protection, the church would be safe from the prying eyes of California's Investigating Grand Jury members—those citizens authorized to oversee and investigate the conduct of government-funded institutions. While the secretive activities of the grand jury were usually reserved for drug trafficking, insurance fraud, organized crime, and public corruption, they always took an active interest when presenting on the topic of ritual abuse. It seemed that the first amendment right was overshadowed here in the otherwise sunny city of San Diego.

San Diego's city fathers had remained vigilant ever since neighboring Los Angeles County undertook the famous McMartin Preschool case—the longest and most expensive criminal trial in American history—lasting seven years and costing fifteen million dollars. Allegations included hidden tunnels, animal sacrifice, Satan worship, child abuse, and orgies—only to end with a hung (tied) jury and no convictions—while the truth was still a subject of debate. San Diego, in its determination to prevent a similar fiasco, was possibly the safest place in the world to be a Satanist.

The conference was headed by a woman from Utah's Ritual Abuse Task Force who worked as an off-the-record expert that law enforcement often consulted when investigating crimes where SRA (Satanic Ritual Abuse) had been alleged. Other speakers on the agenda included a doctor who specialized in treating survivors of ritual abuse, a professional deprogrammer and two survivors who were present to share their stories.

Attendees included members of law enforcement, Mental Health, educational institutions, Victim Witness, and the nonprofits—domestic violence and sexual assault crisis center staff, volunteers, and advocates. Scanning the room, I noticed that the attire varied from East Coast professional to California casual, but the expressions were uniform: somewhere between curious and dubious.

Women made up the majority and flitted about like a flock of colorful birds, but my eyes were drawn to the back of the room where they landed on a solitary young man: tall, thin and pale. He sat with his knees together, hands clasped in his lap and eyes trained on his hands. He was casually dressed with his brown hair carefully combed and hanging in soft waves to his shoulders. He was invisible to the majority of attendees, but I knew the look of a survivor when I saw one.

The day went as planned. Presentations were given, handouts provided, a healthy lunch served, questions asked and answered. I said farewell to my colleagues as they departed and busied myself with packing up my equipment. I had forgotten all about the young man until I looked up.

The sadness in the young man's eyes would haunt me for as many days as my Maker granted me on this earth. The yellow flower in his hand would become the mysterious keepsake, forever pressed between the pages of my Bible. He had likely picked the single flower from the landscaped beds just outside of the front door. That didn't matter. What mattered was the time we spent sitting together on the trim lawn beneath the towering rock cathedral. What mattered was his story.

"I just want to thank you," said the young man with no name, holding a yellow daisy. "I need to thank you for believing. I knew I wasn't crazy—even though everyone tried to make me think I was. No one else has ever believed me." His tears came, as shy and as soft as his voice—gentle and dignified.

He cleared his throat. "My father is a politician, a wealthy politician who throws a lot of parties. Everyone comes to my dad's parties—other politicians, movie stars, even famous athletes." The smooth lines on the young man's face pinched in disgust. "A couple from up north almost always shows up with the kids." He shivered. "Scary. You see . . . like, there was a different kind of party going on upstairs." The young man took a deep breath and twirled the daisy between his fingers. "That's where the kids waited. That's where friends of my dad's other 'family' would have sex with us during the parties."

I blinked. "Whose kids were they? Were they children of the guests?"

"Some of them were, like me. The kids with rich parents were saved for the privileged, but most of the kids come from Mexico." A bitter laugh escaped between tightly pressed lips, his eyes brimming with emotion as he resurrected buried memories. "I know this sounds weird, but it was the couple from Northern California that brought them. They would show up with a van full of kids the night before the party. They would give us treats, like pizza and cake and ice cream"—he sniffed—"but we weren't stupid.

"When I was little, 'playing games' meant being tied up . . . with duct tape on my mouth so the guests wouldn't hear me scream. I was just a kid. They finally left me alone when I got older—nine or ten. When I finally told my teacher, the school went straight to my parents." He bit his lip and twirled the daisy in the opposite direction. "They didn't get mad. They just sent me to a shrink who told me that I had an overactive imagination."

I looked into the eyes of a man who was still in bondage—knowing that emotional bondage is as strong as any cord and as effective as duct tape—society had effectively kept his hands tied and his mouth taped through denial, mockery, and humiliation.

The young man's face twisted in pain, his eyes glittering like fragments of broken glass. "I'm glad he's dead," he spewed.

"Your father?"

"No. The Ghost. My keeper."

"The Ghost?"

"The creepy guy from up north—the biker dude. A white man with white eyes.

My world went sideways. Lights exploded in my head as he talked, but I couldn't make out his words.

"I'm sorry," I said. "What did you say?"

The boy-man looked puzzled for a moment. "He was the man who drove the van. An albino who called himself Miasma. He was seriously scary, with an even scarier wife."

"His wife . . ." I choked out the words, "Tell me about his wife."

Again, the young man looked puzzled. "A black woman. Really dark. I think her name is Day-Day. At least that's what the kids were told to call her."

Taylor had called her parents Me-Ma and Day-Day. Not mommy and daddy after all, but a kiddie version of Miasma and Deirdre. Of course. I felt like a fool—but an elated fool. My head whirled with information overload.

Paige—daughter of a wealthy man. Her last word to me, "Ma-e-ma." The albino who had stalked me and attacked me in the hospital. The black woman who had taken Quincy. A judge from San Bernardino.

The nameless young man grew nervous and started glancing around before turning a pair of bewildered eyes on me.

"You know these people?"

I reached out and placed a reassuring hand on his arm. "Yes. No. What I mean is—I have worked with victims of people with those names, only I didn't realize it until now. Victims in Northern California."

"I have to go." The young man stood and dusted his pants with his hands as he prepared to leave.

"The children—where were the other kids kept when they weren't at the parties? The kids from Mexico? Please. Please tell me. Please, I beg you—trust me."

His answer was a long time coming as I waited, torn between fear and hope.

His eyes moistened, and he licked his lips. "You did a brave thing today," he said at last. "You set me free. I know I'm not crazy now—because you believe me." He glanced around again. "I owe you, Mrs. McLane." He handed me the yellow daisy and asked me for a pen and paper. Then he wrote the location of where the children were kept.

CHAPTER 47

ॐ ☥ ∞

Fear followed me back to the hotel and overshadowed my every move. Everyone looked suspicious. Everyone was watching me. I used my cell phone instead of the phone in my room.

"Travis?"

The tremor in my voice made him ask, "Sunny—what's wrong?"

I told him where I was and what I had learned.

"Can you drive?"

"Yes, I'm okay. I have a car."

"Okay. I'm in Southern California. I want you to drive north on I-15. I'll meet you at the car rental at the Ontario Airport. You can turn your car in there. I'll make some calls, and we'll go out to the property together." He was quiet for a couple of beats and then added, "And, Sunny. Make sure no one followed you."

Travis arrived driving his Lexus, dressed in Levi's, T-shirt, and a lightweight jacket. His face was etched with concern. I put my electronics in the trunk of his car and my suitcase on the backseat, pausing to consider the items piled there: a child's pink Minnie Mouse sweatshirt and a stuffed striped Cheshire cat perched atop a Pirates of the Caribbean DVD Treasure Chest. I swallowed.

Not my business.

It was clear that Travis had a life of his own. He had moved on, and I tried to feel happy for him. "What are you doing down here?" I asked.

"Disneyland. What else? Isn't that why everyone comes to LA?"

"Not me. I was in a different kind of Magic Kingdom."

"No kidding. How did you manage to give a lecture on ritual abuse in San Diego without being arrested?"

"No problem. The organizers held it inside an Episcopal church—and its good thing they did. It felt like a miracle, like a divine appointment."

Travis tilted his head, glancing at me as we merged onto a freeway. "Did Mystery Man have a name?"

"He didn't want to give it to me, and I don't blame him."

"It might have helped when trying to get a search warrant."

"How's that?"

"A little thing called 'probable cause.' But it doesn't matter now because we are definitely on our own. No judge is going to issue a groundless warrant." Travis fished a stick of gum from his pocket and handed one to me. "I'm just hoping no one is expecting us."

"Why would anyone be expecting us?"

"Because Deirdre is a retired judge from San Bernardino. We're driving into the lion's den, and I hope the Lion King I talked to about a warrant isn't making any unwarranted calls."

"Such as?"

"I hope the judge isn't calling Deirdre."

I knew the truth, yet it still came as a shock. While evil crossed all socioeconomic backgrounds, there remained a place inside me that clung to the lie: Cowboys in white hats run our country, and they are there to protect and serve. Bad guys are heartless lowlifes, stealers, and dealers. I guess I was like most people wanting to recognize a threat—so I gave it a face.

"What are we going to do? We can't go in without a warrant."

Travis just smiled and chewed his gum.

We found ourselves on a graveled road heading toward the hills. Other routes, probably used for off-road vehicles, veered off left and right, but we continued straight ahead until we saw a massive black wrought-iron gate looming in the distance.

Travis stopped and backed up, then turned around and parked about a half a mile down a cutoff road. He retrieved two handguns, a nine mil from the glove box and a revolver from the trunk of the car. Handing me the revolver, he asked, "You remember how to use this?"

"Ass."

"What did you say?"

"I said 'yes.'" There was no time to gather evidence and hope for a warrant. It was a long shot and we both knew it. Still, we hoped that Quincy would be inside. If Deirdre still kept abducted children here.

"As my father would say—'Let's do this.'"

Travis looked doubtful. "I don't want you getting hurt. These guys are pros."

"Yeah, well, sometimes you have to make do with what you have. You should know all about that."

"What's that supposed to mean?"

What did I mean? "It means you're a cop. Improvise."

The look of doubt returned, but Travis heaved a sigh and caved in. "Stay behind me—and do what I say."

"Yes sir, Boss." I saluted him and set off cross-country toward the gate. Travis followed.

The cavern at the top of the hill was larger than a house, more grandiose than a mansion, and more imposing than a fortress. I crouched low, although there was little to hide behind as we scrambled past clumps of sage brush as we dashed from boulder to boulder. The hillside looked as though an ogre the size of Godzilla had ripped slabs from the hillside and piled them at crazy angles against one another. A broad paved driveway swept up the hill into the mouth of the yawning cavern framed by the slabs. It looked like a great place to hold up if you were a survivalist, a doomsday prepper, a nudist, or a kidnapper holding children for sex trafficking.

There were no fences other than the massive gate that spanned the two-lane driveway that led up the hill and into the mouth of the cavern. Circling around to enter from the side, we were drawn, impossibly, to the sound of splashing and children's laughter.

Travis took me by the arm and pulled me behind him, giving me signals that meant nothing to me: two fingers poking toward his eyes, pointing at me and then pointing at himself, clenching his fists, patting the air, making me crazy—until I finally returned the only hand signal I knew. Travis looked pained while pointing at his butt.

We had come to a small private lake in the middle of the desert. Amazing stuff for sure. I had expected to find a dungeon filled with chained children, not a swimming hole resonating with the sound of laughter.

A cell phone playing a snappy tune went off nearby. We dropped and flattened ourselves against the ground behind a rock pile. Eyes widened, heart thrashing as I found myself eye to eye with a scorpion large enough to saddle and ride out of there. The scorpion made a short dash at my face. My eyes bulged as his tail swung up in an arch over his back. I froze. My heart stopped, my breathing stopped, time stopped.

A rock whipped down, turning the creature into scorpion jelly with only a couple of twitching legs remaining. Travis let go of the stone. "Let's go," he mouthed.

Better than hand signals.

Travis led, bent over as we skirted the lake—running behind the wall of boulders that shouldered the bank with the exception of some narrow openings that led down to the water. I paused at one such path to peek around the corner and gasped at the sight of naked children swimming and sitting on the rocks. A man's back was to me, a rifle hanging easily at his side, more interested in watching than guarding. We slipped across the trail and headed for the cavern that looked a whole lot like the scorpion's house.

The entry to the structure was recessed. Two Harleys were parked to one side. A surveillance camera goose necked from the wall above an intercom. Travis drew back, frowning in thought.

"What do we do?" I asked.

Travis shrugged. "Beats me."

I rolled my eyes and made a face. "What kind of superhero are you? Superheroes never say, 'Beats me.'"

Travis's eyes widened, and I grimaced in reply. Just because a door is closed doesn't mean it's locked. Gun clenched in both hands and pressed tight to my chest, I darted around the corner, opened the door, and slipped in. Travis followed on my heels.

The room in front of us looked like a millionaire's version of the Chinese tunnels turned whorehouse. The great room was decorated in every shade of red on red: from plush ruby-colored furniture to the thick crimson carpet beneath our feet. The rock walls and ceiling remained untouched. Half-dozen overstuffed chairs and three imposing U-shaped sofas that could comfortably seat ten, arced before three giant plasma screens designed for viewing God knows what. I didn't want to know. Several doors spoked off at the back of the room. One was open.

Travis finally gave me a signal I could understand, and we separated, moving along opposing walls so we would approach the open door from opposite sides.

Travis crouched low. Holding his gun in front of him, he pivoted into the hallway. A woman's voice with a distinctive Cajun accent bounced down the hall and grew louder as we approached.

"Oui. Miasma se mouri." Followed by a pause. "Biznis kòm dabitid." The woman raised her voice, saying, "Of course. Ah, not stupid. You haf till tonight. You want— you come get. Nou fini," followed by a resounding clack of a phone being slammed onto a desk.

Travis spun into the room where Latisha sat behind a sleek oversized desk. "You want—you get. Give me reason shoot you, yeah?" Travis said, aiming his gun. The whites of her eyes grew as round as twin crescent moons. "You unna arress."

"Fo' wha'? You got warran'? Shew me a warran'," she said in a singsong voice, and then tipped her chair backward. "Ey, I know you. You da Paige bump-bump." Her dark face lit with a lewd smile. "Sheet."

"Sunny." Travis fired off instructions. "Shoot her if she moves. I'm going to look for Quincy."

The gun shook in my hands, alerting the voodoo queen. The wolf inside of her smelled fear. Deirdre spoke a bastard mix of French and Cajun in an oily lilt, probably tailored for its hypnotic effect. She rambled on about chillens and bebes, moving her hips, hands, and mouth in explicit ways that sickened and angered me. Travis told me to shoot if Deirdre made any moves, but he didn't say what to do about her mouth.

"Shut up. Where's the baby?" I snarled.

"Just so. Shut up or talk? Bebe? Lemme tink now." She lifted her brows, arching and flexing them like a pair black cats on Halloween night. "Wha' kine you like you? Blaa, brow', got no mo whi' . . . all gone." She shrugged.

"Where is Paige's daughter?" I took a step closer and pressed the gun to her forehead.

Her wicked grin stretched from ear to ear as she tipped her head away and tapped a finger on her jaw. "Lemme tink, you. Ahhhh, yeah." Her fingers slid to the leather gris-gris bag around her neck, stroking the small leather bag that traditionally contained items infused with black magick and was etched with verses from the Qur'an. "Whi' girl. Much much money. She be wit yo' honee, you . . . Monsieur Logan."

My face scrunched like a piece of wadded foil, wrinkled with disdain, fury, and disbelief. I jabbed the pistol hard, smack between her eyes. "Why would Logan have her?"

"Much, much money. Yes? Chillins much money. Bebes so much mo'. You like money, you?" She lowered her voice, soft and seductive. "Deirdre make you very rich. Maybe some powda? Maybe some movie? Efryone wan's someting. Whacho wan'? New bebe? Git you one. Git you two."

A voice came from behind. "Shoot that bitch," said Travis.

I squeezed the trigger.

ೞ ♀ ೞ

A surreal time warp encompassed me—the kind where everything happens so fast that time slams on the brakes and slides into slow motion. A delicate spray of blood-red mist seemed to shimmer and hang in the air—like a soft red fog rolling in off the ocean. There was a burst of automatic weapon fire from the front room as Deirdre's head dissipated and I dropped to the floor. Somewhere in the background, children's screams magnified and echoed, their cries intermingling with the chatter of gunfire ripping down the corridor. A short pause, and then a series of shots were exchanged as Travis jumped, shooting into the hall. I heard the bawl of a man whose life force was leaving him—then three rapid-fire shots—and then silence, except for the wailing of children.

"Sunny?" Travis called from outside of the room. "Sunny—you okay?"

It didn't matter that Deirdre had been reaching for a gun under her desk. I was still sickened by the knowledge that I had killed someone.

"I think so," my voice quavered. I joined Travis in the hallway where he was bent over the body of one of the men we had seen at the lake, pressing his hand to the man's throat as he searched for signs of life. There was none. We didn't have to search the second man whose head had a tight pattern of three holes tapped across it.

"Just the two?" I found my voice, keeping my gun trained on the hall door.

"For now," said Travis.

"Quincy?" I asked anxiously.

Travis shook his head and slapped a fresh clip into his gun, his face set, hard and grim. He glanced toward the great room and the sound of children. "Put all the kids in one room," he said, "and make it fast! I'll try to get help. Other people will be here soon."

I lowered the gun and tried to steady my breathing. "I don't want to be trapped in a room. Let's run—we can hide out in the desert."

"No, we'll be targets. They'll kill those kids before they let them escape. We have to protect them until help comes. I need to make calls."

Naked, big-eyed children were crouched in the great room, trembling and quiet now, except for the sound of sniffles and the muffled sobs. One little boy's face was buried in the shoulder of a pretty girl who looked about nine or ten, going on thirty. She had long blond hair and purple-blue eyes that were the color of the Pacific Ocean, but without any depth, as if painted on a flat canvas.

"We're here to help you. What's your name?" I asked the pretty girl.

"Tiffy," she said, mouthing the word more than speaking it.

"Is that your real name? The name your mommy and daddy gave you?"

The waters stirred, and she seemed to wake. "Jakki."

"Nice to meet you, Jakki. My name is Sunny. My friend and I are going to help you. We need a big girl like you to help us. Can you do that?" I was careful not to touch her without permission. "Would you like a hug?"

She shook her head no.

"That's okay. Do you know this house? Someplace safe where we can hi—" The girl dove into my arms, shaking and sobbing as the other children, about eight in all, watched, clinging to one another.

Travis went outside to place his calls.

"Where are your bedrooms?" I asked Jakki. She pointed to a different hall at the back of the great room. "Quickly now, everyone, find your clothes and get dressed. Hurry, hurry." The children raced down the hall, their voices freed, once again sounding like children.

I follow Jakki to a room that she shared with three other children and they busied themselves climbing into clothes. They looked so very young and vulnerable, somewhere between the ages of five and ten. They seemed well-fed and absent any obvious physical injuries. But then, I understood that the children were an investment to the cartel, and all farmers take good care of valuable livestock.

"Jakki?" I asked. "Was there a baby here? A little newborn baby?"

She smiled and nodded her head yes.

"Do you know where the baby is?"

She tugged a T-shirt over her head. "A man took her."

"How long ago?"

Jakki bit her bottom lip, concentrating. "I don't know. A long time."

I wondered what "a long time" meant to a child prisoner. Chance had been dead for almost six weeks, and that seemed like a "long time" in some ways, but also felt like yesterday.

Jakki and I hurried to help the younger children finish dressing. A Hispanic boy had put on a frilly little girl's dress, and a little Asian girl had put on black fishnet stockings with a black leather miniskirt and a Dora the Explorer pajama top.

Travis appeared in the doorway. "Follow me and hurry—there's a van coming up the driveway."

Travis quickly led us to a large commercial kitchen where we promptly shelved the children like so many groceries in cupboards, closets, and under the sinks. Travis pressed his finger to his lips each time. "Shh. Quiet. Don't move—no matter what," he said emphatically. "Silencio. Ni una palabra. No te muevas." I put the youngest child, the little boy who had been crying earlier in a closet with Jackie. "Shh. Shh." The children understood and quickly settled themselves amid pans, cans, boxes, and bags of food.

Then Travis led me back down the hall, entering the great room just as a fist pounded on the door.

"Come on Deirdre. Open the damned door. We don't have all day," the voice boomed as loudly as the thumping on the door.

Travis and I slipped back down the original hall, stepping over the two dead bikers and moving to Deirdre, collecting weapons as we went. Travis shouldered the automatics and gave his handgun to me, then put me in a bedroom located a little in front of where the dead bikers lay.

"Stay in this room. Got it? Keep your head inside this room. Reach into the hall one-handed and fire once in a while with my gun. Save the revolver in case they make it past me." He slid into the room directly across from me as the first shots rang out, blasting at the locks on the front door, followed by the sound of the door being kicked open.

I clutched the gun tight against my chest, partly to control my erratic heartbeat and to suppress sounds of fear that struggled to escape. Taking a deep breath, I peeked across the hall and was amazed to see Travis peeling back the wrapper on a stick of gum. He raised his eyebrows and thrust his hand out in a silent offer— You want some? I must have looked stunned because he popped it in his mouth and winked at me with a devilish smile. The man made me crazy.

The next sounds were that of cursing, jostling men coming through the door, accompanied by metallic clicks and other solid sounds of weapons being readied; unsheathed, raised, cocked, or whatever it is they do. It was all happening in the front room and in a minute, it would all be aimed down the hall at us.

A single voice directed the men to fan out when someone at the end of our hall spotted the bodies and called out. Everyone redirected to our corridor, and Travis let loose with a hail of gunfire to keep their attention from the kitchen.

I didn't move—I couldn't breathe. Bullets were flying everywhere, and people were yelling in the background. The chattering of gunfire seemed to go on forever before I realized that Travis was no longer returning fire.

He's dead. He's dead—I know it.

The sound of boots moved down the hall, closer, closer. Still, I pressed myself tight against the wall by the door and waited. Remembering something I had seen Travis do, I slid down the wall into a crouch.

As a gun and a pair of forearms swung into my room firing above my head. I turned to meet him and fired and fired and fired, sending his body flying backward. Jumping up and over the body, I continued to shoot down the hall until the only sound was a series of hollow clicks. Still, I squeezed the trigger. Click-click-click.

There was scrambling and cursing from the great room, and something more. New voices joining in the tumult shouting, "Police! Police!" A couple of more single shots rang out—and then . . . silence.

"Dang Sunny, you can back me up anytime." Travis came up from behind me and looked down the hall in awe at three new bodies. The gun clattered to the floor as I dropped it and jumped into his arms, clinging to him, shaking and crying.

"Hey—hey, it's okay. It's okay. Nice work." He held me close, his strong arms wrapping around me, his face pressed tightly against mine. "I was out of bullets. Sunny—you saved my life. You saved the children."

I had never killed anyone before, and now I had killed four people in a matter of minutes.

Travis turned his attention to the police at the end of the hall, calling out, "Hold your fire. ATF. Hold your fire!"

ဆ ✞ object

"How can people be so evil?" I presented my naive question to Travis on the drive back to the airport.

Travis turned to look at me curiously. "I thought you believed in the Devil. Didn't you just give a seminar on Satanic Ritual Abuse?"

I acknowledged his remark with a sad smirk.

Travis reached over to the console and pulled out a fresh pack of gum. "It's all about the money, honey. It's the wave of the future. The profit in human trafficking is second only to sales of illegal drugs." We merged onto a freeway, and as always, I was taken aback by the sheer number of people that lived in the city.

Travis continued. "Look at it this way—a dealer can only sell his drugs once, but a child can be sold twenty or thirty times a day. That adds up fast in the criminal economy."

My jaw dropped in wide-mouthed amazement and then closed. I shook my head and took the pack of proffered gum, removing the label and pulling out a piece for each of us.

"How much money?" I asked, as I peeled back the wrapper and put the gum in my mouth.

Travis pushed his sunglasses higher on his nose. "About ten billion dollars a year—just in the United States. That's about fifty thousand kids coming into the US a year—in addition to the three hundred thousand that are already here."

I about choked on the gum. "Oh my God," I gasped. "How can that be? In America—of all places." I continued to mull it over with a growing sense of righteous anger.

"Yes, America, and all across the world," said Travis. "California, to its great shame, ranks among the top five highest trafficking cities in America."

"Which are?"

"The port cities of San Francisco, Los Angeles, and beautiful San Diego." Travis reached for the remaining gum that I still held in my hand and added, "In case you're wondering, the other two cities are in New York and Texas—which makes sense since they have the highest immigration rates."

We drove in silence for a time.

"My father may have been a Hells Angel, and he may have been an outlaw, but he was still an American who fought for his country. Even after all he went through, he still taught me that America was the best country in the world." I fairly shook with anger. "How can 'moral' America spend ten billion dollars a year on human trafficking?"

Travis chewed his gum thoughtfully before replying. "Moral America doesn't," he said.

CHAPTER 48

ഔ ✝ ഔ

"I'm sorry, Sunny. It's not the way I wanted things to turn out. It wasn't an easy decision, but you've left me no choice. I am going to have to let you go." Jack Savage leaned forward over his desk, chin up, eyes narrowed, not really looking all that sad as he tapped his thumb on an unsigned Notice of Resignation—with my name typed across the top. "I am not firing you. It's better that you resign. I can give you strong letters of recommendation for your next job."

"You're firing me, and I haven't done anything wrong." Hot, angry tears swam at the corner of my eyes, dissolving mascara, adding to the burn and sting that chafed at my sense of justice.

Jack raised his voice, determined. "I am not firing you," he repeated as he ran a manicured hand through his hair. "Let me be blunt—"

"Have you ever been any other way when the cameras aren't rolling?"

Jack sidestepped the low blow. "I can't have my victim advocate running around killing people. You're supposed to be helping victims, not shooting perps."

"What should I have done? Let those children be trafficked? Turn a blind eye like everyone else and let them be brutalized and victimized in some new location?"

Jack's nostrils flared, and his face flushed as war drums began to throb at his temples. "You were supposed to do your job."

"I was doing my job!" I leaned over his desk to meet his gaze, thrusting my own jaw forward in equally fierce determination. "I was protecting victims when nobody else would."

"You were breaking and entering with a loaded gun. Your job does not include killing people. If you want to kill people, go back to school, and I will give you a letter of recommendation to take to Mark Anderson for the SWAT Team."

"That is so—"

"Everywhere you go—people end up dead!"

A chill fell, as stark and icy as anything I had experienced in the wilderness.

Jack retracted. "That was wrong . . . I am sorry. Really, I didn't mean—"

The sound of the door slamming behind me echoed throughout the complex.

ఈ ♀ ℞

I woke to Kissme's nudges and tongue lashes the next morning; it took a moment to realize that the events of the previous day had actually happened. In fact, it took a while for the reality of the entire week to settle in with me. It was time to take stock. Lord knew I certainly had time now.

Jack was right. Paige had died because I left her alone. Quincy had probably been sold for chattel and doomed to eke out her days in some Third World country, all because I had taken her from her mother. Cali's death was somehow linked to Paige and Quincy. Chance was dead because I distracted him, me being in the wrong place at the wrong time. And now, four people whose names I didn't even know—okay, I knew Deirdre's name, and I knew those three guys had been trying to kill me—were dead, but Jack had been right to fire me.

Kissme leaped down from the sofa, whirling and barking in a Pomeranian frenzy in response to the knocking at the front door. I opened to an excited Shane, whose joyous expression froze, then melted faster than soft ice cream under hot fudge. "Sunny—are you sick? Ashley told me to come get you."

I was still in my pajamas. "No, Shane, I'm great." Never better, I thought dryly. "What's up?"

Shane shook it off, too buoyant with joy to be weighed down. "Ashley's water broke. Come on. We're on our way to the hospital. We're gonna be a father—I mean, I'm gonna be a father. You know what I mean." Shane swooped me into a bear hug and planted a big wet, sloppy kiss on my cheek. "Hurry up, double-time." He spun me around and pushed me back into the house. "Get it together and get dressed. Ashley's packing for the hospital. Go-go-go. Meet us at the hospital."

Ashley wasn't the only one whose water broke. Shane's heart was overflowing, and he looked weirdly out of character—big, burly, tough-guy biker Shane with tears of happiness running down his face as he laughed and cried and sprinted back to their car. "We're leaving in five," he called back as he jumped in and slammed the door, peeling out and leaving me staring wistfully after him.

Ash and Shane were like the sun and moon all shining at once, and it was impossible not to be touched and enlightened by their radiant glow. Ashley had never been more beautiful in all her life, and burly Shane put Santa Claus to shame with his sparkling eyes and generous spirit of love that he freely passed out like gifts from a bottomless bag. There was magic in the air, and the magic was called love.

"Hello, Mac. Hello . . . uh . . . Oma." Within an hour the waiting room had begun to look like church. Most of the congregation had shown up, everyone laughing or praying together for Ashley, the doctor, and the babies. Everyone was happy for the soon-to-be parents. My clothes were clean, my hair was brushed, and I had gargled. What I needed now was to ask God to "create in me a clean heart."

I asked. He listened. He answered.

I found myself sitting at a little patio table outside the front of the building.

"Sunny. I haven't seen you in the longest time. I've missed you." Oma looked happy as she walked up to the table.

"I've missed you too. In fact, I've wanted to talk with you." It was a humbling moment.

"I remember the day my son was born," Oma chatted. "It was the happiest day of my life."

"Is it true—is your son really in prison?" I could feel the warmth of shame traveling from my feet to my face. "I'm sorry. It's none of my business. I have no right to ask you. In fact—"

"No dear, it's okay. I am not ashamed of the fact that my son is in prison. I know it sounds crazy, but I am actually happy for him. He has gotten his GED and has plans for the future. Best of all, thanks to prison ministry, he has come to know the Lord." Oma sat in the chair next to me. "Sometimes things happen in life that seems like the worst thing that could ever happen, and then somehow, it turns out to be the best thing." She gave me an encouraging, knowing smile.

Chance would have called it a God thing.

"There's my girls." Mac came out holding two cups of hot chocolate. "Would you like one?" Mac asked, holding a cup out to me. I knew Mac was just being polite.

"Yes." I laughed at the flicker of dismay on his face. "But I'll go get my own. But before I go, I have something I need to tell both of you." Their eyes turned to me expectantly. I hated to be the one to take those smiles from them. I hated to see their love turn to hurt and anger. But I was long overdue. I needed to say it.

"It's all my fault," I said. "All the malicious gossip that went around about Oma—it was me. I did it, and I hope you'll forgive me. I really do feel terrible." The next few seconds seemed like an eternity as I waited for the joyous spirit of the day to turn into scathing rebukes. I stared hard at the table, bracing myself. I was ready. Whatever was going to happen next, I had it coming.

Oma flinched, and the color drained from her face. "Have I done something to offend you?" she asked, placing her hand on mine.

"No—absolutely nothing. Anger couldn't excuse what I did even if I had been angry—and I wasn't angry about anything. I did it because . . . because I was trying to fit in with a group of people who were gossiping. I was lonely, and I wanted them to like me, so I made stuff up." I fidgeted in my chair. I could feel the warm heat of a flush on my cheeks. "I'm embarrassed and ashamed, and so very, very sorry." I stared at their cups of cocoa.

I was surprised at what happened next.

Oma reached over and gave me a kiss on the side of my head and a little squeeze on my shoulder. "Thank you. Thank you for telling us. That was very brave."

My eyes shifted right and left. "So, that it? It's over? You forgive me? God's forgiven me?"

Mac scrunched his face as if I had just stepped on his bare toes with my motorcycle boots on. His lips pressed into a tight line, and he rolled his eyes toward heaven before answering.

"Sunny—here's the thing about grace. With God, it's instant, but it is not a 'Get Out of Jail Free' card. Everything that you set in motion has a ripple effect. Love, hurt, everything. You've thrown a lot of rocks, and you've hit the two of us hard. You've hurt us, Oma and me."

I dropped my gaze. Tears threatened. "I'm sorry. Really sorry." If I said it a hundred times, it would not come close. I could never say it enough.

"The good thing about ripples," said Mac, "is that they stretch out over time until they disappear. I'm not happy with you, but I love you, and Oma and I love each other." Mac turned to Oma with a glow that rivaled Shane's. "In fact, we're getting married."

What a day for new beginnings. My congratulations tumbled over Mac's next words. "And now—I think there are a pair of babies inside waiting to meet us."

"They're born? Oma-gosh!" We all laughed together.

God commands us to "sing a new song." We did, and I was certain that the angels in heaven cracked up, joining us in our laughter.

Mac couldn't have looked happier if he had fathered those babies himself. "Come on, ladies. Let's go say hello to Elijah and Ephraim."

Oma was right. The moment that I thought would be the worst had turned out to be one of the best.

$$\infty \, \maltese \, \infty$$

My heart lit up like a glow stick at the sight of those two little boys in their parents' arms. Ashley had more sparkle than a hundred-carat diamond and Shane looked as bright and solid as pure gold. They were rich, Shane and Ashley. They had wealth and treasure immeasurable. And for a refreshing change, I was not jealous. Not even a little bit.

I hugged my best girlfriend and her amazing husband and caught an apologetic glimmer in their shared expressions as if they felt a twinge of guilt for finding so much happiness in the face of my recent losses. All smiles, I hugged them again and whispered, "It's okay. I'm sorry I've been so distant. We are truly happy for you, me . . . and Chance too. . . you know?" The love we shared was genuine, and it felt good to have my family back again. Their family had grown, and somehow throughout the long cold winter, so had I.

Forgiveness is right up there with sacrifice. Both are about letting go, and every time we let go of anything, our burdens are lightened. That is a God thing.

Home looked good for the first time in a long time. And right when I thought my day couldn't get any better, I froze at the sight of something on the doorstep. A mysterious heart-shaped box of chocolates and a dozen red roses. I had forgotten all about today being Valentine's Day.

ॐ ♀ ☪

So much had happened since coming home from the hospital on New Year's Day. The funerals, the bomb, losing my husband, losing my job. It felt good to celebrate life and love.

I traded in wine for spiced tea, and the smell of oranges and cinnamon perfumed the air.

Paige's scrapbook lay like a colorful autobiography on my lap. I was ready to revisit the young woman who had changed my life in so many ways. In the cool of the evening, I opened the scrapbook that Cali had given Chance. Sitting in bed, propped up by pillows and surrounded by dogs, wrapped in the warmth of one of one of Chance's flannel shirts, I savored the moment. Balancing the heavy book that somehow still smelled like its author, I traced the soft padded cover and corded binding and then opened it up to the journey of a lifetime.

"Hello Paige," I fingered the photograph of a newborn baby dressed in a white lace gown. "Look at you. You never changed," I said, with a short laugh. "Beautiful baby. Beautiful woman." And it was true. The school pictures that followed revealed a growing girl—first grade, second grade, third, and so on up to junior high— always bright and happy, always child-pageant perfect.

Admission tickets were mingled among the pictures. "Look, Kissme, your favorite dog movie, Balto." And Disneyland. "Got to have Disneyland." Other theme parks and events were woven throughout the pages.

I sipped my tea and reached for a chocolate, wondering again who might have left them on my doorstep and why the person didn't include a card with a name. Travis crossed my mind, but I easily dismissed that idea. Travis was living with a lady, and she was his Valentine. Shane and Ashley would have done such a thoughtful thing—had they not been busy birthing love elsewhere. Duncan?

Hmm? Possible.

Seventh and eighth-grade pictures were notably absent. Certificates of completion replaced the traditional school pictures where junior high should have been. Certificates and a couple of pictures of Paige taken at Christmas with her parents. One of her standing next to her birthday cake holding a big-eyed solid white Persian kitten with the name "Snow White" penned beneath.

"Hardly any activities," I mused. "I'm sorry your childhood was stolen and perverted. I know a little bit about that," I said to Paige. "I should have been nicer to you," I added. And I meant it. I hoped it was never too late for kind words, and I hoped that Paige could hear me, wherever she was.

Kissme moved in and put her paws on my chest, begging. I broke off a piece of chocolate and sent her to the bottom of the bed. Mercy whined in protest, so I tossed her one that I ranked "least favorite."

"Just one," I warned the dogs. "Chocolate is bad for dogs—it turns you into cats." They seemed to accept that and settled down.

Paige looked different in the pictures that followed. The glow of childhood was absent. The cuteness was gone, replaced by a young woman who looked more provocative than pretty.

There was the prom. Looking at Paige dressed in her formal, I felt a wistful tug on my heart as I reflected on that period of life. How passionately I had once dreamed of going to the prom. I supposed I was a victim of Cinderella Syndrome at the time, still hoping that Prince Charming was coming to the rescue. Logan just laughed and ridiculed me for asking him to take me to prom night, telling me he had already made plans for porn night.

I turned another page in the scrapbook.

There. It. Was. Right in front of me. Pictures.

The evidence that Chance had wanted to show me on the day he died.

Oh. My. God. "It's not possible," I whispered through my fingers. "Oh, Chance . . . you were right."

CHAPTER 49

ఇా ⊕ ౭

Chocolates flew like confetti in Times Square—much to Mercy's delight and Kissme's dismay—as I leaped from the bed. The clock by the phone showed it was nine p.m.

I know where Logan is. I know, I know, I know!

My brain was on speed dial and fingers shook so hard that I had to redial the number three times before getting through.

My heart thudded in my ears.

I frowned when Travis's girlfriend answered. "This is Sunny McLane. I need to speak with Travis right away. It's urgent."

"I'm sorry. He's not here right now." Her voice was liquid, soft and sweet as Southern tea. "I can give you his cell number."

"Already got it." I hung up and dialed his cell.

"Travis—it's me it's Logan it was him all this time at the cabin I just know it and I am going after him as fast as I can find my keys," the words streamed.

"Whoa! Slow down. Sunny, I mean it, s-l-o-w down. Take a breath, and then tell me what's going on."

"He's at the cabin. I know it, Travis. I can feel it. Gotta go."

Nothing is going to stop me from getting Logan. I turned off my phone. *Not even Superman.* I figured since the Department of Corrections couldn't keep him behind bars; ATF, BCSO, and SWAT combined had let him slip through their fingers when he had been cornered in a tunnel—hell, even the damned cartel couldn't catch him—there was no reason whatsoever for me to wait for backup.

I chose warm jeans and boots and then slipped Chance's shirt back on under a thick coat. My Glock was at the office, but my .22 had been released and returned from evidence after Paige's autopsy. It would work. I loaded the clip and slid the pistol into my pocket.

Then I tore a picture from Paige's scrapbook and tucked it in next to the gun.

This could be goodbye. I took one last lingering look around the house, taking in pictures and memories, the kitchen, the soapstone heater that had warmed us while we made love, the French doors that opened to our favorite place. I wiped my eyes. It was time to go.

I let the dogs out for a minute, then put Kissme back inside. "Guard the house," I told her with a hug and a kiss, then locked the door and called Mercy. She bounded expectantly onto the front seat of the truck with a huff, her tail thunking rhythmically against the door.

A slice of moon shone brightly within the crisp blanket of stars. Blacker than night, the mountains loomed like parapets on nature's castle. I was pumped up, ready to slay the dragon and rescue the princess. Grim and determined as I felt, I was not naive. I knew that sometimes the dragon won.

I parked the truck far from the cabin, up on the logging landing where the dirt road began. "Mercy, come," I said, as I let the big dog out of the truck. Tonight Mercy was like a well-oiled machine without the proper key. She understood basic pet commands, but I could only hope she would respond to the language of love.

The snow was gone, and the road was a deeper shade of night under the trees. Turning down the driveway, I saw the cabin come into sight. A lamp was burning inside.

I led Mercy to the center of the circle drive and kneeled. Holding her head in my hands, I told her to stay. First, she sat, but then crouched down with a soft whine. "Good girl. Stay. Stay," I whispered forcefully. And she did. Giving Mercy a reassuring pat, I repeated "stay" one more time, kissed the .22, and tucked it into my pants at the small of my back.

"God help me," I breathed, as I headed toward the cabin and knocked on the door.

"Logan? Logan! Logan—it's me, Sunny. Open the door. I'm alone, and I'm unarmed. I just want to—"

"Well, well, well. If it isn't the little woman. We have to stop meeting like this." Logan appeared from the dark side of the house. "To what do I owe the honor of your visit?"

Startled, I turned to face the man I once loved, once feared. Emotions gripped like the layers that squeezed around the core of the earth, layers that had developed over our time together and formed around the inner core; my heart, young love. Then came the mantles of disillusion and betrayal, molten anger, fear, and dread. But on the surface, I kept a thick protective layer. A world of evolving emotions—feelings still bubbled and stirred beneath my tough outer exterior. I wouldn't crack. I wouldn't cave. I wouldn't let Logan see anything beneath the shell.

"I just want to talk. Can we talk?" I asked, keeping my tone neutral. Strong, without threat or quaver.

"Well, I don't know. Let me consult my calendar. I'm a busy man," he drawled as he moved out of the shadows. I could see that he hadn't changed much. He was dressed in black jeans and shirt, his black hair disheveled, dark eyes, eagle eyes as hard as onyx peering over a gun that he aimed at my head. "Who's with you?" Logan looked around. "You got a SWAT team workin' their way through the woods?" He seemed casual, even amused by my presence.

"No. It's just me. I swear—I don't care about you. I just want to know how to find Quincy. Is she here? Do you have her?"

"Quincy, huh? I heard you named her." Logan tipped his head back, his sneer stretching from ear to ear. "Still trying to have a kid," he said derisively. "Tsk, tsk. Sorry to disappoint, but since she's not around, maybe you can do like your rich friends and adopt some other kid from a Third World country." Logan laughed. "It's very trendy, and who knows—maybe Quincy'll pop up in some drug lord's house in Mexico . . . or maybe she'll be a sex slave for some oil sheik. Those old guys love diddling little white girls. And it will be All. Your. Fault."

My hand twitched and crept toward the gun. I took a deep breath.

Steady.

"In the house." Logan gestured with his gun.

Crossing the room, I turned to look back at Logan who still held the gun as he closed the door.

"I came to talk. I want to help you. We can work something out if you tell me where Quincy is. I can probably get you a deal. I work for the DA and friends with the head of ATF. They always cut deals for information."

"You think you're so damned smart." Logan laughed long and hard. "You always were stupid. You guys caught Miasma and Deirdre and let the big fish get away. That's my Sunless."

I spread my arms wide with palms out, trying to look disinterested. "What big fish would that be?"

"Perry, stupid." Logan spat the words and shook his head. "The millionaire porn king was right under your noses all the time. You and all your do-gooding, high-minded, dumb-ass notions. All of you blinded by your red, white, and blue while old Perry did business with the biggest warlock and priestess on the West Coast. That slimy bastard pimped his own daughter at parties until she got old enough to talk, and by then no one believed her. Except me. I believed her. The school counselors just laughed. All that talk about ceremonies and black robes and sacrifices." He sniffed. "I wonder what they thought when Paige told them she was going to be Satan's bride."

"The school did nothing?" I asked.

"They told her parents. Cali thought Paige was going through a Ouija Board phase, but Perry wasn't taking any chances. He unloaded her to the cartel." Logan clenched his teeth, seething. "His own daughter!"

I gasped.

Logan gripped the gun so tight, his knuckles turned white, and his hand shook. "And you think old Perry is Mr. Law-Abiding and Upstanding. Seriously Sundown, your naivety never ceases to amaze me."

Not Perry. Not her father. My ever-treacherous stomach churned. "That can't be. You're a lying snake."

Logan's nostrils flared, and the cords on his neck stood out. "Perry is the money man. He wanted those printing presses up and running." Logan erupted with a sharp bark of contempt. "You sure screwed things up for everyone. But then, you have a habit of doing that."

"I don't believe you. If that was true, Perry would never have bought her back from Mexico."

"But he did. You see, poor old innocent Cali was dying of cancer—and a broken heart. He did it for Cali."

He's crazy. Possibly even insane. But he made perfect sense as the final pieces of the puzzle fell into place. I swallowed bits of burning bile that had crept up my throat.

"I just want Quincy. Tell me where she is and I'll go away and leave you alone, forever."

"You're not going anywhere. We have some unfinished business of our own—now that you're the grieving widow and all. Whaddaya say we have a little fun, for old times' sake?"

My brain froze.

"First I'll need to check you for weapons. Take off your shirt."

Then thawed.

"If I had weapons, I would have already stabbed you in the heart, blown off your head, and castrated you."

His eyes narrowed, glittering, as he gestured with his gun. "I said off with the shirt, Sunblock."

Hands on my hips, I raised my chin and glared. "Or what? You'll kill me?"

Logan's mouth twitched. "There are worse things than death. Oh yes. Much worse." He wagged the gun. "Shirt."

I took my time unbuttoning the shirt, feeling the .22 nudging against the small of my back.

Patience.

I threw Logan a sly grin and didn't wait to be told what to do next. Slowly, sensuously, I slipped my fingertips under my bra straps and eased them from my shoulders in a sexy, tempting move. Reaching up from behind, I tipped my breasts forward as I unhooked the bra and let it slip, just a little, then dangle, before letting it slip through my fingers to the floor.

The glitter in Logan's eyes kindled and caught, burning with lust. He moved forward, wolf-like, wetting his lips and reaching out to claim what would always be his. Grinning, he cupped my warm breast in his cold, rough hand and raked my nipple with a calloused thumb.

Throwing my head back in sexual abandon, I arched my back and pushed my breast deeper into his palm, gasping with pleasure. The rat took the bait, quivering as he lowered the gun along with his mouth.

Pulling the .22 from my waistband, I stepped back in one quick motion and fired— once, twice.

Logan jerked, dropping his gun as he was propelled backward by the force of bullets. He fell against the wall and slid to the floor clutching his shoulder.

"Gawd dammit, Sunny. Stop!" Logan's head rolled as he cussed and yelled.

"Shut up, Logan."

"Logan howled, "My arm—my leg. Oh shit!"

The cabin door cracked as it blew inward from an explosive kick to the door. Travis entered fast and straight. "ATF, nobody move!"

"You're late," I said, turning to face him.

Logan made his move, grabbing me by the knees. I buckled and fell on top of him and felt him rip the gun from my hand. He rolled onto his back with me on top and pressed the gun to my neck, triggering the familiar rush of heart-crashing fury and utter helplessness I'd felt each time he'd beaten me.

"She's going with me," Logan warned. He showed no signs of relenting.

"Don't! Don't do it!" I cried out. "Don't shoot him, Travis. You can't. Don't kill him."

"I can and I will. He's already dead." Travis's voice was as steady as his gun; he repositioned himself for the kill shot.

"No, no. Travis. You don't understand." My voice went high and excited as I stuttered, "Travis. Travis. Logan. Logan is . . . Quincy's father."

Travis blinked. His eyebrows formed a solid line. "What?"

Logan staggered to his feet, groaning from the effort, dragging me with him, one hand clutching a fistful of hair, the other pressing the .22 to my temple.

"Oh, this is rich. If it isn't Maxwell Smart and Agent 99. Sweet. You guys don't know shit," Logan hissed.

Travis didn't flinch. "So enlighten us."

"Paige was my ride long before Captain Fucking America here came along. She was mine. You hear me? Mine. And there's never been a sweeter piece of—"

Travis shot him.

The bullet scorched along my shoulder and tore into Logan. The .22 went flying, and Logan bounced off the wall for the second time.

"Gawd damn it . . ." Logan repeated, crying out in agony.

I crawled forward, blood dripping down my bare breast. Travis moved like a cat as he crossed the room and helped me stand.

"I like the outfit," said Travis.

"You shot me!" I howled in disbelief.

"It's just a flesh wound," said Travis.

Okay, it was just a flesh wound, and I was still alive, but it hurt like hell. "What arcade did you learn to shoot at?" I fumed, using my bra to pad my bleeding shoulder before shrugging back into my shirt.

"What is this—fucking comedy night? I need a doctor." Logan moaned. "Call a fucking ambulance."

Stooping to pick up both guns from the floor, I turned Logan's gun back on him.

"Where is Quincy?" I hissed, cocking the trigger. "Do not mess with me, Logan!"

"You guys are such idiots." Logan laughed between clenched teeth as he sat on the floor, still slumped against the wall. "Only, he's dumber. At least you figured out the kid is mine."

The muscles in Travis's face flexed and tightened.

"They were lovers," I interjected. "Have been since high school." I let go of my shoulder long enough to take the picture from my pocket and hand it to Travis—a picture of Logan and Paige at the prom. It seemed like a sad cosmic joke that it would be a prom picture. Of all the possible events they might have shared. Taken almost a decade later in classy Sausalito after I had begged Logan to take me to my little country affair.

Logan snarled. "She didn't have to die. I loved her."

I drew back in revulsion. "You were lovers during our marriage." It was an accusation, not a question.

Logan threw me venomous looks. "You bet your sweet ass. She was worth a dozen of you. She was perfect . . . until her dad—"

Travis tucked the photograph into his pocket. "What about Perry?"

Logan barked a laugh and then groaned as he clutched his shoulder. "Call an ambulance, and I'll talk. I don't want to die on this damned floor."

"This is as good a place as any. You left my father to die in the dirt," I reminded him.

"Paige is dead—because of you, Sunstroke. And now I am going to lose my daughter—all because of you."

"Unbelievable! You say that after killing *our* baby!"

"One at a time." Hans Solo was about to blow a gasket. Travis scrunched his face and flicked the barrel of his gun toward Logan.

"No cell service up here. Tell you what—you talk and I might drive you to the hospital. You're running out of time. You choose."

Logan's brows peaked; his eyes were watery pools of pain. He shook his head and grimaced. "Paige was trying to protect our baby."

Travis and I silently rode the current of Logan's streaming thoughts.

"Everybody wanted the kid. Perry and that dumb-ass Miasma wanted it for their stupid rituals, and the cartel wanted to trade me my daughter for their guns and money. They said if I tried anything this time, they would sell her." Logan moaned again as blood continued to ooze between his fingers, soaking his shirt.

"I almost had her too. Down in the tunnels with their hokey ceremony." Logan's lips pulled back in a twisted grin. "But I screwed 'em all when I put the guns and money in the same room with Perry's gawd damned printing presses." Logan laughed until he coughed and cried out in pain. Beads of sweat popped out on his forehead. "Is that rich, or what? Can't you see it? Everybody shooting everybody trying to get it all?" He smiled and gasped again. "Well, I gave them all what they wanted. Only, the bitch here"—Logan threw me a stabbing glance—"wrecked everything."

"You have one more chance to answer the question, and then I'm going to put a bullet in your other shoulder," said Travis. "Where is the baby?"

Logan staggered to his feet, clutching his shoulder, the circle of blood still flowering on his upper arm and thigh where I had shot him. "Out there," he said, nodding toward the bomb shelter. "Out in the old rec room."

"Sunny." Travis pulled a flashlight from his belt and handed it to me. "Can you do it with your shoulder?"

I shot him a sour look and ripped it from his hand in reply.

"Be careful," Travis cautioned as he started cuffing Logan.

The doors to the bomb shelter were heavy and difficult to open. I couldn't imagine Quincy being in there and still alive. No way, I thought, but clung to hope nonetheless, trembling, fueled by another rush of adrenaline.

I set the flashlight on the top step that led down to the shelter. Both the door and my shoulder groaned in protest as I pulled it back and pushed it wide. Inside was as dark as a coffin, as still as death. The moon was long gone, but as I reached for the flashlight, a blow from behind set stars in motion.

From down below came the plaintive sound of a protesting baby.

"Hush, hush now," a woman's voice said. Footsteps hurried past me, and my head spun. Crawling back to the top step, I called, "Mercy! Mercy!' and the big dog came, whining eagerly and slobbering on my face until I had to push her back. "Get 'em!" I said, doubtful that the term was on her list of commands. A sturdy piece of wood on the stairwell caught my eye. I rubbed the back of my head and stumbled back down the steps, picked it up and held it under Mercy's nose. She sniffed eagerly and looked at me, alert and expectant. "Get her," I snarled with fierce determination. "Go get her, Mercy. Get her." Mercy whirled and sprinted away into the dark. I could only pray she wouldn't return with a half-eaten Quincy.

Travis's voice called out from the house, "Sunny. Hey, Sunny. Can you hear me? Everything okay?"

The sound of snarling came from the woods. Screams of terror shook the night.

I staggered toward the shouts, and there stood Mercy, standing guard over a squalling baby in a torn blanket. The woman had fled.

℘ ☥ ℭ

"What the hell are you doing?" Logan asked from the floor, where he lay handcuffed and dotted with towels that Travis had used to staunch his wounds.

Little noises rose from the baby blanket where I cradled Quincy in one arm, happily oblivious to the gun I held on her father in my other hand. I glanced heavenward and then silently lowered my gaze to the bloody man on the floor.

"Praying."

"Cute. That's just what I need—prayer. Forget Jesus—what I need is some Jack." He groaned and then turned his dark eyes back on me. "Prayin' for my soul, darlin'?"

"Praying for a flat tire."

Logan gave a slight chuckle. "Right—like your boyfriend's really out there calling for an ambulance. Ha! More likely he's out there fucking what's left of Nikki."

"Nikki? Your babysitter? I don't think she's going to be a problem. The cops will probably pick her up when she checks into the ER for dog bites. Anyhow," I added with a growing smile, "you can send her a get well card from High Desert."

Logan wrinkled his nose with disdain. "I'm coming for my kid when I get out. You know that, right? Got it, Sunburn? She's mine. You can play house all you want, but in the end, she's all mine!"

"Hmm . . . I'm thinking hers is one prom you're going to miss."

"Listen, bitch—and you better hear me good. No one—no one—is taking my kid." Logan's voice dropped to a whisper. "She's all . . ." he gasped ". . . Paige . . ." And then he broke.

I didn't know that snakes could cry.

෨ ✚ ෬

The predawn light was pierced by the soft flash of the light bar on the ambulance. Memories trailed me, like Mercy, who had followed me about and now sat close by, watching anxiously as the EMT applied the last of the tape to the thick pad on my shoulder. The technician offered a thoughtful suggestion.

"You can walk through the 'No Admittance' door next to ER if you like. We'll be waiting for you."

"Thank you, because I'd rather die than ride in an ambulance with him," I said, pointing to Logan secured in the back of the ambulance.

The EMT smiled and drove away, leaving Travis and me standing in the driveway. Travis seemed enchanted, under Quincy's spell, as little fingers grabbed at his nose. He leaned in, tenderly kissing her searching fingers.

"I hate Logan, but I glad we didn't kill him," I said.

Travis looked up with a cocked brow. "You're happy we didn't kill him?"

"Mostly. I wouldn't want to have to tell Quincy someday that I killed her father. Telling her that her daddy is a dirtbag will be hard enough."

Both brows were on an even keel as Travis thought about Quincy. Then a slow smile spread across his face, and he replied,

"Maybe she doesn't need to know about Logan at all. Fathers aren't the men who make babies; they're the ones who raise them."

Maybe he was right. It sounded like something Chance would say.

"I never understood why Logan didn't want the baby we had made together. When I wouldn't abort it, he killed it. That's a lot of hate." I dropped my head in shame. "There was a time I loved Logan. I would have . . . did . . . do anything . . . everything . . . for him."

Travis moved close and put a hand alongside my face, drew me in, and kissed me tenderly on the forehead.

"That's the hardest part of what we do," said Travis. "We're trained to see everything— except what's under our noses. I'm a cop, and I not only admired Perry"—Travis dropped his arm and dropped his gaze—"but I loved that guy like a father. And you"—Travis lifted my chin to meet me eye to eye—"are an advocate who has forgotten everything you ever knew about victims of domestic violence."

From somewhere high in the treetops, we heard the lonesome hoots of Kenny's favorite bird: the Who-Who-Me. Somehow, it gave me hope.

"In the end, babe," Travis said with a sad smile, tapping the end of my nose with his finger, "we are just like everyone else— victims of love. We see what we want to see."

My shoulders drooped. "Then how can I know when love is real?"

Travis stared at the ground for a moment.

"I think you already know the answer," he said at last. "You taught it to me. You called it 'faith.'"

CHAPTER 50

I packed the last of my personal possessions into the file box, bowed my head, and prayed, "Lord, please bless the next advocate with patience and wisdom. Let her be a light that shines in dark places, and may she touch the lives of each victim who enters this office seeking protection, direction, and justice."

One long last, lingering look around the room that had been my home-away-from-home for so many years. Not so much taking note of the things that remained but rather the things and people who were gone. I smiled, remembering the fullness of my days.

In my mind I saw Travis lounging in the doorway holding bags of food and cups of coffee, always watching out for me. I saw Paige jangling her bracelet with baby charms, amazed and delighted that someone actually cared. I saw sweet Amanda, the prosecutor with the presence of a lioness and the heart of a kitten. And Gayle, my friend who was always the essence of kindness and thoughtfulness. There also, in a very special place, was Bonita. I laughed to think that I actually hired her because she was a lesbian. I had grown to love that woman, for she was razor sharp and ever perceptive. Closest of all, my dear friend Duncan . . .

"Duncan?" I was ripped from my reverie. "What are you doing here? Don't you know it's Saturday?" I raised a brow and did a slow eye scan from head to toe. "You look fantastic."

Duncan's smile brought light to my otherwise shadowed moment. Other than the trademark blush, he looked a much different man from the day we first met. The shy, geeky, nerdy gentle giant looked both rakish and roguish today. His gelled hair was stylishly messy, and he was wearing contact lenses that accentuate his toffee-brown eyes. He was looking good in his bad-boy earplugs and a Live Free or Die T-shirt that showed off his tats.

"What's with the box?" I asked in amazement, for Duncan held a cardboard box that mirrored my own—except he had a lot more wires and electronic thingies poking out of it.

"We're out of here," Duncan announced with finality. "We're not staying here without you."

"We? What . . . we who? What are you talking about?"

"Me and Bonita." He did his little-boy squirm. "We're starting a security firm."

"You . . . and Bonita? As in you and Bonita?"

Duncan blushed Valentine-red that turned my smile into a grin. "Yeah, we're in love," he said.

"Whoa! Whoa! Timeout. What about her partner? Is this a ménage à trois?" I bounced my eyebrows suggestively.

Duncan laughed but looked genuinely confused. "I am her partner," he said, his face still warm and pink.

"What about the dyke-on-the-bike?"

Duncan winced and drew back. "Rink? Her college roomie? " Pause. "I knew that."

Duncan let loose with a long, heartwarming laugh.

"I just want to thank you, Sunny." He pressed his lips into a tight smile and flushed. "I thought I knew what it meant to be in love. Now I know what it really means."

"Who would've thought?" I heaved a big heart-shaped sigh and shrugged with both palms out. "The women in this place are always stealing the men I love," I said with a wink. "But I'm dying to know—what does Bonita think about SUNNY being tattooed on your arm?"

"Check it out, babe." Duncan rolled his arm toward me with a grin that reached to his eyes. "SUNNY" had morphed into "BUNNY."

"Bunny?" I'm in stitches.

"Yeah, that's what I call her." Duncan blushed furiously. "My Funny Bunny."

"Duke! What's taking you so long?" a voice shouted from the hall. "Hey, it's Miss Chica! How the heck are you?" Bonita gave me a warm hug. She had the outlaw look today: three earrings sparkling from each ear, tight black jeans, and a black tee that matched Duncan's. "I heard you guys recovered la niña."

"Yeah, Quincy. She's with her dad . . . um, Travis."

We hugged again, and I gripped her arm as we drew apart. "Is that a tattoo?" I turned her arm for a closer inspection. "Who the heck is Duke?"

Bunny and Duke turned the glow lights on in each other's eyes. Stranger things have happened.

"I'll send you an invitation to the wedding in Playacar," said Bonita.

Duncan's eyes widened. "Wedding?"

Bonita rolled her eyes and gave Duncan a playful nudge. "As Speedy Gonzales would say: ¡Ándale!—let's get the heck out of here."

I kissed the future groom on his cheek and gave him a lingering look of genuine affection.

The door clicked behind me, but I didn't look. Tears would have just blurred everything anyhow.

౸ ♀ ౳

March flew by, ushering in a magnificent spring. The one thing I could still count on in life was change.

I peeled off my sweatshirt and hung it on the back of a patio chair. The orchard was blooming in shades of pink and white. Tender tips of pine and fir trees had sprouted in succulent shades of green, and even the stark oaks were budding with new life.

A doe crept between the apricot and the nectarine trees, glancing anxiously left and right as she led a pair of playful fawns into the orchard. I sighed, knowing that all too soon she would be leading them to the high country. The stillness was broken by the trumpeting of Canadian geese, like arrows shot from God's quiver, winging their way home as a mountain monkey—my father's affectionate term for squirrels—made a Kamikaze jump from one tree to another.

Life goes on.

Quincy was safe with her adoring father, Travis, who has claimed her as his own. I believed the man was in love, and it did my heart good to see ninja warrior Inspector Lee—Superman— man of steel—making baby kissy noises and talking baby talk to that sweet little bundle, whose favorite pastime was pulling his hair and sticking her fingers up his nose.

I sat in the chair and leaned back thinking, remembering the last time I sat on the porch with Travis sitting next to me.

"What does your girlfriend think of Quincy?" I asked Travis.

"What girlfriend would that be?"

"Your answering machine. The one you take to funerals for date night. That one."

Travis laughed—a long, easy belly laugh as he shook his head. "Are you serious? I told you before about Christy and her kids. She's the wife of my friend, the one that died in Iraq. Remember now? I promised to take care of them."

"Are they living with you?"

Travis grew serious; his green eyes flickered behind a suggestive smile. "Do you care?"

"Nope," I said, pushing out my bottom lip.

Travis grinned. "I flew them out to see California. Christy drove them up to see the redwoods and visit Fisherman's Wharf. And of course, I took them to see the Monterey Bay Aquarium and Alcatraz."

"And Disneyland?" I smiled. "You can't come to California and not visit Disneyland." I hesitated before asking the big one. "Do you love her?"

"Absolutely. But not like that. She met a man in Georgia, and he sounds like a pretty decent guy. Christy went to the funerals with me because she's my friend, and always will be."

We were back on familiar ground. "So . . . what's going to happen to Perry?"

"Probably not much. I filed a report with Internal Affairs, but powerful men like him usually put a lot of buffers between themselves and the ones who do their dirty work. However . . ." Travis let the word trail, as tantalizing and suggestive as an appetizer before a three-course dinner. A twinkle sparked in his gaze, and he cocked his head to one side.

"What we really need to get a conviction on Perry," Travis said—the corners of his mouth turned up, and his dimples deepened—"is one good advocate." Long pause. "Do you know of anyone?"

He paused, stroking his finger thoughtfully along his jaw. "It would have to be someone with experience in working with survivors of ritual abuse. And it would help if the advocate had some experience as an expert witness." Travis let go with a deep sigh and a shrug. "Of course, that would mean a lot of trips together, interviewing victims and going to court. It would require someone with a lot of time on their hands."

ℰ♀ℬ

The pulse of nature always quickened in April, and with it came a stirring in my heart. The truck was packed. It was that time again. Well, actually it was past time. Winter had certainly skewed a budding tradition—the one in which I paid my respects with flowers and song to Lefty every winter, and my mother in the fullness of spring. The tradition hadn't been about their birthdays or even their death days, but rather the seasons that best reflected the lives they'd lived.

We headed to the ocean to visit my father first—the boy who had gone to war and returned a hero. A soldier who had found freedom and family in a custom Harley and an outlaw motorcycle gang, peace in a remote cabin in the Sierra Nevadas, and love for a season with a woman named Starla, and forever in their baby girl.

Kissme copiloted from my lap alongside Mercy, who sat smiling in the passenger seat as we wove our way in and out of the foothills en route to the coast. The land shimmered in shades of green after its long sleep—all the way to the majestic Coastal Range, still robed in royal purple beneath a snowy crown. Heading into the westering sun, it was a long but varied dive. We passed budding orchards that overshadowed swaths of wild mustard whose sunny blossoms danced beneath the pastel canopy. Miles of lime-green rice fields that swirled in the breeze like a glass of fine bouquet, and up into wine country that was as rich and full bodied as its residents—full of themselves and headier than a glass of all things French.

I didn't drive to the veteran cemetery on the hill but down to the ocean below—the place where Lefty's spirit roams like stars across a night sky above the restless waves of the dark Pacific Ocean. A fitting place for a reigning member of Hell's Angels.

I pulled onto a turnout and parked on a shoulder that jutted out toward the ocean and then leaped from the car.

"Hi, Daddy! It's me." I called out, only to be answered by thundering waves and the screech of gulls fishing along the rugged shoreline.

I stumped to the water. "It's been a long winter," I told my dad as I dipped my amputated foot into the surf. "Look, Daddy, I am a 'lefty' too."

I sang him "our song."

"When you're seven, you're in Seventh Heaven
. . . goin' campin' in the wild outdoors.
. . . we turned off on that old dirt road,
I looked at him and swore . . .

Dad, this could be the best day of my life,
I've been dreamin' day and night 'bout the fun we'll have.
It's just me and you, doin' what I've always wanted to,
I'm the luckiest girl alive,
This is the best day of my life . . ."

Before leaving, I sprinkled a bag of dried rose petals on the hungry waves and watched as the current swept them out to sea.

Chance was waiting. A quick blink in the forest just a mile or two from home. Today Chance became the newest addition to my budding tradition. The Ram idled at the intersection of Highway 70; left was home. I smiled and turned right.

Yankee Hill Cemetery found me wandering past occupants in century-old graves. I wondered about their lives and if they had been so different from my own. I wondered about the dramas that had driven them and the heartaches that had broken them.

Chance. The flag in front of his headstone hung limp, and the flowers alongside the flag drooped in the warm afternoon sun.

"Hello, honey." I bent to replace the tired bouquet with fresh flowers. "I miss you . . ." My voice trailed. ". . . I miss us." Falling to my knees, my fingers lingered on the rough edges of his headstone. "Mercy is trying to get Kissme to play tag," I said.

"Good luck with that one," I told the big dog and then turned my attention back to Chance. "I went to see Daddy. Mama's next.

"I don't know how I'm supposed to go forward. I just know that there's no going back. I'm lonely sometimes, but I am not alone. Have you seen the twins? Oh yeah—you were probably there when they were born."

Pause.

"I'm back in church."

Pause.

"What's that you say? About time?" Soft laughter escaped, and I imagined a hundred spirits smiling at the sound.

"You wouldn't believe how fast Quincy is growing. She's doing push-ups. She does them better than me. I get to see her all the time, what with the case and all. Keep an eye on her for me, okay?"

A slow smile grew. "You were always my guardian angel, Chance. I guess you are hers now, huh? I like that."

I was the world's worst singer, but since God tells us to "sing a new song," I did.

> *"Did you ever know that you're my hero . . .*
> *everything I would like to be?*
> *I can fly higher than an eagle . . .*
> *you are the wind beneath my wings."*

It was time to go. I blew a kiss that caught a ride on a freshening breeze that was bound for heaven.

Back at the crossroads. Right turn. Up the Feather River Canyon to visit Starla.

My mother rested in death as she lived in life—completely opposite of Lefty. I drove past Pulga, the ghost town that was once a thriving rail station, onto a familiar dirt road. Up and up, winding along snow-fed tributaries that fed the surging river below, to a sheltered cove and remote waterfall that gave life to rainbows in the mist, lacy ferns, and gentle wildlife.

I was at a loss for a song to sing to my mother. "You deserve a song, Mama, but I don't know what to sing." Songs come from the heart. I searched mine and found it empty. Then I remembered the song from my dream.

> *"You don't know what you've got till it's gone . . ."*

I got another bag of rose petals from the truck and watched them drift and spin and fall into the pool below the falls. They seemed to smile back at me before they leaped, cascading to the river below, where they might just meet the ones I had tossed to Lefty.

My mother, Starla—flower child of the 60s, back-to-the-land birth mother and battered woman of the 70s, drug addict of the 80s, an inmate of the 90s, and ashes in the new millennium. At the ocean, I had told my dad all about the assassin, the bear, the mountain lion, and my amputation. But it was my mother I told about Chance, Travis, and baby Quincy. She listened attentively to my every word—a better mother in death than she had been in life.

I liked to imagine that my mother and Lefty would find each other again one day, perhaps in a forgiving cloud brimming with the promise of a joyous spring shower—but more likely, I was delusional. If against all odds, my parents should find one another, their mingling would likely result in Hurricane Starla.

"It's okay to love the good parts of your parents," Mac had told me. "You've been set free from any generational curse. You are not doomed to repeat their mistakes."

"No," Dano had assured me. "Your parents' bad examples are far more likely to influence your decisions than your DNA. You can choose to be whatever kind of person you want to be."

The pilgrimage ended. It felt good to be home. Rose-petal pink and buttery yellow tufts painted the sky as the sun rose on a new day. The present was mine, and I worshiped a God of the eternal present. Sitting on my deck with my "view of eternity," I had a clear vision for my future. The past was right where it needed to be, and the future looked bright.

છ✟ର

"Explain it to me," I said, wrinkling my brow and twisting my mouth as I complained to Mac. "How is it that I can educate the secular world about ritual abuse and people willingly stand along the walls for hours to hear it? They thank me and even promise to pray for me." I drummed my fingers on the laptop. "But when I create a training specifically tailored for the church—*the church*—which should be on the front lines in the fight against Satanism, only five people show up? Why doesn't the church give a damn? Except for you, of course."

Mac winced and rubbed his forehead. Finally, he said, "Think of the emerging church like Moses. As an institution, it's been wandering in the wilderness for the past forty years in a state of transition.

"A lot of churches focus on keeping their congregation entertained because the world demands entertainment. You know what I'm saying—smartphones, social media, on-demand movies. It's not that they don't care about your topic, it's just . . . bad for business. The last thing those churches want to hear or talk about is Satanism, much less the fact that cult members might be sitting in their pews." Mac ran his fingers through graying hair.

"The church is as susceptible to trends as the people are who make it up. Truth gets buried beneath trends—like vampires and zombies, or the word terrorist. When you take a word and beat it to death, it loses its power and ability to influence."

Mac leaned back in his chair and slowly rubbed his knuckles back and forth along his jaw. "I guess what I'm trying to say, is that the topic of ritual abuse is about as popular at a church as a cat at a dog show."

Mac gave me a half shrug along with a half-smile. "Who knows where your message will go? Anything can happen. Jesus was born in Southside, yet the apostles took his words and changed the world."

Mac sounded so much like Chance.

"I'm happy to be part of a church that cares, Mac, but I am also glad that I don't need the church to affirm what God has put on my heart."

Mac blinked; his laughing blue eyes lit the little schoolhouse. "Oh, Sunny. How you have grown."

Evening arrived. I curled up on the sofa and opened the Bible to Ephesians. A yellow flower lay pressed between the pages, like a bridge connecting the physical to the spiritual. A sunny reminder of a victim whose life had changed—a person set free because an advocate took the time to listen and believe.

I couldn't save the world. I knew that. But tonight . . . tonight I had a choice.

Today I fed dogs, cleaned house, visited Ashley and Shane and their adorable children, made dinner, and started a baby quilt for Travis's—no, make that our—beautiful daughter, for Quincy belongs to all of us: to Paige, Cali, Chance, Travis, me, and even Logan.

The kettle sang on the stove. The hour was late, and I was tired, but now was the time I chose to wage battle. I would fight darkness in the hours of darkness.

I hit the power button, and my computer woke and hummed its song while I made a pot of herbal tea. Tonight the scent of lemon and ginger rose on fragrant fingers, and I was filled with a deep sense of peace and purpose. I am free.

Tonight, I would attempt to reach a disbelieving world that was mostly consumed with the quest for personal pleasure and the pursuit of their next acquisition.

I was up to the challenge.

And when I am done, before wedging myself between pillow and dogs, I will say my prayers, give thanks, and call Travis about that job.

ఐ ✟ ಚ

A silvery slice of moon rose to peek through the window. Eyes heavy, heart light, I closed the computer and picked up the phone.

"Do you think there's any hope?" I asked Travis with all seriousness. "Do you think Quincy can ever have a normal life? Girl Scouts, gymnastics, a pony named Black Beauty?"

Travis rocked the phone with his rich, easy laughter. "With you for a mother—not likely. Maybe karate class and monthly meetings with the NRA. And one day she'll probably ride a motorcycle named Black Beauty."

"Me? Her mother?" An exhilarating thought.

"Isn't that what your friend Kenny and Chance tried to tell you? That children are a gift and belong to the ones who love them?"

Kissme gave an impatient nudge. It was past our bedtime.

A smile danced across my heart. Hope rose and blossomed, as fragrant and sweet as the tea in my cup.

Oh, my.

"Good night, Travis."

"Sweet dreams, babe."

—End—

If you have enjoyed this book, would you kindly take a moment to leave a review on Amazon and Goodreads? Please tell your friends about my books and consider giving them as gifts to survivors of abuse.

AFTERWORD
from
DAWN MATTOX

"Nothing is more chilling than the truth."

I have never been afraid of aliens or zombies. Great horror stories for me are those that fall within the realms of possibility; a rabid St. Bernard, a psycho nurse holding an author hostage, natural disasters, satanic cults, etc.

The story of Ritual Abuse came easily because it is based on truth. I am a nationally recognized expert on the topic of Ritual Abuse, and like Sunny, I was fully resistant. Also, like Sunny, I was stunned by the sheer volume of cases and the horrific nature of the crimes committed "in the name of Satan."

Every law enforcement agency, mental health service, and crisis center is aware of these cases. Friends still send me links as occasional RA cases make headlines. I have given you the gift of entertainment, wrapped in truth.

The story was always there... waiting on me... waiting for you.

Be the Difference!

THE STORY ISN'T OVER

Sunny McLane has a new job at Psychiatric Emergency working with homicidal and suicidal patients.

5150

"Would you kill a stranger to save a friend?"

Available soon on Amazon

www.dawnmattox.com

www.facebook.com/dawn.mattox.author

https://twitter.com/theadvocatebook

www.ingramcontent.com/pod-product-compliance
Lightning Source LLC
Chambersburg PA
CBHW061302170626
46817CB00001B/19